Nothing Special...Just Friends?

Friendship doesn't cost a thing.

A novel by by Toni Staton Harris
Copyright ©2006

Praise for Nothing Special...Just Friends?

"Toni Staton Harris has done it again with this intense novel on a popular hot topic of discussion. After reading this novel, a girl's night out or a conversation with your significant other will never be the same. This is a must read!"

Kenyatta Ingram, founder Sistergirl Book Club

"Through a brilliantly written story, Toni Staton Harris asks and creatively answers the question whether men and women can be just friends. Prepare for a journey with twists and turns that will keep your head spinning, mind racing, pages turning and the candlelight burning."

Jeff Haskins, author of Heavy On My Mind, Freedom Through Poetic Verse, Vols. I&II

Published by Epiphany Publishing House, LLC
PO Box 32308
Newark, New Jersey 07102

Copyright 2006 by Toni Staton Harris

Editor: Chandra Sparks Taylor

Cover Desgn: Lydell A. Jackson
Book Design: About Faces Graphics & Communications

Library of Congress Catalog Card No.: 20059025464
ISBN: 978-0-9710695-1-0

Printed in Canada

First Edition

For Dr. Kimberly M. (Staton) Baldwin

The fining pot is for Silver, the furnace for Gold but the Lord trieth the hearts.

Proverbs 17:3KJV

Prologue

Brandan pulled his freshly polished red Mercedes CLK in front of the wood-planked abortion clinic in Montclair, New Jersey.

He and, Silver, had driven the five-mile trek from home in silence. The clamminess of the day matched their moods.

"I'll meet you inside," Brandan said as the engine purred.

Silver felt she could be incognito coming to this clinic opposed to the one in her own neighborhood that is until she eyed the swarm of people toting posters, banners and bullhorns. Silver heaved heavy a sigh. She had made up her mind and nothing Brandan or her sister said could deter her today. She had to go through with it. She had been through more than any one human should have to take and her decision to discard the fetus growing inside her was final. Any possible romantic future with her child's father was lost and Silver had to accept that. "You know if you're not in there with me, they won't allow me to have the procedure. It's mandatory that someone is present in case of—"

"Silver, I heard you," Brandan interrupted her. He stroked his tie, looked at the tip and rubbed an imaginary spot. "I know all that. I'm just parking around the corner."

"Sounds like you've been here before." Silver huffed. "How did you know there was parking around the corner?"

"I can read," Brandan answered and pointed to the large eyesore of a sign above the building. Brandan turned sideways to face Silver. "You know, if you don't want to do this, then don't, but don't pick a fight with me," he said with a terse rhythm in his voice. He looked out the window. The deafening silence caused him to redeem his tone. "Look, if you're not sure, let's just go to IHOP, get some cakes, and figure this thing out."

The thought was tempting. IHOP pancakes were some of her favorites, but not even the thought of syrupy butter sweetness would block her from what she had to do. "Brandan, I'm making the best of a baaaad situation, man." Silver's words dragged. "I have to do this."

"You don't have to do this. I want to be there for you," he pleaded.

"Brandan, you're still with Daphne, and you can't be there for me if you continue to see that wench," Silver said.

Brandan turned away.

"So much for your solution to this baby thing," Silver said with spewed venom.

"Is my seeing Daphne what this is really about?"

"Listen, Brandan—" she softened her tone, "—this baby was a mistake, and when all is said and done, you and I and everyone else will be happy I've made this decision."

"You're not doing me any favors," Brandan said.

Silver refused to talk about it anymore. She grabbed her bag and catapulted from the car. Before she had walked two steps, the swarm of people converged on her like gnats.

"Don't do this," one protester said. "We can get help for you," another chimed in. "This is not God's purpose for your life or your unborn child."

"Why are you doing this lady?" a little boy with a limp and an empty sleeve shouted. He only had one arm, in which he held the most grotesque picture Silver had seen. It was the photo of a mangled unborn child botched after an abortion.

Silver cupped her mouth. She looked around for support, but Brandan had driven off.

"Come on, miss. Are you okay?" A gracious woman in a white lab coat made her way through the crowd and escorted Silver up the stairs. She gave Silver a cup of ice water and said, "This is your decision. All the people out there protesting wouldn't dare try to take any of these unwanted babies home."

Silver didn't speak. She waved Brandan over when he entered the clinic, filled out the necessary paperwork, paid the money and they waited.

It wasn't too long after watching several women of all ages and ethnicities disappear behind the giant brown door that her name was called. In minutes she found herself stripped of her clothing, in a worn cotton gown, her backside exposed to the world. A nurse with a prominent nose, her bifocals resting on a hairy wart, barreled in asking questions without looking up. "Is anyone forcing you to have the procedure?"

Silver shook her head.

"I need full answers, Miss James."

"Well..."

The nurse looked at Silver's chart. "I'm waiting. Yes or No?"

Silver didn't speak.

The nurse sighed. "Are you sure you want to do this? You can always come back when you're sure."

"Not really. I'm close to ending my first trimester," Silver answered.

The nurse flipped pages on the chart. "I guess you're right. You don't have a lot of time." The nurse continued reading the pages, then placed the chart on her lap, her elbows on top. "I ask again, is anyone forcing you to have this procedure?" This time her tone was lighter, more concern lingered. "Is this contact person, Brandan Savoy, your boyfriend?"

"He doesn't want me to have the procedure," Silver said.

"Then why are you doing it?" The concern the nurse had garnered dissipated.

"Because it's the best thing. I don't know what to do with a child, help or no help from Brandan—"

"Well, it's your body and I'm sure your boyfriend—"

"Brandan isn't my boyfriend. We're nothing special like that. . .I mean we're just friends."

Chapter 1

Rocks and Holes

Silver Alexandra James had hardly any room to open her car door without scratching it. Her garage buddy had once again angled his car over the faded line. It was as if he believed his rusted gray Chevrolet deserved more consideration than her brand-new platinum Mercedes ML320. She sucked her teeth as she carefully slid through the tiny space. If she were a large woman, she would have been trapped. Silver walked around the other side and leaned into her passenger seat where the space between the door and the wall was tighter to retrieve her things. How she wished she could park in front of her apartment building; but the only choice in this dilapidated section of a once premier Newark, New Jersey suburb, was a dirt-floored, dingy carport that stole one hundred and fifty dollars of her hard-earned cash every month. She shook her head and huffed, further disgusted by her parking dilemma when she realized that money could have been better spent on a Chanel scarf or on replacing her Louis Vuitton date book.

Most people who enjoyed the finest things in life would have opted to live in a better neighborhood. However, Silver relished things like her car and designer clothes more than optimal living quarters. Besides this was her childhood neighborhood, having grown up a block away. This town was once prime real estate, and as a child, black folks living in the area was an anomaly. Silver had to admit with the adventitious addition of gangs, drug warfare and a lack of economical luster, the area had been on a slippery slope downward for more than ten years.

Yet instill it was hard to leave a place that she would pay four times the rent she paid for today.

After deciding against leaving another unpleasant, unyielding note on the neighboring car, Silver schlepped down the street and around the corner. She cringed as assorted debris from crack vials to chicken bones to discarded fast food containers papered the street.

The stilled air elevated the stench that bombarded her nose and assaulted her clothes. Rain would have been an answered prayer, she thought as she used her forearm to halt the perspiration flowing from her forehead. Her hair had flattened under the humidity and the usually sparkling white patch in front, her birthmark, looked like a landing strip. Silver approached her front gate, worn from the walk, sweating as if she ran three miles. She looked down to open the gate that would only be closed today, the day her hands were full. She shook her head as she noticed a used condom lying at her feet.

"Hey, Miss Silver. N-need a hand?" Bowman the neighborhood degenerate stuttered. He smacked the few teeth he had left and looked at Silver like she was prime rib, after a marijuana binge.

She would have put her hand on her hip and declared, "hell no" if she had any hands to spare, but they were filled with groceries and her laptop, and she still needed to retrieve her mail. Silver thought it best not to get smart with Bowman because she did need him to open the gate. "Actually, Bowman, if you don't mind..."

Bowman stepped to her immediately, tugging at the soft leather briefcase that held her notebook-sized laptop and files. "No, Bowman, just open the gate and close it back when I'm through, please," Silver said, remembering to at least be polite.

"Anything for ya, ya fine female you." He laughed and tipped his hat in her direction.

"Bowman, please. I can't get to my wallet right now. Damn," Silver said, dismissing Bowman's silent request for a tip and everything else about him. "Next time." She looked him up and down and wondered how a man with no job and seemingly no life could keep brand-new Adidas sneakers so white against the backdrop of the grunge of his clothes.

Safely avoiding a confrontation with Bowman, Silver continued with her journey to her second-floor walk-up. Her cell phone rang, and the distinctive ring let her know her dinner partner for the evening, Todd Boyd, was calling. With caution she answered. "What's up? I'm home but I'm just getting through the door... No, Todd, I'm not going back out to the store. Why don't you pick it up on your way over? No, baby, it's not like that, but I'm hot and sticky, and I don't feel like going back out. What time are you coming over?"

Even though Todd's request to get a bottle of his favorite wine was selfish and disconcerting, Silver still looked forward to his visit. She'd had a rough week at work, hadn't seen him in three, and frankly a piece of his *Sex and the City* would serve her well tonight.

Silver concluded her conversation and picked up her mail. With a giraffe-like stride, she made her way up to her apartment. She kicked her pumps off into a cherry-wood custom-built shoe tree in the foyer adjacent to her front door. Silver then made a beeline to the kitchen, placed her groceries away and pulled out her All-Clad pots. She gave her countertops and table a quick wipe down and filled one pot with water and another with olive oil, garlic cloves and lemon essence. She turned the burners on low and made her way to the bedroom.

On her journey, she thumbed through her mail and noticed two pink envelopes. One was her Dell account for her desktop computer on which she owed a thousand dollars. She hadn't paid on the account in three months, and the company was threatening repossession.

"I'd like to see them try to repossess something from this neighborhood," she said snickering aloud.

The second pink envelope was an overdue Nordstrom's account. Silver threw all of the mail atop another pile of bills on the corner of her desk and decided to deal with them at another time. She continued toward her bedroom, aligned a few magazines, tapped photograph frames in place and ran her finger across her crystal chess set to check for dust. Not that she had to; her anal neatness gave her apartment a fine furniture-store feel. After peeling her tangerine suit off her sticky body, she turned the skirt and jacket inside out and hung it on a soft padded hanger in the far left corner, the only spot she designated for soiled clothes. She spritzed her clothes with Febreeze and breathed, happy to be out of her monkey suit for the weekend.

Now comfortable in a thong and bra, her russet complexion still shimmered from perspiration, Silver returned to the kitchen to set the table as a knock came at her door. She cocked her head to the side and checked her watch. It couldn't be Todd, she thought. He said he'd be over around seven. It was only six, and it was rare for him to be on time, much less early. Silver grabbed a wrap from the bathroom and stomped to the door. "Who is it?" she asked with obvious agitation.

"It's me, girl. Open up."

Quickly she unbolted three locks. "Hey, boy. What the heck are you doing here?" Silver asked as she gripped her best friend Brandan Lemar Savoy. "You said your dimmers weren't working, and I figured I'd check them out on my lunch break. I might not even go back to the dealership this evening. It was slow," Brandan said as he entered the apartment.

"Hold it, dawg. Shoes." She pointed to the shoe tree Brandan built for her. "Socks are in the bottom drawer." Silver pointed again. She kept socks for visitors who felt uncomfortable walking around in their own.

Without hesitation, Brandan complied. He knew how anal she was, and it tickled him silly because he was the same way.

"You're slow at the dealership on a Friday? I'm surprised. People aren't burning your door down to buy the newest Mercedes?" Silver headed back into the kitchen and Brandan followed her.

"Not in this economy. Smells good in here. What's the occasion? You didn't know I was coming, but it doesn't mean I can't stay and hang out," Brandan said, retrieving a brew from the fridge.

Silver pulled an emergency standby bottle of White Zinfandel from her cabinet and placed it in the freezer. "You can't," she said.

"I can't what?" Brandan searched a drawer for a bottle opener, and when he couldn't find one, he used his key.

"You can't stay. I'm having company," Silver said, tinkering with the stove's flame. "Oh, Brandan, you have to get me the color scheme you want for your website. I might have some time to work on it next week after my project ends."

"I'm still not sure, but I'll let you know. I don't want to spend the money to set up the business yet, so it doesn't make sense for me to put up a website. And I have to give you something for designing it for me, even if designing is only your hobby. I mean it's what you do—"

"Boy, please. Did you take money for helping me get my ride on your family plan?" Brandan didn't answer. "Well then. That's what we do for each other. You know that. Now, get me the color specs. We'll figure the rest out later." Silver popped his arm.

"What's this?" Brandan asked, peeking in her pot.

"Chicken picatta," Silver answered.

"For who?" Brandan took a long swig of his beer.

Silver looked away without a word.

"Oh, Sil, why are you still hanging with that cat? He's a bum. You'd be better off with Bowman down there, who, by the way, hit me up for some change. He said he helped you with your stuff and you wouldn't give him anything." Brandan laughed.

———————————————————————————————— *Toni Staton Harris*

"Whatever. How much did *you* give him?" Silver asked, hoping to throw Brandan off from his initial conversation about Todd.

"A five spot," Brandan answered.

"Are you crazy? Five dollars, Brandan? It's because of you Bowman won't ever have to get a job."

"He said he was hungry." Brandan shrugged.

"You know he's going to spend that money on drugs, alcohol or worse." Silver continued stirring the pot.

"That's between him and his god. Now back to you..." Silver had hoped the conversation about her and Todd was diffused, but her distraction hadn't worked. "So like I was saying..."

"Brandan, please let it go. I like Todd a lot. He's different with me, you know?"

"That's the problem. We don't know. He's never around when you need him or want him, just when he thinks you're hanging with someone else. It's like he has a lo-jack on your ass or something. He doesn't come around for cook-outs, bar-mitzvahs or anything."

Silver punched Brandan on the arm. "Boy, shut up. We don't have bar-mitzvahs, we ain't Jewish. Unless you're trying to tell me something..." She laughed.

"You know what I'm saying..."

"I do. But, I'm having company, it's Todd, and I don't want to hear another word about it. You know where your tools are. I'm taking a shower." Silver placed lids on her pots and turned off the flames. She wouldn't fry the cutlets and immerse them in the gravy until after Todd arrived—that is, if they didn't have dessert before dinner.

"I shouldn't fix 'em," Brandan said, pouting.

"Do you," Silver shot back. But that was a bluff. She wanted her lights fixed, and she knew Brandan wouldn't let her down. They had just talked about her having a problem with the dimmers earlier, and Brandan was already there, but that was the kind of friend he was, always had been, since grade school.

Silver emerged from the shower refreshed. The twelve-speed dual spout showerhead—another installment from Brandan—helped her relax. She had been tense since her new overbearing female boss started barking orders and demanding the impossible. It was a sheer miracle that Silver could even tear herself away that night, but nothing and nobody was going to keep her from the moments she craved and needed.

"All done," Brandan said, tossing the screwdriver in the air.

"That was quick." Silver moved swiftly to the light panel. The dimmers worked perfectly. She then turned on the stereo and leafed through several CDs before landing on one of her favorites, Ledisi, an underground singer from Oakland, California, whose CD she found at a record store in D.C.

"Wow. You look fantastic," Brandan said, noticing how Silver's platinum negligee hugged every curve of her long, lean torso and slender hips. "He doesn't deserve it, Sil, I'm telling you. He doesn't deserve you. He's a bum," Brandan said as Silver sashayed past him back into the kitchen. "Whoa, and you smell good, too. What's that, the peppermint soap?" Brandan asked. They had picked up several natural soaps on one of their street fair excursions in New York City.

"Yup, it's the peppermint. Had to get the spots right," Silver said, patting herself. She laughed as Brandan turned up his nose. "You know what? You have to go." She looked up at the gold-trimmed clock that hung on the kitchen wall. It was close to seven, and Todd would be there any minute. She pulled the wine from the freezer and gripped the bottle. The temperature was perfect. She didn't drink the stuff herself, but it was like Todd liked it—just below freezing, almost slushy.

"I don't know why you're rushing me out. Todd ain't gonna be here anytime soon. Hell, we could play a full game of chess before he gets here, and you know how long it takes you to make a move." Brandan rifled through Silver's pantry, found a bottle of Hennessy and poured himself a shot before sitting at the table.

"We could, but we won't because I don't need another episode with you guys meeting up. I don't want that kind of testosterone up in here." Silver looked at Brandan as he gulped down the drink. "Ooh, that looks good."

"It's your house, have one." Brandan offered the bottle to her.

"Nope. Todd hates when I drink Hennessy. He said it leaves my breath smelling rank. Now you have to go, for real, Brandan. I love you but you gotta go," Silver said, pulling Brandan from the table.

"Why don't you let me hook you up with my best client, the one I told you about? His name is Kendrick Armstrong, and he's an attorney in the city. The brother is loaded. He just paid cash for a Maybach like his name is Oprah."

"Isn't that the new top-of-the-line Mercedes you talked about?"

Brandan sipped his drink. "One of the most expensive cars you can buy. The seats are luxury airline recliners. It makes your boy's Escalade look like a Hyundai."

Silver had a pensive look, pondering the opportunity. Finally she shook her head. "Nah. I'm not letting you hook me up. I'll stick with what I have—at least I know it." She took Brandan's drink out of his hand, placed it on the table and pulled him toward the door.

"I'm out. Oh, by the way, we have to do our Monday pool night on Sunday." Brandan rolled his sleeves back down and secured his cuffs. He grabbed his suit jacket from the back of the chair and shook it vigorously before putting it back on.

"Why're you changing our game night? What? You have a date?"

"As a matter of fact, I do. So Sunday, you and me, and be prepared to get that ass spanked." Brandan shrugged and looked into his friend's eyes. "Sometimes I just want to shake some sense into you."

"Brandan, I know what I'm doing. Have a good night," she said, leaning against the door. "Where did you park?"

"In front of your house," Brandan answered as he used the shoe horn to put on his shoes.

"Are you crazy? I hope your car is still there," Silver said.

"This is your crazy neighborhood. I'm with Jill. I don't know why you stay here," Brandan said, referring to her sister's stark opposition to Silver's living arrangements.

"You have some nerve. You only live five minutes from here, so it's your 'hood too," Silver answered, deflecting Brandan's joke.

"Yeah, that's true." Brandan chuckled. "Unlike you, I can park in front of your place. Your drunks, crack heads and gang bangers act more civilized than mine. Look how Bowman takes care of me." Brandan laughed and descended the stairs.

Silver closed and locked the door and ran to her bedroom where she peered out of the bay window that faced the street. Folks surrounded Brandan's car like he was the mayor. She watched as Bowman pulled what resembled a dirty rag from his pocket, wiped the side of the car and opened the door for Brandan's entrée. Silver looked on as Brandan handed Bowman another bill. Bowman gave Brandan a military salute, and Brandan sped off, leaving his constituents in his dust.

Ledisi's CD had played three times in its entirety, and Silver had long changed out of her negligee into a pink velour sweat suit. Angrily, she typed away at her laptop, putting the finishing touches on a document that wasn't due for two weeks. It would be just another task completed and well done under her belt.

Silver picked up her watch from the desk. Looking at the clock on the wall would only make her angrier. The numbers on her watch were tiny, and she could make herself believe that more than three hours had not passed since Todd was supposed to show.

She closed her document, accessed her DSL and sent the work to the mainframe at her office. The output would be on her desk by Monday morning and maybe she would even present it to her new boss then. She quickly decided against the plan of action because instead of a needed break, Silver's outstanding work seemed to push more tasks her way. As the small accounts project leader for the computer firm, Sci-gex, where she worked, Silver had more than enough to do with six ongoing projects and several colleagues to mentor as well.

She shut down her computer and moved to the kitchen where she pulled out Gladware to house her gourmet meal. The sauce looked like lumpy gravy instead of a culinary delight. She covered the raw chicken and placed it in the fridge, determined to cook it the next day before it spoiled.

Looking at the clock was inevitable, and Silver pounded her fists at the fact that it was almost midnight and Todd still hadn't shown. *Brandan was right again*, she thought. But something could be wrong, she quickly reasoned. It wasn't unusual for Todd to be late, but to completely stand her up? He hadn't done that in the year they had dated. Silver poured herself a glass of room temperature wine. As soon as she sipped, she spit it out, even angrier that she had spent money on sugar water. She pulled out the Hennessy and poured herself a double shot. The first gulp went down smooth and easy. She rolled it on her tongue.

Once again, firmly planted in her chair, she became nervous. What if something went wrong just as Todd was about to get off work? Silver turned on a small color television set. After realizing she was long past the news broadcasts and seeing no breaking stories on the local channels, she reasoned Todd was probably okay. He was a cop in her town, although Todd didn't live there. Silver's heart raced, thinking something had actually happened. She hoped not. She wouldn't forgive herself if Todd was trying to get to her and she didn't think enough of him and their relationship to give him the benefit of the doubt.

Thoroughly spooked and praying he was okay, Silver picked up the phone to hear an interrupted dial tone. Perhaps he had called her when she was online, she thought, dialing the access number to her voice mail. It was Jill reminding Silver of her promise to hang out with her niece,

Abigail, the next day. After erasing that message, Silver dialed Todd's cell phone. She was surprised when he picked up.

"Yo," Todd said. Silver could hear the loud rumblings in the background.

"Yo? Yo? You don't sound sick or like something happened. Todd, where the hell are you? It's almost midnight and you said you'd be here hours ago."

"Oh you, yo, bay, I'm sorry. It's my partner Diego's birthday, and the boys decided to get together for a quick drink or two after work…Yeah, man, hit me again," Todd said, obviously not paying attention to his conversation with Silver.

"I don't believe you. You couldn't call me? I've been waiting here all night for you. I went back out and bought your wine," she lied. "I cooked, and you mean to tell me you'd rather spend time with your partner Diego, who I'm sure you can see anytime than fulfill your promise to see me?" Silver yelled.

"Bay, hold up. Let me go outside—"

"Go outside? You should be leaving to bring your ass over here." Silver was furious. A conversation that escalated to an intense level with Todd rarely got her anywhere, but that wasn't her concern.

"Bay, calm down. I'm on my way. We just stopped by the Lounge with Ms. Motley to have a few. I can't let my boy go out another year without me being here. Come on, don't be mad. I'm on my way," Todd said.

"All you had to do was call. That's all you had to do. Don't bother coming by. I'm going to bed," Silver said.

"I'm coming now so I can go to bed with you. I'm even staying tonight, bay—"

"Fuck you, Todd," Silver yelled and slammed the phone down. She paced the floor before she grabbed the Hennessy, turned down all the lights and flipped the stereo off so hard she feared she might have damaged it. That was a no-no. No matter how mad she was or who she was mad at, Silver worked hard and wasn't into destroying her own shit.

She pulled off her sweats, pulled out a red satin sleeper and plunged under the cover. She yanked the lamp cord at her bedside and sat up in the darkness. Her arms were crossed so tightly around her chest, it was a good thing her double D's were au natural, otherwise they might have popped out from underneath her skin. In the dark, she listened to the Friday night gang party outside her window. A few minutes later she heard a knock at her door. She waited until she heard it just a little longer and a little harder. Finally, Todd's undeniable voice beckoned his entry.

The Lounge, a popular town watering hole, was less than ten minutes away, but it burned Silver that Todd's trail to her house had taken five and a half hours.

Silver stomped to the door. "What do you want, Todd?" she asked in a steely voice.

"You," he answered.

"If you wanted me, you would have been here."

"I know, bay, please. I got a little carried away with the boys tonight. I planned on being here earlier, but the party got kinda wild, you know.? I have a surprise for you."

"I can't. I can't take this any more, Todd. I'm sick of you using me." Silver pounded her head against the door. It didn't help that she had downed the last of her drink, making her desire him even more. "When does it all end?" she questioned louder than she intended.

"Soon, bay. I promise. Let me give you your gift—"

"You don't change, man. No, no I need to be strong—"

"For both of us. We're almost there. Soon I'll be coming home every night, right here and you're going to wish I did go out with the boys. Just give me time, bay. Come on let me in." She heard his keys rustling. She knew he was looking for his key, but Silver had already engaged the deadbolt.

Silver would have loved to have Todd so into her that she'd have to beg him to give her a break, but the thought that he'd been making that same promise for a year made her resist. "It doesn't matter, your key doesn't work here anymore anyway."

"Why bay? 'Cause I was late?" Todd sighed. "Damn bay, I'm late, it's not like I didn't show up!" Todd said incredulously.

Sometimes it's better never than late. She thought silently Silver rubbed the tips of her fingers and bit down on the inside of her lower lip. She'd been here before, standing on the wrong side of the door, alone. She didn't want to go back to the place of disappointment, but her heart always played a trick her mind fell for every time. "You ain't gonna change," she mumbled, "but I am." Silver leaned into the door, her forehead touching the wooden panel then she turned around. *You're going to come here, use your key and the locks will be changed.*

"Bay, please. Come on. Let's talk about this. I know my job takes up a lot of my time, but I'll be able to retire soon, and when my pension kicks in, I'll take care of you the way you deserve to be taken care of. Come on, open the door," Todd pleaded.

"I don't deserve this," Silver said as the top lock tumbled. Her lips quivered as she grasped the knob and tore off the chain. She released the dead-bolt, and Todd's mouth bombarded hers, traveling to her neck, and her belly button before finally landing behind her right knee. Todd discovered her G-spot on one of their wildest escapades.

Todd pulled the cold wood of his long, dark night stick from his side holster. He rolled it over Silver's thighs. She moaned.

"Just give me a second, bay," he said as he placed what had to be two dozen of the prettiest orchids she ever seen on the chaise outside her bedroom door. "I told you I had a surprise for you," he said, ripping his shirt from his broad shoulders. He unhooked his leather belt, which held his handcuffs, night stick, stun gun and nine millimeter semi-automatic weapon and placed the gun gently on the sofa. He kicked off his shoes in front of the chaise and stood in his briefs, socks and cap. Silver took in every perfectly beveled line on his body, including his twelve-pack, before leading him to the bedroom.

Her thighs felt like liquid-filled clouds begging for Todd's thunder to command them to rain. His touch gave her permission. He dropped the satin from her shoulders and Todd's full lips engulfed her breasts. Her large nipples beaded like sweet raisins as his tongue assaulted them before moving downtown. He licked her womanhood and her juices gushed. Silver moaned. His tongue continued to bathe her wetness, plunging to the back of her spine.

After her second orgasm, Silver positioned herself over him, taking in every delicious drop, making her liquid love flow harder. She engulfed his manhood as far as she could without choking then she tongued his sack. He moaned.

When neither of them could take anymore, Silver spun around and rode Todd's pony like a jockey, orchestrating every turn and hump. Nothing pleased her more than when Todd flipped her on the bottom and then suddenly thrust into her.

Silver arched her back, clenched the sheets and howled so loudly the moon shook. They both collapsed on the edge of the bed where they climaxed together.

Silver's teeth sparkled amid the darkness of the drawn shades. The loud street rumblings occurring outside her window didn't disturb her satisfaction. "Hey…" She ran her finger down Todd's spine to tickle him awake. These were the times she spoke of, that Brandan would never, could ever understand.

"What's up?" Todd's voice was groggy as he rolled over and kissed the tip of her nose. That move still made her chuckle.

"Come with me to my sister's semi-formal dinner next week."

"Gotta work. What time is it?" he asked, turning his back to her and pulling the sheet over his head.

"Now or the affair?" Silver asked.

"Now."

"Four-forty. Why?"

Todd sprung up. It amazed her that after a heart-wrenching session like the one they just had, his manhood was still standing at attention. He always left her wanting more. Todd grabbed his cap and searched for his other clothing before dressing in the threshold of the doorway, near her full-length mirror.

"Where are you going? I thought you said you were staying the night for once." Silver pouted.

"Gotta take my mother to Atlantic City in the morning. I promised," he said, getting dressed in record time.

She wondered why she allowed him to bring so much strife in her life. "Your mother," she mumbled. "I'm tired of this, Todd. You didn't even answer my question." She followed him into the living room where he brushed off his shoes before slipping into them.

"I did, Silver. I have to work next week."

"But you don't even know when the dinner is," she said.

"When is it?" His tone was remarkably different from the one he used when he begged to enter both of her doors.

"The party is on Friday," she answered. It was actually on Saturday, but she figured she'd give him a larger noose to coil around his neck.

"I can't. I have to work on Friday and Saturday, and I promised my mother—"

Silver cut him off before he could finish. "Your mother. Dammit, Todd, you mean you can't spare one Saturday night?"

"I thought you said it was Friday night," Todd said. Silver slumped against the door. "Don't try to play me, Silver. You can't outplay a player. Remember that. And as for my mama, don't go there either. I promised my daddy on his deathbed I would always take care of my mama, and you and nobody else is going to ever change that. Plus, I've spent Saturday nights with you before. Stop acting like a spoiled brat." Todd checked his weapon and placed it in his holster.

"You've spent one Saturday with me, and that was in Atlantic City. And if I were you, I wouldn't go there because that wasn't a good trip," she said, poking at his chest.

It was that trip where her heart broke in two. Todd's mother had taken a week-long vacation to visit her sister in the South. Todd spent every day at Silver's playing house. She fixed him dinner and ran his bath water. The week was to culminate with him taking her to the Policeman's Benevolent Association Ball in Atlantic City. They got a great deal on a suite in Trump Towers and pledged to dance, drink, eat and be merry all night. Silver and Todd were like two honeymooners—until they entered the ballroom for dinner.

Silver wore her best fringe dress, revealing all of her D-cup and slender hips. She tried to ignore the unfriendly stares and whispers that started the moment they stepped into the room. After light cocktails and having won several doubters over, Silver and Todd sat at his table.

"Well, you two make a lovely couple, Todd. And how long have you been together?" One of the women at the table inquired. Sarcasm slithered behind her words, and Silver waited with bated breath for Todd's response.

"Oh no, it's not like that. We're nothing special, you know, just friends," Todd finally responded.

Shock went straight to Silver's heart. He even had the nerve to wipe the sweat from his brow with a handkerchief she'd bought for him. Amidst a haze of embarrassment and disgust, the water Silver was sipping landed squarely in Todd's face. She snatched her purse and stomped to the car determined to go home. She was so distraught; it took Todd to remind her they couldn't leave without packing their things. Besides, he had the car keys.

He schmoozed Silver for about an hour in their room until she agreed to stay the night, but he returned to the party alone. Flowers, cards, candy and several pieces of jewelry later and Todd had re-entry time and time again. It also didn't hurt that Silver was a sucker for light-skinned men—Todd's manila-colored complexion made her weak.

"Todd, you don't have to explain to me how important your mama is but—"

"Sil," Todd interrupted, "don't get your feelings hurt over my mama. Let it go. Now make sure you put these in water. They are very rare and very expensive." Todd shoved the flowers in her face. "Besides, how I take care of my mama should be an indication of how I'm gonna take care of you when the time is right."

"Is that supposed to be a carrot?" Silver asked, sashaying to the light switch. The dimmers popped on emitting the perfect glow she had set before Todd messed up her evening.

Todd pulled her hips back into him. "Come on, bay. We've talked about this. Just give me a little more time and I can work things out a little better for both of us. Now I gotta go. Do me a favor, fix me a plate. I know you made my chicken," he said, smacking her taut buttocks.

Silver didn't say another word. She wrapped up his food like it came from a restaurant. He planted a luscious kiss at the nape of her neck and bid her good night. She didn't even bother to tell him the chicken wasn't cooked. He'd learn soon enough.

"Oh, bay, and for real, leave that cognac shit alone. It's nasty; I don't like the way it tastes." Todd winked and left her leaning against the door frame. One day she wouldn't succumb to him. As she closed the door, she wished that day would come sooner rather than later.

Brandan tightened the last lug on the transmission cap. He rolled from under the car and wiped his pristine hands and nails with a special oil-removing cloth. His hands were so blemish free, he could have modeled them. One would never know his passion was restoring old model cars and making them hum like a Mach 2 glider.

He had become so good at fixing cars that he had to turn down potential customers. If it were up to his general manager—a position for which Brandan vied—he would serve the largest Mercedes car dealership in the state of New Jersey with dual roles, head salesman and head of maintenance. But the dealership wouldn't pay two salaries. Brandan's degree from C.W. Post in Long Island made him keenly aware of his potential and capabilities to always strive for more. Besides, he preferred wearing a good suit as opposed to coveralls.

It was getting late, and Brandan decided it was time to quit. He took a swig of water from his ice-filled Thermos and flipped off his spotlight. His eyes adjusted to the glowing moonlight and blazing stars. He watched a shadow saunter up his gravelly driveway, carrying what looked like a picnic basket.

"Hey, boo. Whatcha doing?" Savannah Thayer asked as she switched her perfect Coca-Cola frame up to him.

Savannah had pursued Brandan with vigor from the time she and "Daddy" perused the newest Mercedes at Brandan's dealership. If it were up to her, Brandan would have been included with the bill of sale, but she settled for a phone number behind Daddy's back instead.

As hard as Savannah tried, things never quite clicked for she and Brandan. She was extremely attractive and a feline in bed, but she was also very used to getting her own way. That alone shut Brandan down faster than an oil-less engine.

"I called you this evening. I thought we'd share a midnight picnic basket. Got all your favorites: fruit platter with kiwi, star fruit, mangos and strawberries; Fromage; Brie and cracked pepper crackers. I even found a nice bottle of Chardonnay," Savannah said, pulling items from her basket.

"I like Merlot," Brandan said, sipping his water and eyeing her frame. It was because of her breasts that she maintained a slot on Brandan's likes list.

"I know you like Merlot, but you'll come around." She tossed her sandy-brown hair. Brandan just looked at her. "Anyway, I called and you were nowhere to be found. Hanging out today?"

"Yup."

She walked up and rubbed her thigh against his manhood. Brandan couldn't hide that he was turned on.

"I thought we were hanging out on Monday," Brandan said, following Savannah's circular motion.

"Oh, sweetie, did the surgeon general put out a warning advising we should only see each other once a week?" She plunged her tongue down his throat. "Why don't we go inside?"

"I have a lot to do and—"

She placed her strawberry-coated finger to his lips. "Ssh…"

Brandan closed the garage door then whisked her up in his arms and carried her inside. He was always a sucker for strawberries.

Chapter 2

The Sting

Silver was scrubbing everything in sight throughout her apartment when the phone rang. She answered and delightfully embarked on a three-hour conversation with Kendrick Armstrong, a possible contender in her ring of love.

"So what else did Brandan tell you about me?" Kendrick's voice was so enticing, Silver's panties would have been wet had she worn any that day.

Brandan finally convinced Silver she should call Kendrick and get to know him. "Brandan spoke very highly of you. He said you were really a nice guy and that we would enjoy each other's company," Silver said without breaking stride with her cleaning, a ritual she endured after every one of Todd's visits.

"Brandan said you enjoy sports as much as any guy. He says your TV is tuned to ESPN more than the Lifetime channel." Kendrick's odd nasally laugh sounded more like a snort.

"He's right. My TV is on ESPN right now, just on mute. Football is my favorite sport. I like basketball, too, but you can keep baseball and hockey."

Silver continued working on a stubborn spot on her chocolate-colored nightstand where Todd had placed a glass. She used everything, including orange oil, but nothing seemed to do the trick.

"So what did you think about Rush Limbaugh's comment? I don't know if you're an Eagles fan or not, but his statement certainly sparked enough controversy." Kendrick seemed to take pleasure in inciting a debate. He had an accusatory tone as if he was setting Silver up for an argument before the court.

"Actually, I don't have a problem that Limbaugh believes McNabb is only celebrated because the media wants a star black quarterback. Limbaugh is a druggie racist and is just doing his job. My problem was with the fact that the other commentators didn't do their jobs and debate him on the issue. What Limbaugh said was unfounded. Donovan McNabb and the Eagles happen to be my favorite team, but McNabb has been seventy percent of the team's offense for at least three years. The Eagles have to strengthen their offensive line. McNabb can't continue to carry the team by himself. Furthermore, the media has not long championed for a star black quarterback because there have been plenty—Doug Williams, Warren Moon and others. That's why I'm ecstatic they signed Terrell Owens—"

"Don't you think he's a hotdog?" Kendrick interrupted her.

"Why is it when a black man is confident and strong, he's being a hotdog and when you have someone like Jeremy Shockey from the Giants, he's passionate about the game?" Silver asked. "I know one thing, T.O. will put his money where his mouth is, mark my words."

"Okay, okay. I'm sorry I brought the whole thing up. You're right. You do know the game," Kendrick said. "I'm impressed."

What else is new? Silver thought. She always impressed guys with her sports knowledge, and she never failed to use her true love for the game as a mating call.

"I own a box at the Garden. I would love for you to accompany me sometime," Kendrick said.

"That would be cool. Too bad we have to wait until next season because we all know the Knicks are not making the playoffs this year." Silver laughed.

"So what else do you like to do?" Kendrick asked. "I can't imagine that your only passion is terrorizing people about your team, geez."

"I also love chess, playing pool and things like that," Silver said, even though she wanted to talk more about the Donovan McNabb situation.

"So how good are you at chess and pool?"

"I'm very good, if I say so myself."

"I would love to see you in action. I have a genuine Brunswick table in my game parlor that we could shoot a few rounds on. It hasn't seen any action in a while." Kendrick's sexual overture was apparent, and Silver acknowledged it with a chuckle. "So why don't you come over to my place? I'd love to see how good you really are. I'll have my chef cook us a wonderful exotic dinner, and we'll get to know each other even better." Silver's silence prompted Kendrick to further try to convince her of a visit. "I live right in midtown. I could even have my car pick you up." Kendrick's invitation was tempting, but Silver wasn't big on meeting men at their homes for the first time, no matter who referred them. She remained silent. "...or I could meet you at your place. I don't mind crossing the river," Kendrick said. "I really want to meet you."

"I don't feel comfortable with you coming to my place just yet." The words tumbled out of Silver's mouth before she could harness them. She sat at the edge of the bed and bit her lip. She wanted to see Kendrick, but meeting at his place by herself was risky, and him coming to her place was even less of an option. The last guy who appeared at North Seventeenth Street with an interest in Silver received Todd Boyd's brand of the welcoming committee: He was frisked, his driver's license scanned and he was told if he ever graced the premises again, he'd be locked up. Silver thought of Kendrick's voice, his obvious cultured intelligence and thought he might be worth the risk. If his personality was as authentic as he portrayed and his looks matched a quarter of everything she learned to date, she could only say a prayer for him. "Ken, you don't mind if I call you Ken do you?"

"Not at all."

"Ken, I know you've been asked this before, but why aren't you married or dating or anything?"

"I have been asked that, and I could ask you the same thing. The simple answer is I was in a relationship with a woman with three children who I thought was single. When I found out she wasn't and realized our relationship wasn't going any farther, I walked. And as for my being attached, you women have got to understand that we all—men and women—want the same things: love, commitment and no games. A lot of women want my money and want to change me, but I want someone who likes me, can eventually love me and we can have fun spending my money together." Kendrick took a deep breath.

Silver placed her rag at the foot of the bed, positioning herself comfortably in the center. She appreciated his honesty.

"Why don't we do this? Come to the city, and I'll book us a spot for dinner at the 21 Club. We could meet tomorrow and get this party started," Kendrick said.

"Ken, that really sounds great. I would love to have dinner there. You can get a reservation tomorrow? I've heard that place has a waiting list for celebrities, and we'll probably walk out of there having spent about a thousand dollars just to eat." Silver didn't want to sound like she wasn't used to having nice things, but the possibility of dining next to Donald Trump or Russell Simmons almost had her contemplating birthing Kendrick's babies, and motherhood had never been in her plans.

"Oh, a reservation tomorrow isn't a feat. That's easier than convincing you to come over here." Kendrick laughed again.

"Well, it's a date. I know the address of the restaurant. We could meet there and—"

"I don't think that's a good idea. First of all, the host won't allow you to linger, and she won't seat you without my presence." Kendrick cleared his throat. "Besides, I don't want some other billionaire to snatch you up before I've had my chance with you."

Kendrick's explanation about her meeting him at the restaurant sounded lame, but she was flattered he seemed so protective of her. "Well, you could always describe yourself and we could time our arrivals. I'm never late."

"I'd feel odd just out and out describing myself to you," Kendrick said, "but I assure you, you won't be disappointed."

"Good sign," Silver said louder than she intended. "Well describe someone famous you look like."

"That's fair. I don't know if you know these cats, they're probably before your time." Kendrick laughed again.

Silver enjoyed his sense of humor. "Hey, you're not that much older than me. I'm proud to say I'm thirty-two and damn good for any age. Besides, I was raised old school, so try me. As long as you're not describing Moses, I think I can hang." Her wittiness extracted a hearty laugh from both of them.

"Okay, I feel you as the kids say. Well, I work out religiously five times a week. I have a private gym in my penthouse, and I'm a vegetarian so I'm able to keep my weight proportioned."

"Keep going. Sounds good," Silver said.

"Um, cocoa complexion, not too dark but not so light that you question my ethnic background...um, you heard of Fred Williamson or Teddy Pendergrass?"

"Yeah, I have. I know Fred Williamson played ball and he later became an actor. And Teddy, whoa you can't get any better than '50/50 Love' unless your name is Brian McKnight," Silver answered.

"I would say I'm a cross between the two of them."

Silver surrendered. This man sounded like a dream come true. Brandan had really hit the jackpot this time. "Now where did you say you lived again?"

Silver emerged from the subway and brushed the dust from her Felicia Ferrar Original, a line of clothing she scooped from the New York–based designer's store on Fashion Avenue. The black and white wrapped dress, frayed at the knee and accentuated Silver's bold bust-line and twenty-five inch waist.

Confidently, she strolled the New York City streets in open-toed four-inch heels. The fact that several people gazed at her intently made it obvious that Silver had picked the perfect outfit, showing just enough skin and cleavage to entice but covering enough to suffice.

Just north of Forty-fourth Street and Ninth Avenue she came upon an immaculate green-glass-and-brick skyscraper. Silver cautiously walked through the door, awed at the palatial lobby and uniformed lobby workers. "Mr. Kendrick Armstrong, please," she said, approaching the concierge.

The woman slowly lifted her head and placed her glasses at the tip of her nose. "I.D. please." She stuck out her hand, looking annoyed.

Silver rummaged through her frou-frou purse, too small to carry much more than her keys, cell phone and driver's license. The concierge cleared her throat.

Silver slapped the license in the woman's palm and fluffed her hair in the mirror behind the podium. Every square inch was in place. "Is there a problem?" Silver asked, responding to the concierge's forced breath.

"Mr. Armstrong is expecting you. Please take this pass to the far end of the vestibule, make a quick left and your first right. Hand the pass to the elevator operator, and he'll escort you to the penthouse," the concierge said.

Silver snatched her license and placed it back in her purse. "Thank you," she said with an air of disdain. She sauntered away and turned the corner, admiring the female workers in black dresses and white-collared doilies polishing the grand brass-and-glass structure and watering the lush greenery that adorned her path.

Just before the elevator, Silver noticed a window display of mulberry-colored roses with blooms larger than a big man's hands. She followed her instincts and walked into a flower shop where she was greeted by a robust sister-girlfriend dressing an elaborate bouquet.

"Good evening," the woman said. "Wow, your hair is beautiful. Is that natural?" she asked, referring to the white streak in the front of Silver's hair.

"It is. Thank you. It's my birthmark," Silver said, patting her patch. "I tried to dye it once and it turned green." They both laughed. "I couldn't help but notice, you have some gorgeous flowers in here. It's my goal to have fresh flowers in my home daily. I love them."

"Flowers are therapeutic, and we supply to some of the finest homes, offices, spas and catering halls in the country. In fact, this arrangement I'm working on is going to a catering hall in Jersey that only uses Hawaiian exotics," she said, pointing to the array in front of her.

"Oh, Jersey. I'm from Jersey. Hi, I'm Silver." She extended her hand.

"I'm from Jersey, too. I'm Cheryl." She put down her shears, wiped her hands on her apron and grabbed Silver's. "It's nice to meet you."

"You too," Silver said, recoiling from Cheryl's man-like grip. "Are these real?" she asked, feeling the petals beside Cheryl's worktable.

"About a thousand dollars worth of real. These are some of the Hawaiians I spoke about. So what can I help you with today?" Cheryl resumed working.

Silver walked back to the window display. "I saw these and thought about buying a bouquet and presenting one to my blind date tonight."

Cheryl followed Silver's lead and smiled. "These are something. They are Brazilian roses and quite expensive," she cautioned.

That's okay." Silver became unnerved about this woman's assumption that she couldn't afford a bouquet of flowers. Besides, Kendrick would be spending a heck of a lot more on her, so it wouldn't hurt for her to splurge a little.

"Well, we can deliver the balance of the dozen to your home, and I'll dress one stem for you. Delivery would be free..." Cheryl pulled out a pocket-size calculator and typed away. "With taxes and because it's the last set I have, I'll give you a discount." She tapped a few more keys. "I can give them to you for this." Cheryl shoved the calculator in Silver's direction. "They also come in white but you don't want white for a first date. In some cultures white roses are equated with death..."

Silver's eyes bugged when she saw $325. "As in hundred dollars?" Silver's voice raised an octave.

Cheryl nodded sheepishly. "For someone special yes, but blind date, I wouldn't suggest it. Listen, how about I fix up a single pink oriental orchid." Cheryl led Silver away from the roses. "I'm having a sale. Pink is a safe color for friendship, and I could give you a single stem for twenty."

Barely hearing Cheryl's compromise, Silver became fixated on a small cobalt blue vase that held a familiar exotic-looking flower.

Cheryl followed her gaze. "Yeah, now these are really something. They're called Lady's Slipper Orchids, and they're more costly than the roses you like. You really do have expensive taste," Cheryl said. "The three stems go for two hundred seventy-five dollars, and that doesn't include the blown glass vase from the Metropolitan Museum line. The vase alone is about three hundred dollars." Cheryl smiled. "You okay?"

Silver emerged from her trance. "Yeah, I am. I just received two dozen of these last week."

"Really? Whoever you received them from must really be special because these are rare. I'm the only shop in the tri-state area that carries them fresh without special ordering. Now the Lady's Slipper has a less expensive cousin over here that you may have received—"

"No, I think I got these, but anyway, how much did you say for the pink. . .what is it?"

"Oriental." Cheryl's voice became less friendly. "Um, I said twenty, but I'll give it to you for fifteen. How about that?"

"Sold." Silver looked at her watch and realized she'd spent a lot more time in the shop than she'd planned. "Well, thanks for your help," Silver said a few minutes later after accepting her change and the well-dressed orchid.

Silver turned around to give the shop one final glance. She saw that Cheryl stared intently. An eeriness overpowered Silver, but she continued walking and decided the feeling was attributed to the anticipation of meeting Kendrick.

Silver entered the elevator, and the criss-crossed brass gates closed. The elevator then soared Silver and her temperature to the top. Her heart palpitations, which ascended with each floor, stopped when the gates opened to the most opulent mahogany wood-paneled foyer she'd ever seen.

"Have a good evening, ma'am," the operator said as he tipped his hat and disappeared, leaving her standing in the middle of heaven. She pressed a dim button near brass curved handles. The doors fanned open instantly at her release. She spoke to whom she believed was the butler. Hi, I'm Silver James. Kendrick Armstrong is expecting me."

"Yes. Welcome." The gentleman's dull smile altered the romantic glow of the room.

Something was strange, Silver thought as she walked inside and was met by a grand white piano against the backdrop of some of the most exquisite art she'd ever seen. Everyone else from the concierge to the elevator worker was appropriately uniformed and coiffed except Kendrick's butler. He was an older man, probably a lifelong friend, and he had on a worn pair of jean overalls, a white dress shirt and red bow tie. He could have used time in Kendrick's gym as his gut protruded past the sides of his turned-over shoes. His jolly and wrinkled jaw could have used a skilled plastic surgeon, and his receding hairline brought attention to a patch of misplaced crabgrass crumpled at the top of his head. He grabbed Silver's hand and kissed it, his beard felt so much like sandpaper, she checked her hand for blood.

Silver found her way to a gold Victorian settee. She placed the flower on her lap and gazed at the magnificent room, which was grander than the lobby and foyer. She gawked at shiny oak floors complemented by white butter leather furniture and a full glass wall that gave a panoramic view of the Manhattan skyline on one side and New Jersey on the other.

"You like it, I take." The butler's statement rang with an air of familiarity.

"I do. I don't mean to be rude, but would you please get Mr. Armstrong. It's getting late, and I don't want to miss our reservation." Silver turned her attention to the room.

"I'm sorry. I'm the rude one." Just as he said the word *one,* Silver's heart dropped and landed on her knees. She looked into the man's eyes as his voice resonated through her brain.

No, no, nooooooooooooooooooo, she thought. This had to be a cruel joke, and Brandan was the jester.

"I'm Kendrick. I was so taken by your beauty, I neglected to introduce myself properly. Cocktail?" He pointed to a bar so elaborate, it should have been in a restaurant. "It's Hennessy. That's your drink, right? Brandan told me."

Silver accepted the drink and threw it to the back of her throat. She coughed at its harshness.

"Wow, that was quick. Would you like something else? Anything you want, I have it, even some Louis the Fourteenth."

"Um, no, I'm okay," she said as a bewildered expression crossed her face. "May I use your bathroom?" She coughed and pounded her chest.

"Sure. It's just around the corner. Don't worry about the light. It'll pop on once you enter."

Silver scrambled to her feet and placed the lone flower she'd purchase on the piano. "For you," she said. She couldn't bear to put it in his hand. She tipped in the direction he'd told her, grateful for the distance.

Silver walked into the bathroom and stopped in front of a man-size mirror. "He should have looked into this," she said aloud as she pulled her cell from her purse. She pressed the number one and waited to hear Brandan's voice. When the machine picked up, Silver left a menacing message. "I can't believe you hooked me up with Jethro. I'm not going anywhere with this clown, 21 Club or not. I don't care how much money he has, you are dead meat." She hung up and swished cold water in her mouth.

When Silver re-entered the room, natural moonlight brightened it. Kendrick was on the phone, so Silver glided toward the view where she felt a breeze. Half of the wall had been retracted so that the room was a part of the skyline. The sight was breathtaking. If not for the railing beyond the patio and greenery, she would have sworn she would have plunged fifty floors to the pavement. Looking back at Kendrick, she almost thought to do just that.

"Man, I need an oxygen tank. She's everything you said and more," she heard Kendrick say.

"Is that Brandan?"

Kendrick continued talking.

"May I speak with him please?"

Kendrick hung up abruptly. "He said he had to go. He had company. Another drink before we head to the restaurant?" He handed her a freshly filled glass.

Silver accepted it and walked back to the patio. She couldn't take her eyes away from the view.

"This is my favorite feature of the house. The place was designed by—"

"Roderick N. Shade," Silver said, taking a sip of her drink. It rolled down like her throat was coated with marble.

"Wow, I'm really impressed. How did you know?" Kendrick asked, inching closer.

"I'm very familiar with his work. He designed Star Jones's home as well. My brother-in-law is an architect and often encourages people to contact Shade for designs. I love his work. I wish I could afford a house to have him decorate for me."

"Well, maybe you can. I sure wouldn't be opposed to getting some help on changing this place." Kendrick was so close Silver cold smell his breath, a mixture of cognac and cigar. She thought she was going to be sick. "Would you like to see the rest of the house before we go?"

Silver thought about it. It was rare to see a place of this magnitude, and opportunities of grandeur at this level were even rarer. She pondered just a moment longer and decided she wasn't interested in this man and prolonging the night's fate would only cause more pain, for her. She gulped the last of her second drink. "Um, I'm going to go. I'm sorry Kendrick, but this isn't going to work." Fewer words and firmness were the keys to her freedom. "Thanks for your time, and take care." Silver made her own path to the door.

"Oh no, wait. There's no reason to be hasty. Have another drink. My chef is on call. He can prepare us something. We don't have to go out, but please let's continue with the great conversation we started," Kendrick pleaded.

"No. If I go now I'll catch my train without waiting too long."

"Well then, I can have my car take you. Just give me a minute to call my driver." Kendrick picked up the phone and began dialing.

"I'd rather take the train." She walked through the door and pressed the button for the elevator. The operator opened the gates and greeted her with a smile. Just as he tried to close them, Kendrick slipped through.

"I could at least walk you to the train," he said, trying to catch his breath. When the elevator landed on the bottom floor, Kendrick huffed and puffed to keep up with Silver's stride. Cheryl, the florist, was still in the window and gave a faint wave. In half the time it took Silver to walk to Kendrick's building she was back at the subway.

"Can we at least be friends? Can I call you from time to time?" Kendrick bent over with his hands on his knees breathing so hard he could have blown a hole in the pavement.

"No, I'd prefer not. Thanks and take care."

Kendrick stood, grabbed her hand and kissed it, leaving a mixture of perspiration and slob. She shook her head and entered into the underground tunnel, grateful to have gotten away.

Silver cussed the entire New York City transit system as she marched through Penn Station, Newark and the Gateway buildings to the lot that held her car. A subway delay had her sprinting to catch the last Jersey transit train to cross the Hudson at almost 1:00 A.M.

She approached the gate that normally stayed open twenty-four hours, but for some reason it was closed and the attendant's kiosk was dark. She shook the gate to see if it would open but it didn't budge. "Hello," she cried. "Anybody there?" All she heard were the sounds of rustling paper in the streets.

This can't be happening. *What else could go wrong tonight?* she thought as she tapped her foot and pulled her cell phone from her purse. She speed-dialed number one.

"Hello?" a groggy female voice answered.

"Brandan please," Silver said, annoyed.

"Excuse you. Who is this?"

"Excuse nothing. Who is this? I said Brandan," Silver retorted.

"Hold up…"

Silver heard movement, then mumbling before Brandan finally came to the phone. "Sil, is that you? You okay?" he asked, sounding frantic.

"Yeah. Listen. My car is stuck in the lot across the street from my job. For some reason the lot is locked, and I can't find the attendant, and he has my car and house keys. I just wanted to make sure you were there. I'm coming to your place to get my spare keys. I'll worry about my car in the morning."

"I'll come get you. You can stay here and then I'll take you back to your car in the morning."

"Brandan, I'm not staying there while you have some hooch in your bed," Silver spewed. "And besides, I'm mad at you. Why didn't you tell me that man looked like Jethro?"

"Silver, this isn't a request. I'll be there in about twenty minutes. See if you can wait in the lobby next door. I'll pull into that circular driveway."

"Twenty minutes? How about ten? You don't live that far away."

"Okay, ten. Just wait inside and leave your cell phone on."

"Do I ever cut it off?" Silver asked. Brandan didn't bother to answer. She closed the phone and placed it in her purse.

She limped next door. Her feet were killing her since she had to stand for the entire ride on both trains. She knew she didn't look like a vagrant but she couldn't imagine the guard would allow her to wait inside. Suddenly, she remembered her co-worker mentioning that their boss, Daphne Dix, lived in the building. Silver didn't want to use Daphne's name for fear she might bring some indiscretion to a woman she was just getting to know and needed to impress, but she'd do almost anything to grab a seat inside the building.

Luckily, the front doors were unlocked and the security guard was snoring loudly. Silver sat on the very bottom of marble steps just beyond the doors.

Brandan finally pulled up some thirty minutes later to find Silver puffed up. She peered through the tinted glass windows to make sure the front seat was vacant. "What took you so long?" she asked as she slammed the door. "I've been waiting for you forever. I can't believe you took so long." Silver folded her arms across her chest, and threw herself against the seat. She opened her mouth to speak, but before words could escape, her stomach growled, indicating she was hungry.

"Wow, thanks for coming to get me, Brandan," he responded sarcastically. "You are so sweet even though it's almost two in the morning. Stop complaining."

"Like I said, what took you so long? You had to get your last piece?" Silver smoothed her dress over her legs, rubbing some warmth into them as they headed to Brandan's apartment. "You know your dick is going to fall off. Which hooch this time? Mona or Savannah?"

Brandan cocked his head and rolled his eyes. "I don't hang with hooches as you call them. And it was Savannah."

Silver stepped in the apartment behind Brandan. She loved his loft but its open airiness had its drawbacks. The smell of sex permeated the room. She ruffled under the counter and found some citrus deodorizer and sprayed until they choked on the fumes.

"Stop it. What are you doing?" Brandan asked.

Silver pursed her lips and headed to the bathroom. She rummaged underneath the sink until she found what she wanted.

"Now what are you looking for?" Brandan appeared in the doorway.

"Bath salts." She turned on the water and poured what lingered at the bottom of an old bubble bath bottle. "Do you have any salts, like Epsom? My dogs are hurting." She rubbed her feet while she sat at the edge of the tub.

"Why are you taking a bath this late?"

"'Cause I can't sleep without one, even if it is on your funky couch."

"Well I don't have any Epsom salt." Brandan placed his hand over his mouth as if to contain laughter. "So how did your date go?"

Silver put her chin to her chest and rolled her eyes. "Why did you hook me up with Jethro? You knew I wouldn't be seen with him. I don't care how long his dollars are."

"He called me after he walked you to the train. He said you jetted like you were in a haunted mansion." Brandan laughed openly.

"That man described himself as a cross between Fred Williamson and Teddy Pendergrass. He should have said Fred Sanford and Grady, even though Redd Foxx at his worse would have been insulted. Anyway, you should have told me how that man looked." She tested the bath water, and it was perfect.

"You never asked. I'm going to bed." Brandan turned. "I'll throw you down a jersey or something to sleep in."

"Yeah, give me one of your shirts and not something one of your hooches left behind." Silver loosened the belt on her dress. "Keep it up, you won't have a dick left to stick them with. You know your dick is going to fall off."

"Please, girl, I use a condom every time I bone anybody. Besides, Savannah's a sweet girl." The conversation stopped Brandan from retreating upstairs.

"Sweet, and stupid I might add."

"Why do you say that?"

"That woman spends time with you and will do anything for you, including sleep with you on a moment's notice when it's convenient for you and still goes for that let's-play-it-by-ear bull—you know, just friends for now. Please. Y'all aren't friends. You're lovers pretending." Silver stretched. "You know that girl wants more and you just keep stringing her along."

"You sure it's Savannah you're speaking of?" Brandan asked bluntly. "Hey, I don't mean anything mean by it, but Todd isn't worthy of you, baby girl. Todd's a punk, and that's why I set you up with Kendrick. He's a good guy with a decent heart, and that's what you want for your peeps, even when they don't want the best for themselves." Brandan gave her a warm bear hug.

"But he looks like Elmer Fudd. I can't do it, Brandan." Silver playfully pounded his chest.

"Hey, it was worth a try. I'll see you in the morning, and don't snore because I can hear everything upstairs."

Silver spent about twenty minutes thinking about the evening with Kendrick and why she couldn't shake Todd out of her system. She knew Todd was jive, but the truth was, if Todd straightened up his act, he'd be perfect for her. She liked his rugged, take-charge attitude and his assertion of his manhood. When she was around him she felt protected, invincible. She only wished that Todd showed that he felt the same way.

Thoroughly relaxed, she unfolded the blankets Brandan left on the couch for her. He was snoring right above her head louder than the security guard from the building she'd waited in earlier. She picked up the jersey he'd left for her and turned it inside out. "Ooh. He's gonna get it for sure now." She laughed. Brandan had thrown down a Roger Staubach throw-back jersey. Silver hated the Dallas Cowboys, and Brandan knew it. He was probably laughing in his sleep.

This morning was not the day for Silver to be late. She rushed around her apartment willing herself to get ready and get to her meeting with Daphne at 8:30 sharp. Even though she only lived ten minutes away from her downtown Newark office, she found herself dragging after standing in a line of early-morning angry patrons trying to retrieve their cars. Apparently the night guard had gone AWOL and caused a band of controversy that set Silver back an hour and a half.

She stepped out of her dress and bra. She had discarded her thong at Brandan's. The thought of soiled panties touching her clean body repulsed her. The bra would have suffered the same fate if it hadn't set her back fifty-five bucks apiece at Victoria's Secret. She eased herself under the pulsating beat of the water, hoping it would invigorate her.

Silver submerged her full body under the water and against the cold wall tile, not caring that she'd have to wear a white girl slicked-back wet look for the day. A few minutes later, she pushed herself away from the wall and allowed the water to pound against her voluptuous breasts and slender hips. She lathered up first with an antibacterial soap then a perfumed one. Just as she turned to rinse her back, the shower curtain was jerked open, causing her to scream.

"Todd, what in the hell are you doing here?"

Chapter 3

Save the Drama for Your Mama

Silver trotted past the receptionist, failing to grab her mail or say hello. She rounded the corner to her cubicle and hurled her Coach briefcase on the desk. She was pulling out several binders when her coworker, Pat Ghanem, halted her flow.

"Wow, somebody got some last night, recently or something." Pat stepped into Silver's space and stared into her eyes.

Silver continued looking for her presentation without a word. It was 8:30 A.M. In the past few weeks she had been at her desk early. Todd's surprise visit broke that streak.

"Look at that glow. No wonder you're late. Couldn't get up, huh?"

"I'm not late. Our official work day begins now, so technically at eight-thirty I'm on time. Now excuse me. I have to go into to Daphne's office." Silver gingerly brushed past Pat who was eight and a half months pregnant and looked ready to burst any minute.

"Don't bother. She left."

Silver stopped. She pinched the bridge of her nose and rubbed the wrinkle at her brow. "Did she say anything before she left, like when she'd be back or that she was looking for me? We were supposed to have a meeting this morning."

"She did come looking for you but said she won't be back until this afternoon. After my baby shower I'm sure, so you might as well sit down and tell me all about it. Was he as good as Brandan said?" Pat's smile widened. "I don't know why Brandan would hook you up with his friend anyway because—"

"Pat, enough." Silver's frown let Pat know that she was dangerously close to a forbidden line.

"Okay, just tell me then, was it good at least? Must have been for you to have boned him on the first date, 'cause that sure ain't like you." Pat sat down and rested her legs on the top of Silver's garbage pail.

"My date was a bust." Silver sat behind her desk and placed her papers in organized piles. "Then I got locked out of my car and...Pat, I have a lot to do. Maybe we can talk during a coffee break or lunch." Silver's thoughts were jumbled and torn. Todd still lingered on her mind.

"We could talk during lunch but then you'd miss my shower."

Pat's baby shower was supposed to be a surprise and Silver couldn't fake it. She sat forward and cradled her head in her hand. "Okay, how did you find out?"

Pat pulled a bright yellow flyer that peeped from under Silver's desk calendar. She smiled triumphantly at her successful snooping. "When Daphne left early and said she wasn't returning until this afternoon that confirmed my suspicion because you know how Daphne hates baby showers and maternity leaves. The only reason she signed off on my leave was because I threatened to sue her ass."

Silver twisted her lips. She knew Pat was telling the truth about Daphne's dislike for Pat. When Daphne first arrived three months ago, Silver thought she challenged Pat because Pat was white. Silver still wasn't convinced that racism wasn't a part of Daphne's vendetta. Whether a small or large part, it was apparent that Daphne had other issues affecting their relationship. Daphne had made her disdain for trivialities such as pregnancy, matrimony or familial concession painfully clear upon her arrival.

"Well, do me a big favor and try to act surprised. The girls went through a lot of trouble for you," Silver said.

"I'll try, but hiding anything these days is getting harder." Pat rubbed her belly. "Well, I'll let you attempt to get some work done, but I'm not letting you off the hook." Pat struggled to rise and circled Silver's desk. "I know you got some. It's all over your face, and you know a sistah has to live vicariously through you."

"You kill me switching to urban vernacular, Ms. Suburbia." Silver laughed.

"Don't laugh, sistah," Pat said, emphasizing the word again.

"You're a sistah now?"

"I'm always your sistah, and don't you forget it. A little cream in the coffee is always a good thing." Pat winked and retreated. "Hey, Lynne, I heard there's a shower going on today. Care to tell me about it..." Silver heard Pat yelling beyond the cubicle. She didn't know why she had tried to convince Pat to keep a confidence.

Since she had some additional time, Silver thought it best to complete another project by re-vamping some of her requirements documents for her presentation to Daphne. She wanted to be ready when and if she still had a chance to meet with her that day.

As much as she tried to concentrate, Silver's mind reverted to Todd's strange behavior. She had seen him twice in one week. Normally, twice a month was a deluge. On any other day, she would have been long gone for work at the hour he showed up. Furthermore, since when did he resume using his key? She thought he lost it when he didn't use it the other night. She would purposely neglect to replace it. Maybe he wanted to get more serious with her. She thought. She couldn't help to wonder what had happened to allow him more time, which he so veraciously protected?

Once again Todd took up space in her soul, and Silver hated that. She placed her mechanical pencil on her desk and decided to leave well enough alone. A Grande Caramel Apple Cider would do her well at the moment. She snuck past Pat's slightly ajar door, wanting a moment for herself. She dodged morning Mulberry Street traffic and headed over to the downtown Starbucks where the store manager allowed her to usurp the line by placing her favorite steamy beverage on the side bar. Silver stuffed a generous tip into the jar and sipped her drink on her way back to the office.

The walk temporarily did some good. Relieved that Daphne still hadn't returned, Silver was startled when she stumbled into a vase containing two dozen white Brazilian roses similar to the ones she had seen in the flower shop the night before.

Silver placed the hot cup down and eyed the card which read, Thanks for a wonderful evening...looking forward to many more. The card wasn't signed. She sighed and grabbed her head. The ache returned just as the phone rang. She quickly picked it up. "Sci-gex Systems, Silver speaking."

"Cool. Glad I caught you. I need a favor." Brandan was on the phone.

"Whew."

"What's that for?"

"Nothing. I thought you were Kendrick. I'll explain later. What's the favor, Brandan?"

"I need you to go down neck," Brandan said, referring to a place where native Jerseyans traveled to Newark's Portuguese section for seafood, "and pick up a bag of colossal shrimp for my dish tonight. I'm getting out of the dealership late, and the market will be closed by the time I get there."

"Brandan, it's hotter than July out there. Beside Pat's shower is starting in a few minutes, and I might not have time during lunch. Ferry Street traffic is a bear after work. I'm tired and—"

"If you weren't messing with that damn Todd this morning, you wouldn't be so tired," Brandan interrupted.

"Todd wasn't at my place this morning, smart-ass."

"Don't lie. I saw his car in front of your place when I drove by on my way to work."

"Whatever. Guess what?" Silver changed the subject. "Your boy sent me two-dozen flowers, but get this, they're worth hundreds of dollars."

"How do you know how much they cost?"

"Because I saw the same flowers at the floral shop in his building last night. The clerk probably told him I was looking at them or something. He didn't sign the card, but I know they came from him."

"Well if he didn't sign the card, how do you know they came from him instead of Todd's latest fuck-you gift?"

"Because Todd never sends me flowers at work, and it would be too coincidental for him to send the same flowers I saw last night. Anyway, the dozen goes for about three hundred dollars and Todd ain't spending that kind of money on one dozen much less two. You have to call Kendrick for me and tell him I'm not interested."

"Oh, come on, Sil. I'm not getting in the middle of that."

"You will if you want me to get your shrimp."

"Silver, the shower is about to start," a coworker said, peeking around her cubicle wall.

"What's it going to be 'cause I gotta go? Pat's shower is starting."

"All right, all right. You got me. Use your key and put the shrimp in my fridge please. And get the colossal, not the extra large. Oh, and make sure they're de-veined."

"You sure are asking for a lot. When are you going to call Kendrick?"

"Now," Brandan said reluctantly.

"Cool. Later." Silver hung up, picked up the bouquet and inhaled their fragrant beauty. She pulled out an extra ribbon she had used to wrap Pat's gift and tied a huge red bow around the stem of six of the full blooms. She then took them to present them to Pat. "No sense in them going to

Toni Staton Harris

waste," she said aloud as she sauntered into the party.

Silver was helping Pat's husband with the last of the gifts when Daphne breezed through the conference room, giving shallow congratulations and requesting to meet with Silver immediately.

Daphne was incredibly jovial when Silver entered the office.

"Have a seat," Daphne said, strutting around the desk. She closed and locked the door before returning to her desk. "I don't have a lot of time, but I have great news to share."

Silver looked around the office. She didn't see the inside of it very often. It resembled a mortuary, barely allowing any light to shine through the institutional brown blinds.

Daphne sat in the chair opposite Silver. "I'll get straight to the point. I like what you do around here. Your work is good, precise, exact even. Well today I've booked an account that is going to put Sci-gex on the map. A great firm, HRL Equities, a major player in the real estate investment and development industry, has agreed to allow us to overhaul its network for all of its offices, including the ones in L.A., Baltimore, D.C. and right here in Newark. This is a priority, mid-level, million-dollar account that has the capacity to span for five years. Isn't that exciting?" Daphne reached over the desk and pumped her fists in the air.

"It sounds wonderful, Daphne. Congratulations." Silver's voice wasn't convincing as she squared her shoulders to maintain her guarded posture.

Daphne continued to explain the operation and the perks for landing such a laudable account. Silver listened intently. "Well, this all sounds great, but I'm not sure how everything affects me. I mean Pat will return from maternity leave soon, and she'll handle priority accounts as she has been."

"Not quite." Daphne stood and twirled around to open the blinds a bit. "Actually, plans have been altered. After landing the account, I met with Sci-gex's board. There are going to be some changes around here. I hope you're prepared for them." Daphne poured herself a glass of water. She pulled a decorative pill box from her desk. Her thick fingers fumbled through the tiny compartments until she grabbed two tiny light blue pills. She sipped some water, then placed the pills at the back of her throat, threw her head back and took a gulp of water. "Silver, I want you to work with me," Daphne said with her back to Silver, peering out the window to the parking lot.

"Sounds good. In what capacity?"

Daphne returned her attention to Silver. "You'll be working on priority and supervising mid-level accounts. Of course you'd be expected to handle your duties in your department, but I'll be happy to divert your workload to other associates as the projects increase. The HRL account won't get started for another month or so. It sounds like a lot, but I promise you that you'll have my support, a fully apprised staff and the nod of senior management."

Silver crossed her legs, feeling slightly more relaxed, taking in everything that was being said very carefully. "Sounds challenging but I'm up for it. Is there a pay raise and title adjustment with all of this responsibility?"

"That's what I like about you, Silver. You are so sharp."

Silver raised an eyebrow.

"Yes and no," Daphne answered, pouring more water. This time she offered Silver a glass, but Silver declined. "You'll get a small bonus during your six-month probation. You shine, and within a year we offer a substantial salary increase and title."

"Well, I know I can do it. Once Pat returns, she'll get her group back and that'll ease me up a bit."

"No it won't." Daphne perched her petite body on the edge of her desk and crossed her arms. "Pat won't be coming back in the same capacity if she's allowed to come back at all."

"Excuse me?"

"You heard me. When and if Pat returns, she'll be assisting you. You will of course assume her office space, which moves you out of that silly cubicle thing." Daphne waved her hands in the air. She turned back to the blinds and rubbed her chin. "I think I'm going to leave early tonight. I really need to look for a new car. My Jaguar is just giving me a fit. Maybe I'll trade it in for a new Mercedes. You drive a nice one. What is it exactly?"

"It's an ML 320. Daphne, I don't understand. Is Pat being demoted?"

"Oh, where did you get yours?" Daphne asked, ignoring the question.

"Luxury Motors in Little Falls," Silver answered with a slight annoyance in her voice.

"What did you say?" Daphne turned back.

"Little Falls. Luxury Motors is where I got my Mercedes. My best friend, Brandan, sold me mine."

"Oh yes." Daphne tugged her suit jacket. "Is yours a lease or purchase?"

"Lease." Silver was fast getting tired of Daphne's charade.

"Oh, that makes sense. I'd heard you drove a Mercedes, and frankly, I was surprised. I knew you couldn't afford one on your salary."

Silver sat forward, ready to strike. Daphne was dangerously close to crossing the line so Silver dropped her head, and her eyes shot to the top of her brow. "Wait a minute. My car is not the issue. What's going on and what does my new position, if I take it, have to do with Pat being demoted, and why is she being demoted? She has done a great job around here." Silver was so annoyed her voice trembled.

Daphne patted her hair and scratched her scalp. Silver knew it was a sign that she was wearing a weave—and wearing it quite attractively. "I've been with this firm for five years now. It's my job to get this office in tip-top shape, or it's closing for lack of revenue. I can bring the money in, but I can't keep it here if I can't service the big boys the way high-end firms are accustomed to being taken care of. That means I need everyone's cooperation. Families, babies...all of that block one's commitment, and I'm not here to pacify anyone. Family ties are cute, fun even, but not in the workplace. Your work is impeccable, and you don't have children. You are my perfect candidate for the position that's going to change with or without you." Daphne tilted her head.

"Are you saying that if I choose to have children, my job would be in jeopardy?" Silver was seething. She leaned forward with one hand on her knee and her elbow cocked. She pounded the thin carpet rapidly with her heel.

"Children would be your choice, but not a wise one." Daphne planted herself on the edge of the desk, waving her leg in Silver's direction. "You're thirty-two years old, no obvious ties. You're on the upward bound career track. Why would you want to spoil all of that?"

Daphne turned and then sat in her oversized cherry leather chair. "Listen, you can take it or leave it, Silver. Now I admire—" she clasped her hands together then leaned on her desk and searched for the right words—"your loyalty to your little friend. It's cute," she said with a listless laugh. "The truth of the matter is that if you don't take this position, someone else who doesn't resemble you or me will, and if an outsider comes in, you might not be needed here. Now, I'm looking out for your best interest. It's up to you."

Silver stood and forced herself to remain composed. "I don't do threats."

"Threats. Cute." Daphne's tone suddenly softened. "Silver, I'm not threatening you. I'm trying to give you a gift here. It is truly up to you."

Daphne stood and touched Silver's arm. "You have forty-eight hours to get back to me with an answer. Please see yourself out." Silver fidgeted under the heaviness of Daphne's large hand. "Don't let me down." Daphne pranced back around to her desk as if Silver wasn't still standing there. Silver turned the knob and walked through the door. "Oh, Silver," Daphne called out, "where did you say you purchased your car again?"

Silver took it upon herself to take the rest of the day off. She sped up Market Street to drop off Brandan's shrimp and planned on heading to her sister's to talk about Daphne's proposal. Everything in her gut told her to tell Daphne to take her position and shove it, but there was a lot to consider. It wouldn't be easy or pleasing for Silver to concede defeat. She was a hard worker and should be rewarded for such. To have an outsider come in and ruin her chances for progress, the opportunity to make more money and achieve a higher status would be foolish on her part, especially if Pat's dismissal was inevitable. She couldn't help but feel conflicted. She had to talk to someone.

Silver skipped up the brick steps to Brandan's apartment. She inserted her key, and before she could shove open the door, Savannah stood in a black leather cat suit, her naked breasts were pointing through cutouts. "Welcome home, sweetie," Savannah said, not realizing that it wasn't Brandan at the front door.

Silver cleared her throat.

"Oh my goodness. Silver, I thought you were Brandan coming home early. I'm sorry, please, oh my goodness." She darted up the stairs to the loft bedroom.

Silver's eyes widened as she tried to contain her laughter. She placed the shrimp in the fridge as Brandan asked and retrieved a beer. "Savannah, I'm leaving. Just tell Brandan I was here and I'll call him tomorrow. Sorry. Didn't mean to scare you." Silver made her way to the door. "Oh, and tell Brandan that my boss is coming by his job sometime this week to probably buy a car from him. Details at eleven."

"Wait, wait, Silver, please don't go. I need to talk to you. I'm just changing into something more presentable," Savannah yelled from upstairs.

"I really can't stay. I have to meet my sister and…"

Savannah was down the stairs before Silver finished her statement. She had changed from the cat lady to a southern belle in a clingy peach sundress and matching heels. "May I offer you something to drank?"

Silver held up the beer bottle, showing she had helped herself.

"Oh. Yes. Of course. Silver, may I talk to you for just a minute?" Savannah positioned herself at Brandan's island counter in a swivel chair. "Please." She patted the seat next to her.

"Savannah, I really can't stay. I have a lot to do, and I'm on my way to my sister's and…"

"Please?"

Whatever Savannah wanted to talk about seemed serious. Silver wasn't sure she could take another heavy conversation. Savannah's tone reeked of a topic Silver eagerly avoided with all of Brandan's girlfriends. Every one of them had it eventually. "Silver does Brandan love me?' or 'Is he seeing someone else?' or 'How can I get closer to his heart?'"

"I don't mean to be rude, Savannah, but I can't imagine that you have anything you need to discuss with me." She attempted to save Savannah from being dismissed because of placing Silver in the middle of Brandan's relationship.

"It won't take long. I promise."

Silver sat down at the island and sipped her beer quietly, waiting for the bomb to drop.

"I have to get to the point."

Here's another one, getting straight to the point, supposedly, Silver thought as she took another sip, running out of patience.

"This really bothers me." Savannah pointed to Silver's beer bottle.

"The fact that I'm drinking one of Brandan's beers?" That statement wasn't what Silver expected.

"No, the fact that you just walk into my man's place, grab yourself a beer like this is your place. I understand you guys are close—"

"Best friends," Silver corrected.

"Best friends, but your actions certainly don't make me feel any better. I mean, Brandan kicked me out of his bed to come get you. I can't so much as breathe a word about your relationship without Brandan becoming incredibly defensive. Everything about you is off limits. I don't have a problem with you per se. I'm just at a loss as to how to be in a meaningful relationship with a man I adore without your interference. Do you understand what I'm saying? I mean, think about it. I've been around for a while, a little over a year to be exact. Put yourself in my shoes. How would you handle this situation if the shoe was on the other foot?"

Sincerity was sensed as Savannah got a beer for herself and offered another one to Silver.

She catches on quickly, Silver thought, declining the offer. Tears began to well innocently in Savannah's eyes. *Wrong move, girlfriend. Never show your weakness.*

"It's like this, Savannah. Brandan and I are best friends. We have been since we were ten. I moved in with a sister I didn't know I had after my mom passed. My sister is the daughter of a dad I never knew. If she didn't take me in, I would have ended up in New York City foster homes without a prayer. My father's family refused to acknowledge me, and to top it all off, I don't get along with my sister's mother because I'm a constant reminder of my father's infidelity."

"I'm sorry."

"Don't feel sorry for me, Savannah. That's not why I'm telling you this. I'm trying to give you an understanding of my connection with Brandan." Silver tapped her finger on the ceramic countertop for emphasis. "When I moved to Jersey, I might as well have moved to the moon. I withdrew. I didn't speak to anyone for a month, and I didn't eat or drink for almost as long. Finally, my sister had to put me in the hospital for dehydration and malnutrition. They had to feed me intravenously.

"My sister was convinced I was trying to die. Then my next-door neighbor and her son with all of the sweet potatoes, collards and smothered chicken one could eat, showed up. I still wouldn't eat, but her son talked me out of my depression, then he taught me how to play chess—a ten-year-old boy with the wisdom of a grown man. By the end of the month I was laughing so hard and eating so much that the doctor thought my sister would have to put me on a diet. From that day forward, Brandan's been my rock, my friend, my brother and sometimes my father, even though I buck that. I would do anything for Brandan, literally sacrifice my life for him 'cause he puts it on the line for me every time. So you don't have to worry about any blurred lines between us. And better than that, you don't have to ever worry about Brandan's or my feelings blocking his feelings for you."

Savannah looked down at her feet. "I wish Brandan trusted me enough to share this with me."

"It's not for him to share with anyone, Savannah." Silver didn't mean to be cold, but she could tell her comment offended Savannah. "Now let's be real about you. A year ago I met a man I thought—no, I knew—I was in love with. I would have sworn on my life—on my mother's grave—he was in love with me too. Now he's just developed into a bad habit. It took me some time, but I'm finally realizing that he doesn't see me the way I see him or us."

"You sure you don't want another beer?" Savannah asked.

Silver smiled and shook her head. "But to make a long story longer, we did a lot of things together, but always in the dark and not in the light. You ever heard of the singing group Brownstone?"

Savannah nodded.

"Listen carefully to the cut, 'If You Love Me' then ask yourself the question, 'if he loves me...' If the answer is no, accept the relationship for what it is and when you're ready to move on, you'll stop deceiving yourself."

"Thanks, Silver."

Silver gave her a closed-lip plastic smile and made her way to the door. She was really surprised, but Savannah had actually passed the test of not including Silver in her and Brandan's relationship. The conversation was really about a woman who cared for Brandan and wanted to truly be a part of his life without any perceived interference.

Silver turned to apologize to Savannah for the previous night's catfight over the phone but Savannah trumped her move. They accepted each other's unspoken truce.

"Oh, and Silver..." Savannah caught her going out the door.

Silver turned.

"Is Brandan seeing anyone else?"

Chapter 4

Housequake

A week later, following a hectic time full of decisions, Silver and her sister, Jill, milled about the formal dining room where most of the dinner party would take place. The wait staff and chef of the day had just arrived and Jill wanted to add her finishing touches before turning over the reigns to the professionals.

Silver opened the pane-glass French doors off the dining room to allow a fresh honeysuckled breeze. Jill's husband, Sebastian Drummond, had planted the patch the previous spring.

"So did Pat and her husband change their minds about coming?" Jill asked, placing Plexiglas prism place cards on chartreuse charger platters.

"No. I spoke with her, and she really isn't feeling up to it. In fact, she thinks she may go into labor early, possibly this weekend." Silver picked up pewter glass identifiers and started placing them around the stems of the champagne flutes, so that as the evening progressed people wouldn't forget which glass was theirs.

"So, did you tell her about the position and everything you and Daphne talked about?"

"No. I told you Daphne asked me—rather warned me—to keep everything confidential until a formal announcement is made. Besides, I didn't know what to say to Pat. She said she's going to take her maternity leave early. She's not coming back to the office next week."

"Oh good."

"Why is that good?" Silver balled up the tissue paper that held her trinkets and shot it in the trash.

"Not good about the office thing, good that Pat and her husband aren't coming because I have a surprise for you." Jill was obviously excited about the party because her mind seemed to jump without warning. "I know it's a tough decision but Sil, Sebastian and I discussed it, and we both feel it's the best decision you can make. You really have to look out for yourself, your future."

Silver didn't respond. She wanted to figure out everything in her own mind. She felt awful about deceiving Pat. She wanted to give her co-worker a heads-up, but Brandan and Jill had advised against it. Silver followed her sister around the table straightening the place cards even though they were perfect. She stopped in front of the setting marked PAULA MITCHELL. "I'm surprised your mom agreed to eat in the same room with me. Why didn't she want to sit in the informal dining room with Brandan's mother and sisters?"

"Don't worry yourself about that. I've placed her on the far end of the table, away from you, Brandan and Savannah. I wouldn't dare put her in the room with Brandan's sisters. I didn't even want to invite them, but Sebastian insisted that they're family, so...you know it's getting close to time. You better go get dressed," Jill said, changing the subject.

Silver smiled.

"What? What?" Jill asked.

"You. If you didn't want to invite his sisters, Ghetto Fab and Ghetto Fool, why did you?"

Jill shrugged.

"You are too polite for your own good. If it were up to me, I wouldn't invite them or your mother and her ol' evil ass self."

"Silver, I don't allow my mother to speak ill of you, and I won't tolerate that from you either. She'll get herself together one day." Jill stopped in her tracks and turned with her hand on her hip. "You know, I dropped Abigail off the other day and my mother was going through her old wedding photos and stuff. If I didn't know better, I'd think she was pining after that old man. I believe she'd take him back if she knew where he was." Jill shook her head in disgust.

It pained Silver to see her sister's apathy concerning her father who had skipped out on his family the day Silver was made known to everyone. It had been twenty years, and Jill didn't know if he was still alive since he hadn't contacted the family. For Silver, it wasn't as bad.

She'd never known him so she felt her loss could never be as great as Jill's.

"I'm gonna get dressed. Everything cool down here?" Silver asked.

Jill nodded.

"Oh, I forgot to mention, do you have a blank place card or one that reads Guest for Brandan? Savannah isn't coming."

"Whoa, another one bites the dust?" Jill followed Silver out the dining room through the kitchen.

"Yup. I don't think it's permanent though. She asked me the death question the other day so Brandan put her on a time-out. I was trying to help Savannah, but Brandan said he doesn't have time for silliness."

Jill blocked Silver's path. "Then why did you tell him? You didn't have to, you know." Her voice had a slight hum like she was saying less than what she wanted to.

"Brandan and I don't have secrets. You know that."

"Um-hmm," Jill said. "Do you know who he's bringing?"

"I'm sure he'll be able to pull one of his standby hooches, even though I don't know which one. I have to get dressed, Jill. Show me my surprise, please."

Jill pulled out a half of sheet cake with the words *Congratulations, Silver, on a job well deserved* inscribed in platinum.

"That's why I wanted to find out if Pat was coming. You like?"

"Red Velvet?"

Jill grinned.

"No." Silver turned to walk away then turned back. "I love it. Thanks, sister."

"You're welcome, baby girl. Now go get dressed."

The chef was bustling around the kitchen. Clearly, Jill and Silver's presence annoyed her. "Anything or anyone in my way is getting thrown into the pot with the lobsters," she said.

Both Silver and Jill laughed at the harried Cajun chef and scurried out of her way. Silver ran upstairs to ready herself for what was sure to be a night she would not forget.

In the mirror Silver ran her fingers across her sleek black mane. As usual, the streak fell right into place. She was tickled pink at her reflection—the image of a strong woman who had made it despite the odds. She delighted in her attractiveness. When she was younger, she thought her beauty mark to be a curse.

Silver had been called Lily Monster for the last time when she and Brandan at twelve years old had the bright idea to dye her patch. Jill had previously forbade Silver to touch her birthmark but Silver and Brandan decided that once Jill caught a glimpse of the new-and-improved Silver, reprimand would be the farthest thought from Jill's mind.

With the remnants of Silver's monthly allowance and the money Brandan could collect, Silver made a stop at Fourth Avenue's Five and Dime to purchase a box of Toni permanent hair color. She was thrilled as she tore open the box, ready to erase all the ridicule that had ever come her way.

Silver poured the entire bottle of what looked like pen ink on her head. Brandan skipped out for Pop Warner practice. After an hour, Silver found that the dye dripped everywhere—through her sister's towels, onto her school clothes and all over the white porcelain sink.

Silver got a hold of Brandan in a panic. He was sauntering up the block. He dutifully found some bleach to help her clean up. Despite the mess, she was pleased her white patch seemed to be concealed.

"You washed your hair?" Jill asked when she returned home, dragging through the house after a heavy day, and noticed the towel on Silver's head. "Why would you wash your hair on a weekday, Silver? I'm too tired to braid it, and it won't be dry for school tomorrow." Silver's hair was so thick, it took up to two days for it to air dry. Blow drying made it so hard and brittle that Jill couldn't do much after that either. Jill started unwrapping the towel. "What is this?" She removed the towel to reveal the big black spot in the center. "What have you done? Oh my God..."

Jill didn't punish Silver. She didn't have to. Silver no longer had a white patch resembling Lily Monster because as her hair dried, the patch turned green. Her nickname became Kermit the Frog until a year later when the dye finally grew out.

Silver had come a long way from any name she'd been labeled. She slipped her arms through a rhinestone-studded top with a sexy plunging neckline, then she stepped into a form-fitting black skirt with thigh-high splits on both sides and adorned her ears with Chanel chandelier earrings.

She slipped her size tens into three-inch glass slipper heels that made her stand slightly over six feet. The see-through straps, while alluring did nothing to hide her double corns, but that was nothing a little foundation on the toes and invisible bandages couldn't solve. She gave herself one final wiggle and another once-over before stepping into the party like the Queen of Sheba had arrived.

Silver mixed and mingled, noticing the time and Brandan's absence. Brandan was missing prime networking time, which was not like him.

——————————————————— *Toni Staton Harris*

Silver accepted another glass of Veuve Clicquot, and as she headed behind the bar to ring Brandan's cell, he appeared. He looked fantastic sporting an off-white dinner jacket, a royal purple silk mock, black pants and a half-carat stud sparkling in his left ear.

"It's about time. I was getting worried." Silver pecked him on the cheek and interlocked her arm in his. She tried to lead him toward the dining room but he didn't budge.

"One second," he said.

"Oh, there you are." Another person interlocked arms with Brandan on the other side. "Silver, how are you this evening?"

"Daphne? What in the world are you doing here?"

Sebastian tapped his Waterford flute with Jill at his side. "I'd like to thank everyone for coming tonight and my wife for putting together a fantastic evening to celebrate the company's fifth anniversary." Everyone clapped. "I'd like to thank our chef, Wanda Juzang Cooper of Juzang Thang Catering, all the way from Philly. The food was awesome, Wanda. If you'd like her card—she does private dining catering as well as big affairs—please see one of the members of her staff. Now before we retire to the game parlor for pool or the solarium for a Black Shark—some of the men smiled in admiration as Sebastian offered the rare Cuban cigars, which were prohibited from entering the country—"I would like to thank and congratulate someone very dear to me and my wife. She's just accepted a huge promotion at her technology firm. Please help me celebrate my sister-in-law, Silver James."

Applause burst over the room with the exception of Jill's mother, Paula, who gave a subdued two-fingered tap. As the chef rolled in the cake full of sparkles, Silver surveyed the room, gauging everyone's reaction, especially Daphne's whose expression was unreadable.

When the noise finally subsided, Silver spoke. "Thank you, everyone. I didn't expect all of this, even though my sister did show me the cake earlier."

"Aw, Jill…" people cried in unison.

"Please, we all know Jill can't keep a secret. Anyway, I'd like to thank my brother-in-law, my sister, my brother Brandan and also a special surprise guest, my boss, Daphne Dix. She's here, and none of this would have been possible without her. Daphne, please take a bow."

Daphne obliged and looked delighted. Brandan clapped wildly.

Silver was the perfect cohost, and she showed no sign of slowing down. She plopped herself at the bar next to Daphne. "You having a good time?" she asked before turning to the bartender. "An Imoya, please."

Daphne swallowed her drink. "I am. Your sister's place is exquisite, and this is some party. We're going to have to get her to plan an event for us." Daphne tipped her glass toward Silver, and they had a wordless toast. "What's that you're drinking? It looks strong."

Silver took a swig, then shook her head as if the drink put some hair on her chest. "It's brandy from South Africa. Sebastian and Jill traveled through Central and South Africa for three months last summer, and they brought back this and some other delights."

"I hope you're not driving home tonight."

Silver straightened up in her chair. The last thing she wanted was to allow Daphne to see her at ease. Silver understood that it was never good business to have your boss to see a less than professional demeanor. At that moment Silver despised the fact that Brandan invited Daphne since she wanted to relax. She needed to be cool, even though her insides burned with the slight giddiness of being tipsy. "I hope you didn't mind my sharing with my family about my promotion. I didn't find out about the announcement and cake until today."

"I didn't have a problem with it. You're the one who's worried about your friend. The patio looks empty. Why don't we talk out there?" Daphne led Silver through the game parlor where Brandan was playing pool, touched his shoulder and exited to the patio like she owned the place.

Once outside, Daphne pulled a metallic case about the size of a card deck from her purse. She retrieved a long slender, brown cigarette with a distinctive white tip. The odd-looking stick emitted a newly cured tobacco smell as Daphne lit and inhaled hard enough to cause the bushes to sway. "This," she said, making a heavy circle of smoke, "is my one and only true vice. I can't handle hard liquor like that tar-stripping stuff you were drinking, but this, this I can't shake."

"I would have never known."

"My point exactly." Daphne inhaled some more before stomping the butt into the pavement with one of her pointy European shoes that looked like an elf's ski. She immediately pulled out another cigarette. "People should only know what you want them to know. Anything else is damage control."

Silver didn't appreciate riddles, and she was getting tired of the stirring night breeze beating on her corns.

"Plainly speaking, you are a bright girl." Daphne reached up and placed her hard rough hand on Silver's shoulder. Silver wiggled in discomfort. "I really do like you, but if you're going to succeed in this business, or any business for that matter, you have to learn and yearn to play the game. You see, I'm used to this—"

"To what?" Silver asked, placing a safe distance between them.

"To being the only one—you know, standing out. Most of the time I like it but it does get lonely. Anyway, you being at the firm sparked my interest to bring up a young exec in my vein that I can mold, but you have to want success. You have to want more for yourself. I'll tell you a little secret." Daphne extinguished another butt and placed her hand on Silver's shoulder, causing Silver to bend. "Pat was offered this position first."

"So. She's already a supervisor of mid-accounts."

"Silver sweetie, you've got to grab information and run with it. Information is power. It is knowledge. It always keeps you ahead of the competition, and sometimes you have to read between the lines."

Silver was reading between the lines, and she didn't like what she wasn't hearing. "I'm not dumb or slow if that's what you're saying. You don't have to spell things out, but I don't appreciate games, so please get to the point. I have a party to rejoin."

Daphne readjusted her dress and continued to speak in hushed tones. "The only reason Pat didn't take that position was because she was pregnant and expecting to be out for at least six months. Furthermore, had she taken it, you would have been out of your job, but I fought for you." Daphne pulled out another cigarette and lit it. "I'm starting to regret my decision."

Silver allowed the words to seep into her brain. On one hand she was ticked at Daphne for calling her dumb and on the other, she was feeling dreadful about climbing her way up the corporate ladder at the expense of someone she thought to be a friend. "How long had Pat known about the shift in the company?"

"For about a month. You look angry." Daphne inhaled and shot ringlets in the air. "A penny for your thoughts? Hell, with your expression right about now, I'd give you a dollar."

Silver crossed her arms and sucked her teeth. "I guess you can't trust anyone these days, huh?"

"Silver, I don't know about you but that's why I don't have a whole lot of female friends. Friends of the female persuasion are better left to thank-you cards and wish-you-a-speedy-recovery greetings."

Silver snickered before her smile turned to a frown. Daphne had confirmed another reason to keep her circle close and tightly knit, and Pat had just exed herself out. "You know what, Daphne, I need to be candid..."

Daphne, with her cigarette clenched between her fingers, gestured for Silver to continue.

"...I haven't agreed with much of what you said but I agree with your take on female friendships." Silver paced. "I know I seemed tentative but you just gave me every reason to go for this thing with everything I've got. I will be the best damn manager you've seen at Sci-gex."

"Now that's the fire I want to see. Keep it." Daphne extinguished another cigarette and squashed it to oblivion. She extended her hand.

Silver seized it but couldn't help feeling like she had just made a deal with Satan incarnate. They continued talking as Daphne led Silver back inside.

"So Daphne, how did you and Brandan hook up?" Silver asked.

"With your direction, I went to the dealership to purchase my new S320, which will be here in about six weeks. Brandan sold it to me. We talked for a long time over post paperwork. He bowed out of the conversation to take a frantic call from some woman he seemed to be having trouble with. I just sat back, but when I heard Brandan mentioning something about an important party he was attending, we talked some more and I inquired. I told him I'd love to come as I'm getting acquainted in the area and when he said it was your sister, I thought a date would be perfect."

"Oh, well I hope you're having a good time," Silver said, her guard once again being raised.

"I am, and don't worry, I'll be gentle on him." Daphne winked.

"Oh, trust me, it's not Brandan I'm worried about." Silver winked back, and they re-entered the game room where a tornado of a conversation ensued. Brandan seemed to be at the center of the controversy.

"Get this, Sil, folks here seem to think men and woman can't be platonic friends. Give 'em your take" Brandan said. He put down his pool stick. With the game obviously over, Daphne grabbed a cue and took a spin around the table.

"That's easy. Men and women can absolutely be platonic friends. It's never been any other way with us, and neither one of us have ever felt the desire to go in any other direction," Silver said.

"My girl. You see, gentlemen, your theory of men and women having to always go sexual is primitive thinking. Your belief reduces us men to animalistic behavior without control. If that's the case, there's no difference between us and beasts."

"Now I know that's a crock of crap. Darlin', I wouldn't believe that if I were you. Your friend who still has sand behind the ears fell into your friendship zone. I'm going to tell you straight, if a man can hit it, he will, given the right circumstances," one of the partygoers said to Silver, much to the agreement of most of the men in the room.

"You know, women aren't only sustained in friendship by women. Some are sustained by the honesty, nurturance and the primal instincts of a man," Daphne said as she made a striped ball slide to the side pocket. Brandan joined her game.

"The only way men and women can be friends is if one or both is gay or one is so dog unattractive the other finds him or her physically deplorable," a male party guest said.

"Awww..." several people shouted.

"It's time for me to save you because it looks like the crowd is turning on you, bruh," Brandan said.

The conversation escalated with some people dropping out while others seemed to have their disagreements in the corners of the room.

"Who started this conversation?" Jill asked, entering with selections from the gourmet Viennese table. She handed the tray of truffles, chocolate strawberries and chocolate peanut butter cups to a waiter who took over the offerings.

"Brandan probably started it." Silver laughed.

"Well stop it, Brandan." Jill popped him on the arm. "You're running my guests away."

Brandan laughed. He didn't notice that Daphne had beaten him at pool with a clean sweep.

"Everything was wonderful," Silver said, helping Jill with cleanup.

"So you staying or going home tonight?" Jill asked.

"Home. I don't feel like staying. I want my own bed. You know I saw a catalog that sells the same beds you sleep in at the Westin Hotels. I'm thinking about purchasing one. I love those beds... the mattresses are only about two thousand dollars, they're called Heaven..."

"I'm not trying to tell you how to be grown but Silver you really should curb your spending." Jill placed the last champagne flute in the dishwasher, setting the machine for the crystal cycle.

"Yeah, yeah, yeah, mommy dearest. You need any more help?"

"I think everything is under control. I still wish you would stay. It's so late, and I don't like you having to walk in the house by yourself in that dreadful neighborhood of yours."

"I'll be all right. Hey, who was the dude in the corner arguing with the plain-jane girl with the corny black suit?" Silver inquired.

With a bewildered look, Jill thought. "Oh, I think you're talking about Calvin. Smooth brown skin, about five-ten?"

"Yeah. He was fine."

"He works at Sack Enterprises. Remember the account I told you Sebastian is trying to land?"

Silver nodded.

"Well Calvin is an exec for the firm. He was here representing Sack's management team because Sack and his wife were traveling. I can't stand Calvin though."

Silver's head jerked up in a surprise. She'd never heard Jill speak of anyone in such a repulsive tone.

"Sack is having a twenty-million-dollar estate built in either Alpine or Upper Montclair. Sebastian is trying to land the architectural account, so we invited Sack and all of his top management. Unfortunately, Calvin Jones was the only manager who could make it." Jill shook her head and walked over to the stove and turned on the burner.

"So why don't you like him?"

"'Cause he's a dog. That plain jane he was with wasn't his wife, and he's married."

"I didn't think they were together, that's why I asked about him."

"Oh, they were together all right. Why you think he was so quiet in the corner when you all were discussing the platonic friends thing? Please, she works for Sack Enterprises as well, and they were in the corner arguing, but later he was nibbling on her neck and ear."

"Oh."

"He's married to a woman named Candace but China was his date, you know like the country, but she spelled it differently on the response. Candace advised she couldn't attend but that her husband would be. Candace didn't mention his date would be his lover."

"Honey boom, I just got over him. I don't want anybody's married leftovers."

"That's exactly why I didn't introduce you." Jill poured two cups of tea. She and Silver sat at the table.

"So how do you feel about your boss hanging out with Brandan? Do you sense a conflict?" Jill asked as she sipped.

"I don't really know. I mean I don't suspect they'll be a couple or anything. I just hope Brandan doesn't mess anything up for me," Silver answered.

"I know what you mean. Just do yourself a huge favor."

"What's that?"

"Stay far away from anything to do with Brandan and your boss. If I were you, I wouldn't mention anything about their casual date to either one of them and I wouldn't allow them to mention anything to me."

"Jill, you sound cautious, overprotective even."

"Heed my warning, baby girl."

Silver drank as much tea as her bladder would allow for her not to have to run to the bathroom before arriving home. She heard Jill's words but decided her focus should be on her new position, not Brandan, Savannah, Daphne or Todd. "Thanks for everything, sister, I'm out." Silver said as she rose.

"Are you sure you're okay to drive?"

"I'll ring you when I get in. How's that?" Silver asked.

"Better than nothing." They kissed and bid good night.

Chapter 5

Beware of Sleeping Green-Eyed Monsters

On the first day of summer Silver was so tired she dragged herself into her apartment neglecting to shed her shoes at the door. Moments after she entered she noticed a strange odor. She twitched her nose and looked behind her chairs. She also looked under the sofa and behind the chaise that sat outside her bedroom door, thinking perhaps a creature might have suffered an ill fate.

When everything seemed to be in place but still awkward, Silver twirled around and chalked the strange experience to fatigue. She had been working fourteen-hour shifts.

Tonight wasn't the moment to get reacquainted with her place. Silver had plans. When Brandan called earlier and begged her to meet him at the Nickel Bar to watch Game 3 of the Lakers versus Nets, wild stallions nor the bags under her eyes could keep her away.

Since Brandan had started seeing Daphne a month ago, Silver hadn't seen much of him. Considering the responsibility Daphne had been dumping Silver's way, Silver hadn't even seen much of Todd, a proud fact she was ready to put before Brandan. Silver skipped out of the office earlier than usual, relieved that Daphne had extended her out-of-town trip and that she would have Brandan all to herself.

Silver checked her watch, silenced her yawn and drew some energy from her toes to get moving. She wanted to be at the front table before tip-off with a beer poised at her lips and her best friend at her side.

It was an exciting night. The Nets hadn't been in the NBA finals since before Silver was born and even though they were battling the Lakers—she and Brandan were die-hard Lakers fans—rooting for the home team was a great reason to justify their switch from Lakers to the Nets, even for a New York minute.

Changed and refreshed, Silver arrived at the bar, found a decent parking space and moved inside, swiftly searching the dark, smoke-filled room for Brandan. Every person in Newark must have planned to watch the game because the place was packed. Silver was disappointed when she didn't spot Brandan but even more disappointed that all the tables directly in front of all three movie-sized screens were filled.

She turned her attention to the back where the pool table stood. It, too, was occupied by a taut and perfectly V-shaped man bent over a complicated shot. She walked over and watched him study intently before moving his stick to sink a shot she would have paid someone to make for her. "I'm impressed," she said.

The man looked up and smirked. He moved his shoulder-length dread-locks off of his face. He remained silent and maneuvered himself to the opposite side of the table.

"Okay, I wouldn't try that one. There's an easier angle." Silver said as she leaned in and studied a difficult shot.

"Want to bet?" he said, refusing to lose focus.

Silver reached in her front pocket and pulled out a small wad of bills. She leafed through and found a dollar and slammed it on the table. The gesture caused him to look up and smile. Silver couldn't have been more pleased. His teeth were all white and all there.

He studied a little more and then contorted his body before slamming the ball into a corner pocket.

"My bad. I'm really impressed now." Silver tapped the dollar bill and turned to walk away.

"That's how you do it? Wham bam thank you, ma'am?"

Silver turned back around to see the man straddling the corner of the table with the cue stick standing upright between his widely spread legs. "You made the shot. My debt is paid."

"That it is. Your debt is paid, but I'd prefer a beer and perhaps some company, maybe a game?"

Silver smiled. "A beer is more than I bet. You could extend the same courtesy, you know your request for a game or company."

"Touché. I would love to." He motioned to the bartender, held up an empty Heineken and signaled for two. "Diego." He placed the bottle down and extended his hand.

"Silver," she responded as she enjoyed his firm grip. His hands were thick and the muscles in his arms bulged.

"So how about that company on the game table?" Diego pulled the balls from the pocket and placed them in the rack.

"How do you know I play?"

"Women don't make bets on things they're not sure of. My shots were difficult and to know that you have to play." Diego rolled the balls in place. "You're probably pretty good at it too."

Silver's attention was diverted to the door and the clock. It was almost game time, and Brandan hadn't shown or called.

"Am I disturbing you?" Diego asked, handing her a beer.

"Oh, I'm sorry. I'm supposed to meet a friend, and I'm surprised he's not here, and he hasn't called. I don't want to start a game and then. . . excuse me." Her cell rang and she walked a few paces beyond the table. It was Brandan. "Hey, where are you? The game is about to start....Really?" she asked excitedly. "Cool. Well, can't you...What? Come on, Brandan. We planned this, and I was looking forward to...Fine, fine...yeah, have a good time without me." Her shoulders sank as she swallowed a sip of beer and turned to her companion. "Looks like I can take you up on that game after all."

"Don't sound so excited."

"Sorry. It's not you. I was supposed to meet somebody, but he's standing me up." Silver flipped her phone to make sure the call ended; she placed it back in her purse.

"Oh. Well, I don't mind being the guy on the rebound."

"Oh no, it's not like that. He's my best friend, nothing like a boyfriend or anything." Silver pulled up a stool and sat. "And please no in-depth conversation about men and women being friends. That topic of discussion is played." Silver looked around, hoping a seat in front of the tube had miraculously opened up.

"You won't get any argument from me. My best friend is a woman. She's my sister, but she's my best friend." Diego circled the table. "So what happened to your *friend* anyway?"

"Don't say it like that." Silver swiveled and scooped a handful of cashews from a dish beside the pool table. "We said we weren't going to get into that conversation." She popped a few nuts in her mouth.

"So what happened?"

"The woman he's been seeing too much of lately whisked back into town. They're going to the game, without me, of course. The woman, who incidentally is my boss, reserved the company skybox at the Arena."

"At the finals?"

"Yup. So there goes my plan." Silver slid her foot from the metal base of the stool to the floor. She got up and motioned to leave. She didn't feel much like hanging around, considering she wouldn't be seeing Brandan.

"Where are you going? I'm not exactly chopped meat you know."

"Thanks, but no thanks."

"Oh, come on. You're already out. The game is about to start in a few minutes. I have a booth reserved in perfect distance to the screen. Hell, I'll even spring for another couple of beers, just don't leave yet."

Silver twisted her lips and raised her eyebrows, considering Diego's proposition. Finally, after careful thought, she figured she was already out and nothing was happening at home, so why not stay. Diego seemed pleasant enough. "So where is that booth you promised?"

"I guess that means you'll stay."

"Yup."

"If you want to just talk, I could be a good ear. You really seem disappointed."

"No, I'm fine. I am disappointed, though. Besides, now that my boss is back in town, I know I'm gonna have a lot of work tomorrow, so I might as well enjoy one night out."

"Sounds like you have more of a problem with the fact your boss is dating your friend. Jealous perhaps?"

"Diego, I don't know you and you don't know me, but I do know you're over-stepping your boundaries."

"I didn't mean to. I know how you feel. My sister hooked up with my boy, and when they did, it was like I lost both of them. I admit, I was jealous at first too."

Silver's interest was perked. "How did you adjust?"

"I learned to stay out of their business, that's all. Now they're married and everything's cool."

Silver sipped the beer, which had grown warm, wearing a blank expression. "So I should just sit back and let the cards play?"

"That's what I'd do. Why don't you go on to the booth across from screen number two. I'll be there in a second."

Silver stood and shook her pants legs down over her Burberry slides. She liked that Diego seemed to enjoy the view. "You still have that dollar?" she asked.

"Yeah, why?" Diego placed his cue stick on the rack.

"Hand it over," she commanded.

"You lost the bet. I made the shot."

"I know, but I'll turn it in for another beer. How's that?"

"I'm flattered but I'll handle the next couple of rounds."

Silver's head jerked in surprised. She liked that. She watched him disappear in the far dark corner near the restrooms. *Now if only he could grow a few more inches,* she thought, disappointed that the top of Diego's head didn't quite reach hers.

Brandan and Daphne entered the vast arena filled with screaming excitement. They maneuvered their way to the elevators, which took them to an already full glass-enclosed skybox, with enough food to feed the stadium twice over.

Daphne introduced herself and her date, swiftly making her way through to the seafood table that held more varieties of shellfish than the sea. She dropped roasted prawns, a dollop of rosemary-ginger cocktail sauce, Norwegian steamed mussels in their own juices and clams on the half shell on a china plate. "How's this?" she asked Brandan, sliding a clam on his tongue.

"It's delicious." He savored the flavor. "And so are you." Brandan wrapped his arms around her waist as Daphne continued to feed him. "Thanks for this. I'm having a great time already, and the Nets haven't won yet."

"Seems like we got a win-win situation going on here right now," Daphne said, responding to Brandan's light kisses.

Brandan led Daphne to plush high-back seats in front of the glass. The panoramic view of everything and everyone was fantastic, but Brandan couldn't take his eyes off Daphne.

"What are you staring at?" Daphne tilted her head to the side and smiled.

"You. You look great, Dee."

"Thanks, sweetie," she answered as she brushed crumbs from her turquoise duster jacket and very miniskirt. "What are you grinning at?"

"One of the most incredible women I've ever met."

"Brandan, that is so sweet. Thanks, honey. I enjoy being with you. You give me love and attention. I couldn't ask for a better time with a better person."

He kissed her hand. Brandan loved the way Daphne handled herself and more importantly how she handled him. Whenever it was her turn to plan something for them, she took meticulous care to find out what he adored then added her own special twist. In a month's time they had attended their share of car shows, the race track and the traveling black rodeo in South Jersey, which they topped off with a quiet picnic for two. She even brought the merlot. Daphne was always on time and never fussy about her hair and makeup, which always looked flawless. He didn't have to worry about her not participating in something because her hair might get wet, and she'd spent long hours and long dollars on some hairdo he couldn't feel. But the clincher was that in the mornings before they readied themselves for work, ESPN would already be on and the coffee was made before he wiped the crust from his eyes.

"I hope you brought plenty of business cards." She motioned to the door, turning their attention to several NBA legends who had just walked in.

"I always have cards." He smiled.

"Well do your thing, sweetheart. I'll be fine right here." Daphne crossed her legs and squeezed his hand for assurance.

Brandan stepped away and shook his head to make sure he wasn't dreaming.

The morning show blared from the radio, waking Silver from a rock-like sleep. She rolled over and slammed the top of her dream machine silent. She looked over and rubbed her eyes, grateful that she was in bed, alone.

The night before had been a bust all around. Silver didn't get to spend any time with Brandan, choosing to love the one she was with. That effort, however, was futile considering Diego's height deficiency and the fact that he served as a police officer on the same squad as Todd. That along with his subtle arrogance forced her away from his reserved table early. She planted herself at the bar, and as the Lakers rolled over the Nets, she drowned herself in more Heinekens than she cared to recount.

On top of it, when she came home, she found Todd waiting in her bed and ready. She was left dissatisfied, disgusted and sore.

Silver licked the fur from her teeth with her tongue and spent more than half her dressing time in the shower trying to wake up. Finally, her head still in a fog, she rolled into the office past the gossiping about her being Daphne's right hand girl and the questions of why she was handling two groups of programmers despite her efficiency and competence in each task.

Silver sorted some papers on her desk before sitting and putting her head in her hands. Secretly, her concerns about work were growing. Her workload had become more demanding, and her love life was spinning out of control. There was a time when she begged for Todd's attention and presence. But of late, his unauthorized and unannounced arrivals were becoming more of a nuisance. She felt her body growing steadily weary of their relationship, freeing tiny spaces in her mind of a life without Todd for good.

Silver was still sulking when a light tap at her door disturbed her. It was Daphne's assistant. "Daphne called. She won't be present for the eleven o'clock meeting, and she asked that you not only give your presentation, but that you take over the entire agenda. I took the liberty of printing it out for you. If you need any files or anything, I'll be at my desk."

Silver took the paper. She wasn't alarmed by the listing since she was familiar with most of the tasks. She was just frustrated by the amount of responsibility, which had increased for her and seemingly decreased for Daphne.

She snatched the phone from the cradle. She needed to vent. "Brandan Savoy, please...Yes, this is Silver." Now was not the time for the car dealer's receptionist to act snooty. Silver was convinced she had a crush on Brandan and seemed to offer attitude every time Silver called.

"I'm sorry, Miss James, but Brandan hasn't arrived at the office yet. He won't be in until after noon today." A smile seemed to seep through the phone. "Should I tell him you called?"

"Of course you should tell him I called. What kind of question is that?" Silver huffed and slammed the phone down. She immediately dialed Brandan's cell. She didn't even hear the ringer before his voice mail kicked in, letting her know his cell phone was turned off. "Brandan, we definitely need to talk. I'm leaving early today after my meeting so give me a call so we can meet. I'm not taking no for an answer. It's important," she said before slamming the phone down again.

Somehow, some way and to somebody Silver had to blow off steam, so she called her sister. "It seems like Daphne's pushing everything on me so that I don't have time for anything else. And she and Brandan are joined at the hip. Neither one of them is at work yet, and I can't even get a hold of Brandan on his cell or anything."

"Silver, if you interfere with that man's relationship with this woman, whom he obviously cares a great deal about, you are going to jeopardize your friendship," Jill warned.

"I just want to talk to him and sort out what's going on with me." She paused at another rap at the door. "Come in," she whined.

Daphne's assistant tiptoed through the door with a huge bouquet of wildflowers and calla lilies.

"Over there, please," Silver whispered and pointed to the bare credenza opposite her desk. The assistant did as instructed and left. Silver continued her conversation with Jill, complaining about Daphne, the job and Brandan.

"Well, you're doing a great job, and I don't think there's anything wrong with approaching Daphne professionally and giving her a heads-up on what's going on in the department and expressing that you need the help she promised when you took the job. But Silver whatever you do, leave your underlying anger about her dating Brandan out of it."

"Is it that apparent?" Silver asked.

"Uh, yeah."

Silver rested her elbow on the desk, her head in the palm of her hand. She looked over at the magnificent blooms and wanted to toss them. She was getting flowers at work regularly now. She no longer believed they came from Kendrick, even though the bouquets became more elaborate, and the unsigned cards furthered her suspicions.

"You know Daphne's not Savannah or any of the other girls Brandan has dated. From what you say and how I've see Brandan glowing lately, Daphne is good for him and different. Now if you think otherwise, maybe because there is someone better in your mind—"

"Cut it, Jill," Silver interrupted. "I know you're trying to say that I think I'm better for Brandan and it's not working. I'm just a concerned friend, that's all. No different than how Brandan feels about Todd."

"Oh, there's a difference…"

"Jill, I have to go. Someone just walked in. Later." Silver hung up abruptly. No one had entered her office but she wasn't in the mood to listen to what her sister was saying.

Silver walked over and sniffed the fragrant flowers. She picked up the

———————————————————————— *Toni Staton Harris*

card, which read, *ANOTHER GREAT EVENING...LOOKING FORWARD TO MANY MORE.* In very small print the note further read, *mark number 1.* Again, it was unsigned. Silver figured maybe Todd felt her pulling away and this was another stunt. For once her heart didn't jump at the thought. She pushed the arrangement to the back of the credenza and proceeded to gather her thoughts for the meeting. The note slightly jumbled her thoughts but she had more important things on her mind.

"Good work, Silver. Congratulations," a coworker said.

"Thanks."

"Silver, you think I could come by your office later and use your requirements document as a prototype?" another coworker asked.

"Of course," Silver said, greeting her newly acquired fans on the way to her desk. She was on cloud eleven after Sci-gex's regional director praised her at the meeting, and nothing would spoil her high, not even the fact that as she sat down, Daphne barged into her office, closing the door behind her. "Do come in," Silver said.

"I'm sure Brandan will be happy to hear the news that your meeting went well." A smile crept across Daphne's face. Daphne made her entrée into the meeting during the last ten minutes of Silver's presentation.

"Hadn't thought about sharing it with him yet, but I'm sure it will."

"Hey, great work in there. You are really something."

"Thanks, Daphne." Silver paused. "Is there something you'd like to go over or something I can help you with?" she asked cautiously.

"Well yes, actually. I just finished talking to Jim," Daphne flaunted calling the director by his first name. "Jim furthered some information about your performance." Daphne stood and walked to the flowers. She smelled them and frowned before twirling and flipping her hair with such force, her head should have rolled off her neck. "Well, Jim likes your work but there are some definite areas of improvement needed."

"Really? What areas?"

"Well your R.D. lacked Visio. He wanted to know why it didn't include the program Visio like my documents. I told him that I know Visio like the back of my hand, a skill you haven't acquired just yet, but I'd be happy to instruct you." Daphne sat back down and crossed her legs.

"That's really odd, Daphne. Why would he praise me in public then pull you aside and say something completely different?"

"I don't know. That's Jim's style. I'm just telling you what he told me. Now, as I promised I will conduct a seminar on Visio. I need you to set it up. Invite all of the techs and assistants. There's no sense in making it painfully obvious how much I want you to succeed." Daphne smiled.

"Well speaking of success, Daphne, I'm a little overwhelmed right now. When we first spoke about this position, you promised support. I'm thinking that my small group could be delegated to someone else. That would free me up to some degree—"

"Nonsense. You're doing so well. As a matter of fact, I hear that Mark Ackin or Adam or whatever his name is, is leaving tech support for tech development. When I got wind of it this morning, I was shocked to learn that you signed off on the transfer without my knowledge or consent. How industrious of you."

"I hope that wasn't a problem. You had been out of the office and he was threatening to leave. He's a valued employee and—"

"Silver, no need to explain. You acted on instinct. As I said, you're doing just fine. Keep up the good work." Daphne stood to leave, bracing herself on the door. "Oh, and one more thing. Pat is on her way to the office to talk about a return date. It's a premature announcement but you are going to have the pleasure of telling Pat that her position is included in the downsizing. I'll make sure my assistant sends her your way." Daphne pranced out of the door.

Silver was close behind. "Hold up, wait. Daphne," she called out, "you want me to fire Pat? I can't do that Daphne, please—"

"Remember big business is war, and war is big business. No room for friendship." Daphne continued to her office with Silver right on her heels. She closed Daphne's door.

"I have no authority to fire a level five. I'm only level four in case you don't remember. I haven't signed a contract or salary binder. I won't do it," Silver said firmly. This game Daphne was playing was going too far, and Silver wasn't about to be pushed around like some flunky.

Her declaration stopped Daphne cold. Silver towered over her with ease. Daphne backed off and sat back at her desk. "You will do it. And Silver, do yourself a big favor, don't ever tell me what you won't do again." Her voice was like dry ice. "I like you but I don't tolerate insubordination. And do yourself another favor…"

"What's that?"

"Don't fuck with me. When I play, I play for keeps, and this ain't my first time at the rodeo…" Daphne howled in laughter. "I just love that movie, don't you?"

"What, *Mommie Dearest*? No, I don't love that movie. And for the record, don't fuck with me either. I always land on my feet."

Daphne's laughter was borderline hysteria. "You really don't know who or what you're dealing with. My name isn't Mona or Savannah. You won't push me aside, sweetie. Like I said, when I play, it's for keeps."

"Hold up, Brandan is not the issue here—"

"Oh yes, he is," Daphne interrupted. "And that's as clear as day." Daphne stood and smoothed her suit. "I'm going to forget about this little tête-a-tête. I would hate for the firm to learn that their two best African-American protégées didn't get along." Daphne sat back down and proceeded to go over some papers. She stopped Silver once more. "Oh, and Silver, you have the authority because I say you do when I say you do. Be gentle, okay? Good day." She placed her head back into a folder, and Silver stormed out.

A light tap sounded upon Silver's door. When she looked up, Pat was standing there with a huge grin on her face, holding the sweetest angel Silver had ever seen. She wasn't big on children, but Pat's little wrapped in delicate pink evoked a rumble in Silver's heart.

"Oh my goodness." Silver said approaching Pat cautiously. "Sit down." Pat complied and unwrapped baby Emmy who rustled quietly in her lap.

"You want to hold her?" Pat asked.

Silver stepped back around her desk, feeling dis-eased about what she had to do. "No, I'll hold her when she grows just a little bigger."

"You're looking good girl, sitting behind that desk. Don't get too comfortable because before long I'll be back." Pat bugged her eyes and imitated The Terminator with a chuckle.

Silver stifled a laugh. "Pat I need to talk to you."

"Don't make it sound so serious." Pat paused. "Everything okay?"

"Well not really. There really is no great way to tell you this but, the company condensed our department and eliminated your position." Silver regretted being so blunt but it was too late.

"What, Silver why are *you* telling me this?" Pat said intensely. She leaned forward and Emmy seemed to fidget. "Eliminated my position? So what position are you in and why are you sitting at what used to be my desk?" Pat huffed after her tirade.

"Pat we've always been straight with one another and it seems-"

"It seems you and Daphne have schemed behind my back to take my position while I wasn't here. I'd expect this bullshit from someone else

Silver, but you, not you." Pat stood and gently placed Emmy on the edge of what used to be her desk. When Silver tried to move papers out of the way to give Pat space, Pat slapped Silver's hand away. "Don't you dare, don't you come near me or my child!" Pat seethed. Emmy obviously startled wailed uncontrollably.

Silver pinched the bridge of her nose. "It's not like that Pat, please listen to what is going on around here."

Pat wrapped Emmy in her blanket, yanked her baby bag, flung it over her shoulder and walked toward the door. "No need to explain the next step to me, I'm on my way to HR. And to think, I looked at you like my sister and you go and stab me in the back!" Tears formed a track around her bulging red veins. "So much for fucking friendship, but I'll tell you this, If I were you, I'd watch my back around Daphne. You are riding high because you're her girl today, but just wait, she'll pull the same shit with you." Pat stormed out of Silver's office.

Silver could hear Pat pleading for Emmy to stop crying. Somehow Silver sensed there was a whole lot more to Daphne demanding that Silver carry out this task. And she knew just where to go to find out.

What started out to be a bad day, turned good and finished in horror. Silver left for the day, right after her meeting with Pat. She didn't consult Daphne or anyone else that she'd be gone. She told the receptionist to ring her cell if she was needed. Silver started to make a B-line straight to Jyll's but remembered that Jill wouldn't be around until late so she strolled over to the PSEG fountain off Raymond Boulevard. She watched the water dance across the penny stone wall as children frolicked about. She called Brandan to meet her downtown as soon as he could get away. They decided on a Thursday night hotspot in the Newark area.

A stone's throw away from the job was the hottest spot in the Northeast on a Thursday night. At the outdoor bar of New Jersey's premier Performing Arts Center, Silver sought to get an early start on Thursday Night at the PAC by ordering a Heineken, impatiently waiting for Brandan to join her. The PAC, during the summer was when New Jersey's professional finest loosened their ties and buffed their high heels for an evening of networking and cocktails. Coined as the meat market the latest up-and-coming R&B or rock band provided great background music.

Silver was on her second bottle when she spotted Brandan amid the swell of the crowd. She waved him over, grateful that the only thing behind or beside him were several female admirers giggling and pointing like little schoolgirls.

"I almost forgot what you looked like," Silver said. She pecked him on the cheek. "What are you drinking?"

"The usual," Brandan said as he loosened his tie and unbuttoned the neck of his shirt.

Silver slapped six bucks on the bar, retrieved his beer and led Brandan to a grass hill.

"I thought you needed to talk." Brandan raised his eyebrows as she thought a father might, positioning himself to scold her.

"I do want to talk but after this group's set. They sound pretty good."

Brandan shook his head, acknowledging Silver's stall tactic. She sat on an iron bench about a hundred feet from the stage and tapped her foot, playfully patting Brandan's thigh to the beat.

The group finished to rousing applause and accolades. Brandan looked at his watch.

"Sorry I'm boring you," Silver said.

"I'm not bored, but we do need to talk," Brandan said. "Besides, it's time to get out of here. It's seven and you know the meat market gets started after a little liquor gets in folks."

"There was a time you rather enjoyed the show at the meat market," Silver yelled back.

Brandan shrugged. "Yeah, sometimes things change."

Silver snapped her neck and widened her eyes. She drained her last sip of beer.

"Why don't we go to the park and talk, away from the noise? My car's on the street so I'll drive," Brandan said.

"And what am I supposed to do with my car?" Silver asked.

"I'll drive you back to yours. I'm coming back down this way anyway," Brandan said.

"Oh, I see. Hanging out with Daphne again tonight? Have you seen your place in the last few weeks?"

"Let's just go and talk," Brandan said, leading her by the arm to his car in uncomfortable silence. They drove to Branch Brook Park where they stopped in front of the fully bloomed cherry blossoms papering the sky and grass below.

Silver gazed out of the window watching one lone petal as it traveled through the breeze until it disappeared. She heard Brandan fumble about in his console. He slipped in a disc and Kindred's music spirited the atmosphere. She looked over as he turned the volume down to a hum.

"I had to tell Pat that her position was downsized today." Silver had an uncertain air of sadness in her voice.

"How did she take it?" Brandan sighed heavily and stroked his tie.

"How do you think? She's hurt, betrayed. She was more hurt that I didn't clue her in about the changes at the job. I couldn't look her in the face or hold her baby Emmy. I felt so bad. And Daphne was way out of line today. Obviously you know we had a huge fight."

Brandan tilted his head and bit his lip.

"Anyway, what's going on with you and Daphne? Are y'all really serious?"

"Yeah, we're serious. She's probably the one," Brandan said without hesitation.

"Is that some code for 'I love her'?" Brandan didn't deny her statement, and Silver placed her chin in her chest and rolled her eyes. "You don't know her, Brandan, I'm telling you. What do you see in her that has you so open?"

"She's no pressure, and we have a great time. I like the way she's into me." Brandan's voice didn't waver.

"I would have never guessed new pussy would have your nose as wide as your ass."

"Sil, it ain't only about the pussy." Brandan turned the music completely off and looked in her direction. "I've already talked to Daphne, and now it's about you. You are forever my dawg. You and me, this won't ever go anywhere. Nobody has ever come between us, and nobody will."

"Brandan, you're already letting that happen. Last night we were supposed to hang out but Daphne called. We were supposed to continue our Monday night pool but Daphne called. This morning I tried to call you, you're not at work, which is not like you. You don't answer your cell and you're not at home. I guess you were with Daphne and couldn't be disturbed."

Brandan yanked off his jacket and tie and threw them on the backseat. He rolled the sleeves of his monogrammed shirt back to his elbows. "You don't get it. Daphne doesn't want to come between us. She is in support of our relationship—"

"Hold up. Who is she to be in support of our relationship?" Silver yelled.

"No, you hold up." Brandan's voice was steady and deep. "What happened today, you were way out of line. And when Daphne tried to explain it to you, you bucked up at her."

Silver didn't interject.

"You don't realize what you did, do you?"

"Brandan," she said methodically, "if anybody else came off on me the way Daphne jumped off today, I woulda slapped the shit out of them. You should have heard the things she said to me."

"You know where Daphne was this morning?" Brandan asked.

"No," Silver answered.

"She was in an off-site human resources meeting discussing the downsizing—you—didn't know about it. Anyway, that dude whose job you saved was about to be terminated, and the directive from upper management was to fire him. Your upper management was going over the list and saw his name as part of another department. Daphne didn't know anything about it and was reprimanded for it. She investigated and found out you signed off on the transfer. You put Daphne in a real bad position." Brandan continued to explain how and why Daphne was so incensed with her and how she thought Silver was allowing her jealousy to adversely affect her decision-making. Daphne's directive for Silver to downsize Pat was Daphne's way of reminding Silver who was in charge.

"Baby girl, you stompin' with the big dawgs now. You have to learn to play the game. And for the record, your bosses were really upset with you, and Daphne covered your butt." Brandan's tone indicated he agreed with Daphne's style of management.

"Just 'cause Daphne said it happened that way doesn't mean it's true. Daphne had it out for the guy the same way she's had it out for Pat, all because he embarrassed her in a meeting a few weeks ago and called her out on something she should have known. Daphne has no clue about interface systems and Mark called her on it and-" Silver took a breath and realized she was defending herself to Brandan. Of all people, he should have been on her side, but here he was making a case for a woman who had fast become her sworn enemy. "Look, I was doing my job. Daphne wasn't around, and it was one less transaction for her to worry about."

"Okay, okay," Brandan said calmly. "Silver, I'm telling you for your own good, you have to learn to play the game. Now the job is one thing but why did you bring my personal life into your conversation?"

Silver squinted. "What are you talking about now?"

"You told Dee that she was insignificant in my life and that she'd end up like Mona and Savannah."

"No." Silver was emphatic. "You must have mentioned them because I never said a word about them. As a matter of fact, Daphne brought them up, not me." Silver couldn't believe Daphne had magically turned the entire situation around to suit herself.

"Well Daphne said—"

"Brandan, I don't care what Daphne said."

"Okay, let's just drop this. I love you, Sil, but I won't let you choose my women for me. I never have and I won't start now. I'm going to be with Daphne, and if things go the way I'd like them to go, I hope for a long time. You all are going to have to find a way to get along."

Silver was dealing with a different breed. On top of turning everything around in her favor, Daphne had acted fast, and Brandan was buying the entire sordid situation. She'd never seen Brandan so smitten with somebody, and she couldn't fathom how she should counter his behavior and unfounded accusations.

"...So, can I count on you? I mean are we cool?" Brandan had been speaking, and Silver had conveniently tuned out. He turned the car on and took the scenic route back downtown to get Silver's car, traveling through the East Orange border and her block.

Silver's brain couldn't hold much more at the moment, so she conceded. When Brandan turned down her street, her heart sank. Todd's glistening pearl-white Escalade was parked in front of her house. Silver grunted. The day was disastrous enough without having to deal with Todd. Besides, she'd just seen him the night before and wasn't in the mood for another dry run.

"Brandan, you're going to Daphne's tonight, right?"

"Yes, I am, and don't start—"

"No, I'm asking because Todd is at my place and I don't feel like dealing with him tonight. I can stay at your place and hang out until I know he's gone."

Brandan looked over and noticed Silver's worn and dejected expression. He felt bad. He wanted to have a conversation to smooth things out, not get her upset. He adjusted his cell earpiece and commanded the phone to dial Daphne.

Silver rolled her eyes, disgusted that this woman had space in his automatic Rolodex already.

"Hey, Dee, I'm not going to make it by tonight. Yeah sure...How about tomorrow?...Okay, cool...I'll call you in the morning...Good night."

"What did you cancel for?" Silver asked.

"Because we're going to deal with this Todd mess once and for all." Brandan was stern. "Tell me this, do you want to be with him?"

Silver thought, then shook her head.

"Then let's go up there, get your key and kick his ass to the curb."

"Brandan, I don't know—"

"Do you want to be with him or not?" Brandan asked.

"No, but I'll handle it—"

Before Silver could finish her statement Brandan had positioned his car in park behind Todd's Escalade. He got out, waved to Bowman and bolted toward the stairs.

Silver was stunned. She left her belongings in the car and ran after Brandan. Fortunately, his car had an automatic locking system that activated forty-five seconds after inactivity.

Silver darted past Bowman without saying a word and stumbled upon a staunch, dark man. She didn't have time to inquire about the man's presence since she could hear that Brandan was almost to her door.

Silver almost dropped at what she saw. Todd had pushed her laptop aside and was seated at her desk with a mound of white powder in front of him. His gun was out of its holster, facing the door on her coffee table. Everything was out of place and the apartment smelled like a tobacco factory.

"What the fuck is going on in my house, Todd?" Silver asked. She stopped Brandan from moving closer.

Todd looked up like he was drunk and laughed like a hyena.

"Todd. Todd!" Silver shouted.

"He's high, Silver." Brandan relaxed his shoulders.

"I don't give a fuck what he is. He's out of his mind that's for damn sure. Todd, Todd!" Silver stooped over and shook him. She noticed her fine crystal had been used and discarded all over the floor. A cigarette butt had obviously been extinguished in the end table next to her couch, and ashes were everywhere.

"Todd. Todd!" Silver slapped him so hard, the liberty bell rang in her ears.

"What, baby?" Todd asked, laughing.

"What the fuck are you doing using my place like it's a bar?"

"Aw, baby." Todd grabbed her waist and fell off his chair.

"No, no, Todd, I swear...where's my key? Where's my key?" Silver repeated as she frantically searched him. She moved to his stuff strewn over the table and found the key she'd given him during better times. "You have one hour and I mean one hour to get your shit and get out of my house, or I swear I'll kill you my damn self. One hour, Todd." Silver stomped out of the house and Brandan followed her.

When they reached the street, the mysterious man had disappeared.

"Sil, did you have your deadbolt on?" Brandan asked as he clicked his car remote.

"Yeah. Why?" Silver answered, still fuming at how Todd destroyed her place.

"Because taking your key doesn't mean anything. He bypassed the deadbolt." Brandan opened the passenger door and helped Silver into the car. He got in on the other side and revved the engine. "Why don't you stay at my place tonight? We'll get your car, you can come back in the morning and I'll change your locks while you're at work. I'll even get your new keys to you before day's end." Brandan pulled off.

Silver blew a hard breath, determined not to allow the tears to fall.

The next morning Silver took long lunges up her apartment stairs with a steadfast goal to kick Todd's ass. She couldn't believe he had the gall to stay at her place all night. His car was in the exact spot he'd left it hours before. She wasn't surprised that his car, unlike her own, had not been touched, considering everyone in the neighborhood knew who Todd was and dared not damage it. Silver bypassed Bowman who was brushing his rag over Todd's spinning rims. When she reached her apartment, she noticed the door to her apartment had been left ajar.

She pushed her way through to find her place in more of a shambles than the previous night. Drawers were overturned, her console flipped upside down and her big screen was in tiny pieces in the middle of the living room.

"Todd," Silver called, so angry her voice shook. "Todd, where the fuck are you?" she yelled louder.

Her gaze landed upon her crystal chess set, most of which was shattered. If she hadn't dismissed him for anything else, this would be her reason to get rid of him for good.

Silver realized she heard water running. "And this motherfucker has the nerve to be taking a shower?" she said aloud. "Todd, Todd, I'm not fucking playing with you, this—" She jerked the shower curtain back. "Oh my God. Oh my Gooooooodddddd," she screamed.

Chapter 6

On Your Mark,
Get Ready, Set...Chaos!

The image of Todd's decapitated body was cemented in Silver's brain. Jill sat a cup of tea before her but when Silver tried to lift the cup to her mouth, her hand shook so hard, more tea landed on the table than her tongue.

Brandan and Sebastian, Silver's brother-in-law, were busy on their cell phones. A barrage of police, coroners and internal investigators invaded Silver's place like a scene straight out of *CSI*. Silver sat at her kitchen table with a down comforter wrapped around her shoulders.

A female officer had tried to question Silver only to receive broken, unintelligible answers. Finally the woman gave up. It was another detective's voice, a looming man, that spawned some sign of life. He was pointed and focused but his soothing baritone caused Silver to look up and take notice from her almost drunken-like stupor. "Silver, I'm Detective Dowdy. Now I need to ask you some very uncomfortable questions but you need to give me some honest answers. The more we do here, the less we'll have to do at the station, okay?"

Silver nodded.

"Actually she won't be answering anything right now, thank you very much," Kendrick Armstrong, said. Silver faced Kendrick, one would have never thought she'd be grateful to see him again after their blind date fiasco, but she was. He was slightly out of breath having trotted up the stairs. Silver vaguely remembered Brandan calling him in desperation since Kendrick was the only attorney of whom he could think of at the time.

"Ken, what brings you to these parts? I know you're not trying to interfere with an official investigation," Detective Dowdy said. "Is this your client?"

"Obviously," Kendrick answered. "Silver, don't say a word."

"Doesn't matter. This is a criminal case, and in case you've forgotten, this is Jersey, not New York. No high priced widows or divorcee's here. Just good old fashioned blood and gore." Detective Dowdy said.

"You can't stop me from advising someone to avoid piranhas such as yourself." Kendrick placed his briefcase on the table in front of Silver as if it provided the necessary barrier for her not to speak.

"She's a material witness, Ken, and you're not going to whisk her away. We can do this here or at the station. It's up to you," Detective Dowdy said.

Kendrick removed his briefcase from blocking Silver's face and placed it on the floor near her foot, which she tapped repetitively.

"Thank you," Detective Dowdy said. "So Miss James, what exactly did you see when you came home?"

Silver took a small sip of tea and immediately threw up. She wiped her mouth with the blanket hanging from her shoulders and began to talk. "Um, I came in and the pl-place, h-ha-here, 'cause I s-sss-saw his tru—" She tried to take another sip, this time with a little more success.

"Did you see anyone at all fleeing the scene?" the detective asked.

Silver shook her head.

"What about anything strange on your block, like cars or people lurking around?"

She shook her head again.

"Where were you coming from this time of morning?"

"She stayed at my place all night," Brandan answered.

"And who are you?" the detective turned and asked.

"I'm Silver's friend. We're like family," Brandan answered.

"Oh, okay." The detective circled the table and eyed Brandan intently. "A little jealous rage perhaps? Were you upset Boyd was here with your woman or something?"

"Man, go somewhere with that bullshit. I said family. You don't see any blood or anything on me," Brandan answered and threw his palms in the air.

The detective met Brandan nose to nose, refusing to back down. "Just because O.J. didn't have any blood on him didn't mean he didn't do it, now does it?"

"I didn't have shit to do with O.J." Brandan's voice elevated.

The detective retreated and scribbled wildly on a small pad. "So tell me, Miss James, why was Todd Boyd here?" He returned his attention to Silver.

"My-ma—" she breathed heavily—"ma-ma boyfriend," she managed to get out.

"Oh. Officer Todd Boyd was your boyfriend?" the detective asked incredulously.

Silver nodded. The other officers present looked around with rampant smirks painted across their faces.

Suddenly Kendrick had buckets of sweat pouring from his forehead to the armpits of his stained dress shirt. "Did you say Todd Boyd? Officer Todd Boyd?"

"The one and only." The detective stepped toward Kendrick. "Know 'im?"

"Uh-uh, only because he's been on a few of my cases, or former cases. That's enough." Kendrick tugged on Silver's chair with her still in it. "This questioning is over. My client is not well. This is traumatic, and I'm taking her home."

"But she is home, Kendrick," the detective reminded him.

"Then she's going elsewhere. Brandan?"

"No, Mr. Armstrong, I'll be taking my sister with me." Jill finally spoke.

"Fine. She is going elsewhere," Kendrick said as he almost pushed Silver out of her chair.

"Ken, make sure she makes an official statement soon, and when I say soon I mean ASAP. This case is going to be high-profile considering the decedent is a city cop. In fact, you may want to get a blood sample taken and forwarded to the lab so that we can compare it to the blood in the apartment, just to speed things up," the detective said smugly.

"You have a warrant for that request?" Kendrick shot back. "I didn't think so. We'll be in touch," Kendrick said as Silver paced gingerly through the muck and mire of the place she once treasured.

"Okay, people, declare this a crime scene, talk to every man, woman, child and dog on the block. No comments to the press and I want this under wraps from all media until we can figure this out," the detective barked.

"Too late for that, boss. City Line News and all of the majors are lining up across the street as we speak," a uniformed cop said as he entered the apartment.

"Great. Has anyone contacted Todd's wife?"

No one spoke.

"Okay, Daniels get to Boyd's place quickly. We don't want his wife and kids hearing through the media that Todd was decapitated."

Silver hadn't made it to the door, when she managed her question with lucent clarity. "Wife and kids? You mean Ta-Todd has a wife and kids?"

"Silver, let's go, honey." Jill tried to usher her along.

"St-st-op," Silver yelled. She quickly made her way back to Detective Dowdy. "W-What wife and kids?"

"Oh come now, Miss James. You didn't know?" Detective Dowdy asked sarcastically.

Silver shook her head and allowed Jill, Sebastian and Brandan to escort her out. Kendrick lagged behind. At the bottom of the stairs, she collapsed. The next day in the paper, the picture: Officer Todd Boyd's headless body, draped in a body bag being carried away by the official coroner's office. The caption: Decorated Officer Todd Boyd killed in a possible jealous rage. News at eleven.

Silver, Jill and Brandan slipped in on a back pew, long after the service began. After weeks of unsuccessfully searching for Todd Boyd's head, the media reported that the family had consented to hold a closed casket funeral.

Brandan stroked his tie as he peered around the room. He tried to shake an eerie feeling, a mixture of grief and odd curiosity. Jill removed her oversized Jackie O glasses out of respect, and Silver kept her head down as perspiration formed a horizontal line under her blue-tinted Got Rocks shades.

The soloist was concluding her soul version of "On the Arms of An Angel" when Jill whispered over Silver to Brandan. "That woman has a glorious voice. Who is that?"

Brandan flipped through the program, too caught up in the atmosphere to call the singer by name. "Oh, it's Gem. She's hot on the R&B charts right now."

"Oh," Jill said. Silver sat stiffly.

"You okay?" Brandan asked as he tugged on Silver's arm and tightly clasped her hand to get her attention.

She nodded.

Silver had been warned by Kendrick not to attend Todd's funeral before he withdrew all advisement from the case, but Silver was determined to be present. She needed closure. Even Silver's new attorney, Sir Elias "Mac" MacDuffie along with her brother-in-law Sebastian insisted Silver's attendance was a bad idea, but she couldn't deny her last opportunity to say goodbye.

"You were the girlfriend, the mistress. The papers are even calling you the concubine. Why would you want to subject yourself to that?" Mac questioned. Silver didn't answer nor did she waver. Silver felt Todd's wife was the big secret, the other woman, but that fight was left to the media who hadn't stopped reporting the incident as prime news for three weeks since it happened.

Not long after the service ended, six model-like men in dress blues marched down the center aisle of the church to carry the pearl white casket.

Todd's wife, a robust, short woman adorned in a black dress, matching veil and gloves followed closely behind. She was flanked by another group of officers and an elderly woman with blue hair.

"You bitch," Todd's wife yelled, her title Widow Boyd had been deemed by the media. Widow Boyd stopped directly in front of Silver's pew. She lurched so fast that if Brandan hadn't been there to block the collision, Silver would have been pummeled.

"Cheryl, please," the blue-haired woman cried. "Not now, baby. Not here in the house of the Lord."

"What are you doing here? My husband is dead all because of you, and you have the nerve to show your face at his funeral?" She lunged again. "You see my babies? They are without their daddy, and you show up like you deserve to be here? I hope you rot in hell..." Her voice trailed far behind the spitball she threw that landed squarely in the center of Silver's right lens. Fortunately, her sunglasses blocked more than the sun.

"I had to be here. I deserve to be here," was all Silver chanted as Jill wiped her sister's glasses then her face with a light blue hanky.

"Silver baby, let's go. Come on, let's go," Jill implored. "Come on, baby girl, let's just go." Jill and Brandan forced Silver to her feet and pushed her through the side door out to the adjacent parking lot and Jill's car.

As Brandan forced Silver into the car and closed the door, he and Jill talked about how they regretted succumbing to Silver's request by attending the funeral. Brandan knew Silver shouldn't have been there and it pained him to watch her stare into oblivion. With the damage already done, however they all watched as the last hearse rolled out, leading the siren clad procession to Todd's final resting place.

Sebastian paced around the room. "I don't care. I told you, you and Brandan should have tied her up if you had to. Silver shouldn't have been at that funeral. It has set her back, and the therapist is having an even harder time with her than when we started. It's been weeks, and she's not making any progress. She hasn't even gotten out of bed in..."

"I'm going to be okay," Silver said, poking her head in the kitchen where Sebastian and Jill had been arguing. "Don't talk about me like I'm not here." Silver's hair was plastered to her head. She made her way to the fridge where she poured herself a glass of water. She was far beyond a healthy weight for her statuesque frame.

"How are you feeling, baby girl?" Jill asked.

Silver didn't answer. She gave her sister a look like she couldn't believe Jill was asking something like that. The answer could be too devastating to face. "I'm going back to bed. Send Dr. Parker up when she comes..." Silver said, referring to the noted therapist for whom Sebastian had paid.

"We'll do, baby girl. Try to get some rest," Jill said.

"So as I was saying..." Sebastian continued, unaware Silver remained in the corridor, listening to every word. "You say she needed closure, but closure won't mean a damn thing behind bars. Silver has been charged with murder. You all going to that funeral against the attorney's wishes undermines the case," Sebastian argued.

"Did the attorney call?" Jill asked.

"Hon, I would have told you if the attorney had called." Sebastian paused.

"I'm glad Silver listened to him about submitting to the blood work to determine if any of her blood was in the apartment. We can at least put the suspicion stuff to rest and get this crazy madness thrown out of court."

Jill sighed. "I don't know why she's a suspect. She was with Brandan all night."

Silver had heard enough. It had been two weeks since Todd's funeral, and her concern wasn't whether she should have gone but the unending nausea, lightheadedness and loss of appetite she'd been fighting for some time. She heard the doorbell ring, and she quietly made her way up the remainder of the stairs and pulled a heavy down comforter over her head.

Brandan and Daphne's entrance prompted a momentary truce between Sebastian and Jill. The tension among all of them was heavy. The whole situation was taking such a toll that it prompted Sebastian and Jill to agree on one thing: their daughter, Abigail, should stay with Sebastian's parents for the time being.

"Where's Silver?" Brandan asked as Daphne quietly joined Jill at the kitchen table.

"Upstairs. We had some valium prescribed for her. God only knows if she's taken it," Jill said. She rose to grab the kettle to refresh her tea cup. She offered some to Daphne who refused. "So what did you guys find out about Kendrick?"

"Not much. He just refuses to help us on any level. He won't even talk to me. I had to speak with his assistant." Brandan explained that something was awfully strange about Kendrick's abrupt exit from the case and his waterfall of sweat when Todd's name was mentioned. "Did you notice how the detective kept calling him Ken? Something's fishy."

Sebastian and Jill nodded in agreement. "Well, we can't focus on that now. We have to concentrate on Silver getting well and putting this whole thing behind us," Sebastian said.

The phone rang, and Jill rose to retrieve it. "This phone has been ringing off the hook." She grabbed her head.

Brandan stopped Jill from moving and answered. The group listened intently finally concluding it was another reporter trying to get an exclusive story. "No comment. No comment, I said." Brandan slammed down the phone.

"You might want to get your phone number changed. That might help for the moment," Daphne interjected.

"That's a good idea. Everything's been so crazy we didn't even think of it," Jill said, grabbing Daphne's hand. "We really appreciate everything you're doing, Daphne. It means so much to all of us." Jill referred to how Daphne held things down at work for Silver.

"I'm just glad I can help," Daphne answered. She wrapped her arms around Brandan's waist, pulling him closer to her.

"You know, I wish these damn reporters would find another home. I'm sick of chasing them away. I may have to hire private security," Sebastian said, peering through the front sheers. "I haven't seen this much commotion since the Newark riots."

"You were around then?" Daphne questioned. Sebastian nodded. "I was too. I had never been so scared in my life. My parents had just moved us to South Jersey from Texas. It reminded me of the big KKK rallies we had to endure, only it was a sea of black people angry at the world."

"I was a boy. I barely remember anything except everything and everybody being on lockdown. The police didn't bother me as much, they had a hard time identifying which race I belonged to, so to play it safe they left me alone." Sebastian said.

"So what's the plan?" Brandan interrupted the trip down memory lane.

"The plan is to follow the attorney's orders to a tee. I was just saying to Jill that going to the funeral was not a good idea..."

"With all due respect, Sebastian, Brandan did try to talk Silver out of going but no offense, we all know how stubborn Silver can be." Daphne let out a nervous chuckle.

Jill's neck snapped. "How dare you make derogatory comments about my sister in my home?" Jill squinted and balled her fist.

"She didn't mean anything, Jill. Dee is really trying to help," Brandan said.

"I know, I know. We're on edge." Jill placed her hand on Daphne's shoulder, but her attention was on the door and the ringing bell. "I'll get it, and it better not be another one of those damn reporters." As soon as Jill opened the door, a barrage of flashbulbs and shouted questions greeted her.

Mac hurried in, wearing a navy designer suit and carrying an overstuffed leather briefcase. "Good evening," he finally managed to get out. "We need to talk. Where's Silver?"

"She just went upstairs to sleep. Can we talk without her?" Jill asked.

"I think not," Mac answered. He planted himself in the living room and spread a ream of paperwork all over Jill and Sebastian's maple wood coffee table.

Jill left to get Silver as Sebastian escorted Mac to the living room with Brandan and Daphne in tow. A few minutes later, Jill helped a wobbly Silver down the stairs. Silver sat down in full view of everyone, although it was apparent her mind was elsewhere.

"I'm glad all of you are here. There's a development in the case that's going to make my work a lot harder. The D.A. has formulated a theory, and the grand jury has returned an indictment against Silver as an accomplice to murder in the first degree of Todd Boyd," Mac said. "They also have an eyewitness."

"What?" Jill shouted as she grabbed her chest.

Silver rocked wildly, trying to get her mind around what Mac was saying.

"Who did she supposedly help if they are charging her as an accomplice?" Sebastian asked, trying to remain calm.

"That's where the bad news comes in. Brandan, you're going to have to turn yourself in to the police. The D.A. put forth the argument as a crime of passion and convinced the grand jury that you two conspired to kill Todd. You'll be officially charged, of course, and will have to seek representation because I won't be able to handle Silver's case and yours. Conflict of interest." Mac looked at his watch. "We should turn on the news. They might be breaking the story right now."

Sure enough on every major tri-state channel, female D.A. Dené Hoard stood ready to deliver Silver's and Brandan's fate.

Silver's head was still in a fog but she managed to clearly hear how investigators and the D.A. formulated their theory that Todd's murder was a jealous crime of passion and the perpetrators would pay dearly.

"Oh my God, Brandan, did you hear that? They're talking the death penalty for torturing and executing a cop." Jill Said.

"I heard them, Jill. I heard them," he shouted.

Jill then gasped and Sebastian stood stoically in complete shock.

"What? I can't believe this. They really are calling for Brandan to turn himself in." Daphne repeated the D.A.'s words as if no one else was present. "Brandan, who are you calling?" Daphne asked when he jumped.

"I'm calling Kendrick. Maybe he'll take my arm of the case," Brandan said.

Daphne stepped over and placed her finger on the receiver, disconnecting the call. "Why are you all so bent on this Kendrick thing?"

"Daphne..." Brandan turned.

"No, hear me out. He doesn't want anything to do with the case for whatever reason so stop pressing him. He's not the only great attorney in the world."

"Daphne, I don't have time to go turn myself in and worry about who's going to defend me later," he shouted.

"Okay, everyone, please calm down," Sebastian said.

Silver frantically rocked. Jill held her tight.

"Please, please, we have a lot of work to do. Silver, we need you to calm down and focus," Mac said firmly.

"Give her a minute. This is a lot for her to take in," Jill hissed.

"We don't have a minute." Mac's gaze vacillated between Silver, Jill, Sebastian and Brandan and Daphne. "The biggest problem we have is to refute an eyewitness who claimed they heard a struggle between you Brandan, Silver and Todd. The eyewitness also claims they saw you two running out of the house in a huff and overheard you threatening to kill Todd. Now the culmination of the love triangle theory came from the blood work results, which confirmed Silver's pregnancy. Silver, trust me, you can't keep anything at all, especially something as important as this—"

Silver's voice crackled as she pulled her hair from her face. "What are you talking about pregnancy? Who's pregnant?"

"You, Silver. You're pregnant. The results are here." Mac rifled through several papers until he found a document that read ELEVATED HORMONE LEVELS, PREGNANCY: POSITIVE.

Sebastian snatched the paper from Mac's hand. "And this case came from the blood work that was supposed to clear her from having anything to do with this mess?"

Silver grunted in despair. She fell out of her chair and plastered herself to the floor, making loud guttural sounds.

"Silver, baby girl, it's going to be all right, I promise. Somebody, help me please…" Jill cried. Finally, Sebastian threw down the paper and went to help lift Silver from the floor. Brandan just sat with his head in his hands. Daphne was on the phone.

"I know this is tough but things are going to get worse before they get better, and if each and every one of you don't pull yourselves together immediately, you won't make it through this, I guarantee it," Mac said.

"Brandan, we have to go." Everyone looked up at the sound of Daphne hanging up the phone.

"I'm not going anywhere," Brandan insisted.

"Honey, I know a lot is going on but we have to go. If you don't turn yourself in, the police are coming for you. Come on, Brandan." Daphne was unsuccessful in pulling Brandan's large, brooding frame from the chair.

"I could recommend someone but not Kendrick Armstrong, of course," Mac said.

"Why? What's up with Kendrick Armstrong?" Sebastian asked. Everyone except Silver looked up in anticipation.

"Apparently, he had several run-ins with the very police department involved in our case. I'm not sure exactly what but there is a lot of bad blood between Kendrick and the local police."

"Thanks for the information," Daphne said to the attorney. "Brandan, honey, please trust me. We have to go. I have a former military attorney who will look at our case. He said he's going to meet us at the police station." Daphne tugged at Brandan once more, and he finally rose, making his long, slow exit out the front door. Flashbulbs and shouted questions greeted them. Brandan blocked his face as Daphne navigated them through the crowd, shouting "No comment, no comment."

Back in the house, Mac explained his strategy to have the case thrown out before a jury had the chance to hear it.

Silver exited the bathroom, wiping the residue of regurgitation from her mouth. On top of everything that was going on in her life emotionally, physically it felt as if her body had turned on her. She was pregnant, a situation she thought she'd never be in, and her body rejected almost everything she gave it to sooth herself.

"I bought a Quarter Pounder extra value meal," Brandan said, sitting yoga style in the middle of the family room of Jill and Sebastian's fully furnished basement. He pulled the burger and fries from the bag, then poured the fries in the lid before shoving everything in her direction. "I would pick out the soggy fries for you but I figured I'd let you do something for yourself." Brandan smiled.

Silver sorted through the fries, leaving the hard, crispy ones for Brandan or anyone else to share. She ate one fry before grabbing the soda and gulping down almost half to keep from vomitting.

"Still having a hard time eating, huh?" Brandan asked. He pulled a tiny plastic box from his bag, along with some chopsticks a small plastic container and packets of soy sauce. He poured the soy sauce in the empty container, opened the plastic box and swirled a green pasty substance in the sauce, mixing it until the chunks of green splattered the landscape of the dark brown.

"Other than Daphne, when did you start eating raw fish?"

"Silver, don't start. This is a tuna roll. Daphne's turned me on to this stuff. It's good. You should try some." Brandan lifted the pungent food to Silver's face.

"Okay, tuna roll," Silver said sarcastically, gulping her Coke. "I barely eat cooked fish so you know I'm not trying it raw." She winced. Silver continued gulping her Coke, understanding the soda was probably her dinner for the night because she couldn't hold anything else down. She watched Brandan devour the meal like he really enjoyed it. Her lips were still turned up. "Umph." Silver sipped the last of her Coke, usurping every drop. She bit down on the edge of the cup and rubbed the papery remnants from her mouth. "So are you okay? I mean having spent forty-eight hours in jail and all."

"What are you talking about?"

"Brandan, please don't play coy with me. You have to talk about it. We're in this together," Silver said.

Brandan looked in her eyes. He couldn't face the terror and weathered look he saw. He shook his head and glanced at his tuna roll. "It's no place for a black man," he mumbled.

"Were you mistreated or anything?"

"I was mistreated having to go to the damn police station and turn myself in for something I didn't do and have nothing to do with." He stirred the soy mix with vigor, spilling the contents.

Silver grabbed more napkins from the bathroom to clean the mess. "What do you mean?" She didn't look up as she tried to sop the liquid.

"Come on, Silver. You've seen television or heard about jail. Jail is jail. Damn. What do you want from me?" Brandan threw the last piece of tuna roll in his mouth before rolling together and shoving the paper, Silver's uneaten dinner and the empty containers in a brown handled bag. In another bag next to the trash he pulled out a bottle with what Silver thought was Chinese characters and the word *plum* in bright red letters. Brandan gathered all of the trash and proceeded to discard it.

Silver followed him through the kitchen where he disposed of the trash. When he noticed her, he continued his silent trail through the family room, game parlor and finally out the white-paned French doors to the patio. He took in the fresh air and cracked his neck and knuckles.

"We gotta talk about it, Brandan. I know it's painful but you can't hold it all in."

Brandan looked to the sky, his voice raspy and broken. "What makes you think I'm holding it in?"

"Because I know you." Silver's voice wasn't much stronger but she wanted to be there for her friend, considering over the last few weeks she hadn't been any good to anyone.

"It was fucked up, I mean for real. It was only two nights but I don't want to ever go back. I can't. The air was foul, pissy. Open toilet. I didn't shit and wouldn't even pull my dick out, there was so much dirt and crap in there. But what was worse—" he turned and looked her in the eye— "was all the lost souls crawling from the walls, brothers there just because. That was the worst."

Silver regretted having pushed him to open up because she didn't know what to say. All she could do was listen, and that seemed to be exactly what Brandan needed. Silver led Brandan through the house. She peered out of the windows at all angles. Only a few local reporters sat outside; the others were chasing the newest gory story in another town. Apparently, the media reported, with the arrest of Brandan, the case had been solved. They walked out back to the ground, taking in the dark, cloudy sky. Brandan spoke candidly of the pain he was enduring. Every time he tensed because of a sad thought, his mind reverted to Daphne, and he smiled. She had put up a fifty thousand dollar cash bond.

"Why is it every time I mention Dee's name you get the ugliest look on your face?" Brandan asked.

"I don't."

"Yes, you do. For real, talk to me. Why?" Brandan stopped and grabbed Silver's hands.

"I just don't think her intentions are fully honorable and mean you any good. I think this entire situation is something she's going to hold over your head for a prize, like marriage or something silly."

"You can't be serious, Silver."

"Very. I mean things are changing, like you're changing, Brandan. Here you are calling Daphne Dee and eating sushi…"

"Hold up. I think you really need to consider what you're saying, Sil."

"I am considering what I'm saying."

"No, I don't think you are. I mean Dee has done a lot to help both you and me. Hey, she didn't have to put up a dime for me. She's keeping your job afloat while you get through this, and it has to count for something more than some carrot you're talking about. That's all people want is somebody to stand with us through the good and the bad. And this is pretty damn bad if I say so myself."

"I know it is. It really is. I'm not discounting all that Daphne has done and is doing—"

"You sure sound like it."

"Well, I'm not. I'm just saying…" Silver was at a loss for words.

"What are you just saying?"

"That-that things are changing, Brandan, and I don't like it."

"Silver, yeah things are changing, and we have to stand strong. Shit, we're up on murder charges. This shit is like a damn soap opera. My mind ain't nowhere near wrapped around everything."

"In case you've forgotten, I'm right here with you on it," Silver snapped.

"I know that, but, Silver, it's not just me and you. It's me, you, Jill, Sebastian, my mom and Dee. And whether you like it or not, we need all the help we can get on this." Brandan and Silver went back inside. The quiet stillness lingering there seemed to evoke a calm between them. "All I'm saying is that we have a heavy road ahead of us, and we have much more to worry about than what we're talking about. I tell you what, when Dee brought over my sushi, she gave me a nice chilled bottle of plum wine that I would love to share with you. Let's have some, turn on some music. I can get my Kindred CD from the car. Cool?"

Silver rolled her eyes. "I'm surprised you're sharing it with me. Where is Daphne anyway?"

"She's at the office," Brandan answered. "She had work to do." Silver conceded. She wanted to further her case against Daphne but her energy was running low.

Brandan retrieved his CD from the car and popped it into the stereo system. He finagled a few buttons to ensure sound only emitted through the basement rather than the entire house. He didn't want to disturb anyone else. He looked behind the bar and found two white wineglasses that were in the fridge.

Silver made herself comfortable on the floor with a few oversized throw pillows to cushion her sore buttocks. Brandan sat down and poured the light molasses-like liquid. They clinked glasses, and just as Silver put hers to her mouth, Brandan panicked.

"Oh shoot, you can't have this." He yanked the glass from her lips.

"What is wrong with you?" she shouted.

"You can't have this. We have a little baby to protect," Brandan said, placing the glass down and rubbing her stomach. He half smiled.

"Oh, Brandan, please. This little bit of wine ain't gon' hurt nothin'. Before I knew I was pregnant I had valium and bunch of other stuff to make me sleep, besides…"

"Besides what?" Brandan asked, taking a sip from his glass. "What?"

"In a couple of weeks, it's not going to matter anyway. I'm having it taken care of," Silver said softly. "I would do it sooner but Mac advised against it." She was purposefully vague.

"Taken care of? Silver, what are you talking about?"

"Oh, now who's playing dumb?" she asked.

"I'm not playing. What are you talking about?" Brandan placed his glass down.

"Abortion, Brandan, okay? You happy I said it out loud? I'm having an abortion. I already have the appointment."

"Abortion? Have you talked to Jill or anybody else about this?"

"Jill and Sebastian know."

"When were you going to tell me?" Brandan asked.

"When I thought it was the right time, and right now is better than any." Silver turned her back and held her head.

"As if we're not going through enough, you throw this shit on me now." Brandan stood.

"On you? Please, man, truthfully this has nothing to do with you. I'm the one pregnant, not you, Jill, Sebastian or anyone else, and I ain't about to mess up my life with a child that I have no clue what to do with." Silver jumped up and headed to the fridge. She pulled out a beer, opened it with the built-in bottle opener on the bar and sat back down Silver poised the beer to her mouth but paused. As much as she wanted to prove to Brandan she was serious, a pang in her gut wouldn't allow her to swallow. She placed the beer down on the floor in front between she and Brandan.

"I don't believe this."

"Brandan, when has it come as a surprise to you that I don't want children? I've never wanted them."

"I don't believe this."

"I don't want to be a single parent, you know, all alone," Silver said.

"Since when have you done anything in your life alone?" Brandan asked. His tone was cutting.

"Say what you mean, Brandan. That I've leaned on you and my sister for everything."

"No, I'm saying—"

"Are you saying that all of my accomplishments are only because of you and my sister?"

"No."

"Then dammit, Brandan, what are you saying?" Silver rose and stood firm for emphasis. "I've been alone all my life, sometimes with and without you, and this is one thing I'm not doing alone. So take it or leave it, I'm not having this damn baby, and I don't want to hear anything about adoption and help and all of the other things Jill and Sebastian have thrown my way." Silver turned to walk away. "I won't have the damn beer, alright? But I'm not having this baby, I don't care what you or anybody else has to say. And adoption is not an option!"

"Listen to me. Don't walk away, listen. I'm not talking about adoption. What I'm saying is that in anything you've done in your life, we have all been there for you and will continue to be there for you just like you've been there for us. But Sil, you have another life to think about now. Abortion is not fair, and if anybody knows how important life is regardless of the circumstances, it's you. Your mother didn't get rid of you even though she got pregnant by a married man. And you may not have had a silver spoon all your life but you've always been loved and taken care of."

Silver turned away. She was incensed that Brandan would compare her situation to her mother's. The fact was, her mother wasn't alive and left Silver to fend for herself at a very early age, a fact that haunted Silver every time she thought of her mother. Death was no excuse. Silver had no intention of ending up like the woman she longed for no matter how much she was loved.

"Even if Todd were around, I would be a part of that baby's life—a second father to that kid regardless of Todd. There was no question in my mind that I was going to be a father to that child from the time we found out you was pregnant. When I was sitting in that jail cell, don't you realize one of the reasons and things that kept me going and brought me through was the fact that a new life is coming in the world for all of us. Don't take that from us, Sil, please don't take that from us," Brandan pleaded.

"Brandan, I've made up my mind. I'm doing this with or without you. I'm not keeping this baby, and that's that. It's not fair to bring an unwanted child in this world." The silence from Brandan choked her. "This time, I need you, even if you disagree with me. You say you'll be there for me, then be there for me now."

Brandan didn't say a word. He ended the music, pulled the disc out of the player, gathered his things and gave Silver one final look of disdain before storming out of the house.

Chapter 7

So Help Me God

The tiny room in the Essex County Courthouse barely held Silver, Brandan, Jill, Sebastian, Mom Savoy and Daphne. All, except Silver, waited patiently before entering the courtroom for the pre-trial evidentiary hearing.

Silver paced around the dark-paneled room that smelled of mold and old cigarettes. Daphne and Brandan hovered in the corner, clinging to each other as if this would be the last time they would see each other.

"Silver, honey, why don't you sit down? Walking around is not going to make the proceedings start any quicker," Jill pleaded.

Silver didn't acknowledge the comment or stop, continuing to pace and constantly gazing from the door to the black-and-white clock above it.

Mac and Harry Coles Sr., Silver's and Brandan's attorneys respectively, entered the room.

Mac spoke first. "We should start in a minute. I want you all to be patient. I'll come back and give you updates as they occur. This is an evidentiary hearing, so I along with Mr. Coles here will hear evidence from the D.A. concerning their case against Silver and Brandan. Mr. Coles and I will then present our motion to have the case thrown out for lack of evidence, and if all goes well, we can go home safe and happy then contemplate our action against the city for wrongful arrest and a host of other charges."

Mr. Coles spoke. "Brandan and Silver, you won't be coming in just yet. You may not come in at all—" he directed his attention to the group excluding Brandan and Silver "—so I don't think it's necessary for all of you to wait around all day."

"I hope y'all don't mind, but I want to pray right now," Mom Savoy said, interrupting the legal brief. Brandan smiled, appreciative of his mother's stance on her belief when needed.

Everyone gathered with Mom Savoy directly in the middle as she prayed the Holy Ghost into the room. Amens went forth all over.

With prayers solidified and other business intact, all anyone could do was wait. Daphne advised the group that she'd be going back to the office, and if anything should break to call her immediately. Brandan planted a long, luscious kiss on her lips before grabbing her and holding on tight. Sebastian's fake cough finally broke their grip.

Sebastian and Jill also prepared to leave. "Mom Savoy, I can take you home," Jill said, gathering her things.

"Thanks, baby. Now Brandan and Silver, you have put it in God's hands, don't take it back." Mom Savoy grabbed Brandan's right hand and prompted Silver to join with the other, forming a small circle of wisdom. "Trust in the Lord, babies. He will see you through. Now call Mama if you need her. I put some food over there, not much, just some baked chicken and gravy with stuffing and fresh string beans with white potatoes. Oh, and some pineapple cake, and Silver, I pulled some Red Velvet cake from my freezer for you, and I made a pitcher of sweet tea. Got to keep your strength up, Silver. You eatin' for two now." Mom Savoy patted Silver's belly.

Silver coiled, realizing no one had informed Mom Savoy of her plans.

"Okay, Mama, you go on home now," Brandan urged. The room cleared, leaving Silver and Brandan in an uneasy silence. "So, how you think this thing is going to pan out?" Brandan asked as he paced and Silver looked out the dingy barred window to nowhere.

She shrugged, walked back to the middle of the room and sat at the table. "Jill left her purse."

"Well she'll be back or you'll take it to her." Brandan joined her at the table.

Silver pulled out her laptop and began typing.

"Good to see you getting back to your old self again," Brandan said.

"Whatever that is." Silver didn't look up although the document didn't really hold her interest.

"Sooooo, have you given any thought to reconsidering your actions about the baby?"

Her hopes of the subject being avoided were dashed. "It's not a baby, Brandan. It's a fetus, and no, I'm going through with it, with or without you, especially considering I've never done anything in my life on my own."

Brandan sighed. He knew that comment would come back to haunt him. "Okay, let's settle this once and for all."

"Nothing to settle. You said what you had to say, and I'm doing what I have to do." She turned her back, hoping it would dissuade him from talking to her any further.

That little trick didn't work. "First of all I'm sorry. You took what I meant the wrong way. All I was trying to say is that you'll have my full support, but Silver, I don't believe in abortion. And whether you choose to call it a baby or a fetus, it is still a life."

Silver closed down the program on her computer. She rose and planted herself against the window with her arms folded against her chest and shook her head.

Brandan joined her, wrapping his arms around her and placing his chin on her shoulder. "I know it's hard for you—for us—but as my mom always says, God doesn't put anything on us we can't bear. And as I always say, what doesn't kill you will definitely make you stronger."

"Says you. I feel like a walking dead woman—everything I've come to know is gone, destroyed or lost. I don't want any more parts of it."
Brandan turned her around to face him. He brushed her hair from her eyes. "Everything is hard on all of us."

"I don't want to do this, Brandan. I can't. What if I go to jail? I can't have a baby in jail. That is some ghetto mess."

"Yeah, it's a tough thing." Brandan pulled away. He sat back down and plastered his head against the chair's iron head rest. Here he was asking Silver to consider having a baby, not knowing her fate. He didn't want her to experience even a holding cell for a minute, much less real time for murder in a jail cell, but urging her to keep her baby seemed right in his gut. "You remember when Allencia got pregnant and claimed it was mine?"

Silver was surprised Brandan would bring up his college ex. In proving his point, he was going for broke.

"I thought it was the end of my world. I thought for sure I'd have to leave school, and I just wasn't feeling her like that to have a child with her. I remember my mom saying to me when I laid down to have sex with her, I committed to having a child with her and that I couldn't neglect my responsibilities. I remember thinking I wasn't going to be like my dad—you know, make a bunch of babies and then leave them high and dry with no one to look up to. I mean look at my sister. I think the main reason for her drama is because my dad wasn't around to teach her what true love is about."

"Brandan, if you don't realize it, you're proving my point," Silver said, not in the mood for his argument. She wanted to lash out at him for even bringing up his college incident. It certainly didn't compare to her situation, even though it was later discovered that Brandan wasn't the father of Allencia's baby, a fact he often left out when he brandished his badge of honor.

"No, what I'm trying to say is that with my situation, the greatest joy of life is a child. Things change when children come around. Even you, without a maternal bone in your body, I guarantee will change and be thankful you kept your baby. I mean look at Cariss," Brandan said, referring to one of his sisters. "I think she's so mean because she regrets having V.I.P. status at the abortion clinic. You never get over that shit, man."

"I hear you. I heard you, and trust me, I've considered everything you've said. My mind is not changing, so take it or leave it. I'm not having this baby, and that's that."

Brandan huffed.

Silver sat down.

Brandan gritted his teeth and pounded the table. "Silver, come on. I'll be there for you. I'll be a father to that baby. I want to be a father to the baby—"

"You plan on staying with Daphne?" Silver interjected, looking over the screen.

"Yeah. What does that have to do with anything?" Brandan asked.

"Duh. Please, Brandan. That girl can't stand kids, and she won't even think about going for this arrangement. You being a father to my child and seeing her? It ain't happening."

"No doubt. Daphne's my girl, but she has nothing to do with this situation here. This is my decision."

"Brandan, I'm worn out. I don't want to discuss this anymore." Silver returned to her computer, which still didn't hold her interest. She shut the computer down again and walked back over to the window. "The sky looks like it's about to rip wide open." She looked at her watch. Her silent prayers hadn't been answered. Only minutes had passed. She traveled back to the end of the table and tore into Mom Savoy's delicious food. "Hungry?" She looked at Brandan and brandished the chicken baked so golden and tender that a gentle shaking separated the meat from the bone. Silver filled her plate high with everything. She was tearing into one drumstick and reaching for another when Brandan finally joined her.

After having consumed almost everything, Silver returned to her computer to avoid having Brandan strike up another aspect of their dreaded conversation. Angst filled her gut. She sighed several times before taking in deep breaths. She shook her head and cracked her neck but nothing helped. The bad energy between her and Brandan consumed them both.

Brandan stood from the table, having only picked at a piece of chicken, and went to the dingy wired window trying to find a signal for his phone. Silver turned toward him. Highly agitated, Brandan placed his phone on the ledge and continued to gaze out the window. A somber mood flooded the room. "I don't understand why this baby would be so important to you. You hated Todd."

"Why would you even fix your lips to say something like that? This ain't about Todd. This is about another life, one you don't have a right to take. And since you've known me, when have I ever condoned abortion?" Brandan's words were pointed, even though he didn't bother to turn around and give them. "Nobody killed you."

The heavy door opened, and both were grateful for the interruption by Mac's clerk.

"How are things going in there?" Brandan asked as he walked past Silver like she wasn't present.

"Things are really up in the air right now. The judge was changed due to illness, so the new judge is hearing arguments about dismissal for lack of evidence. The problem is that this is a newly appointed judge. Considering the notoriety of the case, he might want it to go to a jury just because he wouldn't want the heat from the public because an officer was killed."

"Damn, this is crazy." Brandan slammed his fist into his hand. "How much longer do we have to be here?"

"Your attorneys sent me in here to advise you to go home because this argument will probably go on all day. They said to stay close though, together if you can, and leave the number to where you'll be."

"We might as well go back to Jill's." Silver's voice was filled with trepidation. She pulled out a card and wrote a number on the back. "This is my sister's house. Mac has the number but you take it just in case. We'll—she looked over at Brandan for confirmation. He stood with his arms folded, giving none—"we'll be at my sister's house if anyone needs us. Thanks."

"You're welcome," the clerk said and exited.

Silver began cleaning up their garbage. Brandan went to the opposite side of the room to do the same. When he came across Jill's purse, he handed it to Silver. "Here. Hold on to this. You probably want to call Jill and tell her you have it."

Silver took the purse and pulled out her cell phone. She had a signal and proceeded to call Jill while Brandan continued gathering their things. "This isn't Jill's," she said a few minutes later. "She said she has her purse. Must be Daphne's."

Brandan shrugged.

"Come on, Brandan. Talk to me. My head is spinning, and I can't do this alone. I need you," she pleaded. She slumped in a chair and grabbed her temples.

Brandan knelt beside her, cupped her chin and lifted her face to his. His eyes softened immediately. "I know. I'm sorry. There's a lot going on here, and there's pressure on both of us."

Silver nodded without a word. Beads of perspiration popped on her forehead and under her nose. Suddenly she became warm and flushed.

"You okay? You all right?" Brandan asked tenderly, her face still in his hands. "You know I'm here for you, right? You know that, right?" She nodded and Brandan kissed her right cheek, then her left and finally her upper lip, then just below her eye. From the inside out, it was a kiss of reverence, one that screamed "I got your back and we'll get through this like we've made it through everything else."

But from the outside looking in it was a kiss of betrayal, one of longing and fulfilled urge dredged up from the depths of one's soul. From the outside in, the embrace that followed was filled with passion as Silver's arms locked around Brandan's neck, and she whispered to him. From the outside in, another peck, lip to lip and a closed eye embrace spoke volumes.

Daphne stood, watching and waiting.

Shrills filled the courtroom as the judge declared there was not enough evidence to remotely link Brandan or Silver to the death of Todd

Boyd. The eyewitness was a snitch who turned states evidence on another case. Mac planned to tear his so-called story to shreds.

After the murder ordeal was over, Silver got back to the business of abortion plans. She hadn't felt a maternal bone in her body. She never desired children, and while she wouldn't wish any harm on a little one, she had no desire to go through the dreaded morning sickness, swollen feet and out-of-control appetite for the next few months.   She was already having to unzip some of her designer duds for comfort, or was it all in her mind?

Silver tried to shake her thoughts as she walked with new vigor through the doors of Sci-gex a week after the judge's decision. She was eager to get back to work and restore some normalcy to her life. While she still stayed with Jill and Sebastian, as soon as she could muster the courage, she planned to salvage what was left from her old place and move.

As soon as she entered the office she was overwhelmed. Rather than the expected backlash for the scandal she'd endured, she was well received by applause, hugs and flanked by a sea of cards, balloons and flowers. She avoided the flowers as they reminded her how the sordid details of life over the last few months began.

Daphne stood in the doorway of her office, overseeing the glee. "Okay, everyone. I know we're happy to have Silver back, but we do have plenty of work to do. Maybe you all can have turns taking her out to lunch," she said as she ushered Silver into her office.

The hairs on Silver's arms stood. As Daphne closed the door. Silver's recollection of the office being a replica of a vampire's tomb vanished. It had been dramatically brightened by seafoam green paint with yellow trim and adorned with live greenery. Classical music played softly in the background. "Wow, it certainly is different in here," Silver said.

"Yes. I have a different outlook on life now." Daphne tapped loose papers into a neat pile. "Enough about me. How are you?" Her voice was curt, and her smile was too wide.

"Great," Silver answered cautiously.

"Good. Are you sure you're ready to come back? It's only been a week since your case was thrown out." Daphne swiveled her chair around to a steaming hot carafe, poured herself some tea and offered some to Silver who declined although the mint aroma was inviting and soothing. "You know the company has gone through a major overhaul despite your month-long hiatus. Some of your accounts we had been working on have tripled in work to be done."

Silver nodded, praying this meeting would end quickly. She had to go to the bathroom.

Daphne handed over a clasped manila envelope. "I've outlined a few project prelims that I think will move you back into the swing of things without over-exerting you."

Silver perused the documents, feeling the tasks were fair. "Okay, great." She slapped her thighs, ready to leave. "Oh, who's handling my group until I get up to speed with things?"

"The boys and I believe you should take it slowly, one day at a time and we'll go from there." Daphne stood. It was an obvious directive for Silver to exit. "Oh, and you'll find that your desk will be exactly as you left it." She smiled.

"Thanks," Silver said as she walked through the door. Daphne wasn't far behind.

"Oh, Silver, I forgot one little thing.... Maybe we should go back into my office."

We couldn't discuss this while I was in here the first time? Silver thought as she sat at the edge of her seat again. She sensed it wouldn't be long before she found out the meaning behind the blank smile Daphne had been giving her.

"Did you plan on taking off any days during the week?"

"No. Why would you ask me that?"

"Oh, because Brandan shared with me your plans to take care of your pregnancy. And if you needed time to do that, I wanted you to know that I'm totally behind you on your decision, and by all means, I would cover for you."

Daphne continued to whisper as Silver became enraged. Why would Brandan discuss her abortion issue with Daphne? She wondered. He was tripping. They'd never discussed intimate details of their lives and decisions with anyone.

"Daphne," Silver said, stopping the tirade about single parenting and the workplace, "whatever I decide to do, trust me, my job won't be affected. You and I don't need to talk about this." A new wrinkle crowded Silver's forehead.

"Oh, okay. I was just trying to—"

"Daphne, there's no need to discuss this with you," Silver asserted. "I'd better get to work." She marched toward her office, where the first business of the day was to get Brandan straight about discussing her personal business. When she reached her desk, not only had it not been touched as Daphne had advised, but a new body was sitting behind it.

"Pat?"

"One moment," Pat said, covering the phone.

As Silver waited for Pat to conclude her conversation, Silver noticed she hadn't quite lost all of her baby fat.

Pat finally hung up the phone. "Okay, I see Daphne gave you the projects we're going to have you start working on."

"Yeah. I thought you weren't coming back?" Silver said.

"That was the plan, but with your situation, the company needed a sure hand, so Daphne offered me a package I couldn't refuse." She shuffled some papers and called in an assistant who gave Silver a gracious nod.

"So, any questions?"

"Yeah. What the hell is going on here? Daphne said my desk was left untouched."

"She's right. Your desk is the one outside my office."

Silver dropped the envelope at her side. "This is a trip. Okay, what games are you and Daphne playing now?"

"Games?" Me and Daphne? I would ask you the same question, but I don't have a lot of time. I have a meeting to attend. If you have any questions about the projects we've given you, see my assistant, or I'll be back around three." Pat rose and attempted to walk past Silver.

"Pat, for real, wait a minute. What's going on here?"

"I thought Daphne explained everything to you."

"No, she didn't explain anything to me."

"Well, you've been placed in staff writing for small accounts. I'm heading small and mid accounts, and you report directly to me," Pat said.

"So I'm not project manager anymore?"

No, you're not, and I'm surprised Daphne didn't tell you that you were demoted. Don't worry, your salary is the same."

Silver turned around and looked toward Daphne's door, which she'd left wide open. "When did this happen? Who ordered this change?"

"Apparently Daphne brought this up with the director last week. She gave me forty-eight hours to accept her offer. Now I have to go." This time Pat was successful in moving through the doorway.

Silver didn't have the strength to respond or fight. She took her position at her old desk in the wide open space in the middle of Sci-gex's offices for all the world to see.

Two weeks had passed and Silver had settled in nicely. She actually enjoyed the less strenuous atmosphere as opposed to the one she remembered right before her leave.

Pat approached her desk one day. "Silver, are you done with the requirement documents for HRL?"

Silver had finished them the day she was given the assignment, two days after she'd come back. She silently handed everything to Pat.

"Wow, this looks great," Pat said as she read over the information.

Silver kept working, not looking up. Finally she said, "I need to take Monday through Wednesday off. I have a medial procedure, and I'm going to need some recuperation time. I know I'm out of vacation days, but if you have to dock my pay or something—"

"Don't insult me like that. If you need the time, you got it...on one condition."

Silver looked up.

"You come with me to lunch today."

Silver looked back down at her computer and typed ardently. "I don't do requests."

"This isn't a request, but a directive," Pat said with warmth and a touch of firmness.

Silver rolled her eyes. "Pat, I really don't—"

"It is not a request, whether you want the time off or not."

"Let me get to another section in this document first and then I'll be ready."

"Reprogram your voice mail. We'll probably be gone for most of the afternoon."

Silver and Pat entered the office after a three-hour lunch, hoping to one day get on with being true friends again.

They were both confused as to why Daphne was using them as pawns in some lavishly orchestrated scene of revenge. Everything became apparent after the appetizer when their conversation got so heated, the maître d' asked them to quiet down. It was obvious Daphne had something against both of them, and they were a part of her corporate game, but neither of them could think of why Daphne wanted revenge.

Silver knew she and Daphne enjoyed some rivalry over Brandan's attention but Daphne had sought to drive a wedge between Silver and Pat before Daphne and Brandan were deemed a couple. The thought of Daphne's revenge perplexed Silver. What angered her more was the fact

Brandan discussed her pregnancy with Daphne.

Pat interrupted Silver's thoughts. "I really want you to think about what you're doing, Silver. You have the time but I'd wish you'd reconsider," Pat whispered at Silver's desk.

Silver knew that Pat was speaking of the abortion. "Pat, thanks for your concern, but my mind is made up. I only told you because…well…you're so damn nosy I couldn't get out of telling you." Silver really didn't know why she had told Pat. They were on track to being cool again but their friendship in full blast would have to resume in time.

Pat returned to her office, and Silver worked on the file she was working on right before Pat dragged her to lunch. She wanted to get as much done as she possibly could. She had no intention of staying in the office late; she had an appointment for which to ready herself.

"Silver James?" a man-sized cold drink of water on a humid day asked. "Would you mind signing here?" He shoved a clipboard in her face.

"For what?" Silver asked hesitantly, considering her legal troubles of late.

"The bouquet over there," he answered, still forcing the clipboard on her.

Silver bypassed the clipboard and tipped toward the foot-tall surprise wrapped in pink-and-white lace paper. When a white rose popped out from a ripped seam, she tore the paper to reveal two-dozen regal white roses and orchids. The fragrance and arrangement was reminiscent of the same flowers she'd been receiving preceding her discovery of Todd's body.

Her fingers trembled as she picked up an unsigned pale blue card that read, *Welcome back. I knew you weren't guilty.*

"Who sent these?" she shrilled.

"I don't know, lady. I just deliver them. Will you sign?"

"Then who-who sent you?" Silver yelled.

"Central processing. I'm a delivery guy, lady. Call my boss if you want that information."

"What is going on out here? This *is* a place of business," Daphne said, wild-eyed as she rushed out of her office. "Silver, Silver, are you okay? Oh, God…" was all Silver heard before she blacked out.

Silver regained consciousness as Pat tried to shove cold water down her throat. She focused and found Daphne talking to Detective Dowdy, the Prosecutor Investigator who had worked on Todd's murder case. Her head pounded. "How long have I been out?" she asked.

"About twenty minutes," Pat answered. "Brandan's on his way. I couldn't get a hold of your sister. Silver, we think you should go to the hospital."

"No, no, I'm not going to the hospital. I'm just tripping. I'll be all right." Silver stubbornly stood.

"What did the delivery guy say to Miss James?" Detective Dowdy asked Daphne.

"I don't really know. I just heard Silver yelling something about who sent you. I had to come out of my office because I could hear her with the door closed. When I approached, she just blanked out," Daphne answered.

Silver wobbled over to the detective and Daphne. The nausea overwhelmed her; she didn't know what was worse, the pregnancy or the permeating stench of the orchids. "I'm okay. I'm going home."

"I highly recommend you go to the emergency room, Silver," Daphne said with her hand on her hip.

"I'm going home. Pat said Brandan was coming and—"

Before Silver could finish her sentence, Brandan rushed in. He pecked Daphne on the cheek and immediately turned his attention to Silver. "What happened? You all right?"

"Yeah, I'm all right. These damn flowers just unnerved me a little, that's all."

"Flowers. Who sent them?" Brandan asked. He picked up the card and read the contents. "Is this some kind of joke or something? Who sent this?"

"That's what we're trying to find out, Mr. Savoy. Miss James, you have no idea as to who would have sent these flowers?" the detective asked. Silver shook her head.

"The delivery guy really provided no leads. His firm got the order for pickup from a greenhouse in Chinatown. I called the shop, and they barely speak English. I already have one of my guys going over there to investigate," Detective Dowdy said.

"Investigate? I don't understand. Is there a crime?" Brandan asked.

"Well, we don't know. This behavior is odd, stalkerlike, and these flowers may provide some leads to Todd Boyd's death, so we're not taking anything for granted." Detective Dowdy returned his attention to Daphne as she was the only one at the moment who could answer his questions coherently. They continued speaking until a light bulb went off in Silver's head. "Hold up. These flowers could have come from Kendrick Armstrong."

"Why Kendrick?" Detective Dowdy asked.

"Because right before Todd's death, months ago, Kendrick was sending these elaborate bouquets to my office. I never got around to telling him to back off."

"Now you're talking. Tell me more." Detective Dowdy pulled out his pad and wrote.

Silver told the detective everything she could remember, she wanted to get home to nurse her aching head more than answer the questions he was throwing at her about her love life. "Detective, that's all I can give you right now. If you don't mind, I'm going home. Brandan, are you taking me or do I have to call a cab or something?"

"I'll take you home. You sure you don't want to go to the emergency—

"Home," Silver demanded. She gathered her things, handed them to Brandan and told Pat she would call her later. "I'm going to take some time off, Daphne. I can work from home, but right now I don't want to be here. I don't feel safe."

"I understand," Daphne said.

Brandan gave Daphne another peck and signed that he'd call her later. He was on Silver's heels when Daphne yelled, "Take all the time you need, dear."

Chapter 8

The Fall of My Discontent

Silver sat in the chilly room of the abortion clinic. Her feet swept the floor. The nurse had finally concluded her questions and now Silver waited for the prep.

The room grew colder by the minute, and the clouds just outside the window turned black. Silver noticed a long vanity mirror opposite the examination lounger. She stood sideways, the hospital gown barely covering her knees. She pressed the gown to her mid-section and eyed the tiny bulge in her once flat stomach wondering if Todd had been alive would her actions be the same. Would she really go through with this if Todd were still here? She thought of the possibility of Todd committing to her fully and completely once he found out she was pregnant with his child. Silver didn't have much time to revel in her fantasy as she remembered he was never hers to begin with. She couldn't believe she was thinking like the type of woman she despised, a chicken-head so bent on getting what she wanted that the consequences of her actions didn't matter. The truth was that her consequences did matter, and if she'd known Todd was married with children, she would have left him a long time ago.

Silver continued to gaze into the mirror, looking at not only her body, but also her soul. Suddenly, views from every direction flooded her mind. "Have this baby...Don't have this baby...What kind of life can you give a bastard child...He'll never be accepted...He'll be our child...We'll raise him...I'll sign the birth certificate...Don't get rid of my seed...I'm sorry I hurt you, but don't take it out on our seed...You bitch...I'm tired of you trying to steal my man, and now you steal him even in death?...You'll never find a man now...Baby, God doesn't put anything on us we can't bear..." Silver screamed. "Get out of my head," she said aloud.

"Miss James? You okay?" The nurse re-entered and brought Silver back to reality.

Silver shook her head and shoved her thoughts back into her mouth.

"Miss James, we're getting ready to take you now," the nurse said.

Silver didn't say a word as she stumbled back to the examination table where she sat. She snatched her blouse and stuck her arms through the sleeves with her gown still on. "I can't do this," she said. "I won't do this."

"Okay, okay, you don't have to. Why don't you just sit and calm down for a moment?" the nurse tried to reason.

"I don't know. I need more time..."

"If you take anymore time, Miss James, we're going to have to induce labor—should you come back. By then, you'll be out of your first trimester and it will be a lot more costly."

"Labor?"

"Yes, well the fetus is detached from the uterus and—"

"You mean the baby?" Silver grabbed her stomach. Her vision was blurry and the room shifted. "I'm not doing this. I'm outta here." She exited without saying another word. She navigated through the halls and stumbled past the door of the post-operative holding room. The sea of bodies, all lifeless and sedated, lined up on gurneys against the wall, sealed her decision. She stumbled upon two large brown doors. She snatched the metal rods and released herself from the dungeon of the damned, running straight to Brandan who held his head in hands in a dark lone corner of the waiting room. "Let's go," she said in a dry voice.

He slowly lifted his head and wiped his bloodshot eyes. "It's done? That fast you just take a life?" he asked sarcastically. He balled up his newspaper and stood.

"Let's go to IHOP, get some pancakes, strawberries and warm syrup and figure this thing out. I'm *craaaving* pancakes. How about you?"

Brandan smiled from ear to ear before hugging her so tightly she could barely breathe. He helped Silver down the stairs, and she managed to smile. When they approached the street, the crowd that previously circled her like a swarm of cicadas was still there. The one-armed little boy who met her earlier sat on the curb sipping what smelled like hot chocolate. His poster board was at his side.

"I'll get the car," Brandan said, leaving Silver standing there.

Silver sat down. "Whatcha drinking?" she asked the little boy.

He looked up with sparkling doe-brown eyes and answered, "Sweet cocoa."

Silver smiled. She hadn't heard a child use such a term. "You know, you're a little too young to be out here, don't you think?"

"Nope. Gotta do it," the little boy answered. He stopped sipping and looked Silver squarely in the eye, appearing worn and old.

"Gotta do what?" Silver asked.

"Stop people from doing what my mother tried to do to me." His voice was clear.

Silver felt like she was talking to an old soul. "What did your mother try to do to you?"

"Tried to take me away, but it didn't work. I only have one arm but it's okay."

"You *are* okay." Silver hugged the little boy and felt a tingle up and down her spine. "So what's your name?"

"Todd."

Silver's chest lunged. Her eyes were full. "Todd?"

"Yup. Todd Brown the third," the little boy said proudly. "Well, I haveta go. See ya later." Silver watched the little boy as he picked up his sign, placed it under his arm, and grabbed his cocoa and walked off.

"Todd," she called after him. "I didn't do it, Todd. I couldn't..."

Todd Brown III looked back and smiled. "I know." He faded into the crowd.

"Who were you talking to?" Brandan asked as he pulled up.

"The little boy you left me beside. Guess what his name is?" Silver said, struggling to put on the seat belt. "Todd," she answered before Brandan could guess.

"Oh. What did he look like?" Brandan asked.

"Didn't you see him? You left me standing right next to him."

"Silver, I didn't leave you standing next to anyone. He must have walked up on you." Brandan slowly pulled out into the middle of the street, trying to avoid the protestors. "I'm so proud of you. We can raise this baby. You'll have help from me, Jill, my mom, everyone. Daphne will be pleased. She really wants the best for you," Brandan rambled.

Silver continued to look out the window. "Hold up, Brandan. I want to find that little boy 'cause I know I'm not crazy. I'll ask that woman right there. Pull over."

Brandan did as she asked, and Silver hopped out to speak to a woman at a table handing out beverages. Her boom box played a familiar tune, "On the Arms of an Angel."

"May I help you, ma'am?" the woman asked.

"Yes. I'm looking for a little boy who is protesting with you. His name is Todd Brown the third. He was drinking hot chocolate. He's a medium brown complexion, short curly afro, oh and he only has one arm..."

"About how old would you say this little boy is?" The woman continued handing out beverages and additional supplies as she spoke.

"I don't know, about ten or so."

"You're welcome and God bless you, my child," the woman said to someone, seeming to ignore Silver's agitated state. "Ma'am, I don't know of anyone who fits that description. As a matter of fact, we don't have any children protesting with us. It's against the law. They should be in school during this time." She pushed her wire-rimmed glasses up on her nose.

"But I'm telling you I saw this little boy, and—"

"I know what you're saying, ma'am, but trust me, we don't have anyone of that description here. Now here's some information that will help you deal with your decision. It also includes some financial resources once your child is born..."

Silver snatched back her hand. "How do you know I decided to keep my baby?" she asked.

"Let's just say a little angel told me..." She led Silver away from the table.

Silver pulled in a different direction, bewildered by what had just happened. She still heard the song playing in the distance and wondered if that was the only tape the protestors had.

"So did you find him?" Brandan asked as Silver entered the car.

"I think so. I think I found Him."

"So what do you think Daphne's going to say when you and Brandan break the news that your plan is to raise this child together?" Jill asked as she diced scallions for her famous turkey-and-garlic stew.

"Auntie Silver..." Abigail ran into the kitchen. She dropped her book bag in the middle of the floor on her way through the door.

"Excuse me, young lady. Is this a barn?" Jill asked her eleven-year-old daughter.

"Sorry," Abigail said. She climbed down from her aunt's lap and placed her book bag in the corner. "So what are we doing this weekend?"

"I planned on looking at some places I outlined in the paper this morning," Silver said.

"Awe." Abigail sighed.

Silver caught Jill's glance of dismay. "It's time, dumpling. Auntie has to get back to her own life in her own space." She spoke more to Jill than to Abigail. Silver understood how Jill loved having her in their place in Montclair but Silver explained how being in her own space would help her to combat the demons in her life.

"But I don't want you to go," Abigail pleaded.

"I know, sweetie. You can always come and hang out just as soon as I get set up. Give me some time. I just can't stay here forever." She stroked Abigail's long, thick braid, which dangled just above the small of her back.

"Ab, go get ready for dinner, and we'll talk more later, okay?" Jill commanded more than asked. "I really think moving out is a bad idea, baby girl," she said to Silver as she shook her head while she diced.

"I know you do but I can't stay here and hide forever. I need some breathing room," Silver said. She spotted the newspaper and found the real estate section.

"So is Brandan going to actually adopt the baby?" Jill asked.

Silver popped a carrot in her mouth and straddled a stool at the island counter. "He's actually going to sign the birth certificate."

Jill dropped the knife. "Silver, you are opening a can of worms you may regret. That's dishonest. He's not the baby's biological father." She paused. "Is he?"

"Jill, no. Why would you ask me something like that? You know the deal."

Jill started chopping onions. "I thought I did but I don't know anymore, Silver. You and Brandan are making some really dangerous decisions."

"Not really. We've looked into this. Brandan will be considered the parent of record. He's signing the birth certificate knowing he's not the biological father, but the baby will have a father of record. That's important to me. Besides, Brandan wants this. I'm not looking a gift horse in the mouth. This baby needs a father, and who better?" Silver moved back to the table. Jill was getting too close.

"So you two are not a couple?"

"What is wrong with you? No," Silver stated emphatically.

"Okay, I'm going to just come out with it, and I need you to be honest with me." Jill wiped her hands with a dish towel and sat across from

Silver. "What happened between you and Brandan at the courthouse a couple of weeks ago?"

"We were exonerated. Didn't you hear?"

Jill shook her head. "Not that...remember you said that I'd left my purse?"

"Yeah, and you said it wasn't yours," Silver answered.

"Well, when I looked in my drawer my purse wasn't there, so I rushed out thinking that I must have left it. I called your phone but you didn't answer, so I drove back to the courthouse, but when I got to the steps Daphne was coming out and she had venom in her eyes that I've never seen on a woman. I asked if you two were still inside, and she cut me a look. If she were a snake, I would have been bitten..."

"So?" Silver asked, annoyed.

"So, when I caught up with you guys later, I asked Brandan if Daphne found her purse—mine was in the backseat of my car—and he said yeah, but she was acting real funny about it. Now you tell me about this agreement between the two of you, and I'm just saying—"

"Stop saying, Jill. I've done nothing wrong, and neither has Brandan. And if Daphne is upset about anything we've decided, that's her problem. Brandan and I made our choice, and it's ours to make. I'm not thinking about Daphne." Silver rose.

Jill caught her sister's arm and pulled her back down. "You need to think about her. Something tells me in my gut that woman plays dirty, and if she thinks you're screwing her over, you're leaving yourself wide open to whatever may happen."

"So, what do you suggest I do, Jill? Leave the child without a system of support?"

"You have me, us. You don't have to move out. I took care of your stinky butt, and we can help take care of another," Jill offered.

"I know, but I want my own life. I had it before, and I can have it again despite my circumstances. Brandan and I have discussed this thoroughly. I will handle this myself," Silver concluded.

"I know you will. And you know I'm here for you. We all are," Jill said cautiously. "Now go get ready for dinner, and call your niece in here as well."

"Yes, mother." Silver laughed. "I'm going back to work full-time on Monday. The divisions are splitting, and Pat arranged for me to stay in hers, so I won't have to deal with Daphne at all."

"I'm proud of you, baby girl."

"You should be. You raised me."

Silver rode the short escalator in the Gateway IV building where she worked. She passed the Hudson Repro graphics storefront and waved at Rodney, John, Anthony, Dave, Angel and Bernard in the boys-only print shop. It was the first day of taking her life back.

"Silver, welcome back again," the receptionist said as Silver quickly filed past her.

"Thanks."

"Pat needs to see you right away. She said for you to go right in…"
Silver heard the command, dropped her purse in her bottom drawer and made a beeline to Pat's office. "You need to see me?"

Pat was on the phone but motioned for Silver to come in and close the door. When she finished her call, she said, "Welcome back. You feeling okay?"

"Great, thanks. What's up?"

"I don't want to make any fanfare but you have to come up to speed on what's going on with the company. We've landed a huge government account to help design a system that will allow access to personal information at the touch of a button. To do that we all have to be thoroughly screened. There will be background checks as well as fingerprints made."
Silver sat at the edge of her seat. Considering her legal troubles, this didn't sound good.

"I see the worry on your face but don't. We all know of your situation. It's the people with unsavory backgrounds who need to worry. Anyway, submit to the criteria before the end of the week and you'll be fine. An office has been set up at the end of the hall for all employees until every person is checked. In the meantime, we need an outstanding R.D. worked up for the project, and we all know you're the woman to do it. For this document we need everything—the Visio, expanded Gui, the works."

"I'm up for it but I don't know Visio that well," Silver said.

"You'll have support. I've enlisted Mark Adler to help you. He's happy to help you, too, considering you saved him from Daphne months ago."

I've heard that before, she thought.

"Don't look so enthused," Pat said.

"I am."

"Okay, good. If you have any questions, come to me, nobody else, especially Daphne. The less we have to deal with her, the better."

"No problem from me. Pat, I need to tell you, I'm keeping my baby,"

Silver said quietly.

"Oh my God!" Pat jumped up and grabbed Silver. "Wonderful. I have Emmy's things...she's growing so fast that I'll pass them off to you, and we can—"

"Pat, chill. Keep it under your hat. I don't want anyone making a big deal out of this."

Pat's demeanor matched Silver's subdued one. "Fine, but Silver I'm so happy for you."

"Yeah. Don't go planning any showers at work or anything. I don't want people to know until the last minute."

"Sure," Pat said dejectedly. "Hey, if you need anything, just let me know."

Silver acknowledged her with a nod and walked out. She made her way to her desk where some unopened cards from her last return remained. She reorganized things and got to work.

Pat occasionally smiled surreptitiously as she passed by Silver's desk. Silver didn't really mind. She knew Pat was just checking on her but she didn't want to give Pat's excitement any leeway for fear she would go out of control. Silver wanted to take her new life one day at a time.

Toward the end of the day, Silver had organized and prioritized her projects. She even completed her fingerprinting process during lunchtime, which pleased Pat since Silver could be exposed to pertinent information concerning the government project after her results were returned.

As she walked out of the office, Silver was met by a caramel-colored gentleman carrying a large glass bowl. Her brow twitched. The delivery guy smiled and Silver held the door for him as he placed the planter on the ledge at the receptionist desk. He pulled out his clipboard and electronic scanner. "You're dropping this off for..." Silver asked.

The guy continued scanning and then looked at his board. "Silver James," he answered casually. "Is there anyone here who can sign for this?"

"I'm Silver. Who sent this?" she asked, dreading opening the package.

"It was a pickup from Fresh and Pretty this afternoon and—"

"Not the shop, the individual..."

"I don't know, lady. Maybe the card will tell you."

Silver ripped open the envelope. A small card read, YOUR PRESENCE WAS SORELY MISSED. Once again it was unsigned. Silver threw down her purse on the reception desk and retreated to her desk where she dug through her Rolodex and found Detective Dowdy's number. She dialed immediately, pounding her fingers into the keys. "Yes, this is Silver James. I need Detective Dowdy to come to the Gateway building right away at..."

Pat came out of her office, laughing into her cell phone. She stopped short when she saw Silver. "I'll call you back." She flipped her phone down. "Silver, what's wrong? What's going on?"

Silver continued giving information before slamming down the phone. "Somebody's doing this shit again. Another bouquet." Silver pointed.

Pat walked over to the delivery guy who look perplexed. "Who sent this?" Pat asked.

The deliveryman placed his scanner in his pocket and threw his hands in the air. "That's the same thing she asked me. I don't know what's going on, but I don't want any parts of this drama. Are you going to sign for this so I can go?"

"No, sir. Unfortunately, you are very much part of this drama, and you're going to have to wait until the police come. Silver, you called the cops, right?" Pat glanced Silver's way.

"Yeah. Somebody's on their way."

"This is crazy. Silver, you okay?" Pat asked.

"I'm fine. I'm mad now because somebody's fucking with me but they don't know who they're fucking with." Silver paced.

Daphne came out of her office for the first time that day. "Wow, Silver, you must be really popular," she said, passing the package. "Good night. I'm out for the evening, and I won't be in tomorrow."

"Hold up, Daphne," Silver said, grabbing her arm. "Did you send this shit? I mean, it seems you've had a problem with me ever since I came back, and you're the only one other than Pat who knew I'd be coming back today."

"Silver, I suggest you take your hands off me," Daphne said.

She released her grip.

Daphne rolled her eyes and swung around to Pat. "What's going on?"

"Another anonymous bouquet," Pat answered.

"Did you all call the police?" Daphne asked.

"Yes, I called the police, Daphne. Are you sure you didn't have anything to do with this?" Silver asked.

"Silver, I don't appreciate your tone," Daphne said.

An hour passed before Detective Dowdy and another young cop burst in the office.

"Finally. Can I get a signature and go now?" the deliveryman asked.

"Silver, did you open the card?" Detective Dowdy asked, ignoring the question. She nodded and pointed to the card that lay on the desk. Detective Dowdy read its contents aloud and turned his attention to the delivery guy. "Who sent this? Do you know?"

The delivery guy huffed. "Hey, like I told that lady and that lady over there—" he pointed to Silver—"I'm just the guy who picks 'em up and delivers 'em. I don't know who sent them, and frankly I don't care."

The stocky bow-legged cop with shoulder length dreads that perfectly framed his face, who accompanied Detective Dowdy walked over to the guy and asked for his credentials. Detective Dowdy intently eyed the flowers. A dozen white roses and a dozen white calla lilies sprung from the package. "This is serious because the flowers and cards are consistent. We're going to treat this like a threat. You haven't received any packages at home, have you?"

"No," Silver answered then bit her lip.

"Where have you been staying?" Detective Dowdy questioned.

"My sister's, but I'm moving soon," Silver said defiantly.

"Is that wise, Silver?" Pat asked with genuine concern.

"Yes, very wise," Silver asserted.

"Have you received any odd phone calls today, perhaps hang-ups?" the detective asked.

Silver shook her head.

The other cop joined them. "Nothing on the delivery guy. He's clean," he said.

Silence engulfed the room. Everyone looked when the door creaked open. "Hey, babe. Sil, I'm glad you're still here. I tried to call you. How was your first..." Brandan didn't finish his sentence when he noticed the officers. "What's going on now?"

"Silver here got another bouquet." Daphne rushed over to Brandan and planted a kiss on his lips, but it was clear his attention was on Silver, the detective and the news.

"What? Sil, you okay?" Brandan stepped over to Silver and grabbed her by the waist.

"I'm fine. I'm more pissed than anything," she answered.

"We're trying to convince Silver here that we consider this a serious threat and that moving is not a wise thing right now," Detective Dowdy stated.

"Moving? I thought we said we were going to talk about this." Brandan's attention still remained locked on Silver, and Daphne gave them a look of disgust. "Now is not the time to be thinking about moving anywhere."

"I'm sick of everyone trying to tell me what to do," Silver ranted.

"We're not trying to tell you what to do, but if your life is in danger,

———————————————————— *Toni Staton Harris*

you have to act reasonably. You aren't just caring for your life anymore," Brandan said.

Silver swatted his hands from her waist.

Daphne cocked her head.

"Is there any way we can convince you to stay at your sister's or somewhere other than your place a little longer until we get a better handle on this?" Detective Dowdy asked.

"Yes, we can. She can stay with me." Brandan's tone let Silver know she didn't have a choice.

Daphne's eyes widened.

"In fact, I'll take you by Jill's so you can get a few things. You can clear your head at my place for a few days," Brandan commanded.

"What are you doing? We have plans for tonight." Daphne's tone switched mid-sentence from upset to innocence.

"Come on, baby. Clearly, this is more important." He pecked Daphne on her cheek. "Detective Dowdy, it's settled. I'll take Silver home with me and we'll talk later."

Silver slumped her shoulders. There was no use in fighting.

"You gonna be okay?" Pat asked. Silver nodded. "Okay, I'm going to go. I'll see you in the morning." Silver nodded again.

"Lieu, I'll put these flowers in the car so we can backtrack," the cop said to Detective Dowdy.

"Good deal. So Mr. Savoy, I'll be in touch with Silver at your place for the next few days?"

"Yes. Right, Silver?" Brandan asked.

"Oh, I have a say-so now?" Silver tossed her purse over her shoulder and walked out the door.

"You look beat," Silver said as she sliced lime in Brandan's kitchen. "I hope you're prepared to lose tonight because I'm on my A game with this cooking contest."

Brandan wrenched his tie from his neck and hung his jacket and tie together in the hall closet before he rolled up his sleeves and plopped on the couch.

"I'm going to let you sample what's going to whip your ass tonight." Silver shoveled a piece of sea trout with crabmeat and andouille stuffing in his mouth.

He sampled the dish and with his palms forward he surrendered. "You won. I'm not going to try and top that."

"You're giving up that easily? You must be tired. How was your day?" Silver snapped him with her dish towel. She had been looking forward to their cook-off to prove who was the ultimate gourmet champion.

"My day was screwed," he said, following her into the kitchen and picking at the stuffing. "Um, is that andouille sausage?"

She nodded. "Mixed with back fin crab meat and a touch of habanero pepper. That's what gives it the kick." Silver figured it was okay to give out her secret recipe since Brandan had conceded walking through the door. "So what happened that has you so down today?" She pulled more lightly browned trout fillets from the oven and lopped the stuffing mix on top.

"Ben Dwyer got the general manager's position today." Brandan punched his hand.

"Oh, I'm sorry, boo. I know you wanted it."

"The boss gave me the old 'I need you in second position but running the repair division is always an option' speech."

"But Brandan you're a whiz at fixing cars."

"Yeah, and then he'll have me not only fixing the cars but fixing Ben's messes too. That fool doesn't know what he's doing." Brandan grabbed a brew from the fridge and plopped back on his couch.

"So what are you going to do?" Silver asked as she joined him.

"I don't know. Maybe I'll put my résumé in with another dealership, but nobody's hiring right now. This recession is kicking my ass." Brandan took a sip of beer.

Silver looked at the bottle, dying for a taste. "Let me have a swig," she teased.

Brandan just looked at her. "Don't play. How are you feeling? Everything cool at the job?"

"So far, so good. No more flowers if that's what you mean. I plan on resuming my search for a place this week."

"You know you're welcome to stay here as long as you need," Brandan offered.

"I know, but I'm tired of being a burden on you and my sister. Two weeks with you is long enough." The ringing phone prompted Silver to halt the conversation and answer.

"I'm not here, I don't care who it is," Brandan said, swigging another sip of beer.

"Brandan Savoy's residence...Daphne, Brandan didn't get in yet..."

He leaped behind Silver and grabbed the phone.

"So much for not being here no matter who it is," Silver said, feeling awkward. She almost wished she hadn't answered the phone. She went back to the kitchen to clean up.

"...No, baby. I'm really tired and Silver cooked all this food for our cook-off, which I conceded to. With everything she has laid on my counter, I'm sure she cooked enough for an army. Why don't you come over here and..."

Silver braced herself. She had successfully avoided Daphne as Daphne was in and out of the office over the past few weeks, and she certainly didn't feel like putting on a dog and pony show at Brandan's place. "I'll go to Jill's tonight," she mouthed.

Brandan squinted, shook his head and mouthed *no*. "...Okay, babe. Yeah, I won't forget.... Cool. I love you too.... See you tomorrow." He hung up the phone. "I just don't feel like going anywhere tonight, and she didn't feel like coming over here so I'll just see her tomorrow. She got tickets to a midnight premiere happening in the city anyway."

Silver didn't say a word. She was grateful for Daphne's refusal and didn't want to jinx it. She pulled more fish out of the oven, uncovered the deep-fried spinach and took another dish towel off the cake-like corn bread.

"Wow, everything looks great, but if it had been on a good day, this wouldn't have topped my jambalaya," Brandan said as he sat like a king waiting to be served.

Silver fixed their plates and sat down next to him at his bar-stooled counter top.

Brandan dug in before grace was concluded. "Hey, you think you can do some work on my website tonight?"

"Actually, I already did some stuff I wanted to show you. What I did might make you go into business sooner."

"We'll see." He continued to dig in. "Afterward, you up for a game of chess?"

"The board is still set from the last game when I was taxing that ass." She laughed.

"Don't get carried away. You might have won the cook-off this time, but chess, never," Brandan said.

"Yeah, we'll see. We'll see," she repeated as she watched him enjoy his food. There was nothing she wouldn't do for Brandan, and she was glad she could brighten his day a little bit.

Silver sloshed around the office at a snail's pace. She was feeling particularly pregnant well into her second trimester and not at all happy about the heaviness in her legs and around her gut.

But even with the dream of her body and mind returning to normal, she knew her life would never be the same again. Things had already changed, and this pregnancy was just the beginning. Silver thought about how she could handle a child and purchasing the newest pair of leather sock boots she had eyed on the mannequin in Nordstrom's. Thoughts constantly reverberated through her head concerning her safety and the fact that she could not just consider herself. When she was summoned to Daphne's office, she was not in the mood to deal with her.

"So, how are things going?" Daphne asked in a singsong voice as she closed the door behind Silver.

Silver sat, placed her elbows on her knees and cupped her chin. Her position was quite indecent but that was the least of Silver's concerns. At the moment she would do anything to keep from barfing all over Daphne's desk.

"How are the R.D.'s coming for the government project?" Daphne's hands flailed.

"Fine." If Daphne was playing elusive, Silver would follow her lead. An inquisition could have been made another time. "What's this all about, Daphne?"

"I'll get to the heart of the matter soon enough. "I wanted to talk to you about something outside of the office, you know woman to woman." I needed to remind you to get your fingerprints done or you'll be subject to termination. You see I get a human resources report and—"

"My name shouldn't be on that list," Silver interrupted. "I had my fingerprints and passport registered the same day I returned, weeks ago. Look, I have a lot of work to do, so can we skip all the bull and get to the point?"

Daphne flipped through a chart on her desk. She pulled the pencil she'd been biting and placed it on top of the chart then rolled her seat to a new pine credenza that held a heavy crystal water pitcher and matching glasses. She poured two glasses and offered one to Silver who had been sweating so much, she accepted. The water was so cold she held her head to avoid a brain freeze.

"You've been at Brandan's for a couple of weeks now, am I correct?"

Daphne asked after sipping her water slowly.

"So?"

"So?" Daphne laughed. "So." Her tone plummeted. She reared back in her seat and picked up the pencil, waving it like a conductor's wand before setting it on the paper again. She tossed her hair. "Brandan told me you're keeping the baby. Is that the reason for your hormonal moodiness and your lackluster performance of late?"

Silver's eyes bugged.

"Yes, Brandan, told me about the baby, and you must know that your extended stay with him is causing a major strain for him, me, our relationship and your family. Now I understand your desire—Brandan is scrumptious—but you can't have him the way you want him. I suggest you move back to your sister's place, your old place or wherever you deem fit."

"Who the hell do you think you are talking to me like this, especially about Brandan?" Daphne began to speak and Silver held her hand to Daphne's face and shook her head. "Oh no, it's my turn. I don't care what you think about my relationship with Brandan. Those are your hang-ups. You see, I was there before you and will be there long after you—"

"That's assuming I go anywhere, and that's not happening. I will stop at nothing to protect the man I love, even from you." Daphne raised one brow. She smiled and her tone softened. "Frankly, Silver, I'm trying to help you. You won't be able to rely on Brandan much longer, and at the rate your performance is going, you won't even be able to rely on a job at this firm."

Silver closed her eyes and gnashed her teeth. "You can't even go there with me, Daphne. Pat doesn't have a problem with my work, and neither does anyone else. That anchor you're trying to throw has been uprooted, and the ship has sailed. Besides, I'm not even in your group anymore, so why are you all up in my business?"

"I told you once before, when I play, I play for keeps. I see you have a different strategy. Umm-hmm," Daphne stood and circled the desk. "You plan to keep Brandan under your hoof and have him help care for this bastard child, all under the guise of friendship. And that's only because he feels sorry for you..."

Before Daphne finished her statement, Silver's hand connected with her cheek. "Talk about me, but don't you let another word about my child come out of your mouth again." Silver swung Daphne's office door so hard, it hit the back wall and caused several framed portraits to crash to the floor.

Daphne held her face, stunned, trying to recover from the tornado that just blew through.

Chapter 9

Going to the Chapel

"So what really happened between you and Daphne a few weeks ago?" Pat probed.

Silver nor Daphne would confirm anything about the incident. Silver feared damaging her relationship with Brandan, so she didn't tell. She wasn't sure why Daphne had kept her mouth shut. Perhaps she knew Brandan better than Silver thought. If Brandan found out Daphne had referred to "their" child as a bastard, he'd surely break Daphne's spirit. While they remained civil in Brandan's presence, she and Daphne took painstaking measures to avoid one another at work.

"So?" Pat nudged. "Is it true?"

"Is what true?" Silver continued typing as Pat waited anxiously over her shoulder.

"That you hit Daphne so hard she went flying over her desk."

"I can't believe you're buying into office hype," Silver said, not looking up.

"Oh, come on. Something happened. Papers didn't fly off Daphne's desk and glass frames weren't broken because of some strong wind, unless that hurricane was named Silver." Pat smiled.

Silver didn't respond. She entered commands to no avail. Her dialogue box continued reading UNAVAILABLE or UNABLE TO LOCATE DOCUMENT. Her quest continued to come up short, which added to her frustration.

"What are you looking for?" Pat asked.

"I'm looking for a Visio mockup in the mainframe."

"Why don't you just use the prototype Mark set up for you?"

"Because a long time ago Daphne used Visio on an R.D. similar to this one, along time ago, and the director praised her for it. I want to mirror it but I'm not asking the witch for it." Silver continued typing.

"Says who?" Pat asked.

"Says who, what?" Silver looked perplexed.

"Who said Daphne used Visio on an R.D. that the director praised?"

"Daphne, of course." Silver looked over, rolling her eyes and her neck. "But like I said, that was a long time ago, when you first left for maternity leave."

Pat laughed.

"What's so funny?"

"That you're looking for a document on the mainframe that Daphne did. Daphne authors nothing through mainframe, honey. Anything Daphne's done, you'll have to actually go to her computer, but I guarantee you won't find it there either. As far as the director praising her for a document, you should go on the stage when you tell your jokes, you'll get more money for them."

"Why is that a joke?" Silver finally stopped typing and faced Pat.

"Because Daphne doesn't know Visio. She never has. Why do you think she and Mark always went at it? Remember when he showed her hand one day in front of the director, she's had it out for him ever since." Pat wasn't laughing anymore. "That entire presentation was a bust. She even messed up the GUI."

"You have to be kidding me." Silver was astonished. She thought way back when Brandan mentioned that Daphne couldn't help him with his website because she admitted she hadn't known GUIs that well. Silver couldn't understand that and thought Brandan had to be mistaken because GUI design was the basis of computer programming. Even though Daphne wasn't a programmer, as head of the site design area she had to at least know the basics. "How did she get the job if she didn't know about interfaces?"

"Silver, I can't believe you didn't know all of this or at least hadn't put it together. Daphne was in good with the director who owed Daphne's ex-husband a favor. That's the only reason she got the position. She didn't have to know about GUIs."

"Is this fact or rumor?"

"Well, primarily rumor, but it makes sense. Daphne doesn't know anything. That's why she gets rid of anyone who knows more than she does. That's why she's hot on your butt now. The directors like you, which is why they split the group and placed you with me."

Silver was numb. Answers about Daphne's psychotic behavior were falling right into place. She didn't care for Daphne at all, borderline hated her, and now she knew why. Daphne was a fraud.

"Hello. Anyone home?" Pat asked, bringing Silver out of her thoughts. "I thought you knew all about Daphne Fake. I know you don't keep up with the gossip but I really thought you knew."

"No idea," Silver said, sucking her teeth.

"So when do you plan on telling Brandan his woman is a phony?" Pat asked with a grin the size of the Grand Canyon.

Silver didn't answer. Instead, she picked up the phone and dialed. She waited a few seconds and spoke, "Brandan Savoy please. . .Sure, I'll hold." All of a sudden Silver hung up. "Hold up. I can't go to Brandan with just rumor stuff. How could I confirm this information?" Silver thought more aloud than she meant to.

"Technically, you can't." Pat hopped off the desk. "But…you could put a bug in Brandan's ear and get him to confront Daphne, but I wouldn't advise that."

"Why not?"

"Because Daphne could make up a story or flat out deny it. Then you'd have Brandan mad at you because it'll look like you're just picking on her."

"You sound like my sister with her logic."

Pat shrugged.

"I need you to be honest with me," Silver said.

"I always am," Pat said.

"What made you say something about me going to Brandan?"

"I know what you mean." Pat paused. "Everyone who knows you knows that Brandan is your best friend. You asked me to be honest with you. Now you have a legitimate reason to get Daphne out of Brandan's life so you can have him for yourself and stop playing. You two have an undeniable chemistry."

Silver bit her lip.

"What's wrong?" You look sad all of a sudden."

"I don't know if *sad* is the word I'd use but I don't like people thinking I want Brandan for myself."

"You asked for my honesty." Pat moved back to the desk where she fully faced Silver who had leaned back. "I will say this: whether he wants you or you want him, I don't know of any man, best friend or not, who rides his white horse for anyone as hard and as often as Brandan does it for you. And if that's true friendship without anything more, I understand why people think the way I do. I'm saying it's a hard pill to swallow because a relationship like that is rare, unimaginable even, for most."

"Well, it is true. Brandan and I are just friends."

"I think you think that, but Silver ever since Todd's death, your legal troubles and that flower thing, something has changed for you and Brandan. It's like the stakes got higher," Pat said as she hopped off the desk again. Her comments grabbed Silver's attention. "It's okay though. Many people fall in love with their best friends, if the friend is of the opposite sex and cute enough—and not gay. It's said by many that the best lovers are friends."

"Many people like whom?" Silver asked.

"Oh, I don't know. I'm going to get some lunch. You want something?"

"Get me whatever you get yourself. I'll give you the money when you get back," Silver said.

"Oh, before I forget," Pat said, turning. "I was honest with you, now you be honest with me."

"Shoot."

"Did something really happen between you and Daphne, and if so what?"

Silver raised her eyebrows and coyly turned her palms upward.

"Don't play with me. I'm not buying the act," Pat said.

Silver blew a puff of air before following Pat into Pat's office and closing the door. "Keep this to yourself because I haven't even talked to Brandan about it, but Daphne called my child a bastard so I slapped the shit out of her."

"That's it?" Pat asked incredulously.

"Isn't that enough? I haven't talked to Brandan about it because I was so mad that he told Daphne I was keeping the baby before I was ready to say anything," Silver said.

"I'm not saying Brandan didn't tell her but that's not the only way she had to find out. Administrative paperwork still goes to her for her approval. I put your papers in the day you told me so you would be excused for doctor visits and such without penalty." Pat shifted her weight to the other foot. "I'm hungry, and now I have to go to the bathroom. I'll catch you in a minute." She exited the office.

Silver strolled back to her desk and wanted to jump through the ceiling. Everything made sense. Brandan probably didn't babble her business like she thought, even though he hadn't been really acting like himself since he started dating Daphne. Impulsively, Silver decided she needed concrete proof that Daphne was a phony and a liar.

She tapped on Daphne's door and asked if they could speak for a moment. Daphne, engrossed in paperwork, waved her in without looking up. Tension hung stiffly in the air. Silver strolled in confidently with her shoulders squared. Daphne plopped her papers down and squinted at Silver.

"I was looking for some R.D.s you did in the system a few months ago. They had prototypes for Visio, and I was wondering if you had them handy."

"That's why I employ people like you. I don't have any R.D.s," Daphne said in a steely voice. She returned to her file.

"Well do you have the prototype for Visio handy? I could mirror yours and perhaps get a lesson later…"

"If I've never done an R.D. Why would I do Visio, Silver?" Daphne slammed her papers down. "Listen, if you need help, maybe you should ask Mark whatever his name is, you know the one you kept on board without my permission. Now excuse yourself, I have work to do. I'm leaving early today."

Silver left without another word. Daphne's end of the conversation confirmed everything Pat had said and clenched her decision for action. She decided to grab a six-pack for Brandan to enjoy and then break the news that his woman was a conniving con artist who meant him harm. She would tell Brandan everything, and Daphne would be out of Brandan's life for good.

Silver stepped into her sister's house feeling on the verge of vindication. Hopefully after the conversation, Daphne would be gone forever.

Even though Silver wouldn't admit it out loud, Daphne's comments about her being a strain on Brandan worried Silver. She, too, felt Brandan's space was getting cramped with both of them there, even though Brandan was at Daphne's most evenings. She was starting to itch for her own space again, and she found that running from her sister's to Brandan's failed to scratch. The day after she slapped Daphne, Silver packed her things and moved back to Jill's. The walls began to close in immediately, despite the forty-five hundred-square-foot house that Jill and Sebastian enjoyed.

Nevertheless, the time was growing near when Silver knew she had to move forward. How she would move and where was a question to be answered on another day. That night, she was on a mission. She took hard strides into the house, desperate to freshen up, change her clothes and meet Brandan for an evening of conversation and the resolution of a nightmare.

"Silver, we need to talk to you," Jill said, startling Silver as she walked into the kitchen for a glass of water.

"Love to but I have to go. I'm meeting Brandan tonight—"

"It will only take a minute." Jill and Sebastian were solemn. Silver sat down and braced herself. "Your old landlord called. Your place has been restored and Mrs. O'Hara wanted to extend an invitation to you to take the apartment back before she puts an ad in the paper."

"Really?" Silver didn't expect that. Shivers slid up and down her spine.

"I told her that I doubted that you'd want to return. She said she had a few of your things in her basement that were recovered." Jill grabbed Silver's hand. "She needs to know what she should do with them."

"You know, your sister and I could go over and sort things out and bring them here for you to decide what you want to keep," Sebastian said.

"How long do I have before I have to pick through my stuff?" Silver asked.

"Well, she said she's putting the apartment in this Sunday's paper, and she wanted to have everything removed as soon as possible," Jill answered.

"Let me think about it. I may want to go by and look through everything but I'm not sure."

"I could do that for you," Jill said.

"Thanks, I know." Silver rose from the table.

"So what are you doing tonight? You seem like you're in a rush."

"Gotta go by Brandan's. Don't wait up for me. I might have to hang out there for the night."

Jill and Sebastian looked inquisitively.

"I'll explain later, but Brandan and I need to talk about a few things," Silver said, exiting the kitchen.

"Be careful," Jill said. Even though Silver heard her, she opted not to comment.

Silver used her key and entered Brandan's apartment, glad she had beat him home. She didn't see his car and assumed he was still at work. She walked in carefully, wanting to get the chess board set up. A game would be a great reprieve once she dropped the bomb. The house was cool and dark as she made her way to the open kitchen. She turned on a lamp and spotted a path of discarded clothes, then she heard chuckling. Stunned, she listened.

"Now what you plan on doing with that strawberry Twizzler?"

"Do I have to tell you or would you like me to show you?" That was definitely Brandan's voice.

"Um, both, um," Daphne said.

Silver covered her mouth to keep from gagging.

"Yeah, how's that?" Brandan asked.

"Um perfect, just like you, ohhhhhhhhh." Lips smacked after the elongated moan. "That tickles, *hee, hee, hee*...oh baby, um yes, oooooooh. Now that's what I'm talking about. I love you, Brandan. Yes, I love you, baby..."

The bed rocked and squeaked, emitting a rhythmic sound, and Silver took that as her cue to gently turn around and head for the door.

"Whose is it?"

"Yours, daddy, yours..."

Silver tip-toed to the door and quietly turned the knob.

"So who are we going to tell first and when?" she heard Daphne ask breathlessly.

"That we're getting married or that we're pregnant?" Brandan asked.

"Both, silly."

"We have to tell our families first, of course. Tomorrow. What are we waiting for?"

"For real, Brandan? Tomorrow. Oh, baby."

"Yeah, for real, baby. I love you."

"I love you too."

"I want you right here with me, always. You know that, girl?"

"I know it, and I love you too."

Silver ran out the door. She didn't care that Brandan and Daphne would know she was there and had heard everything. When she finally got to her car, she felt like her guts were leaving her. There was nothing left in her stomach to come out. Silver patted her flushed face and eyed the bile that lay in a puddle by her car.

Silver brushed her fingertips across the wall of her new Bloomfield apartment. The painters had informed her the place wouldn't be dry for at least two days, considering the moisture. Silver admired the macaroni-colored walls complemented by plush rust carpet, even though the smell of newness in the air made her sick to her stomach.

Her furnishings were modest compared to those she had in her old place, but adjustments had to be made. Rent was a lot higher than she wanted and she chose not to salvage anything from the apartment—the memories were just too painful.

Two weeks had passed. The move was a hasty decision she'd made after realizing Brandan and everyone else seemed to be going on with their lives.

When she considered Mrs. O'Hara's offer to move back to her old place, Sebastian called some friends. A real estate client offered a quaint two-bedroom apartment in the heart of Bloomfield, only two miles or so away from him and Jill.

Her new place was nice enough. She missed some of the amenities she'd acquired at her old apartment, but she didn't miss having to park blocks away for the security of her SUV. Now, despite being on a busy main drag, she heard chirping snowbirds rather than early-morning sirens. She had an assigned parking space, and according to the police, car burglaries weren't the norm, so she could feel safe and secure.

She sat down on her new couch, courtesy of the insurance money for her vandalism claim. Jill encouraged Silver to sack some of that money away but Silver, fearing it would be a long time to enjoy another spending spree, blew every penny she received on new furniture. She gazed around with a lukewarm attitude. The quietness in the almost dead neighborhood was close to driving her insane. Slowly but surely, the noise of a vibrant life was being silenced and that fact weighed heavy on her mind.

Since announcing his engagement to Daphne, Brandan had acted as if he hadn't been locked up and charged with a crime he didn't commit months ago. He also seemingly forgot that he begged her to keep a child she wasn't sure she wanted, and to top it all off, her feelings were really hurt that it had been almost two weeks since he helped her move in and he hadn't stopped by to see how she was doing. Sure he called to check on her, but phone calls couldn't fill the void of his presence, which she desperately craved. It was hard for Silver to admit she desired companionship or just wanted some company.

Silver rubbed her six-month swollen belly and sighed. Almost overnight her stomach popped out like a basketball stuck in a hoop. While the move seemed to slow her down, her life was changing way too fast for Silver to keep up. Soon there would be yet another change, and she wasn't sure she was ready to wholly consider another life. It was times like these the silence became too loud and her thoughts too jumbled. The question of whether she made the right decision regarding the baby often seeped into Silver's thoughts and caused her to question her motives.

Silver had just risen and decided she would attempt to clear her space of a few boxes when she heard a knock at the door. "Who is it?" she called out as she schlepped over. There was no anticipation in her voice.

"It's me, baby girl. Open up." Brandan's voice caused her to gaily unlock her door. "Hey," he said as he embraced her warmly. "I came by to see how you're doing."

"It's about time." Silver pulled away and rolled her eyes, then a smirk crept across her face. Her heart softened, and she felt her face go flush. "Actually, I'm glad you're here. How are you doing?" She opted against displaying the hole in her heart for their friendship.

"That's what I'm talking about," Brandan said as he walked in and made himself comfortable. He carried a sagging white plastic bag that read THANK YOU in bold red letters. The spicy aroma permeated the room.

"What you got there?" she asked, trying to yank the bag from him. She almost fainted at the thought of what Brandan carried with him.

"Thought I'd bring back a taste of how we used to be," Brandan said, smiling. He made his way to the kitchen and started setting up the plastic ware and Styrofoam plates like the place was his. "I hope you're hungry."

"I am. I thought I was going to have to order a pizza or something." Silver sat down at the table.

"This place is a mess. What have you been doing—or not been doing?" Brandan asked as he lifted Styrofoam containers from the bag.

"I'm tired, Brandan. It's going to take some time for me to get settled," Silver said defensively. As she looked around, she had to admit, it was not her style to leave her place in a shambles like it was, but at the moment, the new apartment was representative of her spirit and her life. "Well, other than a house inspection, to what do I owe this honor?" she asked, arranging her food just right on her plate. "Damn, Brandan, ooh this smells good. I can't believe you went all the way to Just Fish. Boy, do I miss that place." Silver dipped her fork in the homemade tartar sauce and stabbed a fried scallop. She almost died, it was so good. She then bit into the whiting drenched in hot sauce and savored every bite. Finally, she attacked the shrimp. Everything was fried to a golden perfection. When she dipped into the collard greens and macaroni and cheese, she thought she was going to have to kick somebody's mama. "Umm, um, um." She looked up. "You're not eating?" she barely managed to ask between bites.

"Daphne's got me on a diet to lose a little around the middle before the wedding," Brandan said. His plate held raw carrots, celery, mixed greens without dressing and cucumbers. He sprinkled salt and pepper over the meal and squirted lemon juice from a small packet.

"Oh, come on, I know that's not all you're eating. What is that woman doing to you? You're in great shape," Silver declared as she licked her fingers of the savory hot sauce.

"She's not doing anything to me I don't want her to. I was complaining about my middle a little 'cause we eat out so much. Dee just said that she doesn't want to hear me complaining for the next couple of months and she wants her day to be perfect," Brandan answered defensively.

"The next couple of months, huh? Y'all set a date?"

"February fourteenth," he answered. "Two months from now."

"You're about to make me lose my dinner." Silver stood and moved her container to the counter. "Did you bring anything to drink? I only have water and OJ. I don't want to be tempted to have anything else. I'm taking care of my baby. I'm going to breast feed when I deliver too."

"Wow! I'm proud of you baby girl. That's a change. I'm real proud." Brandan repeated like a proud pappa. "Well you don't have to worry I bought you something to drink that you can have and that you'll love." Brandan pulled two jumbo-sized cups from the bag, which had so much depth to it, Silver wondered if he would pull out a rabbit next.

"That's not what I think it is, is it?" she asked.

Brandan smiled.

Silver's eyes lit up. "Dang, Brandan, an Uptown too?" she asked, delighted he remembered the lemonade/sweet tea mix. "What brought all this about?"

"I need a favor," Brandan said candidly.

"Oh, that's how we roll now? Bribes?" She took a sip and again thought she'd gone to heaven. "I'll say this, after a meal like that and then you top it off with this Uptown, I'm liable to do almost anything." She looked at Brandan and quickly added, "Almost."

"I want you to go with me to the diamond district to help me pick out a ring," Brandan said.

"For what?"

"Oh, come on, Sil. You know for what. Don't play dumb with me."

"You the one playing dumb if you think I'm going to help you pick out a ring for that mongrel."

"Hey, don't talk about Dee like that. I'm not playing." Brandan remained calm but the deepening of his voice warned Silver to be careful where she dared to tread.

She ignored the warning since her belly was full, and she was sipping on her sweet drink, which probably had a bucket of sugar. "Then, I'll say this, plain and simple, no."

"No, what? You mean, you just going to leave me out there?" Brandan gripped her arm, his brow wrinkled.

"No, I'll never leave you out there, but I won't be a part of helping you to marry that. . .woman."

"Why, Silver?"

"Because she's not right for you, Brandan. That's why."

"But you don't get to decide that."

"You're right. I don't. But I do get to decide what I'll participate in, and your death as a man, a friend and anything else you are to me and everybody else, I won't—I repeat, I will not—take part in." Silver slammed the cup on the table and sat down.

"I don't believe this," Brandan mumbled.

"Believe it." Silver took another sip. Her lips curled at the taste of the lemon pulp. "I wasn't going to say anything to you about this because you have enough on your mind, but Daphne and I had a fight."

"Go on."

"Daphne and I had a fight, Brandan. She called my child—our child—a bastard, and you know I wasn't standing for that. And that was after—"

"You called her a dried, barren bitch."

"What? I never called her anything. She was telling me that you were—

"I don't want to hear it, Silver. Dee already told me everything."

"Obviously not if you think I provoked that situation." Silver's blood began to curdle.

"What I want to know is why you never told me," Brandan said, crossing his arms over his wide chest.

"Because Jill and I decided it was best. I didn't want to hurt you or drag you into some mess. I thought it was best—"

"You thought it was best." Brandan cut her off again. He laughed eerily.

"Since when did you start listening to your sister? Huh?" His voice was still calm. "Answer me. Since when did you start listening to your sister? You want me to believe Jill encouraged you to lie to me?"

"Well, if you knew, obviously you've been lying to me too."

"Don't try to turn the tables on me, Sil. For the record, I found out two weeks ago. I knew something was wrong but Daphne was acting like everything was okay. I had to pull it out of her. Then she begged me not to get into it with you. She was trying to protect our friendship, which is a lot more than I can say for you."

"Hold up. If anybody's trying to turn the tables, it's you," Silver said.

"No, I'm not. Silver, you should have told me what happened. For the record, don't keep anything from me, especially when it has to do with *our* child. Secondly, I'd always rather you hurt me with the truth than a lie. And finally, just like I told Dee, you two better get it together. You and this baby will always be in my life. Dee is going to be my wife and she's having my child. We all have to make this work like a family. It's not ideal, but it's what we've been dealt. So all this cat fighting shit—yeah I said it, cat fighting shit—has to stop. I'm in the middle, and both of you are going to have to meet me halfway. Now I'm going to the diamond district on Sunday. I want your help, and I don't expect you to let me down, like I'd never let you down. Agreed?"

Silver looked at Brandan with a closed mouth and piercing eyes. She didn't want to believe her ears. Just like Pat said, Daphne had turned everything around like she always had and now Silver was looking like the bad guy.

"Agreed?" Brandan's voice was stern.

"Agreed," Silver said.

"So what time is good for us to go?" Brandan asked like the previous discussion hadn't occurred.

Silver remained in her time warp for another few seconds then answered, "Ten is good. We'll have breakfast and go. I remember a few places I used to deal with."

There are a million plus people on the island of Manhattan, and all of them seemed to converge on the diamond district the same day. Silver trudged down the street with her hands in front of her to prevent people from walking into her or the baby.

It was taking time for her to adjust to being pregnant and while her maternal instincts hadn't totally kicked in, day by day she found herself feeling a little more protective of the life that grew inside of her.

"Brandan, I can't take another step without eating," she whined as he tugged on her hand to cross the street.

"Okay. One more shop, and I promise we'll grab something to eat. I guess a three-egg western omelet and three pancakes doesn't hold a sister anymore?" Brandan said, referring to their breakfast at the Bloomfield

IHOP before the twenty-minute train ride to Manhattan.

"Don't be a smart-ass. Let's just get to this shop, check it out, go back and get the diamond we saw in the first store I took you to so we can get some food," Silver said. She allowed Brandan to drag her to one last shop on the corner of Fifty-fourth Street. They trudged through the doors, and people shouted prices in all directions or baited others to come check out their display. Silver hadn't even known about this shop in her early days of working at a jewelry store, so she realized she probably wouldn't be of much help. She was pleasantly surprised when the very man she'd worked for wobbled to the front, spotted Silver and smiled with glee.

"Seevuh, Seevuh," he called out.

"Mr. Katzenfrieg. Oh my goodness, what are you doing here?" Silver asked, delighted. She extended her hands to him.

"I now work with my brudah. Store too much to handle, so I sold store and now I work heah two days a week."

"It is wonderful to see you," she said.

"You too. I see we in the family way. Here to shop for a diamond with your young man?" Mr. Katzenfrieg asked, extending his wrinkled, shivering hand toward Brandan.

"Oh no, Mr. K. I'm here to help out my friend. You remember Brandan, don't you? He used to pick me up a lot from the shop, and he's the one who convinced you to buy back my jewelry when my bill became too high." Silver chuckled.

"I do. Hello, my friend." Mr. K. shook Brandan's hand. "What can I do for you? When are you two planning to marry?"

"Oh no, Mr. K., not me and Brandan. He's marrying someone else, and I'm just helping him find a stone. You have anything for us?" Silver interjected.

"Come with me." He led them to a private room away from the noise. Mr. Katzenfrieg pulled out several diamonds, including an emerald and a brilliant cut, but the most exquisite was a mine cut. The shape resembled a square round, and because it contained more facets than the average brilliant cut, it could out sparkle the Manhattan sky-line.

Brandan was drawn to the mine cut. He moved closer, picked up the magnifier and studied the stone.

"Good taste, son. I give great deal." Mr. Katzenfrieg walked over to an adding machine, typed in a few numbers and handed a small slip of white paper to Brandan.

"Mr. K," Brandan said, looking at the paper, "I know you can do better than this." Brandan balled up the paper.

"No, son. One of my bedder cuts."

Silver allowed the guys to negotiate. She knew Brandan liked the rock, which they learned was 1.7 carats, by the way he fondled the stone and moved straight to it once Mr. Katzenfrieg pulled it out. It was wise of Brandan not to look too anxious. Mr. Katzenfrieg was a strong business head and could always hook the most savvy on an emotional buy like a diamond engagement ring.

While Brandan and Mr. Katzenfrieg continued their negotiations, Silver decided to take a closer look at the brilliant gem Brandan might be placing on Daphne's finger. She picked up the stone and measured the weight in her hand. It felt good. She twirled it between her fingers. The surface was pleasing. She placed the magnifier on her eye and studied the stone under the light. She then pulled it away, wiped the magnifier and her eye and resumed studying. "Brandan, hold up, sweetie. Come take a look at this." Silver led Brandan away from his conversation toward the very little natural light allowed by a small window.

"This cut is old one but making a greeeeeeeeaaaaaat comeback," Mr. Katzenfrieg emphasized.

Silver held up her hand. "One minute, Mr. K." Silver twirled the diamond on its side and placed it in Brandan's hand. "You see that?" she asked.

"What?" Brandan and Mr. Katzenfrieg asked simultaneously.

"Mr. K, we need to take this one outside and see it in natural light."

"That's no problem. I go with you," he said confidently. He proceeded to lock things up and called for the security guard to escort them outside.

Once out the door Silver donned the magnifier again. "I don't see it now. I thought I saw some yellow. It would have really shown up under the natural light 'cause a yellow tint in a white diamond is unacceptable. I don't see it now. You're okay Brandan."

"Seevuh, I surprised at you. Wouldn't show you a diamond with yellow. It's clean."

"I know, Mr. K., but I have to be sure," Silver said emphatically. She loved Mr. Katzenfrieg and didn't believe he'd cheat her, but this was Brandan, and if he was going to spend upwards of ten thousand dollars, she had to be sure he was getting the best deal.

Brandan pondered over the stone. "So what do you think?" he asked Silver.

"Honestly, I don't think you'll find better," Silver answered.

Brandan looked at Mr. Katzenfrieg and extended his hand. "If you come down just a little, Mr. K., you have a deal."

Mr. Katzenfrieg grabbed Brandan's hand and said, "Okay, okay."

Brandan grabbed the elderly man around the shoulders and they walked back to the store. The deal was sealed. Brandan was buying the diamond and Silver felt she had been officially pushed aside. She followed Brandan and Mr. Katzenfrieg inside where Brandan negotiated the setting he'd purchase along with fabulous diamond that would adorn Daphne's hand.

Silver was knocked out in the car as Brandan drove from Newark's Penn Station straight up Bloomfield Avenue. They'd had a great day, and Brandan couldn't wait to place the ring on Daphne's finger.

Before Silver could roll over and get comfortable, they were in front of her building, and Brandan was around on her side opening the door. Silver sat up and wiped her eyes. The cold air jerked her awake. Brandan helped her out of the car.

"You really came through for me today. Thanks. It means a lot to me," Brandan said.

She yawned and nodded. "You knew I would. Good night. I'm going to bed," she said as she turned her doorknob. "I don't feel like entertaining tonight." She was grateful she could be honest with Brandan.

"I'm not coming in to be entertained. I want to give you something," he said as he pushed his way in behind her.

Silver dropped her coat and purse at the door and headed straight to the bathroom. Brandan planted himself on the couch and kicked up his feet.

"Don't get crazy," she said, swiping his feet off her table when she returned. "Just because I haven't received my new shoe tree yet doesn't mean you get to put your feet all over my stuff. What are you smiling at?"

Brandan slapped the cushion next to him.

Silver rubbed her eyes and sat down. "What, Brandan? It's getting late."

"Just wanted to give you something. I know it wasn't easy for you to help me out today but you did, so I got this," Brandan said. He reached in his pocket and pulled out a navy blue box. He rubbed his hands together as she opened it. "Thought it would be nice for you to get something, too, since everybody else is getting something."

"Thanks, Brandan." Silver was somewhat sentimental. "You're probably just doing this because you know I'm still mad at you about our argument the other day."

"Just open it and stop flapping your gums."

Silver did just that. It was a black pearl pendant wrapped in white gold.

"Wow, this is gorgeous. What's this for?"

Brandan hopped up and clapped. "Told you everybody else would be getting something, thought it'd be nice to hook up my dawg too. The stone is a—"

"Mikimoto pearl," Silver said.

"Dang, girl, you know your stuff." Silver motioned for Brandan to place the pendant around her neck.

He did, then kissed her shoulder.

Silver walked to a full-length mirror in her bathroom and fingered the precious object. "Wow, this is fantastic. It means so much."

"I knew it would. Just know that I always have your back." Brandan kissed her forehead. "Good night."

"Good night." Silver smiled as she let him out the door.

Chapter 10

Destiny's Child

"I don't know what possessed you to agree to stand up for Brandan at his wedding. In my day, women stood on the bride's side and men stood on the men's side regardless of whom they were really standing for. Hold still." Jill had been fussing all morning.

"Jill, just help me get my stockings up, please." Silver had heard Jill's mouth since the day she and Brandan agreed to his bridal party consisting of only Silver on his side and Daphne cajoling one of their co-workers to stand as her maid of honor.

Jill struggled to help Silver get dressed. Silver wished she'd reconsidered being Brandan's best woman, considering every task, from breathing to standing, was a daunting one in her eighth month.

"Okay, you ready?" Jill asked.

Silver just rolled her eyes and wobbled over to the dresser for her earrings. She had agreed to get dressed at Jill and Sebastian's. If she hadn't, she probably would have never made it to the church on time. The baby was healthy the doctor had advised, but Silver felt uncomfortable turning left or right, much less bending over.

"Silver, your pearl is nice but you have too many dark colors on. Daphne asked that you wear white pearls." Jill said.

"I didn't bring other jewelry with me and besides, I want to wear my pearl," Silver insisted. She'd gone back to the store and purchased the matching earrings, bracelet and ring to the pendant Brandan had given her.

"Okay. I don't want to hear your mouth when Daphne asks you to take it off. You know she was pissed when Brandan gave it to you," Jill said.

"Oh, who the hell cares? She has everything she could ever want—the diamond, the man—and her day or not, I'm not letting that witch begrudge me the use of my personal jewelry and taste." Silver tugged on her dress and gave herself one last look in the mirror. "I'm ready."

"Um-hmm. Abigail," Jill called to her daughter, "let's go now."

"I'm coming, Mom. I'm putting on my lip gloss," Abigail yelled back.

"And it better be lip gloss, not lipstick either or—"

"I know, Mom," Abigail shot back.

"Give the girl a break, Jill. She's just experimenting," Silver said, trying to defend her niece.

Abigail came running out, and soon after the family proceeded to the very church where Todd was funeralized. The church had been decorated to Daphne's specifications—pink pew bows and so many pink flowers Silver thought she'd puke. Jill and Sebastian strolled to the front and sat next to Mom Savoy, Brandan's two sisters and Brandan's brother who still looked hung over.

"Where are all of her people?" Jill asked Mom Savoy who threw up her hands and rolled her eyes. The groom's side was filled but the bride's held a sparse number of people who looked like they were forced to be there.

"Is that all of her family?" Jill asked.

"Actually, those people aren't her family. The white ones are our coworkers. It's rumored that Daphne had the director mandate that a few people from each department come for support," Silver whispered.

"Hey, baby. You look lovely," Mom Savoy said to Silver.

"Thanks, Mom," Silver said. "I would kiss you but I can't bend over today."

"I understand, baby. It's okay."

"Well, I guess I better get to the study and find Brandan," Silver said. She gave Mom Savoy a special look that only mothers of the groom and best friends could share. It was an expression of concern. Silver knew she had at least one other person on her side when Daphne fought against getting married at Mom Savoy's storefront Newark church, citing it was too ghetto. That was another fire Brandan had to squelch because Mom Savoy had overheard the comment. While Mom Savoy had forgiven Daphne like she did everyone, Silver knew Mom Savoy didn't have a great feeling about the wedding either.

Silver wobbled down a flight of stairs past a door with a makeshift sign that read BRIDAL SUITE. She heard laughter and pressed on for the place where she and Brandan had to meet the pastor before the ceremony. She knocked on the door and found the pastor and Brandan deep in conversation when she entered.

"Ah, here's your best woman." The reverend presiding over the ceremony stood. "How are you, my child?"

"Great, Reverend. Thanks for asking." Silver smiled.

"Well, are we ready to get this show on the road?" The reverend asked.

"Yes, sir. We're ready," Brandan answered like a kid receiving a special toy on Christmas.

"Follow me," the reverend said, walking out the door.

"Reverend, do you mind if I have two minutes with Brandan?" Silver asked.

The pastor looked to both of them before asking, "Is everything okay?"

"Yes, sir. I just wanted a word with my best friend before his big day," Silver said.

"Sure. But in two minutes I expect to see you walking up to that altar, young man."

Silver smiled again and shut the door. "Brandan, you don't have to do this. We can go to the hall and eat that food and have a big party but, you don't have to do this," she whispered.

"You finished?" Brandan asked. He wasn't whispering.

"Yeah, but—"

"But nothing. Come on now, Silver. Don't do this on my day. My day, my wedding day." He pounded his chest. "Dawg, be happy or step, but don't cloud my stuff with your negativity. Now you going up there with me or not?"

"Brandan—"

"With me or not?" He stared.

"With," Silver answered.

Brandan filed out without another word.

"Don't say I never tried to tell you so," Silver mumbled and trailed behind him.

"…Speak now or forever hold your peace," the minister advised. No one said a word, and the ceremony continued on.

When it was finally over, Silver released the breath she had been holding since the ceremony began. Daphne was Mrs. Brandan Savoy, and Silver couldn't do anything about it except smile when the photographer said, "Say cheese."

Silver was sitting on the front pew as the happy couple continued their photo session with immediate family members. Everything centered around Brandan's family since Daphne's family wasn't present. Silver dabbed at her forehead as she began to sweat profusely. She couldn't imagine why she was so hot all of a sudden since the temperature outside was slightly above freezing. She began to fan frantically.

"You okay?" Jill asked, rushing to Silver's side.

"I'm fine. I'm okay," Silver said, trying to wave her sister off.

"Excuse me. Can we get on with this?" Daphne asked, her comments neglecting to hide her disdain.

"I'm okay," Silver said out of breath.

"No, Silver. You are not okay. Here, lie down." Jill forced Silver horizontally on the pew with one leg touching the floor. "Oh my God, her water broke," Jill yelled.

Silver's eyes rolled back and she seemed to be going in and out of consciousness.

"Somebody call an ambulance. Something's not right here. Help. Silver, Silver, stay with us, honey. You okay? You okay?" Jill asked.

Brandan strolled back into the church with his jacket over his shoulder and his ascot loosely fitted about his neck, his top button exposed. Only a tiny bit of candlelight cast a shadow on the limp body that sat on the opposite side of the front pew where all the action had occurred. "I went by the hall. The guests said you hadn't showed up," he said soberly to Daphne.

"What reason would I have to be at my own reception without my husband?" Daphne's voice trembled. She placed her gown between her legs, the fabric making a rustling sound as she turned her back.

"I'm sorry, baby, but I couldn't just leave Silver here, not like that," Brandan said, moving close to his wife.

"You'll never be able to leave her, Brandan. Silver has more than enough people looking after her. I knew she'd pull something on our wedding day. I was just surprised that it was after the ceremony and not during."

"She didn't do this on purpose, honey. Her heart rate was erratic. She almost lost the baby," Brandan said.

"I take it she didn't."

"No, but she and the baby are in ICU. She's really sorry, Dee."

"I don't want to hear Silver James's apology, Brandan. Are you sorry? Are you sorry for jumping to Silver's every whim? Contrary to what you believe, now you're my husband. You have a responsibility to me and your unborn child." Daphne placed his hand on her stomach. "I don't know that you can fulfill that responsibility with Silver always tugging at your heart strings. I mean, this was our wedding, our wedding day, Brandan." Daphne's voice elevated with each word, and tears rolled down her cheeks.

"I'm sick of this, Brandan. I really am. And if this is how life is going to be—me being second fiddle to Silver every time she needs you—we don't even have to take the honeymoon. We can go to the courthouse right now and file for an annulment because I won't do it. I won't." Daphne faced Brandan with a fierce look in her eye.

Brandan hung his head. He didn't know what to say. Daphne was absolutely right. Being there for everyone was weighing on his spirit. For the first time since he popped the question, he wondered if he might have made a mistake. Maybe everything had happened too soon. They hadn't dated a full year. He looked in Daphne's weary eyes and realized there was nothing else he could do except to make sure she was comfortable and happy being Mrs. Brandan Savoy. "You're right, baby. I'm really sorry."

"I want to believe you. I really do. I know you mean well, but how do I really know I can trust that you'll be here for me and this baby when we need you? How do I know that Silver will come second or not at all?" Daphne stood and strode to the altar. She pulled a stem from the altar bouquet, sniffed then turned around. "Getting married in a church should be special. I'm not religious or anything, never have been but I always dreamed I'd get married in a church. My grandmother used to always read scripture to us. I wasn't into the Bible all that much but I remember my grandmother reading the passage about how a husband cleaves to his wife and..." Daphne laughed and shook her head. She walked back to the pew where she originally sat. "...I'm sure you know the rest. Anyway, how can I be sure that you'll make me and our baby your priority?"

"Because I just promised before God, that's how." Despite Brandan's lack of religiosity, he had stood before God and declared and pledged his love and his life to his woman. Maybe he was caught up in the emotion of everything, but the fact of the matter was that it was said and done and the questions Daphne had weren't unreasonable. All she asked was that he be forthright about his commitment to her. Brandan had never had a problem with commitment, and he didn't see any reason to start. "How can I make this up to you?" he asked, having resolved his current dilemma in his head.

"I don't know, Brandan. I don't know that you can," Daphne said. Her back was to him, her face to the candlelit altar.

"Why don't we go to the reception, greet the guests that are still there and dance with the private band we spent so much money for until our hearts are content. And every uneaten piece of fruit left, I'll dip it into the chocolate fountain you demanded and feed it to you by hand, one by one?" Brandan was almost on his knees.

Daphne wasn't breaking. He could tell she was heartbroken, and at that moment he would have done anything to lift her mood and put a smile on her face.

"I don't want to go to the reception, Brandan."

"What can I do? What do you want to do?"

"It was funny. Whenever I'd think of you, how we met, all we've been through, ups and downs, through all the pain and glory, I always think of you. I believed I didn't want to go through this life another second without you," she paused. "But now I don't know. Maybe I made a huge mistake, putting all of my trust in a man who clearly is in love with someone else." Daphne finally turned to face him. "Brandan, make no mistake, I love you with all my heart. I want to be there with you and for you until we're old and gray. If you're not ready for that, let me know. I'll be hurt and a piece of me will die, but I'll survive and move on. I'd rather know now that you can't love me the way I need to be loved, the way I love you than to live a lie." Tears rolled from her eyes.

Brandan kissed her tears dry. His heart was heavy but he didn't have it in him to back away from a woman who obviously lived to love him. For what more could a man ask? "I promise you here and now before God again, I will never leave you. I will always put you first and do everything in my human power to make you happy, keep you there and love you with the fullness of my being."

Brandan couldn't believe the words dropping from his mouth. He couldn't pinpoint from where they'd come but he knew since he said them, he would stand behind them always. "Please tell me what I can do to make this up to you?" Brandan kissed her hands.

"I just want to go on our honeymoon and forget all the ugliness and just remember when you put your ring on my finger." Daphne looked down at her hand. Both her engagement ring and wedding band sparkled.

"Okay. You don't want to go by the reception?"

Daphne shook her head vigorously.

"Okay, okay. How about we get a suite at the airport and start our honeymoon a day early? Instead of Monday, we'll change our flight to tomorrow and stay under the sun as long as we need."

"Promise?" Daphne asked.

"Promise. You wait here. I'll make all of the arrangements," Brandan said. He stood and passionately kissed her forehead then her lips. Daphne's tongue fell inside of his and from that moment on, no matter how anyone felt, Brandan vowed to make Daphne Savoy his first and only priority.

It was another early morning that Silver had to rise and feed two-week-old Lemar Todd Savoy James. Frost formed at the windowsill and inside the panes. Dim light in the wee hours of darkness provided a perfect picture. Silver turned the lights up so she could see how to latch Lemar to her breast.

The hospital nurses convinced Silver that breastfeeding was the best gift she could give her newborn, so she decided to go through with her original plan. However, she admitted to herself the process was grueling and unpleasant. Every two hours she was up. She couldn't get any sleep, and her nipples hurt so badly she wanted to cry. It took her days to learn how to latch properly and every part of her body seemed raw and sore.

In spite of all of the things she complained about, she also had to admit that something magical happened the day Lemar was born. Almost overnight she'd look at her precious little one, amazed that such beauty came from her. When she smelled the sweet scent of his natural black curls, her heart melted all over again each and every time.

At an even five pounds, Lemar was a miracle. He squirmed and kicked like a three-month-old, and Silver was amazed how bright his eyes shone. That probably came from the fact that out of necessity and certainly not choice, Silver endured natural childbirth. By the time the paramedics arrived at the church, she had no choice but to deliver not long before she went into full shock.

After recovering in the ICU, both mother and son were remanded to the care of Jill, a task Silver believed her sister had orchestrated and with which Jill couldn't be more pleased. Silver didn't even put up a fuss when Jill and Sebastian insisted that she move back to their house until she became used to caring for a newborn.

At first Silver handled Lemar like he was glass, scared if she lifted his toe or finger, he'd break. But remembering how the nurses handled him and seeing how Jill used caution but explained a baby's resilience, Silver was slowly getting the hang of it all. The quirkiest adjustment was that she couldn't just go and do anything and everything like she had in the past. Her world had immediately changed drastically. She wanted to get a breath of fresh air one day but the doctor had advised that frigid temperatures were too harsh for the baby and suggested that Silver wait weeks before venturing outside. Being inside was driving her stir crazy, but every time she thought to complain, she'd just look at Lemar's angelic face and that indescribable feeling would overwhelm her once more.

Silver was so busy, she barely had time to notice that Bali held Brandan and Daphne captive several days longer than originally planned. When they were returning was anyone's guess—even Mom Savoy was in the dark. Silver felt bad that she hadn't seen or talked to Brandan since the wedding. She felt worse that she'd ruined their affair but had quickly gotten over that, deciding that Lemar's agenda for arrival was not her fault and that she had more important issues to worry about.

Detective Dowdy and crew had named another suspect in Todd's murder. Silver promised she would get to the station at her earliest convenience for additional questioning but having just given birth, she wasn't pressed to do anything but learn how to be a good mommy.

"Good morning. Isn't it wonderful how a baby brings so much joy to a household?" Jill asked, popping her head in Silver's room.

She waved Jill in. "What are you doing up so early?"

"Just wanted to see my nephew before I went to work." Jill sat down on the bed and placed a glass of freshly squeezed grapefruit juice on the nightstand.

"You want to hold him?" Silver offered.

"No, it's okay. He's eating."

"You mean he's playing." Silver lifted Lemar off her breast and handed him over to her sister. She then proceeded to gulp down the juice. It was tart but she enjoyed how it perked her taste buds, despite the fact she hadn't brushed her teeth.

"He's just precious," Jill said, rocking him.

"That he is," Silver said. She could finally cross her legs yoga style, and she enjoyed doing so as she watched her sister beam with delight.

"Sebastian and I have a proposition for you," Jill said to Silver. "What's that?" Silver finished the last of the juice and leaned against the chair's headrest.

"Sebastian is designing a mother-daughter house on the backside of the property. We'd like you and Lemar to move in permanently and make it a mother-son house," Jill said. She cooed at the baby and kissed his cheek. "I think he likes me. He just smiled."

"He loves you. Why are you building separately instead of adding on?" Silver asked.

"Thought it would be nice to keep you two here. You could have a house of your own, pay minimal rent, which would eventually contribute to a mortgage of your own. You'd be able to save a lot of money and keep your car. I know you were thinking of turning it in. Now you won't have to."

"Sounds nice, but I'm not sure, Jill. Just before the baby came, I was finally getting used to my place in Bloomfield."

"Silver, it's not every day that someone is offered to live practically rent free, help to take care of their baby and they turn it down."

"How long will it take to build?" Silver asked.

"Sebastian is estimating about six months or so," Jill said.

"That means I have time to think about it."

"Yes, you have time, but I can't understand why you wouldn't jump at this opportunity."

Lemar stuck out his tongue repeatedly. Silver knew it was time to eat again. She held out her arms to receive him.

"I'm going to get ready for work now. We'll talk some more later," Jill said, handing the baby over. "If you need me, just call. I'll be in the office all day."

"I will. Have a good one."

"I love you." Jill blew a kiss.

"I love you, too, auntie," Silver answered for Lemar.

Silver was fiddling around the kitchen when Jill and Abigail burst through the door, laughing like two girlfriends. Silver looked around and smiled, looking forward to the day when she and Lemar might walk through the park after a football game, clowning about how he stiff-armed some tight end who hadn't been schooled on the ways of Lemar

Todd Savoy James.

"Where's the baby?" Jill asked.

"Taking a nap," Silver said, sitting with a cup of hazelnut tea in her hand.

"You're gonna learn that when they sleep, you sleep," Jill stated as she pulled fresh vegetables from a grocery bag.

"I tried," Silver answered. She blew over the cup, but the steam kept coming. "I couldn't sleep. I actually got on the computer and tapped out a few items for Pat."

"Cool. So have you thought about the house deal?"

"Yeah, I did." Silver's voice was upbeat.

Jill's eyes widened.

"But..."

Jill squinted.

"I don't want to give up my place yet. So until the house is done, I'll stay at my place then move in," Silver said.

Jill filled a pot with water to boil. "But you could be saving all of that money."

"I know, but I don't want to stay much longer. I want to get used to being in my own place for a minute. I'm sure you understand that." Silver rose and headed toward the room where Lemar was sleeping. She thought she heard him whimper before the sound displayed on the baby monitor. She waited a few seconds, and she was right. Lemar could be seen rustling on the video monitor.

As Silver exited, the phone rang. I'll get it," Jill yelled. She wiped her hands on a hand towel and picked up the phone. "Heyyy, yeah...oh really. ..I'm so sorry...When...Okay..."

Silver returned with a quieted Lemar. She bounced and encouraged him to settle down as she rubbed his tummy. Jill sat down at the table before hanging up.

"What's wrong?" Silver asked.

"Brandan and Daphne are going to be in Bali for at least two more weeks," Jill answered.

"Okay."

"They lost the baby," Jill said sadly.

"Oh." Silver said.

"Silver, did you hear me? I said—"

"I heard what you said."

"I know you don't like the woman, but that's no reason to act ugly about the situation. We'd all be devastated if something happened to

Lemar before he was born."

Lemar had gone back to sleep, and Silver looked at Jill, silently asking her to quiet down. She exited and placed him in his bassinet. When she returned to the kitchen she adjusted the volume and picture quality on the monitor. "I don't wish bad on any one. But lost the baby? Come on, Jill. I can't believe you're falling for that."

"Silver, Daphne's in the hospital. You can't fake anything like that."

"You remember when Audrey Gibbons was in the hospital and lost her child but we found out that she was never pregnant? I don't know if the woman—Audrey, I mean—was pregnant or not, but I know there's a way to be in the hospital then dramatically break it to your husband that you all lost the baby."

"That's a terrible thing to say." Jill resumed preparing dinner.

"I'm calling it like I see it. I wouldn't be surprised if she didn't have some accident and fell on her stomach or something crazy." Silver flipped her hand and rolled her eyes.

"As a matter of fact, they were horseback riding on the beach, and she did fall. The horse bucked and threw her. Not only did she lose the baby but she broke her arm."

"What was she doing riding a horse knowing she was pregnant?" Silver asked.

"You didn't stop any of your activities while you were pregnant. It was their honeymoon," Jill reasoned.

Silver just glared.

"Well whatever you think, Mom Savoy said the doctor will probably release Daphne over the next few days. She and Brandan opted to stay awhile, hoping to help Daphne to feel better. If I were you, I'd act like I'm very sorry that this tragedy has befallen them."

"I don't know if I need to take your advice," Silver said casually.

"What? Why?"

"The last time I took it and neglected to tell Brandan that Daphne and I had a fight, she was able to turn the whole situation around on me. So puleeze spare me." Silver walked out of the kitchen into the living room and picked up a magazine.

Jill followed her. "What do you mean? I didn't tell you not to tell Brandan about your fight."

"You didn't tell me to tell him either." Silver sat and crossed her legs, flipping through the latest *InStyle* magazine. She reached for her tea but it was cold.

"What I've been trying to teach you is not to run to Brandan about every insignificant point about that woman, especially not with gossip because she'll turn that around on you."

"Whatever. It all backfired. And you know what? It's clear that Brandan has moved on with his life, and it's time I move forward with mine, so if it sounds better for me to say I'm sorry about a baby, catch me next time. I don't believe there ever was a baby, and I'm not losing any sleep over it." Silver walked out of the room.

Two weeks later Silver received a strange message from Detective Dowdy, saying he needed to speak with her about Todd's case immediately. She wasn't a suspect any longer but he felt she and Brandan could help put together some key information.

She'd hope that she and Brandan would attend the questioning together but when Brandan hadn't returned from his honeymoon she realized she couldn't put off the detective's questioning any longer.

Silver looked up at the police station's gray slate doors and recalled excruciating memories of her experience there. She pushed her way through and immediately spotted her attorney, Mac. His cell phone was glued to his ear, and he tended to several papers on his lap. She wondered how he could accomplish anything with the mess that always seemed to accompany him. He pointed for her to sit directly across from him and she did. "Yes, that'll be great, just fine. Okay," she heard him say in a nasally tone before he hung up and turned to her. "Silver, great. Right on time. Encounter much traffic?"

"No I'm not too far. I took the streets."

"Oh, okay. I'm glad you didn't bring your son with you. A place like this isn't good for a child."

"Luckily, Brandan's mom could watch him. Can we get this over with or what?" She rubbed her hands on the sides of her pants leg.

"Sure. Now you're just here to answer some questions. Apparently, there's another suspect but the detective believes you can add some pieces to the puzzle. If I advise you not to answer something, I don't care how riled up you are, don't answer. This isn't *Law and Order*. I'm here for a reason, so let me do my job." Silver nodded. "Great, shall we?"

She stood, and Mac led her to an interrogation room identical to the one Brandan described he was in for hours.

Detective Dowdy walked in as cocky as ever. He threw a brown folder in front of her and asked, "What can you tell me about your association with Todd Boyd's widow?"

Silver took a deep breath and remembered her attorney's words. She didn't respond.

"Rumor has it that you had an encounter with Mrs. Boyd prior to the funeral and that was why she went ballistic on you."

"Is Silver a suspect again, detective?" Mac asked.

"No," Detective Dowdy answered.

"Then, please watch your tone."

Detective Dowdy bent over. "I apologize. Is there anything you can tell me about Mrs. Boyd? Any encounter you may have had with her prior to the murder?"

The murder. Silver couldn't believe Todd's life and the gruesome way he died could be reduced to "the murder." She shook her head.

"I don't understand sign language, Miss James."

"No. I can't tell you anything about Todd's widow because I don't know her, never met her, didn't know she even existed until after he died," Silver said. Mac placed his hand up to stop Silver from saying anything more. She complied. She didn't know where the detective was going, and she wasn't enjoying the journey thus far.

"Who is this new suspect that would prompt you to phone my client? And where are you going with this, sir?" Mac asked.

"Can't say who, counselor, but a very good source advised us that Miss James and Mrs. Boyd had contact prior to the funeral. And since Miss James is not talking about it, I will say this, when everything comes out, and it will, don't even look to us or the D.A. to cop a plea. I guarantee your client's defense won't be thrown out on a technicality."

"This meeting is over." Mac stood. "Silver, gather your things. We're leaving.

"Wait a minute, I have a question," she said as she stood. "Are you planning on trying to drum up charges on me and Brandan Savoy again?"

The detective pulled a toothpick from his pocket and swirled it in his mouth before he answered. "Mr. Savoy satisfied our curiosity. We no longer believe he had anything to do with this. He answered all my questions."

"You conducted an interview with Brandan by phone but made me come all the way down here?"

"No. Mr. Savoy's interview was a week ago. I thought you two were going to come in together." Detective Dowdy looked bewildered.

Silver looked between her lawyer and Detective Dowdy. "Brandan couldn't have been here a week ago, detective. Is he playing some kind of game with me?" she asked her attorney.

"Silver, let's go." Mac ushered her out of the door.

"Miss James," Detective Dowdy said as he trotted to catch her, "if you remember anything, it will be in your best interest to call."

Silver and Mac moved quickly. She wasn't pondering the detective's words about the case, but the fact that Brandan had been home a week and she didn't know. "Did you know Brandan was interviewed last week?"

"His attorney called me. We tried to schedule you two together but Mr. Savoy declined." They darted across the busy street, and Mac led Silver to her car.

"Did Brandan say why?" she asked.

"Why what? Silver, I have another appointment."

"Why Brandan declined to have our meeting with the detective together," she stated.

"I really don't know," Mac said before she entered her car and locked the door. He quickly walked away.

Silver sat in her car bewildered by the latest turn of events.

Silver called Mom Savoy "...yes, I'll be back in an hour or so. I need to make a run. Extra milk is in the freezer. I'll be back before you run out. Okay, thanks." Silver closed her phone and gunned her engine, heading toward Brandan's place.

Everyone was acting strangely, including Mom Savoy whom Silver thought was ineffective at playing coy and evasive. She, too, knew Brandan was back. Silver wondered what was going on that Brandan didn't want her to know he was home and why it was such a secret.

In minutes she was in front of Brandan's place. His car wasn't there but neither was Daphne's. She rang the doorbell, and when no one answered she started to use her key before she remembered the last time she had used it and became sick to her stomach. She peered around. Apparently no one was home because several local circulars sat around his doorstep. Silver picked them up and threw them in the trash. She had another idea of where she could find Brandan LeMarr Savoy.

Silver traveled a little farther east, straight to downtown. Sure enough when she pulled into the lot where she parked her car for work during the week, there sat twin Mercedes at the far end of the blacktop. Brandan was staying at Daphne's.

Silver handed her keys over to the valet who peered at her. She knew he recognized her and probably wondered where she'd been. It had been months since she was at work. She tipped around in the front of the building and up the marble tiled stairs. She wondered how she'd slip past the guard without alerting Brandan and Daphne of her visit.

A stream of chattering people passed her on the stairs, and Silver noticed they just waved at the security guard and proceeded through the echoing hallway. Seconds later when the next group came by, she blended in with them and made her way to the elevators.

She stepped on the elevator with the others, and one girl shouted, "Which floors, everybody?"

Their choices were three, four and nine.

It dawned on Silver, she didn't know where Daphne's apartment was. She didn't have time to scour every apartment in the building—by the time she'd knocked on a few wrong doors, she'd surely be found out and escorted out on her ear. With her luck, residents would contact the police and Detective Dowdy would be the one to answer the call.

The elevator had reached the ninth floor and Silver was one of the few remaining people. She exited with an attractive African-American couple.

"Are you okay?" the woman asked. "You look lost."

"I am. I'm here to meet my girlfriend Daphne Dix, and I can't remember what apartment she's in.

"Daphne Dix?" the fair-skinned gentleman replied.

"You know Daphne. She drives the burgundy Mercedes. Tiny woman on three," the woman said.

"Oh yeah, we met her in the gym," the gentleman said.

"Do you know what apartment she's in? The apartments go from A to Z on some floors." The woman's voice reached a higher pitch. She seemed like she was getting suspicious.

"I think A. I'm pretty sure she's in Apartment 3A," Silver said.

"They should have told you when you checked in at the desk. Sometimes, depending on who you get the guards will question every person who walks through that door and others sit there like a bump on a log," the woman said to her husband. "Anyway, if you're not sure, go back to the lobby and ask which apartment Daphne's in. They'll be able to tell you. Did they buzz you up?"

"Yeah, but they didn't remind me which apartment she's in. Well, thanks." Silver nodded. The elevator had arrived and she was grateful. Once the doors fully closed, Silver hit the third-floor button. She wasn't about to go to the security desk and alert Brandan that she was coming. She only prayed that her guess, Apartment 3A, was right.

She knocked on 3A, but it was the wrong place. A muscular man in workout gear opened the door. "I'm sorry. I'm looking for Daphne Dix. The front desk guy told me 3A. He must have given me the wrong information," Silver gushed.

"No problem. She's in E, right around the corner on your left," he said.

"Thank you," Silver said and rushed away. "Ooh, I'm not sorry," she mumbled. "As fine as you looked." In seconds she landed in front of Daphne's door. It suddenly dawned on her that she didn't know what she was going to say. Without thinking her plan through, she watched her hand connect with the surface of the door like she was having an out-of-body experience. She was grateful when Brandan opened the door.

"Welcome home," she managed to get out.

"Hey." Brandan looked around sheepishly then quietly stepped outside.

"All you can say is 'hey?' You've been home for probably weeks now, and all you can say to me is 'hey?' She rolled her eyes. "How about, 'hey, Sil, sorry I didn't call you when I came back to town or come by to see how Lemar is doing,' or 'how's life with *our* new son?' "

"How about, 'how was your honeymoon? And how is your wife feeling since she had a bad accident and broke her arm?' and 'how are you two handling the fact that you lost your baby?' " Brandan shot back.

Silver didn't know what to say.

"I thought so," Brandan said.

"How could I ask about your honeymoon or express anything when I didn't know you were home?"

"Silver, keep your voice down. Don't embarrass me at my home."

"Your home? Since when is this your home? What about your apartment?" she asked.

Brandan put his head down and rubbed his temples before hugging Silver without warning. He held her tightly for what seemed like hours. She returned the hug with the warmth of a glacier.

"Want to start all over?" he asked.

Silver bit the inside of her lip and took a deep breath. "Yeah, why not."

"I can explain, you know."

"I'm listening, Brandan. No, before I listen, I want to talk. Can we take a walk or something?"

Brandan looked around, placed his finger across his lips and slipped behind the unlocked door. For minutes Silver stood wondering what was going on and why Brandan was acting so strange. He returned with his jacket and his keys jingling in his pocket. "We can go downstairs."

When they reached the ground floor, Silver smiled at the guard who shot her a peculiar look. They sat on the edge of an oversized concrete flowerpot, looking at the fountain in the middle of the building's circular driveway.

"What's going on? Why are you asking so strangely?" Silver asked.

Brandan started to speak.

"No, wait a minute. I said listen." Silver paused. "I don't know what's going on, but everything's changing fast, and I don't like it." She tried her best to be angry but her heart was far too weighed down. "You're married. I respect that, but I don't respect how hanging with me is like a chore or forbidden. You're treating me like a mistress. You're home and I have to hear about it from Detective Dowdy?" Silver's tone revealed that she was incredibly hurt.

"Daphne and I are having a real rough time right now. She lost the baby, and she's been extremely depressed. We came home sooner because she couldn't handle being in the place where she lost our baby," Brandan offered.

"I'm sorry," Silver said as she swung her legs back and forth.

"You don't sound like it."

"Well, I am. I don't know what more you want from me."

"Silver, I need your patience and your understanding. Daphne is still really upset about the wedding and missing out on our reception, and unfortunately, she blames it all on you. I can't get her to shake her anger yet."

"Daphne blames everything on me. What else is new?"

"You just have to understand. For a minute we have to cool out. I have to make sure Daphne is okay before shaking her up with hanging out and around you. I promised her, and I have to show her she comes first. Right now that means me sacrificing some of my time with you."

Silver's head snapped back. "What are you saying?"

Brandan shrugged.

"Are you saying that to be comfortable and cozy with your wife, you have to cut me out of your life?"

"Not permanently."

Silver squinted as if that would make her vision clearer. "I don't believe I'm hearing this. Twenty plus years comes to this? Over some broad?" Silver stood.

"Daphne's my wife, Silver."

"And she's made you choose and you're choosing her. What about Lemar, your namesake? What about..." Words escaped her.

"I'm trying to work everything out, Sil. It's just hard." Brandan hung his head, his voice guttural. "I have a wife now who needs me as much as anyone, maybe more. You have to let me handle this the way I see fit."

Silver searched her purse for her keys. "When you figure out your way, holla." She turned to walk away. "Or better yet, how about I call you when I'm ready to hear about your way." She stomped off.

"Silver, Silver," Brandan called out in a loud whisper.

She didn't turn around. She couldn't for fear he would see something that hadn't escaped her since she could remember—a tear.

Silver was on the Garden State Parkway North, exiting through the 140 toll booth when her cell phone's special ring indicated urgency. She fumbled with her headset. Finally she threw the headset on the floor and dared to answer the phone without it.

Jill was frantically on the other end. "Where are you?" she asked.

"Turning on Bloomfield. Everything okay? Lemar's okay?"

"Yeah. It's not Lemar, baby girl. You might want to turn around and go to your old apartment. The kids and I will meet you there," Jill said.

"Why would I go back to where Todd was killed? You're not taking my baby over there. How did you get him from Mom Savoy anyway?" Silver asked. Her voice rose. "Just tell me. What's going on?"

"I picked Lemar up on my way home and dropped Mom Savoy off at her house." There was a frightful break in Jill's voice. "Your old place is on fire. The new tenant may be trapped and Mrs. O'Hara too. It's all over the news. The reports say you may be in the building. Where they got that information I don't know. . ."

Silver hung up before Jill could finish. She swung the car around and took Grove Street heading east. She could only hope that Jill heeded her words by not uprooting Lemar and Abigail and rushing over there.

When she arrived, Silver couldn't get through the blockade on the street. One of the cops let her through after she explained she lived in the building, adding her relative might still be in there.

The flames ripped through the cold blue sky and heated the frost from the barren branches. Silver approached cautiously and watched mountainous streams of water pelt the old wood. Cracking sounds and burnt smells permeated the air. The flames seemed to come directly from her old apartment. The fire raged. It didn't feel like an accident, and the tingles in her body told Silver someone may have been after her.

Chapter 11

Ashes, Ashes We All Fall Down

In the Northeast, March was usually still under a snow-capped spell. However, the weatherman offered a present. The forecast was a high of fifty degrees, and Silver couldn't have been more pleased. Winter depressed her, and the tiniest bit of sun seemed to awaken her and the city.

Pat wanted to try a new restaurant in the area where live jazz was played nightly. Silver declined, opting to take a long walk to the main downtown drag where a new bookstore had opened.

She'd promised Jill she'd pick up a few of the latest releases for Jill's insatiable reading list. Silver pulled a crumpled piece of paper from her purse and read the selections. She walked into the oak-finished store.

"I'm looking for *The Prodigal Husband* by Jacquelin Thomas, *No Strings Attached* by Nancey Flowers, oh and *Sugar* by Bernice McFadden," Silver said, hoping she had the titles correct since she couldn't quite read her own handwriting.

"Excellent selections," the salesclerk said, grabbing the books without hesitation. "You're in luck. We can't keep these on the shelf. Will that be it?"

"Yes, thank you," Silver said and went to patiently wait in line. The store was getting too crowded, and Silver turned to ask the person behind her to back up. She could feel his breath on her neck.

He smiled pleasantly, and before she could say anything, he said, "I'm sorry. I didn't mean to bump you. It's getting crowded in here."

"Um-hmm," Silver acknowledged.

"I guess that's a good thing, don't you think?" he asked.

Silver smiled and didn't respond. She wasn't in the mood for small talk.

"What do you have there?" he persisted, glancing at the titles. "Good reads. I see you like a variety."

Silver cleared her throat and remembered to be polite. "These aren't for me."

"I know another one that whomever they're for might like," the stranger said and placed a small paperback book on her stack.

"*When We Practice to Deceive* by Gloria Mallette," Silver read aloud. It sounded interesting enough. "What's this one about?"

"Intrigue, double identities. It's a smart book," he answered.

"My sister might like it." Silver pondered the selection.

"I thought you might like a book on how to shoot pool or something. You won't find that here, though." The gentleman chuckled.

Silver studied him intently. "Do I know you?" she asked, clearly perturbed.

Before he could respond, the clerk called for her. Silver placed the books on the clear glass counter and fumbled in her purse for her debit card. Before she could hand it over, the gentleman behind her handed the clerk his credit card and placed his books next to hers.

"Two bags, please." He tapped the piles.

Silver's neck snapped. "Again, do I know you? I don't need for you to buy my books."

The clerk didn't pay Silver any mind and had the purchases tallied before Silver finished her sentence.

I met you sometime ago at the pool hall. I thought we kind of hit it off and then you ran out on me. The Nickel Bar." He reared back on his heels and stroked his bare chin. His face had a boyish quality.

"That must have been a really long time ago." Silver smiled at the clerk and picked up her purchase.

"Yeah, it was. When your friend didn't show up, you got in a huff and left like you're doing now." The gentleman followed her outside.

Silver stopped and placed her sunglasses on her head, before pulling them down on her nose. "Thanks," she said, still trying to place him. The streets were crowded and noisy and Silver tried to avoid the many vendors trying to hock their goods.

Toni Staton Harris

"No thanks needed. Just tell me what you think about the book," he said.

"How would I get in contact with you to tell you?"

"I found you this time. I'm sure I'll bump into you again, Silver."

Silver thought she should have been taken aback, especially after noticing the revolver on his hip, but instead, she appreciated his style, his forwardness. Considering her lack of companionship, she decided he could be a pleasant distraction. "Okay, you win. You know my name, but I don't remember yours."

"Diego." He extended his hand. There was something familiar and tingly in his touch.

"It's a pleasure to meet you, Diego," Silver conceded.

"So..."

"How can I get in contact with you to let you know how I like your purchases?"

Diego nodded slightly. "I'm sure we'll see each other again." He waved and walked off.

Silver couldn't believe how fast Lemar was growing. At two months old the family had declared him a genius. In spite of the joy she found in her son, Silver was still really disappointed at Brandan's limited involvement—or lack thereof—in Lemar's life. He had only seen Lemar twice, and his interaction with Silver was strained.

Jill also was quite surprised by Brandan's actions and decided to host a party to celebrate Lemar's naming ceremony and baptism. She decided a shot of family unity was needed and sooner was far better than later. So, in a week's time Jill enlisted her favorite event planning service, Eclectic Designs, and her tried and true chef.

It was early Saturday morning before the party when Silver thought to run some last-minute errands. Months ago she would have still been asleep but now that Lemar was present, sleep was an anomaly, so she bundled her boy and headed out.

Her SUV had been doing the jerk, so while she was in the area picking up some items, she decided to stop at the dealership, hoping Brandan could work some magic.

She drove around the small customer parking lot until a spot near the door became available. She developed a slight attitude when she realized a white Escalade had blocked two spaces. Silver squeezed out of the driver's side and pulled Lemar's stroller from the trunk. She was ready to have a nervous breakdown trying to open it when a kindly pregnant stranger with two little ones in tow had the stroller unfolded, upright and locked in seconds.

"Thank you," Silver said, out of breath.

"You're welcome. You need help getting the baby in the seat?" the woman asked.

"No, I'll be okay, but thanks anyway." Silver smiled at the woman's children and proceeded to remove Lemar from the car. "You're getting heavy, little man." Lemar was half asleep and clearly paying his mother no mind as he clutched a tiny green rattle.

Silver checked her hair and makeup in the mirror of the deluxe stroller before heading inside. She didn't have to wait long before she was ushered into Brandan's office.

Brandan's eyes twinkled when he saw Silver standing there with the stroller in front of her. He practically jumped over his desk to get to her. Just seeing that look alone made her glad she'd stopped by.

"Hey, baby girl. How are you doing?" He hugged her tightly. "What brings you around to these parts?" Brandan set his sights on a dozing Lemar and lifted him from the stroller. "He's getting big, huh?"

"Yeah, he is. How are you doing?" Silver asked. She noticed after Brandan's initial shock, his smile faded and sadness seemed to engulf him.

"I'm all right, hanging in there, you know," Brandan said as Lemar rustled in his arms. A couple of the other salesmen popped in and asked Brandan a few questions. When they inquired about who the newborn was, Brandan proudly replied, "This is my boy." By their puzzled expressions, it was apparently known that Brandan's new bride had lost their baby. Brandan ignored their quizzical stares. "So what brings you around?"

"I have to get my car serviced. I was in the area, and I was hoping you could get someone to slide me in front of some people."

"I could work on it myself. It's slow here today." Brandan cleared his throat and looked at Lemar. "So. . . the naming ceremony and baptism is tomorrow, huh?"

"Yeah, it is. You coming?" Silver sat on the edge of a chair and rubbed her sweaty hands on her knees.

"Yeah, I'll be there," Brandan said and cleared his throat.

"Your wife coming?"

Brandan shrugged, refusing to meet her gaze.

"Trouble in paradise?" Silver asked.

"You think you know people, but then you realize you have the same shit just a different day." Another salesperson stepped in and Brandan directed his attention to him before writing on an order bill and handing it to Silver. "Meet me in the service bay. Where did you park?"

"In the first row, near the door."

"I'll be right there. Just follow the blue arrows on the floor."

Silver held Lemar tightly as she jumped in front of several people who had been waiting for their cars to be serviced. It took only minutes for Brandan to cure the jerking in her car and quickly she and Lemar were back inside, ready to go.

"Thanks," she said casually. Having secured Lemar, she buckled her seat belt and spoke through the lowered window.

"You're welcome," he said leaning in.

"I miss you, man. I really do." Silver's throat tightened.

"I miss you two too." Brandan laughed. "But it won't be like that for long."

Silver's eyes widened. "Why? Is something going to change about your situation that I should be forewarned about?"

"No," Brandan answered quickly, "but some things are going to change. I think Daphne's had her time long enough. She has to take responsibility for her own healing and stop blaming everyone else for her misery."

"I don't understand."

"You're really getting the hang of this motherhood thing, huh?" Brandan said, looking at a peaceful Lemar.

She wouldn't tell him this scene was far better than the earlier one. "It's getting better."

"I see."

"Brandan, I need to say this."

"I don't want a lecture."

"No lecture. I really need you to be at the ceremony. And I want to be here for you. I miss you. I need you to be more than just there, though. Lemar needs you too. I don't appreciate Daphne for you but I'm willing to respect her as your wife. I want to meet her halfway but she can't just take you away from us because of her silly whims."

"I hear you. Trust me, baby girl. I'm here for you and Lemar."

"But I want to be there for you too. So if you need to talk, you know where I am," Silver said and gunned her engine. "Sounds good."

"Yeah, it does." Brandan kissed Silver on the forehead.

"I was talking about the engine." Silver laughed. As she drove off, she felt lighter than she had in months. She took a chance, opened her mind and heart, was true and clear, and she liked the way Brandan responded. Silver adjusted her rearview mirror, gazed at her bundle of joy for a moment and smiled. Things were getting better. She felt like she was getting control of her life in a positive way.

Brandan had returned to clean up some of the mess he had made while working on Silver's car when he spotted one of his sales members rolling a white Escalade into the service area. "If you haven't noticed, we service Mercedes not Cadillac," he said.

"Oh no, I need an assessment done. It's a trade-in. This client has been in my office for the last couple of hours. I'm gonna have a mega sale." The salesman tried to give Brandan's fist a pound but missed.

Brandan chuckled. "Good for you."

"Would you do me a huge favor?" the salesman asked.

Brandan raised one brow.

"I'll owe you."

"Maybe," Brandan said as he observed the car. It was immaculate, almost like it was never driven.

"Could you detail the assessment and run the report for trade-in-value? This is a cash client."

"All the bells and whistles?" Brandan asked.

"And the kitchen sink too."

"Who's buying, Whitney Houston?" Brandan laughed.

"Nope. Some widow who just got a death insurance settlement. She wants to spend it on a car. I'll owe you."

"Yes, you will because you're cutting into my break, but cool, I'll have it to you in about twenty," Brandan said.

"Great. If I'm not in my office I'm probably by the general manager."

"No problem," Brandan said as he popped the hood. Just like he thought, everything was clean. He ran several tests. The gauges matched the level of driving for the car. The paint still sparkled, and the trade-in value on the seventeen thousand dollar wheel package alone would substantially bring down the client's new car bill.

Brandan jotted several things down on his clipboard and proceeded to the final area of the car. He tested the bumper's strength—everything was intact. He popped the trunk. "Aw man, whoever she is didn't clean out her stuff," he said aloud. Brandan pulled several boxes of dried petals and plastic vases and placed them on the ground. He wasn't about to take them to the owner's new car—her salesperson would have to give her that kind of treatment, considering he was receiving a sizeable commission. As he slowly closed the door, he noticed he had missed a crate lodged near the back of the seat. Brandan yanked it toward him. It was full of white flower heads. A cold shiver embraced him.

"Thanks, man. If you have any more to do, I'll take over from here," the salesman said, interrupting Brandan. "My customer is happily driving off the lot as we speak with her new, top-of-the-line Mercedes." The salesman reeled back on his heels. "She'll come back tomorrow to sign the transfer papers."

"Can I see the paperwork?" Brandan asked.

"Why? You trying to cut in on my sale?" the man asked defensively.

"No, fool. I just want to know who you sold a car to and who turned this car in," Brandan said.

"Oh, a really nice lady. She had her mom with her—with the strangest blue hair. I think she was flirting with me…"

Brandan shot out of the bay in a flash. The customer was nowhere to be found. Brandan turned, picked up the crate and left.

"Where are you going?" the salesman called out.

Brandan headed straight for the police department to see an old friend, Detective Dowdy. Something was strange about that Escalade and even stranger about the flowers he'd found in it.

Brandan pulled a hand-size shrimp from the decorative mound on the dining room server and popped the whole delicacy in his mouth. Jill and Sebastian had outdone themselves again, throwing the most lavish name ceremony and baptism anyone had ever seen.

Silver ran around having a ball, greeting guests and being more social than she'd been in months. Motherhood was challenging but times like this—family gathered together on a peace-filled playing field—made her smile. Even Paula Mitchell, Jill's mother spoke, cordially and managed to make her lips curl up at the ends, ever so slightly.

Silver was off to the side talking business to the proprietor of the decorating service Jill used. The company, Up, Up and Away, a local balloon specialist, would be an ideal candidate for new accounts for Silver to flash in front of Pat and the big boys. Her conversation was cut short when she couldn't take her eyes off Brandan who seemed to be sulking in a corner by himself.

Silver politely ended her talk, took the woman's card and sauntered in Brandan's direction. Daphne hadn't shown up and had completely skipped out on the church ceremony. Silver could tell Brandan was steaming. When anyone questioned him about Daphne's whereabouts, he'd just bark, "I don't know," and pop another goody in his mouth.

"Somebody loves the corner, huh?" she asked.

Brandan shrugged. His ringing cell phone allowed him to avoid any of Silver's questions. He answered his phone and whispered obscenities in hushed tones. Silver nudged him to the kitchen away from the guests and then downstairs to the game parlor where he could talk in private.

He hung up the phone, and laughed cynically. Brandan made sure his phone was off and placed it back in his breast pocket. "You know she's not coming."

"Who? Daphne?"

"Yeah, Silver. Who else?" Brandan was distraught. He looked up and shook his head.

"What's going on between you two?" I've never seen you like this," Silver said, very concerned. "Hey." She shook him. "It's probably hard on her, considering the loss of the baby and all. Think about it. This is a baptism."

"Photo. Anybody seen Silver and Brandan?" Jill called out.

"Down here," Silver answered. "Come on. I know you want your wife here, and if you have to go, I understand, but will you take a few more photos with the family? Can't leave the godfather out, you know." Silver rubbed his back.

Brandan put on his happy face and followed Silver up the stairs.

"There you two are. What's going on?" Jill asked.

"Nothing, nothing. Let's just take the picture." Silver looked back to check that Brandan was okay. He'd straightened his face all for Lemar's sake.

Silver was in the middle holding Lemar, Jill flanked on her left and Brandan on her right. Sebastian, Abigail and Mom Savoy filled in. Silver stopped the photographer's shot, looked around and then called out, "Paula, you want to join in, please?" Her request was sincere. Everyone looked at Silver like she had three heads, each representing a different personality. "Seriously Paula, come on. You're family."

When Paula cautiously approached the group and then took a stiff stance on the end, the room grew silent. After the final bulb flashed, the entire family burst into laughter and applause, almost forming a huddle. The flashbulbs continued, catching the candids of something magical.

The end of a long and fruitful night had come. Guests filed out one by one, carrying plates full of exotic seafood and other delicacies Jill swore would go to waste if they didn't take them. Just as Silver said good night to Pat, a familiar-looking Mercedes rolled onto the graveled circular drive then ran into a bush and parked. The driver passed the valet sign. A figure draped in black emerged from the car and stumbled to the front door. It was Daphne. Pat didn't bother to speak. She gave Silver a quizzical look and handed the valet her ticket to retrieve her car.

"Welcome, but everything is over, Daphne," Silver said.

Daphne pushed past Silver without speaking and let herself into the house.

"Welcome to Transylvania," Silver said, referring to Daphne's outfit. She followed Daphne inside.

"What are you doing here?" Brandan asked unabashedly.

"I'm here for the festivities of course." Daphne's voice was light and bubbly like she'd been drinking.

Brandan frowned. "Let me talk to you for a minute." He grabbed her arm so hard, he practically lifted her off the ground. He led her through the French doors off the living room, out the back.

Silver and Paula began to clean up, making their way near the door where Brandan and Daphne were having an argument. Every so often Brandan threw his hands in the air. Daphne clasped her hands across her chest, her head down.

"Let it go, deah. The worst place you can be is between someone's marriage," Paula said eloquently.

Silver looked at Paula, and instead of being angry at her statement, Silver wondered why Paula never remarried and never seemed to have anyone.

Brandan's voice boomed so loudly that the few remaining guests paused. Silver thought the glass pane doors were going to shatter. Despite Paula's advice, Silver slipped on to the patio to try and calm Brandan and Daphne.

"Excuse me, excuse me." Her tone was firm. "I don't know what's going on between you two but you're making a spectacle of yourselves. People are still here, and they're watching. Maybe y'all should take this argument home."

"Silver," Daphne said, raising her hand, "this is between me and my husband so you better back off. I've had enough of your shit ass meddling. We wouldn't even be in this crap if—"

"Hold up, bitch. You've lost your fucking mind. Don't you tell me to shut up in my own house." Silver stepped in closer.

"Your sister's house," Daphne said.

"Bitch, I will—"

"Daphne, go home, now," Brandan insisted.

"Yeah, bitch, go home now. We were doing fine without you," Silver interjected from where she stood partially behind Brandan.

"Silver, go in the house." Brandan cut his eyes at her.

Silver complied but stayed near the cracked door.

"Where are you staying tonight?" Silver heard Daphne ask.

"Don't worry about it," Brandan answered.

"Come on, baby. I told you the truth. You have nothing to worry about…"

Silver had never heard Daphne sound so desperate and frail. She couldn't imagine what they were talking about but surmised whatever it was, it had Brandan's mind warped all day long.

"Are you ready to tell me everything? I mean every last detail? I don't want anymore surprises, Daphne, because if I find out another piece of information that you left out, it's over, and I mean it."

"Oh shoot." Silver's head jerked.

"Don't gloat, deah. Come. Jill needs help in the kitchen." Paula led Silver from the glass wall. Silver's mind filled with the plethora of reasons Brandan could be so furious. There were only a few actions—lying and infidelity—that would evoke such a response. "Whoa, that must be it," Silver said aloud.

"What must be it, deah?" Paula asked.

"I bet you that witch is cheating on, Brandan. If that's the case, whew-we…" Silver shook her head.

"That's not your concern, deah. Your job is to be there for your friend no matter what he and his wife are going through," Paula explained.

"What's your deal, lady? Why all of the advice all of a sudden? You've said more to me today than you have my whole life."

Paula wasn't dismayed nor was she dissuaded. "I'm always concerned, deah. I am a psychiatrist." Paula's words rang with superiority. "But my trepidation at the moment is not for Daphne and Brandan, but you."

"Why me? You never were concerned before," Silver snapped. "I'm doing better than I have in a long time."

"You've overcome some serious obstacles—remarkably well might I add. We're all very proud of you."

Silver didn't respond.

"Howevuh," Paula said, her chin lifted, "I would strongly encourage you to continue on the journey of healing that you seek. Your trials and tribulations are not over yet, not by a long shot." Paula exited the room.

"What's not over by a long shot?" Silver asked Jill who continued packing food.

"I'm not sure. My mother often speaks in riddles, but they always ring true eventually. Then you learn exactly what she meant."

"Yeah, from the looks of things, if Brandan and Daphne are not over yet, they will be soon," Silver said.

"Don't sound so happy about that." Jill scraped the last of a crab-and-cheese dip into a bowl. "You want to take this home?"

"No. I'll be right back. I'm gonna see what's going on with Brandan and Daphne."

Jill raised her eyebrows and continued putting food away. It wasn't long before Silver returned. "What's happening?" Jill asked.

"They left, but Brandan's car is here. Your mother said he said he'll pick it up in the morning, before work. I don't know what's going on," Silver said, gathering her things.

"Maybe it's not for you to know," Jill said.

"Whatever. Hey, I'll see you tomorrow," Silver said. She kissed Jill on the cheek, gathered her things, including Lemar, and left.

Silver was warming up at the pool table. It had been a long time since she picked up a cue stick and even longer since she and Brandan met to do it together. He had called her during the week to set up a time for them to get together to talk. It was obvious that last week's events at the naming ceremony and blow-out with Daphne had not been resolved.

"I see we meet again," a familiar voice rang behind her. "How'd you like the books?"

Silver turned around, and this time had no problem placing Diego the cop. "So we do meet again. How are you doing?"

"A little better than you with the cue stick." He laughed.

"Has anyone ever told you arrogance is a turn-off?" Silver turned back around. She didn't care if the man had spent fifty bucks on her books.

"So how were the books?" he repeated.

"I don't know. I told you the purchases, including your

recommendation, were for my sister. I guess you would have to ask her." Silver circled the table and banked a difficult shot.

"Now if you leaned to the left and turned your forefinger just a little bit, your ball would have barely cracked a sound," Diego said.

"Excuse me," Silver said, huffing. "I didn't ask for your opinion or for your help, so if you don't mind…"

"Actually I do mind because in five, four, three, two, one, ah this table is reserved in my name," Diego chided. Silver threw the stick down and started to walk away before he grabbed her arm. Silver's stare made him retract immediately. "You're welcome to stay, though. I would love the company again."

Silver looked him up and down. He had tried her patience, but something about him intrigued her. She crossed her arms and stood firm.

"I take that as a yes," he said. "Come on, why don't we start all over? Hi, my name is Diego."

She smiled, softened and grabbed his extended hand, and with weary caution said, "Okay. I'm Silver."

"Great, Silver. Would you mind playing a round with me?"

"Until my best friend comes. I'm meeting him for a beer," she said, picking up her cue stick once again.

Diego racked the balls. "You were in this position the first time I met you too. It was here, and the NBA finals were playing. Your best friend was supposed to meet you then too. You sure he's going to show up this time?"

It all came flooding back to Silver. The first time she'd met Diego at the Nickel Bar she was waiting for Brandan, who stood her up for a date with Daphne to the finals. "I remember you now," she said, recalling what besides his height turned her off to spending more time with him.

"Good. Great things I hope." Diego laughed.

"Ummm."

Despite Silver's reservations, they played a round, laughing with vigor about various things. They found they had a lot in common. Silver looked up at a clock and noticed two hours had passed. Once again, Brandan hadn't showed.

"It's time I put up my stick," she said, trying her best to hide her disappointment.

"You can't leave now. We're just getting started, and besides, I'd like a chance to win a beer or something. I see somebody hasn't lost her touch."

"Yeah, I miss it," Silver said somberly.

"The game or your boy?"

"Both really," she answered with renewed ease.

"What's up with him not showing up all the time, not calling? That's not cool," Diego said. He continued playing, trying to tempt her back to the table.

"I don't know. My boy hasn't been the same since he married this woman."

"Oh, your boy married the woman he stood you up for the first time?" Diego asked.

"You have a great memory, and yes, he married her. I tell you, she is the most manipulative person I know. She was pregnant but lost the baby and now she's acting all crazy, putting demands on him that he's not to see me as much and trying to block him from being a valued part of my son's life." Silver couldn't believe she was spilling her guts but Diego had a way about him that resonated calm and resolve.

"Your son's life?" Diego seemed shocked. He stuttered, "You know she can't keep him from being a father to his son."

"My son is not my friend's son, biologically," Silver said, slightly annoyed at Diego's inference.

"Oh. Oh okay. Well, how does his father feel about your boy taking over the father figure position?"

"His father has nothing to say. He's out of the picture permanently," Silver said casually.

"You say that like the man's dead or something." Diego laughed.

"He is. And I mean figuratively and literally."

When Silver didn't laugh, Diego's facial expression changed dramatically. "I'm sorry. I didn't mean to—"

"Just let it go please. I better leave." Silver walked off.

Diego trotted after her. "Listen, I'm sorry. Please let me make it up to you. I've had my share of baby daddy drama lately but I really would like the time to get to know you. I just didn't want some overbearing jealous father or father figure interfering with our getting acquainted. Please? Come on, give me another chance." He grabbed her arm.

"Diego, I remember you clearly. You're a cop."

"Yeah, I am. Why? Does that bother you?"

"It could," Silver said.

"It shouldn't. I make a great living. That is if you aren't a criminal on parole or something." His laughter lightened the mood, and he led her back to the table.

"Do you know who I am?" Silver asked.

"You're a fine-ass woman who is as hard as nails to crack who I'd love to have more time to see—with or without a son." Diego reached in his pocket and pulled out a pen and handed it to her. Then he extended his hand for her to write on it.

"That's so childish," she said, giggling.

"Just give me the digits so I don't have to keep bumping into you like a mad stalker, please," he pleaded.

"How about I take your number?" she asked.

Without hesitation, he pulled out a business card with only his name and cell number. He wrote his e-mail address on back.

Silver's ease suddenly switched to dis-ease. "Are you that popular that you have to have business cards for personal information?"

"A business card is quick and easy. No games, no fuss. All of my information is right there out in the open for you to see," Diego said with confidence.

"Yeah, thanks." Silver slipped the card in her purse. "Maybe we'll talk again. Really, I have to go now."

"Only if you promise to give me a call."

"I can't go unless I promise to call you?" Silver stared at him and frowned.

"Yeah," Diego said playfully.

"Okay. I promise, I'll call you."

Silver popped into the office early on Tuesday morning. It was the official day of Daphne's return.

Silver pulled out her Palm Pilot and other items she'd need for the day. The card with Diego's number fell onto the desk. Weeks had passed, and she hadn't called him. She promised she would, she just didn't say when. There was some hesitancy about dealing with him. He obviously had some concern about her being a single mother, and for the first time Silver realized the angst it caused her that a man might not want to deal with her because she had a son.

Her freedom had been compromised. Silver wondered how many others would question her potential as mate material. For once, she realized why she leaned so heavily on Brandan for support. It was an unsettling feeling, and she vowed to move past it, knowing her son needed and loved her unconditionally. As his mother and only living parent, she would sacrifice everything, especially the affection of a stranger she wasn't sure about.

—————————————————————————— *Toni Staton Harris*

Chapter 12

Love Child

Pat, the directors and several members of the Sci-gex board paraded around the office, whispering in hushed tones. The word was that Sci-gex was going through a major overhaul, possibly merging with another computer firm and that several jobs could be in jeopardy. While Pat couldn't disclose any real information, she assured Silver that her job was safe.

Despite the buzzing and Silver pitching in for Pat where needed while Pat entertained the big boys, Silver had a peaceful week. Daphne hadn't returned to work and Silver hadn't had the chance to find out why.

It looked like Brandan and Daphne were trying to work things out, and hard as it was for Silver to give them space, she did, choosing to focus on her and Lemar's affairs. Every so often after Lemar had been put to bed or when she had a moment of quiet time to think, Silver would get lonely and long for some companionship.

Another week had passed and she'd come across Diego's card and thought about calling him. She couldn't shake the notion that he seemed unwelcoming to the fact that she had a son. He never really said having a child was a problem and maybe she was reading too much into his words, as Jill had suggested. Maybe it was her own hang-up and a manifestation of her original reservations about having children, but nevertheless his awkwardness about Lemar rendered her uneasy and unwilling to make that call. So she took the card, ripped it up and threw it in the trash.

Silver picked up the phone and called Jill to inquire about her plans for the evening. Satisfied that her sister, Sebastian and Abigail were to have a quiet evening at home, she suckered Jill into spending some time with Lemar while she had an evening out on the town.

"Who are you going with?" Jill asked.

"Nobody—by myself. I just want to get out a little."

Jill was ecstatic to spend time with Lemar and prouder that Silver was finally starting to do something about her social life. After squaring arrangements to drop Lemar off for a few hours, Silver hung up the phone only to have it ring several seconds later. "This is Silver."

"Hey, girl. What are you up to?" Brandan said.

"I was just thinking of you," Silver said.

"Cool. Dee's in Texas taking care of some business. I was hoping we could get together, play some pool or have a drink. I have some good news to share."

"Brandan, you read my mind. I'd love to hang out. Why don't we go to this new restaurant downtown? It's called—"

"The Grille," Brandan answered. "Dee and I just had dinner there last week."

"It's settled. Can you get off at seven?" Silver asked.

"I can do you one better. How about six?"

Brandan sounded excited, which in turn excited Silver.

"I can't wait to hear your news," Silver said. She was skeptical about it, but still excited to hang out. "Seven is better for me. I have to drop Lemar off at Jill's then meet you at the restaurant."

"Cool. See you then."

"Yeah, then." Silver started to hang up. "Oh, and Brandan…"

"Yeah?"

"Don't stand me up this time."

"I promise I won't," he said.

As happy as Silver was she and Brandan would be getting together, the distance and formality of their relationship was as obvious as a pink elephant. If nothing else, she hoped that night would erase all of the uncertainty between them.

When Silver arrived at the restaurant, Brandan was already seated at the bar. As she neared, she became nervous. She eyed two glasses of wine in front of him. She didn't want to imagine that Brandan would spoil the little time they had with an uninvited guest. "What's this?" she asked, pointing to the red wine.

"Hey." He was the consummate gentleman, rising from his stool and helping her with her seat.

"I ordered some wine for both of us—you know change of pace, grownup stuff." He smiled.

Silver smiled back. She tasted the wine and almost choked. It just wasn't her thing.

"You want a beer instead?" Brandan laughed.

"Naaa, I'll try and be grown for a minute. So what's this great news you have?" Silver took another sip. The second one rolled slightly easier, though not much.

"Daphne and I found a place, a house. We're moving." Brandan lifted his glass. Silver clinked it hesitantly. She didn't know if this was good or bad. She decided her reaction was contingent upon the rest of his announcement. "Where are you moving to?"

"We found a nice three-bedroom starter in Willingboro. Daphne's transferring out to the Philly branch as soon as her paperwork clears. She's not coming back to work in the Newark office."

"Why?"

"She wants a fresh start. We need a fresh start," Brandan answered.

"So are you going to commute from South Jersey every day?"

"Yup. If I can find a good dealership down there, I'll transfer. We're going to have enough land for me to put up a shed for my tools. Maybe I'll get my car refurbishing business started or work my way up to my own dealership and stop begging folks to give me their jobs."

"I'll drink to that one." The wine had a bitter aftertaste, much like Brandan's announcement. "So what brought this on other than a new start for the two of you? And what's going on with Daphne and the office?"

"Somebody got a hold of her social security number and has been opening online accounts and stuff in her name. Her government background check at the job hasn't cleared. She thinks her paperwork problems will undermine her authority in Newark."

Silver fingered the rim of her glass.

"I was hoping you would be happy for me."

"I can't lie. This will just take us farther apart."

"No, it won't. I'm not keeping my place, so if I ever get stuck, especially in the winter, I'll need somewhere to stay. Your apartment will have to be it."

"Brandan, you say that now, but trust me, once you're away, it'll be impossible for us to remain friends. You're moving on, man. I just never thought the day would come when you'd move on without me...us."

The silence was thick. If it weren't for the hostess advising them a table was ready, neither of them would have spoken.

"I've lost my appetite. I'm gonna get going." Silver placed her purse strap on her shoulder.

"Silver, you can't run every time something doesn't go your way. You have to stop it. This is big girl and big boy stuff, and we're going to deal with it."

"I'm not good on your words and promises much lately, Brandan. You have a life to live, and Lemar and I aren't included in it. What else do you want me to say?" She huffed. "Good night, Brandan." Silver exited from the bar and took the long green mile walk to her car. She looked back and became more upset Brandan didn't come after her.

Silver drove down Bloomfield Avenue in silence. Lemar was asleep when she arrived to pick him up. She almost stayed at Jill's since she felt so drained after the night's news. She didn't discuss Brandan's announcement with anyone. She didn't feel like explaining or exploring. Brandan was right. Life was big girl and big boy stuff, and either she was going to participate in having the life she imagined or it was apparent she would be eaten alive.

Silver made a few turns, hoping to avoid the heavy traffic that had accumulated on the main avenue. As she inched closer to her street, a police blockade complete with vehicles and wooden barriers was set up and an ambulance appeared. The enraged flames were bright and familiar. She made sure all of her windows were up and turned the air conditioner on full blast.

Silently she prayed that the trouble was nowhere near her house, but as she approached she realized that the very building she had been calling home was in a burst of flames. "Oh my God," she cried so loud she woke Lemar. He immediately started bawling, more out of the shock of hearing Silver's piercing voice.

Silver quickly moved to get her head together. She turned the car around, the tires making an ear-biting screech. She dipped and dodged the traffic as best she could. She had to get Lemar out of there. Thank God they weren't home, she thought. She didn't know what she'd do if something happened to him.

Silver sped to her sister's. She stopped in the circular drive, praying that

———————————————————————— *Toni Staton Harris*

the car didn't go through the front door. She grabbed Lemar out of the backseat and rung the doorbell. She didn't have time to call Jill and tell her what was happening.

When Sebastian opened the door, Silver shoved Lemar into his arms and shouted, "I'll be back."

"Trouble seems to follow you wherever you go, Miss James. Is there a reason for that?" Detective Dowdy asked. "Have you received anymore flowers?" Detective Dowdy twirled a toothpick in his mouth and leaned back.

"No," Silver said, quivering.

"That lead was a bust anyway," Detective Dowdy said.

"What lead?" Silver asked.

"The lead I gave them," Brandan said. He and Sebastian had accompanied Silver to the precinct. Both were afraid Silver was in danger and that the cops weren't doing enough to protect her.

Silver looked inquisitively at Brandan. "You want to explain?"

"I had to do an inventory check at the dealership and trade-out paperwork on an Escalade. It was the day you came by with Lemar before the christening. I found crates of flowers in the trunk. They looked similar to the ones you were getting a while back. I remembered Todd had a white Escalade and thought there might be some connection, so I brought a sample of the flowers to Detective Dowdy to check out—"

"But when we got back to the dealership, the truck had been sold off the lot and the flowers were gone," Detective Dowdy added.

"When did you get back to the dealership?" Brandan asked.

"It took some time to get the search warrant—" Detective Dowdy said.

"Answer my question," Brandan demanded.

"It was about a week later and—"

"No wonder. You all couldn't solve a crime if the clues were right in front of you," Brandan shouted.

"Son, you are way out of line. Now I know you're upset because you believe your friend is in danger, but we have this under control. We ran the plates and the paperwork of the person we suspected sent the flowers, but there was no connection." Detective Dowdy excused himself for a brief moment. Silver, Sebastian and Brandan sat in a cold, eerie silence like it was best to remain quiet. When he returned Detective

Dowdy threw a folder in front of Silver. "Take a look at this."

Silver opened it. A duplicate copy of a receipt dated May 8, in the amount of fifteen dollars, was applied to her credit card.

"Do you remember this?" Detective Dowdy asked.

Silver squinted. "Not really."

"This is proof of purchase of a flower from a shop located in a residential building on Forty-fourth and Ninth in Manhattan." Detective Dowdy cupped his hand to his chin. "Ring a bell?"

"Kendrick Armstrong lives there. I don't understand," Brandan said.

"Okay, so I did purchase a flower from that shop. I had a blind date with Kendrick Armstrong. Is that a crime?" Silver snapped.

"No. A blind date isn't a crime but covering up evidence is. You said that you never had any contact with Cheryl Boyd before the funeral." Detective Dowdy slammed his fist into the metal table and stood.

"I hadn't." Silver matched his tone.

"Well according to Todd's widow, Cheryl Boyd, the proprietor of the shop you visited, you not only had contact with her, you also made arrangements for additional purchases."

"The lady in the floral shop is Todd's wife?" Silver asked.

Detective Dowdy nodded.

"How would I know that?" she asked.

"It's too coincidental not to know," Detective Dowdy settled back in his seat.

"You think she was sending me the flowers? But what would be Cheryl's motive for trying to scare me like that?" Silver asked when he got off the phone.

"I was hoping you could tell me. The Escalade Brandan found was not in Cheryl's name, and the flowers were not traced to her shop or anyone near her. Is there anything else you remember that you could tell us about this whole situation?" Detective Dowdy asked.

Silver didn't like his tone. She could tell that he didn't buy her sudden remembrance. "What do you mean?"

"I mean, Silver, I believe you're holding out information that could be crucial to this case. I can help you now but if you're tied to this case, you'll be on your own." Detective Dowdy ceased twirling the toothpick in his mouth. His voice was intense and that fact alone boiled Silver's senses to overload.

"I don't know anything I'm not telling you. I'm not the criminal here. My house was just burned to the ground, and you're treating me like I'm the one who did it."

"I'm trying to get to the bottom as to why two residences of yours have been burnt to a crisp, magically when you weren't home. You sure you aren't trying to hide anything?" Detective Dowdy began twirling his toothpick again.

"This interview is over. It's obvious you aren't going to help me, and I'm not taking your shit." Silver rose and Brandan and Sebastian followed. As she exited through the wired glass door, she ran smack into Diego, the pool-playing cop whose card she had ripped up.

"Silver?"

"Diego." She looked at him with disdain.

"What are you doing here?" Diego asked.

Silver twitched her lips, looked at Detective Dowdy and proceeded out the door.

"Silver, wait up. What's going on? What are you doing, here?" Silver stopped, and Brandan swiftly placed himself between them.

"Brandan, it's okay. I know him." She moved Brandan aside and spoke to Diego. "I'm here taking care of business. What are you doing here?"

"I work here. Remember, I'm a cop," Diego answered.

"Silver, let's get out of here. We don't have time for this clown," Brandan said.

"Clown? Nigga, who you calling a clown, in my house?" Diego stepped up in Brandan's face, barely reaching Brandan's chin.

"Okay, you two, cut it out. This is not the time or the place. Brandan, let's go," Sebastian insisted.

Brandan sized Diego up then relaxed.

Sebastian pulled Silver through the doors where they were met by a sea of reporters, including Talise Grimes who had been covering the case from the beginning.

Silver descended the steps; Brandan and Sebastian flanked her.

Shouts and flashbulbs appeared from everywhere. "Miss James, is it true that you have a lovechild by Officer Todd Boyd?" "How do you feel about the wrongful death suit having been filed by Widow Boyd?"

"Is it true that the love nest you once shared with Officer Boyd was recently burned down?"

Silver tried to shield the reporters with her forearm but nothing seemed to help. Brandan and Sebastian took bold strides in front of her to get her to the car, but the mob scene made it difficult.

"Get me out of here," Silver shouted.

They finally got to the car, and Silver could hold back no longer. Her knees buckled before she could get in. The last thing she remembered was Brandan and Sebastian lifting her inside.

It was 10:30 P.M. and Silver and Brandan had driven an hour away from home. When Silver awakened after falling asleep before they reached the highway, she couldn't make out their whereabouts for all of the trees. She wiped the drool caked around her mouth and asked, "Where are we going?"

Brandan kept his eyes fixed on the dark road, "As far away as we can get from reporters."

"I need to call Jill and Sebastian and check on Lemar." Silver searched for her cell phone in her purse.

"Lemar is fine. Jill and Sebastian are taking good care of him. I didn't want to go back to the house because Jill said the reporters are still there," Brandan said as he kept his eyes focused on the road.

Silver looked out the window to nothingness, trying desperately to focus.

"Who's Diego?" Brandan asked out the blue.

"Diego? Oh, he's nobody," Silver said dryly.

"Nobody? He sure didn't seem like nobody at the precinct. He tried to step to me like he was your man or something."

"Why do you care? You jealous?" Silver wasn't in the mood for twenty questions. She thought they had escaped the questions when they fled from the media.

"Nothing to be jealous about. I just didn't like the way dude stepped to me. I was ready to teach the little boy a lesson, had he stayed in my face any longer."

"Um-hmm. Men and their testosterone. I'm hungry. Are we going to stop to eat?" she asked. "Where are we?"

Brandan didn't answer. He pulled up to a gas station, filled up and asked for directions. Moments later they were in front of a small dive called The Whitehouse. This place served better Philly Cheese steaks than Philly even though it was near Atlantic City. Every body that was anybody paid tribute to the famous eatery that boasted visits from any entertainer—from Gladys Knight to Frank Sinatra to a young Whitney Houston. The aroma of the cooked onions and peppers was heavenly, and instead of taking their foot-long steak subs to go, Silver wished they could demolish them right there in one of the small booths the restaurant provided.

"Where are we going now?" Silver asked after they had been traveling in silence for a few minutes.

Brandan still didn't respond. Instead he pulled on a quiet, dark cul de

Toni Staton Harris

sac. The only lights were the sparingly placed street lamps that emitted no more of a glow than a penlight. Brandan stopped in front of a quaint cottage-style one-level home and bade her to stay in the car. He jiggled the house's door lock for a few moments then waved her inside.

She turned off the engine, grabbed the keys and the greasy paper sacks and skipped inside, looking all around, wondering where Brandan had them stationed. The ants sounded louder than her footsteps.

"Whose house have you broken into?" she asked.

Brandan fumbled around a little and found the lights. He flipped them on and stumbled through the house while Silver stood firmly near the front door.

"This is our place," Brandan said proudly. "You might as well make yourself at home 'cause we're going to have to be here for at least the night."

"And where are we supposed to sleep?" Silver asked, looking around the empty space.

"The heat is on," Brandan said, adjusting the digital gauge. "I know there are some blankets from the contractors. We'll make use of whatever we find around the house."

Silver looked around with a snarl. She couldn't believe she was reduced to camping out because of some loud mouth reporters who didn't know when to leave well enough alone. What repulsed her more was her inability to bathe. Reluctantly she squatted in the middle of the high-gloss hardwood floors and set up to eat her sandwich. She was so hungry that she all but inhaled it.

Brandan pulled out two beers he brought with the sandwiches and sat down next to Silver. "You like the house?"

"It's nice," she said, wiping her mouth. "How many rooms?" She walked around, admiring the sand-colored sheers against the bay window and choice of yellow paint for what seemed to be the living area.

"There are three bedrooms, two and a half baths, this living room, a casual den and a full eat-in kitchen. I'll take you around when we finish," Brandan said as he bit into his sandwich.

"I don't need a tour. You all closed rather quickly on this place. Heck, I just found out you were moving," Silver said.

"I didn't mean to put it on you like that. Daphne found the place, and she's been coming down almost every weekend, buying and sizing stuff up."

"But I thought you said the house was in attorney review," Silver said.

"Actually, we have the pre-deed on the house. Since the owners moved already, they've given us some leeway to come almost any time we want. I just didn't have a key on me because I didn't expect we'd have to come, especially under these circumstances."

"You broke the lock?"

"Yeah. I'll fix it in the morning. You won't even know it was broken."

"That's Mr. Fix-it for you." Silver smiled.

"I'm not Mr. Fix-it...Well, maybe I am, but not how you mean." Brandan continued chomping away on his sandwich.

Silver returned to sit next to him. "It's not a bad thing, Brandan. You're everyone's savior—Mr. Fix-it, get it right, get it done."

"Too bad I can't always fix what's going on in my marriage like a car or that lock." Brandan's tone was gloomy.

"Like what?" Silver asked instinctively.

"Marriage is tough. We've been faced with some serious stuff, like my lock-up, Dee losing the baby. The good thing is that we know we can make it through the big stuff. She's down for me, and I appreciate that. I'm always down for her, too, you know. That's why I had to do things the way I've been doing them. Our relationship—Brandan pointed back and forth, to indicate he was talking about him and Silver—has taken its toll on Daphne. She's jealous of me and you, and I have to respect that and leave both of you whole."

Silver was warmed. This was the Brandan she was used to, the one who communicated with her, the one who let his guard down and was unafraid to be the man, the person he really was—kind, considerate and wise.

"So what's eating you? It seems like the big things are on track," she said.

"It's the little things that irk me. Dee's messy, and when I'm home with her I can't think. Sometimes she has shit all over the place, so when we argue, it's not about bills or anything like that, it's the fact that she won't make the bed when she gets out of it or that her drawers are at the foot of the bed."

"Jill always said it's the little things that count, and the little things will take care of the big things," Silver said. She picked an onion off his sandwich and ate it.

"I keep telling her that we won't be blessed with more if we don't show good stewardship over what we have."

"You sound like your mother." Silver laughed.

"That's not a bad thing, for sure. What really bugs me is that I have to go over everything she does, like housework. Whenever she folds clothes, she pats them down, but they aren't folded well, and she doesn't even fold her bras and underwear. She just throws them in the drawer."

Toni Staton Harris

"Brandan, delicates like that don't hold a fold. I fold mine, but most women don't."

He shrugged. "Oh, okay, but she's messy, and that's a problem for me."

"But Brandan, this doesn't sound like what you two were arguing about the night of the christening. What really is the deal?"

"Oh that," he responded and rose. "I don't want to talk about it." A furor seemed to stir inside. He gathered the garbage, balled it up and placed it into the plastic bag they'd brought everything in. "I'm taking this out. You want anything else?"

Silver shook her head. She surveyed the area, looking for something appropriate with which to bed down. She found a felt-like tarp and some old towels and laid them down as best she could. By the time Brandan returned, she was smoothing out the nest. "Make sure you stay on your side of the bed," she joked.

Silver rustled at the sound of Brandan entering the house. "You sleep okay?" he asked.

"Believe it or not, that was some of the best sleep I've had in a long time. What do you have there?" she asked, pointing at the bag he held.

"Breakfast," he answered, pulling out two breakfast sandwiches and a six pack of Guinness Stout.

"Don't you think it's a little early to have beer?"

"When Dee and I were in the Caribbean, we drank Guinness with breakfast. I thought it'd be nice since we were hanging out."

Silver yawned. "Ooh, I have to call and see about Lemar. Ooh." She frowned, referring to her own stale breath. "I know you don't have a toothbrush anywhere around here."

Brandan flipped a packaged brush her way and a tube of travel-size toothpaste.

"You just thought of everything, huh?" she said.

"You could say that. Lemar is fine. I called this morning and told Jill you were snoring. She said to let you sleep."

Silver nodded, wrapped the tarp around her waist and made her way to the closest bathroom. She found the light and admired the rust and orange tile, glass shower, separate tub and seashell pedestal sink. "This is nice, Brandan. Everything looks new."

"The previous owners allowed Daphne to pick out the

improvements," Brandan shouted from the living room. "Oh damn."

"What?" Silver asked.

"Nothing"

"That wasn't a nothing. What is it?" she questioned as she re-entered the living room. She wiped her hands on the felt tarp. For the first time in her adult life she kept her panties on, neglecting to discard them as she had nothing else to put on. "What is it Brandan?"

He tossed her Northern Jersey's premier paper. The headline read: MOTHER OF LOVECHILD COLLAPSES AFTER ARSON AND MURDER QUESTIONING.

"Damn they are ruthless," she said and read on. A horrific-looking picture showed Silver falling with Brandan and Sebastian trying to catch her. Brandan looked like he was caught in a crossfire. Under the picture the caption read: LOVECHILD'S MOTHER, SILVER JAMES, LEAVES THE PRECINCT AMID A CLOUD OF DOUBT AND INDISCRETION. The article then detailed the sensation: "Held up by whom is believed to be her partner in crime and latest married lover…" Silver slammed down the paper. She couldn't read anymore without breaking down again. She didn't know what else she could take.

"How did they get this information? Is there a leak in Dowdy's camp or what? How did they know I was there?" she asked rhetorically.

"Still think it's too early for a beer?" Brandan handed her an open can.

Silver gulped the strong stout like it was water.

"I spoke to Sebastian this morning. He's working from home. He said the reporters finally left around two A.M. We can head back up after we eat. Hopefully no one's lurking around in the bushes."

"I'll call Pat later. She's sympathetic to my situation considering the fire and all. Thank God your wife isn't back to work or I'd be fired by now." Silver reached for her sandwich and began to eat heartily. "So when do you think your move will actually go through?" Silver needed to change the subject.

"As soon as Daphne clears up this identity crap. The pre-deed is like a pre-cursor to the actual closing but if things don't get rolling I may have to put the house in my name alone, or Daphne won't be able to move as quickly as she'd like to, like yesterday." Brandan's gloom returned and Silver sensed he still wasn't telling her everything. Discarded underwear and lack of folding them couldn't be his biggest source of mental contention. It just didn't ring true.

"What is bothering you, Brandan? Come on, man. This is me. I'm not buying that other stuff."

"I don't really know what's going on." He popped another can and paced around the room, gulping the beer. "I just keep finding stuff that doesn't add up. I saw the police report, I've even spoken with authorities in Texas on Daphne's behalf but I've also found pieces of paper with a strange name on them, incoming and outgoing phone calls at strange hours in the middle of the night..."

"It sounds like she's a victim of circumstance and she's working hard to get it straight." Silver grabbed Brandan's leg. His pacing was making her dizzy. "Do you think she's cheating on you?"

Brandan crushed his beer can. Some beer was still inside and took residence on the hardwood floor. His demeanor changed instantly. "I swear if she is, this shit is over. I will drop her ass, married under a year or not. Now that shit is a deal breaker and you can believe fatback is greasy on that one."

"Sometimes you sound like an old man," Silver said, grinning.

Brandan didn't crack a smile.

"Okay, do you have anything else to go on?" she asked.

"Everything feels different."

"Different?"

"Silver, don't play dumb with me. Different," Brandan said as he stomped off.

Silver remained on the floor with her knees supporting her chin. Her best friend was in turmoil, and she was saddened because there wasn't a thing she could do about it.

A sudden jerking movement from the front doorknob startled her. Someone was trying to get in. "What the hell?" she heard the offender curse. She remembered Brandan had changed the lock before she arose. Silver started to sweat. She knew that voice belonged to Daphne. She wanted to run and hide, but with only a tarp wrapped around her waist, there wasn't anywhere else to go.

Silver jumped up, found her pants and hurried to put them on. It was bad enough she was going to have to open the door to let Daphne in her own house but to be in nothing more than her panties was unacceptable. As Silver was getting the other leg in her pants, she saw a shadow dart from the door to the bay window, where there was almost a clear view of the inside.

"Oh hell no," she heard Daphne exclaim. Daphne ran back to the front door. "Open the damn door, Silver. I see your bitch ass in my fucking house. Open the damn door." She began pounding.

Brandan heard the banging and ran out. "What's going on in here?" He walked to the front door and opened it. Daphne came bursting in. "Hey, babe. You're home early."

"You're damn right. I'm home early, and I come to my house to catch your ass here with this bitch. Damn, Brandan. You mean to tell me not only did you disrespect me by being with her, your so-called friend, but in my house? A house that we're not even in yet? And you have the nerve to ask me what I'm doing home so early in my house, with this bitch?"

"I'm not going to be too many more bitches, Daphne. You're overreacting. It's not what it seems."

"I don't give a fuck what it seems like," Daphne spewed. Every hair on her head was out of place as she ranted and raved. She lunged at Silver like a rabid dog.

They tussled, and Brandan pulled Daphne off. "Calm down. Stop it. It's not like that. You have to listen to me." Brandan held Daphne's face in his hands. He smoothed her hair out of her eyes.

Daphne was heaving and crying at the same time. "I can't believe you would do this to me. You promised, Brandan. You promised."

"I know, but it's not like what you think. Let me explain," Brandan pleaded.

"I can't wait to hear this one," Daphne said as she folded her arms. Her foot tapped incessantly.

"I went to the precinct with Silver yesterday. Things got out of hand. I had to get her away from the reporters who mobbed her, so—"

"You brought her down here to our place that's not even ours? How did you get the key? I have it on my ring?" Daphne asked.

"I had to break the lock. I changed it and was going to leave the key with the realtor."

"Brandan, why didn't you call me after you left the precinct? I tried to call your cell but I guess you were too busy taking care of this bitch again, and you promised," Daphne yelled.

"I told you I'm not going to be too many more bitches, Daphne."

"Shut up, Silver," Daphne insisted. "That's why I called the damn press in the first place. You are forever getting away with shit, but not this time, that's for damn sure."

"You did what?" Silver and Brandan asked in unison.

"You heard me." Daphne's attention was completely turned on Silver. "I called the damn press to let them know your ass was at the precinct again. I thought they might be interested, and I guess I was right because your ass was on the front page."

Silver saw stars as she processed the information. Her hands met Daphne's throat with a hold to choke the very life out of her.

"Silver, stop it. Stop it." Brandan pulled Silver off a coughing Daphne, shoving Silver so hard she fell.

"What's going on in here?" a voice asked. Two officers were standing at the front door. "We got a call from the neighbors. What's going on in here?"

"Officer," Daphne said, stomping over to the door, "she's trespassing. I demand she be arrested immediately."

"Who are you?" one officer asked.

"I'm the owner of this house. This is my husband," she said, pointing at Brandan. She shoved her finger at Silver. "She doesn't belong here."

The officers looked around and one questioned, "You are slated to move in, I take it?"

Daphne nodded.

"I need to see some identification and proof of ownership because you look like squatters," the other officer said.

Daphne moved to her purse, which she had dropped outside the door. She yanked her wallet from her bag along with a stack of neatly creased papers. "Officer, here is my license, and I have my pre-deed in the car. Daphne stomped off to the car, snarling at Silver all the way to the door.

Silver fixed herself up and Brandan gathered the tarp. Daphne returned with a briefcase. She pulled out a laminated folder that contained all sorts of documents for the house.
Daphne licked her fingers and flipped through them one by one.

"Where is the survey from Chicago Title? Oh, here it is. Here it is," Daphne said triumphantly.

"Officer, my name is on that pre-deed too," Brandan said, brandishing his license.

The officer took his time gazing at Daphne's license and photo and back at her several times. Obviously satisfied that Daphne was the license bearer, he unfolded the deed like it was the holy scroll, bringing the paper close to his face. "Look at this," he said to the other officer.

"That's right. This is my place, and I want this woman arrested for trespassing. She even coaxed my husband into breaking the lock," Daphne said.

"Hold on. Mr. Dixon, may I see your license please," one cop said to Brandan.

"My name isn't Dixon. It's Savoy. Brandan Savoy." Brandan held his license out to the officer.

"Then we have a problem. This pre-deed doesn't list either one of you," the officer overlooking the document said. "It lists a Darnel Dixon."

Daphne snatched the papers almost ripping them. "This can't be." She flipped through the pages. "This is wrong. How did they get my brother's name mixed up with mine? This is crazy."

"Your brother? Daphne, what the hell are you talking about?" Brandan stepped closer to her. He stopped when one of the officers extended his arm.

"Wait a minute, people. Are you Mrs. Dixon?" one of the officers asked Daphne.

"No sir, I'm Mrs. Savoy, but—"

"Then we're back at square one. All of you are trespassing. Unless somebody can produce identification that reads Darnel Dixon, you all are in trouble," the officer explained.

Daphne ran to Brandan. "I didn't want to tell you, but my brother's been using my social security number to open credit card accounts. I found out when I went back to Texas. I may be forced to prosecute him," she said.

"She's lying, Brandan. Can't you tell? That doesn't even make sense," Silver shouted.

"Shut up, bitch," Daphne growled.

"I told you, I'm not going to be any more bitches." Silver lunged, only to be blocked by Brandan who faced Daphne, waiting for an explanation.

"Officers, I can't think right now, please have this. . . this woman escorted off my premises," Daphne said.

"Actually, ma'am, all of you need to leave because according to this document you are all trespassing. "And buddy—" the officer directed his statement to Brandan— "if I were you, I wouldn't bring my mistress to my wife." Both officers chuckled and parted for all to exit.

Daphne stomped off first, followed by Brandan and Silver. The officers closed the door behind them.

"Brother, Daphne? All of a sudden this Darnel character is your brother? You're full of shit," Brandan said, hopping in the driver's seat of Silver's truck.

"Where are you going?" Daphne cried.

"Far away from your ass. I'm done, Daphne. I'm done. That mothafucker's name is on my deed. How did you swing that, Daphne? How did you get my name off the paperwork?" Brandan shouted through the window. "Now this Darnel person is your brother and has been stealing your identity? You must think I'm a brand-new fool. Silver, let's go or this train is leaving without you."

Silver rolled her eyes at Daphne and gritted her teeth. "Your day will come," she mouthed to Daphne as she jumped in the passenger's seat. Brandan gunned the engine, screeched out of the cul de sac and sped off, leaving Daphne standing with her mouth open.

"Okay, Brandan, calm down. You're speeding in this one-horse town. We don't need another encounter with the police." They rode through town and passed the Cherry Hill Mall. "Who is Darnel?" Silver questioned.

"The motherfucker that Daphne's sleeping with, that's who. Her brother my ass. Darnel Dixon has been all over my house on papers and stuff. Do you know some mail came to Daphne's in his name? She's been sending that shit back, no addressee, but it keeps coming." Brandan ranted from exit five on the New Jersey Turnpike to exit eleven.

Silver now understood all that was going on with her friend. His sadness, his angst and all of his torture and turmoil had a face, and it belonged to Daphne Dix Savoy.

Chapter 13

All the Queen's Horses, All the Queen's Men

"Good morning," Silver said blandly as she stopped in the kitchen, rifling through the cabinets for her favorite of Jill's mugs. As much as Silver enjoyed tea with her sister and brother-in-law, she longed to have it in her own space. Over a year had passed since Todd's murder and a change was due. The second arson incident was not solved and Detective Dowdy and the boys, including Diego who now worked closely on her case, chalked it up to circumstance.

In her gut, Silver knew differently, but she concluded that she had to focus her attention on creating a solid environment for her and Lemar, now four months old, in the face of all adversity. Single motherhood, in spite of the enormous support she had, was a task in itself. The amount of uncertainty and effort placed on her in her new role was enough to drive a person to sit under a rock until it was all over. The reality was that Lemar and all children were blessings to those whom they were bequeathed, and it was her honor and her job to do the best she could with what she had. Those were Jill's words, but Silver tried to buy into them.

"So, where are you rushing off to this morning?" Jill asked.

"I need to get to work early. I'm presenting to Up, Up and Away today." Silver was somewhat pensive. She really wanted the account; it would be a staple with the company. She ran around the kitchen swiftly, tackling her full regimen of getting prepared. Today, she was up so early that Lemar was stretched out in his playpen, fully dressed, having eaten much earlier.

"Up, Up and Away? Is that the balloon company that decorated for the christening?" Jill asked.

"Yes, and I have a good shot at it too." Silver gulped the last of her tea and placed the mug in the sink.

"Good for you. You worked that christening, huh?"

"You could say that," Silver answered with confidence.

"I know, I understand. Is Daphne back at work yet?"

"No. Since she and Brandan aren't moving to South Jersey, I thought she was going to nix the transfer thing, but she hasn't come back to the Newark office, and nobody's talking about anything."

"Is Brandan still at his place or have he and Daphne reconciled?" Jill asked.

"They haven't reconciled, and he said they're not going to. He's still on Park Avenue."

"Wow, he must really be upset. It's been about two months, right?" Jill said.

"He's really hurt. He won't admit it, but I know he's down. He loves Daphne, but he says nothing adds up with her, and he's tired of her lies, finding truth in bits and pieces."

"It's good that you're there for him." Jill rubbed Silver's arm.

"I wouldn't have it any other way." Silver clasped her hands and checked her watch. "I better get going."

"Great. By the way, don't wait for me tonight. Sebastian and I have a dinner meeting with some of his clients. Abigail is going to hang with my mother."

"Okay. I'll probably be home late too. Brandan's picking Lemar up from day care and is going to spend time with him while I run a few errands," Silver answered.

"Abigail," Jill yelled as she was walking out the door, "if you aren't down here this instant, you'll be walking to school, and then you'll be late and you know what that means—detention—young lady. I don't care that it is the end of the semester. Let's go."

Abigail came rushing down the stairs. Silver smiled at her niece's feeble attempt to wipe off some shade of sparsely applied lipstick. Abigail had just turned twelve and Silver briefly reminisced of her own pre-teen years. Silver could hear Jill fussing through the front door. Silver thought fondly that being with her sister's family wasn't so bad. She gathered a nodding Lemar and his things and headed out. She could only pray her day would be a peaceful one.

The prolonged daylight was a delight to Silver because it was 5:30 P.M., and it wasn't dark yet. She landed her account and her errand running concluded much earlier than she thought. She drove up to Brandan's to find him and Lemar in the front yard. Lemar, who squealed with joy, was bundled in a heavy sweatshirt despite the mild weather. Silver watched them for a moment, appreciating every inch of their relationship.

"How did your appointment with the attorney go?" Brandan asked Silver as she walked toward them. Lemar laughed heartily, loving every minute of the attention Brandan bestowed on him.

"Better than expected. I got the account today. My presentation was so good, Pat agreed that I could manage it completely. I'm getting back on track," Silver said, her excitement bubbling just before the bursting point.

"That's fantastic. I'm proud of you, baby girl." Brandan stopped tickling Lemar and together they hugged Silver so hard she screamed. "Let's go celebrate. You want something?"

"What you got?" Silver asked, smiling. She followed Brandan and Lemar into the house with Lemar giggling at his mom over Brandan's shoulder.

Once inside, Silver unrolled Lemar from his bandagelike clothing and shed herself of her suit jacket.

Brandan re-entered the living room with two full pilsners and a bottle of milk. He set everything down and made a toast. "To Mommy—" he looked at Lemar who clearly had no clue as to what was going on—"and to my girl, my friend for putting it all back together and being my catcher in the rye." He clinked Silver's glass, put Lemar's bottle to his lips, then drank a sip of beer.

Brandan looked over at Silver who hadn't sipped. Real tears formed at the corners of her eyes. "Cut it with the waterworks," Brandan said. He cleared his throat. "So what happened at the attorney's office?"

Silver acknowledged Brandan's changing of the subject and obliged. "The attorney said that I have a good shot at getting a piece of Todd's pension for Lemar. And get this, Cheryl and Todd weren't legally married, so technically because all of his kids were out of wedlock, Lemar is entitled to social security like the others."

"How did this information come out?" Brandan asked as he maneuvered Lemar's bottle.

"When Mac was setting up financial accounts for Lemar, he had to inquire about all avenues from me and Todd. He did some digging and got access to information I think people hoped would stay a secret, especially Cheryl Boyd." Silver continued sipping.

"Yeah, but there has to be some verification like a DNA test or something," Brandan stated with concern. "I don't agree with Lemar being subjected to DNA testing. Silver, do you need the money? Why put him through this?"

"Because whether I need the money or not, it's about Lemar's future. What if something happens to me?" Silver asked.

"I'd be here, and Jill and Sebastian would be here to treat Lemar like he's our own, because he is," Brandan answered.

"No offense, dawg, but that's not enough. I never want Lemar to be in the position I was in when my mother died."

"But he wouldn't. What happened with your mother and father wouldn't happen with Lemar and you know that." Brandan said.

"The bottom line is that Lemar is entitled to part of Todd's pension, and with my attorney I'm going to see that he gets it, no matter what you or anyone else thinks," Silver said indignantly.

"Have you told Jill about your plans?"

Silver started playing with Lemar, purposely ignoring Brandan's question.

"Again, have you talked to your sister about your plans?" Brandan pressed.

"No, I haven't. I'm grown, Brandan, and I don't need yours or her permission," Silver said, sounding like a stubborn child.

"Yeah, okay," Brandan said. He got up to answer a knock at the door for which Silver was grateful.

Daphne burst in. "I'm not surprised that you're here, but I need to speak with my husband in private."

Silver held her tongue. She refused to be ghetto in front of her son, even if it meant missing an opportunity to put Daphne in her place.

Luckily, Brandan stepped in. "We don't have anything to talk about. Get out. Be gone."

"No, Brandan, we have something serious to talk about," Daphne whined.

"Come on, sweetie. Let Mommy change your diaper." Silver swooped Lemar up and took him upstairs to Brandan's bedroom. She knew this burned Daphne's butt.

Brandan watched Silver go up the stairs. "What do you want?" he asked abruptly refocusing on Daphne.

"To talk."

"Nothing left to talk about. You lied, you're cheating, and I'm done with it." Brandan flipped his hand and walked away.

"The only thing I lied about was that I knew my brother was messing up my credit, using my social security number. Even though we're estranged, I didn't want to bring him down. I was trying to handle the situation my own way." Daphne's voice was weak and hollow.

"Your brother? Now I know you're full of shit. How could your brother use a credit card with your name on it Daphne?"

"Because he'd use it online or over the phone. He didn't use it in person."

"I don't know anything about this brother and all of a sudden you're willing to sacrifice our lifestyle for him? We're family, and we come first and—"

"Don't you dare lecture me about us being a family and us coming first. I have not cheated on you and never will. Dammit, since the day you stepped into my life you've come first. You can't say that I've come first. Shall I name—"

"Don't start bringing up past shit that's done." Brandan paced away from Daphne.

"Oh, not too distant past might I add. You were arrested. I put my entire financial life on the line for you, and we weren't even married—"

"I knew that shit would come back to haunt me. I don't care if it takes the rest of my life well after our divorce, I'll pay your ass back."

"I don't want your money," Daphne yelled. "I want you. I've always wanted you. We've talked about my family and why there's no contact." Daphne rifled through her purse and pulled out a photograph. "You don't believe I have a brother? Here's a family photo of when we were children. My family exists. We're just not on good terms. You knew this before we got married."

Brandan picked up the photo and studied it intently. "Your family is not my problem. You never thought to include me before or acted like you cared about your parents or your brother. Why start now?" He tossed the picture back on the coffee table.

"Because you've taught me the meaning and importance of family."

"Daphne, don't try to lay that bullshit on me. I'm not having it." Brandan walked away.

"You just don't get it. Yes, I lied about my brother, but I never lied about us. Silver, on the other hand—"

"Don't you try and blame this on Silver," Brandan yelled.

"I'm not blaming this on Silver, but you can't preach to me about putting us first because from the day we got together, Silver has come first in your life—before, during and after our marriage.

"You've always run to her defense in everything. We didn't enjoy our own reception because you had to turn to Silver's defense. Yes, I called the press on her because I'm tired of Silver being the beneficiary of your time, efforts and emotion." Daphne turned from Brandan then twirled back. "Please don't talk about me putting us first and me not considering the well-being of my brother." Daphne planted herself comfortably on Brandan's couch. "Well, say something."

Brandan bit his lip. "Daphne, bringing up the press incident is not helping you right now. Plus, you had my name removed from the pre-deed. Don't think I didn't catch that shit."

"All I wanted was to do something special for you, with my own money, on my own accord. I figured—"

"You figured wrong. You figured I was going for the okeydoke again," Brandan said.

"No, Brandan. I'm just owning up to mine," Daphne pleaded. She paused for a moment as if to think. Suddenly her tone changed. "You should own up to all the crap you've put me through. You're no angel." She crossed her arms, her purse dangling in front of her. "Silver is the real problem here and always has been, but no matter what, I've always stood by you and always worked with you."

Brandan shook his head and smirked. "You're good, you know that? So good I don't know what to believe. You see, when you lie once, I can forgive you but twice... three times, I don't believe anything that comes out of your mouth." He leaned over her with a menacing stare.

"Brandan, what are you really saying?"

"You want me to spell it out for you? Here it goes: I want you to get your ass out of my place and out of my life. I don't want anything else to do with you."

"Brandan, we have to go." Silver briskly walked down the stairs with Lemar in her arms. She'd heard everything from Brandan's open-air loft bedroom.

"Don't worry. Daphne was just leaving," Brandan said.

"It's always about Silver, isn't it? It always will be, won't it?" Daphne stood and touched Brandan's chest.

He forced his chin to the ceiling, his arms folded. "Silver, hold up. Don't leave, 'cause Daphne's getting ready to."

"So it's like that? You're just going to discard me like three-day-old trash?" Daphne asked, tremors in her voice.

Lemar was starting to get antsy at the tension in the room, and Silver became uncomfortable as well. "Y'all need to stop arguing like this in front of the baby."

"Then leave, bitch," Daphne chided.

"Hold up, I'm not going to have you talking like that in front of my son. You leave," Brandan yelled. With that Lemar wailed. "Do you remember the last conversation we had? Do you?" Brandan stepped in Daphne's face. "Well, let me remind you. I told you no more games, no more lies. I told you to tell me everything because if I found out any more information that you could've told me in that moment, it was over. And not only do you put my son, my best friend and entire family in jeopardy by calling the press on us, but you lie about some phantom brother you all of a sudden have and then you get my name removed from the pre-deed." He laughed. "And I'm supposed to trust you?" He paused and thought for a moment. "Get out of my house."

Lemar wasn't the only one wailing. Tears flowed effortlessly from Daphne's eyes. She started dry heaving and Brandan turned his back like she wasn't there. "I'm leaving. Your son. He's not even your son—"

"Daphne, watch it. Don't say a bad word about my son," Silver warned.

"Oh, you don't have to worry about me anymore. Either of you." Daphne was eerily calm. "In fact, Brandan, your check in the mail will suffice because when I get through with you, and after I bear the child I have growing inside of me, you'll have nothing left to care for anyone or anything else." She stormed past Brandan and brushed Silver's shoulder with her own.

Brandan grabbed her arm just before she exited. "Oh, so you're pregnant now? Again? Well, I want a paternity test because I don't trust you, and I don't believe a word you say. Get out of my house," Brandan bellowed so forcefully Lemar became hysterical. Silver stood wearing a startled look.

"Oh, you don't have to worry about a paternity test," Daphne said, "because when I'm done with your ass you'll be sorry you even met me."

"I already am," Brandan shouted back, but Daphne had stormed away. He mumbled something but all Silver could make out was "bitch."

"Brandan, enough. Enough now. Get yourself together," Silver said.

Brandan looked around and saw that Lemar was still upset and Silver couldn't comfort him. Brandan picked up Lemar, rubbed his back and apologized profusely until Lemar quieted down.

Silver scooped her son in her arms and kissed Brandan on the forehead. "I'll call you after I get him settled."
Brandan nodded.

Silver was struggling to get a squirmish Lemar into his car seat when they heard a bang so loud, it sounded as if a bomb was dropped. Silver looked around and hit the ground. Nervous that Lemar might jump out of his unbuckled car seat, she reached over, pulled him out of the car and ran to Brandan's door.

Brandan was already looking around to see what was going on. "Wait here," he told them.

"Silver," Brandan yelled, "call an ambulance. I think I see Daphne's car."

"Oh no," Silver said. "I hope that girl didn't do anything stupid." She placed Lemar on the couch and dialed 911.

The waiting room at Beth Israel hospital was so congested Silver had to nudge herself between an obese man and a screeching kid. After she left Brandan at the hospital, she dropped Lemar off at Paula Mitchell's with Abigail. The waiting room, full of Friday night specials gone wrong, was no place for a kid.

Silver yawned then checked her watch. It had been an hour and a half since they heard anything from Brandan who waited somberly in the surgical lounge area. Silver wanted to console him, but the lounge was reserved for immediate family, and by the looks of the nurse on duty, if Silver dared to venture that way again, she might be thrown out of the hospital altogether.

Silver paced to the other side of the room where Mom Savoy sat and kneeled beside her. "Why don't you go to the room just to check on Brandan and see if we can get any status?" Silver prodded.

"No, baby, I'm staying right here before Nurse Hatchet yells again. She said mom-in-law ain't immediate family." Mom Savoy's comments solidified Silver's reluctance to barge over to where Brandan was. "Have a sit-down, chile. Stop worrying. Brandan'll be over here before long to tell us Daphne's gon' be just fine."

Silver smiled at Mom Savoy's steadfast faith and ability to be calm when everything seemed to be falling apart. But Mom Savoy's faith that Daphne would be okay hadn't transfixed itself on Silver just yet. The image of Daphne being pulled from the wreckage was way too fresh in her mind for any optimism.

Daphne's entire body was melded to the wheel, and if the impact hadn't crushed any bones, the way the paramedics beat on her chest to get her heart pumping surely did. The onlookers predicted Daphne's death, many times over; even Silver thought it was over. But some of Mom Savoy's faith must have had long-reaching arms because miraculously the paramedics had Daphne on a stretcher, breathing and her heart pumping.

Standing by the door with Mom Savoy caused Silver to get cold, so she moved to the other end of the room where an automatic cappuccino machine dispensed fresh, hot cups of java.

"Place gettin' mighty fancy," Mom Savoy said, joining Silver. "How you work this thing?"

Silver didn't really know, but after pressing a few buttons, the java flowed freely, and Silver enjoyed warming up before she spotted her sister.

"There's Jill." Silver placed the cup on the table where the machine sat and waved so Jill could see them.

Jill walked over, kissing Mom Savoy first, then Silver. "Where's Brandan?" she asked.

"In the surgical waiting room, and you better not try to go in there. You'll be met with a hatchet," Silver said.

"Well, the kids are at home with Sebastian in bed. My mother gave Lemar a soothing bath, and it knocked him out. I couldn't even wake him when I put him in the car on the way to the house," Jill said. "So now what happened?" Jill grabbed Mom Savoy and Silver's hands then led them to a small corner near the door so they could talk freely.

"Well, like I told you on the phone, Daphne came over to Brandan's. It didn't help to see me there, and they argued. Daphne stormed out, and the next thing you know we heard a loud noise."

"They argued in front of Lemar?" Jill asked.

"Yes. That's why I was trying to get out of there because Lemar was getting upset," Silver answered.

"Poor baby." Jill shook her head.

"Lemar or Brandan?" Silver asked.

"Both," Jill answered.

"I tell you, I know that girl's gon' be all right but I don't have a good feeling about this. My bones are starting to ache," Mom Savoy said. She rubbed her shoulder.

Silver and Jill looked at each other. Mom Savoy's premonitions could be a scary thing because good or bad they always seemed to come true.

"But Mom Savoy you just told me to have faith. Your shoulder changed your mind?" Silver asked.

"My shoulder is telling me this here situation ain't good, baby. I'm not saying she ain't gonna be all right. I'm going to the ladies' room. Where is it?" Silver pointed through the swinging door, and Mom Savoy followed her finger.

With Mom Savoy gone Silver felt she could be free about what she really thought. "Jill, that was the worse accident I've ever seen in real life or on TV."

"It was that bad, huh?"

Silver nodded. "I didn't get a chance to tell you earlier, but they had to use the "jaws of life" to open the roof and pull Daphne out. But it just didn't seem right."

"What didn't seem right?" Jill asked.

Silver pulled Jill into a corner of the hallway so they had more privacy. She looked around to make sure no one was in ear shot. "Don't get me wrong. I feel bad for Daphne, but I feel worse for Brandan. He's been blaming himself since we left for the hospital. By the time we got here, he was delirious, talking about if he got another chance, he didn't care what she did, he's going to be a better person."

Jill contorted her brows inward, looking at Silver inquisitively. "You shouldn't feel guilty about feeling bad for Brandan. That's natural. Just like he shouldn't feel guilty about the accident. It's unfortunate, but it wasn't his fault."

"That's it. I don't think it was accident." Silver was relieved to admit her true suspicions.

"Oh, come on. That's pretty extreme. You said yourself that Daphne hit the back of a truck."

"Yeah, but the eighteen wheeler was double parked and the driver wasn't in it. I heard one of the kids telling the cop that Daphne's car stopped at the corner then gunned the engine and ran into the back of the truck," Silver said.

"Wow, that's still pretty extreme. I'd hold my tongue on that if I were you."

"Why hold her tongue now? She doesn't hold on anything else," Brandan said, appearing like a shadow. "Answer my question. Why hold your tongue for that? You don't for anything else." He walked in front of Jill, coming nose to nose with Silver.

"Brandan, back up. I didn't mean any harm. I was just—"

"You were just putting your damn foot in your mouth like you always do."

Silver backed away. "Okay, I know you're upset, but you need to calm down. I didn't mean any harm."

"You didn't mean any harm. You never mean any harm," Brandan yelled and spun around. He started to walk away, but turned back to face

Silver again. "That woman is in there fighting with everything she has for her life. We don't even know if she'll walk again her pelvic bone was so crushed, and all you can do out here is stand and gossip?"

"Brandan, it's not my fault. I was only repeating what I heard some of the witnesses say. You heard it too," Silver yelled back.

"Okay, you two, cut it out. Cut it." Jill tried to intervene. It was too late. Silver and Brandan's yelling had elevated to full scale.

"Excuse me. Ex-cuse-me!" Nurse Hatchet appeared. "This is a hospital, not your hippety-hop bar room. Now you two better shut it down, or I'll see that both of you are escorted out." She poked each of them on the shoulder. "Mr. Savoy, the doctor will see you now." She turned and walked away.

"I want you out of here," Brandan said in a low voice.

"You are being ridiculous, Brandan," Silver said.

"I said I want you out of here," he yelled so loud they all thought the walls shook. "Now," he whispered.

Silver's chest heaved; her eyes bugged wide. She pulled her keys from her pocket and stomped off.

"Silver wait. Wait," Jill called out, but it was too late. When she finally caught up with her, Silver was sobbing on the side of a brick wall.

"Baby, oh, baby girl, I'm sorry. You know Brandan didn't mean any of that. He's just in pain and feeling guilty right now. We always lash out at the one's closest to us." Jill held her sister, trying to console her.

"I'm tired, Jill." Silver pulled away and wiped her eyes. "I can't do this anymore. I'm not going to be a doormat for Brandan and his wife. I'm not going to be the scapegoat for their ridiculous bullshit."

"I know, honey. I know how you feel."

"No, Jill, you don't. From the moment Daphne showed up at your party on Brandan's arm, things have never been the same with us or him.

He's a different person, almost manic. And I'm tired of being the brunt of Brandan and Daphne gone wrong." Silver's voice was hollow, her words lifeless. She walked aimlessly across the street to the parking lot.

"Where are you going, honey?" Jill called out.

"Home. I'm going home to be with my son. I'm done, Jill, and what happens to Brandan from here is no longer my problem or my concern."

"Okay, I'll drive you." Jill ran up to her.

Silver was miraculously calm. She nodded.

"Wait a minute. Please wait here. I left my purse upstairs. I hope it's still there," Jill said. Silver nodded again. Jill turned and ran back across the street into the building.

Silver looked above. The stars shone brighter than they had in months. There wasn't a cloud in the sky. Nothing there could mask the onslaught of tears and pain of knowing her friendship with Brandan had served its reason and season.

Chapter 14

Reason, a Season or a Lifetime

Jill burst through Silver's bedroom door, flipped on the lights and pulled back the covers. "No time for sleeping. Come on, follow me," Jill said as she pulled the covers completely off Silver's bed. According to the baby monitor, Lemar was sound asleep in his crib.

Silver grumbled, she wished she had her own place. As much as she loved her family, she missed her privacy. Remaining at Jill and Sebastian's longer than she hoped was her fault. She'd saved enough for a nice apartment or starter home. Jill's whining convinced her to stay, save more money, and assured her that waiting for the right time to move would be worth it. Silver could admit every time she looked at her savings statement, she couldn't imagine having so much of her money in one place at one time. She could pay off her lease and a substantial mortgage with cash to spare.

"Come on, I want you to see something," Jill said, pulling Silver from the bed. Jill grabbed Silver's robe, threw it over her shoulders and kicked Silver's fur slippers to her. "Ooh, maybe you should put on your sneakers. We're going outside."

Silver complied. She pulled a clean sweat suit from her drawer, put it on and placed her robe around it. She put on her socks and sneakers and followed a gleeful Jill through the back door.

The darkness prompted Jill to grab a flashlight. She led them through a few trees that eventually would be cut down. "Okay now close your eyes."

Silver did and felt Jill tug her arm, prompting her to move a little farther. "Be careful," Silver said, losing her balance on what felt like a large branch. They stopped and Jill sighed. "Open your eyes now."

Silver did, and what she saw made her clasp her hands to her mouth. The house was done. Silver dropped her hands and walked closer. It was beautiful, but most importantly it was hers, and it was done. Silver moved back to Jill, grabbed the flashlight and pointed it into the windowed entrance door.

"The inspector comes next week, then the electricity gets turned on and you're in business, baby girl. Your first house," Jill screamed. "We have to go pick your appliances, your bedroom sets, some modest furnishings..."

All Silver could do was jump up and down. After doing so for what seemed like minutes, she hugged her sister so hard, she lifted Jill from the ground.

"I'll take it you're happy," Jill said, struggling.

Silver was speechless; her smile was wide.

"If you want, we can go to the Design Center in Union and pick out some things after work. You still need to choose some light and bathroom fixtures and stuff like that," Jill said.

"Oh, okay." Silver's smile dimmed. 'I guess I could cancel my date. I was going to ask you to baby-sit tonight."

"Oh no. We can go tomorrow or over the weekend. Who's your date with?" Jill asked.

"Diego," Silver said casually as she peered at the house's sturdy structure.

"Is that the cop guy you told me about who bought those books for me some time ago?"

"Yup. We're playing pool," Silver answered.

"Um-hmm." Jill looked questionable.

"Oh, come on. Don't give me that look. It's nothing serious. We're just hanging out. It would do me some good to hang out with the opposite sex. I haven't had a date in what feels like years."

"God knows that's the truth. I just don't know if it's wise to get involved with..." Jill stopped short. "Just take it slow, okay? Remember, he and Todd were on the same force. Do you all talk about Todd at all?"

"Nope. We agree that subject is too serious for casual acquaintances," Silver said.

"Speaking of friends, Brandan called last night. He asked about Lemar. I told him Lemar was doing well and that he should come by and—"

"I was thinking of a southwestern theme—orange, yellow and reds throughout the house and mocha for Lemar's bedroom and mauve for mine. What do you think?" Silver asked as she and Jill walked inside.

"I know you don't want to talk about it, Silver, but I think estrangement from Brandan for two months is long enough," Jill prodded.

"Jill, I'm not going to be enrolled in Brandan's drama. Whenever he's ready to come out of it, he knows where I live." Silver continued to look around. She pushed her feet into the gravel.

"Daphne's coming home today," Jill announced.

"Good for them," Silver said. She tightened the robe's belt around her waist.

"You are not trying to hear anything about Brandan and Daphne, are you?" Jill asked softly.

"I'm really not."

"But Silver, it's been too long. He's your best friend, and this silence between you is not good for anyone. Your situation with Todd should have taught you that life is way too short."

"Why is it every time someone wants to guilt me into doing something they bring up Todd? I'm not calling Brandan. If he wants to see Lemar, he's more than welcome to as long as his wife is not around. She won't be allowed to take her frustration for me out on my child because then she'd wish she was dead."

"Fine, Silver."

"Listen, Brandan's made his bed with that witch and he must lie in it. It's time to go inside," Silver said and walked back into the house.

Silver's office was abuzz. The government project had finally been completed, and the website was about to go live. Everyone gathered around as the director talked about the future of Sci-gex and how the staff could expect significant bonuses at the end of the year. Peopled clapped and cheered.

"There are going to be big changes around here. We've landed key accounts with the help of some industrious associates, and these accounts have been critical to our success. Of course we're looking to you to carry the torch forward. New direction never comes without new leadership, so with that I'm pleased to present to you, your new managing director of accounts, Patricia Ghanem." The office went wild. Pat bowed her head. It was obvious from her serene expression that she wasn't surprised.

"We're expecting great things from you, Pat," the director continued. Pat nodded. "Our next announcement is coming as a surprise to the recipient as well as most others. Whatever task given, this person has taken it on with fervor and enthusiasm despite the odds. Help me welcome as a permanent member of our management team, Silver A. James who is being promoted to director of large accounts."

Everyone including Silver gasped. That meant Daphne was not coming back. "Well let's give her a warm welcome." The director jolted everyone to wild applause and verbal accolades. Silver sat with her mouth open, accepting Pat's wink.

After the meeting, Silver dodged several well wishes and caught up with Pat, shoving her into Pat's old office. "You couldn't even tell me?"

"No, I couldn't, Silver, as badly as I wanted to. This government project is really top secret and requires clearance for every phase. I couldn't talk about it."

Pat sat down at her desk and put her face in her hands.

"What's going on? You're acting strange. I don't like it, and I'm not going through another crazy Daphne episode. Be straight with me or keep your position and your attitude."

"Silver, I can't talk about it. Know that you are well liked and the big boys are pleased with your selection to the position. Trust me, my mood has nothing to do with you or your new position," Pat said.

"Fine. So what's going to happen with Daphne? She must be definitely transferring to the Philly office now."

"Daphne's been fired, Silver. She's not coming back to Sci-gex and probably won't work in this industry again," Pat said.

"What? Why? What is going on around here?" Silver gawked. She couldn't help it, but she felt glad.

"I've said way too much already. Just leave it at that. You won't have to worry about Daphne ever again as far as this job is concerned."

"And you can't say anything else?"

"I can't and I won't." Pat paused. "I take it you and Brandan aren't talking yet?"

"No. Why are you asking?" Silver crossed her arms over her chest.

"Because if you two were talking, you would have known Daphne was fired and you wouldn't be asking so many questions. She was fired before the accident."

"But she and Brandan weren't back together before the accident,"

Silver said, trying to size everything up.

"Then that's why he called here about her medical insurance," Pat said.

"What about her medical insurance? She doesn't have any?" Silver was getting more confused, and Pat wasn't helping any.

"The hospital called to verify coverage, and it was denied. Medical insurance expires ninety days after termination—"

"She's been terminated for more than ninety days?" Silver questioned.

"You guessed it, I didn't give it."

"Then that's what Brandan was talking about her constant lying. He must have known but didn't tell me. Exactly when—"

Pat held her hand up. "I can't answer anymore of your questions, Silver, and I mean it. Whatever else you need to know, you need to take up with your friend and his wife." Pat's eyes looked sullen. She tried to change her expression, but Silver still caught the hollowness in her voice. "I'll be out of this office at the end of the week. Make sure your stuff is packed and labeled so it can be moved in when I leave. Your name is going to be gold leafed on the door a week after you move in. Your new business cards should arrive over the next few days. Congratulations, director. You deserve it," Pat said and extended her hand.

"Thanks, friend," Silver said. She tugged on Pat's arm, whipped her from around the desk and hugged her tightly.

Silver pulled away and saw tears in Pat's eyes. Silver decided not to push. She grabbed a tissue from Pat's desk and handed it to her. Pat tried to laugh her sorrow off while dabbing her eyes. "Now get out of here, director. Take the rest of the day off and celebrate." Pat sniffled.

"Why don't you come with me, just you and me?" Silver prodded.

"No. Too much work to do, but you enjoy."

"Thanks. I will. I'll talk to you later?" Silver added a sing-song tone to her question.

"Yup. Later."

Silver walked out of Pat's office, not sure how she felt. Pat was the one who often brought sunshine into her life when things were really going bad, and now for whatever reason, Pat needed a lift and Silver couldn't help her. She wanted to feel bad but she couldn't. She had a new house, a new position, more money than she ever dreamed of having in the bank and a son who was growing well. If only she had someone with whom to share all of her good fortune. It was times like this, she missed Brandan more than anything. Her life was really turning around.

She got her desk in order and headed out. It was time to celebrate.

"So where would you like to go, Miss Manager of . . . What did you say your title was?" Diego asked.

"Director of large accounts, but I supervise mid and small accounts as well," Silver answered.

"Where would you like to go?"

"Want to shoot a game of pool and get a beer?"

"Works for me. Nickel Bar okay?" Diego asked.

"Cool."

"That's what I like about you," Diego said as he passed through the toll booth onto the Garden State Parkway South.

"What? Because I like guy stuff like beer and pool?" Silver laughed.

"That helps and the fact that you're so down to earth. I wasn't feeling anything fancy tonight, even though if you had asked, I would have obliged."

Silver smiled. She liked that Diego was hospitable and the fact that she could have an intelligent conversation with a man who knew how to correctly use multi-syllabic words.

"I have a karate competition in a few weeks. Would you be interested in coming?" Diego asked.

"Can I bring my son?" Silver asked.

"Of course. Why would you ask something silly like that?" Diego sounded sincerely offended.

"That's why it took me so long to call you, because you acted so stank when you found out I had a son." Silver's mood changed drastically. She was prepared to have Diego take her home or she would call a cab if need be, but she wasn't about to deal with a man who was going to be shady about her son.

"I tried to explain to you, I had had a lot of baby daddy drama and I wasn't for any with you. No offense." Diego looked out the side window.

"I can buy that. You know whose son Lemar is, right?" Silver asked.

"I know now. I wasn't sure though. Every time I saw you, with the exception of the bookstore, you had that big dude hanging around you. I thought he could have been your man, and I didn't want to tussle with him. Even though I know I could take him." Diego laughed.

"That's not true because Brandan stood me up twice when you were around. Besides, no offense to you, but you're probably half Brandan's size." Silver laughed.

"But not half his strength. You know what they say, the bigger they are..." Diego turned into the full parking lot of the Nickel Bar. He walked around Silver's side of the car and opened her door, then extended his arm. As she exited the car, Diego pecked her on the lips.

Silver was somewhat taken aback. "I don't know you well enough for you to be putting your lips on me."

"I'm sorry. I couldn't resist. Just want you to know that I look forward to spending time with you and your son, God and you willing."

"Okay, that's fine, but keep your lips to yourself," Silver reiterated.

"That's fair."

"Oh, and you don't have to worry about my friend Brandan either. He's out of my life." Silver tried to sound casual, but her private thoughts resounded loud and sad. She wished she could retract her words the moment they escaped her lips. "And I don't feel like talking about it," she warned before Diego could question her.

"I wasn't going to ask. Sounds like that's deep. I'm sure you'll talk about it when and if you're ready," Diego said, touching the small of her back to lead her inside.

Silver felt at ease. Diego had great instincts, and she loved that he didn't pressure her. She smiled as he led her to the pool table.

The weekend had come faster than Silver had anticipated, and after a wonderful evening of conversation, Diego had asked her out again for early afternoon ice cream. She loved nothing more than Applegate Farms ice cream parlor in Montclair. Diego had even begged her to bring Lemar but Silver wasn't completely comfortable with Diego yet to bring her son on a date with them. She just wanted to be sure Diego didn't have a problem when she did bring him.

"What do you want to do with your life?" Silver asked as they climbed the small hill from the parking lot to the sprawling farm house. More than fifteen high school and college students waited to take their order for everything from Italian gelato to Cinnamon Rum Raisin ice cream.

"To ask that question leads me to believe you think I'm not content where I am," Diego said.

"No. I've just never met a cop who only wants to be a cop." Silver smiled. "No offense."

"Believe it or not, for years that's all I ever wanted to do was be a cop, but recently I've had my sights set on other things." Diego and Silver moved to the edge of the grass where long lines had already formed.

"What are the other things that you're interested in?" Silver asked. She looked over and her heart dropped. A red Mercedes pulled up to the handicap parking spot. Brandan emerged looking worn. His clothes sagged and his car had so much dust that the inscription *clean me,* would have been an understatement. Silver watched as Brandan walked to the other side of the car. He pulled a wheelchair from the backseat and set it up, then he gingerly placed Daphne in it. Brandan checked her seat and rolled her to the back of one of the lines. Silver turned abruptly for fear Brandan might catch her staring.

"...then my ultimate dream would be to start a karate school in the inner city, much like the one I attended on Fourth Avenue."

"Oh, okay, that's cool," Silver said, neglecting to acknowledge she and Diego were from the same neighborhood.

"What has you so preoccupied?" Diego waved his hand in front of her face.

"Oh, I saw somebody, and I don't want to get into it right now."

"Who? Your boy who just got out of the red Mercedes?" Diego asked.

"How did you know?"

"I'm a cop. Besides, he's hard to miss, even though he looks different, not the mass I remember," Diego said. "You should go over there and at least say hello."

"No can do," Silver said as they reached the window to order. "I'll have a double scoop of Red Velvet and Butter Cream Almond."

Diego ordered and paid for both. Silver tried hard to get into her ice cream rather than Brandan and Daphne's movements. Daphne clinched the armrest of the wheelchair like an invalid as Brandan pushed. When Diego joined Silver, practically sucking up his banana split sundae, she asked, "Ready to leave?"

"Not really but you are," he said.

Silver and Jill jumped around Silver's new house like two Mexican jumping beans. It was ready for Silver and Lemar to move in. Almost everyone was present—Sebastian and Jill, Paula, Abigail and Diego, who met the family for the first time. Everyone seemed skeptical about Diego at first but he seemed to win them over with ease. Mom Savoy was there, too, but she stayed far away from Diego, barely allowing him to shake her hand.

The contractor had done an amazing job. Light was everywhere and shone perfectly against the southwestern theme Silver had picked.

Silver stood in the middle of the living room in front of the wood-burning fireplace and looked around. She recalled her entire eighteen months and reveled in how far she'd come from Todd's murder to her charge and ultimately becoming a single mom.

"Congratulations, deah," Paula Mitchell said, entering the living room. "I'm taking Lemar and Abigail to the big house for a snack. Abigail, come help me with your cousin. Do you mind?" Jill's place was now called the big house considering the new addition.

"No, not at all. Thanks, Paula," Silver said sincerely. Paula had come around more since she and Silver enjoyed an unspoken truce. Paula seemed particularly attached to Lemar.

Nevertheless, Paula's words could still be minced with Silver and vice versa. There was no reason for them to take their new way of relating to each other in giant steps. Baby steps were appropriate and palatable, but the wheels of miracle steel turned slowly for both Paula and Silver. Jill was just grateful the once adversaries were cordial to each other.

"How about some tea?" Jill offered from Silver's kitchen.

"Don't mind if I do." Silver laughed.

Sebastian and Diego walked around the house, surveying the structure and entertaining each other with their knowledge of all things boy.

"Silver, my cab is outside. I best be going now. That pan over there is full of fresh apple cobbler. Dig in and make sure you return my baking dish," Mom Savoy said.

"Why did you call a cab? I would have taken you home if you needed to leave early," Jill said.

"It's all right, baby. Y'all just have a good time," Mom Savoy said and left.

"Mom Savoy didn't feel comfortable being here. You notice how she was when Diego tried to kiss her hand?" Silver asked.

"Yeah. She's depressed. She said Brandan is miserable. Apparently Daphne is running him ragged," Jill said.

Silver cringed at the mention of Daphne's name. She'd hoped her silence would steer Jill away from the topic.

"Did Pat ever give you a clue why Daphne got fired?"

Silver poured water into two mugs she'd retrieved from a gift box from Abigail. "All I could get out of her was that Daphne lied on her original application. Because it's a signed document, there's no statutory limit to the company exercising the falsification rule. That I found out on my own."

Jill poured honey in her tea and stirred. "It's a shame that Brandan got caught up in mess with that girl. His insurance is not footing all of the bill for her hospital stay, which has reached hundreds of thousands of dollars. With Daphne not working, Brandan is spent. Their dream for a house is long gone." Jill sipped the tea.

"I'd offer to help, but I know he wouldn't take it," Silver said somberly. She sipped her tea as well.

"I know. I offered help, but Brandan wouldn't even talk to me or Mom Savoy about it. He just said no."

"Oh well, he's grown," Silver said. She recalled seeing Brandan at the ice-cream parlor. She hadn't mentioned to anyone other than Diego how bad Brandan looked.

"So how does it feel having been officially named the director for a month now?" Jill asked.

"You know, I have to admit, Daphne was on her game about a lot. Some of her records were impeccable," Silver answered.

"Why only some?"

"Because I haven't gone through everything as of yet," Silver answered.

"You have really grown. I'm so proud of you," Jill said.

"Why? I didn't do anything."

"Oh yes you did. You've weathered some serious storms and came out on top. And now you're giving props to Daphne Savoy. Whew, you've really grown," Jill said.

"Don't get carried away now." Silver laughed.

Silver was milling about her office, going through some file cabinets when she came across a bulky file that seemed out of place. It contained a mountain of loose pictures. Silver gathered all of the pictures, but one stood out among the rest. She pulled it out and studied it closely. The photo included a "big mama" type woman in the center, her hands wrung with anticipation. Daphne on one side, who must have been her puny little brother, displaying a wry smile, on the other. Silver could imagine the deviousness Daphne mentioned. The woman looked sad. Silver turned the picture over and read in Daphne's handwriting: *Grandma, Daphne and me.*

Silver turned the picture back over and wondered what the story was. What could have happened in their family that caused Daphne to act out so? What pain had Daphne endured to cut off her family without so much as an invitation to her own wedding. Silver knew these were questions that would probably never be answered. Still, she wondered why the folder was left.

Silver worked steadily on several projects until the end of the day, but the picture file continued to plague her. She realized most of her Co-workers were gone and thought it the best time to return the folder to Pat since Pat was senior management. She knocked on her door and entered. Pat was on the phone but waved for Silver to wait. She ended her call, and Silver placed the folder on her desk. "I would have given this to your secretary to send out to Daphne, but I wanted you to be aware of it first."

Pat picked up the folder, looked through it and dropped it back on her desk. "Thanks. It must have gotten mixed up with some other folders I sent you. Thanks," Pat repeated. "I'm surprised you found that thing."

Silver squinted and crossed her legs.

"I can't spell it out for you, Silver, but if you happen to find things out on your own, I wouldn't be able to stop you." Pat placed a thick reference book on the bookshelf adjacent to her desk. She swiveled back around and continued speaking. "You know technology can be our friend, but sometimes it can be our worst enemy. How torturous it must have been to be a part of a system that revealed your ultimate demise." Pat shook her head.

"Stop speaking in riddles, dammit," Silver demanded. "I'm not Batman and you're sure not the Joker."

"I'm going home for the evening. Be sure to lock up when you're done. Perhaps you want to peruse the classified system we've installed. If you're caught, it'll be your word against mine as to how you got in here. I promise you that one."

Pat gathered her things and left. It didn't take a mathematician to compute that Pat was leaving definite, undeniable clues. But clues to what? It was obvious Pat wanted her to figure something out, so she checked her watch, called on her sister to take care of Lemar and got to work.

Silver had been typing for hours when she stumbled upon a classified field of top management dossiers. She studied some of the head directors', including Pat's and found nothing of alarm. A separate file held past director's files, including Daphne's. Silver's heart raced. When she tried to access the file, she discovered a password was required. Silver tried several times to no avail. Something in her bones clued her to type in *Darnel*. She did, and a huge document opened up.

According to the document Daphne was forty, not in her early thirties as she had led everyone to believe. The file also revealed Daphne was born to a Brazilian mother and African-American father, which explained her thick wavy hair, which Silver swore was a fantastic weave. According to the history section, Daphne's father was enlisted in the armed forces, allowing Daphne and her family to live all over the world until the family settled in a small town near Corpus Christi, Texas.

Silver scrolled through several pages about Daphne's life, stopping at the final one, which documented her employment with Sci-gex. Next to her name was the code 999, which was foreign to Silver. She skipped around and found the key that explained all the codes There she read, 999: FALSIFICATION OF RECORDS AND/OR FELONY RECORD IMPRISONMENT. Silver skipped back to Daphne's history and learned she had served time in a juvenile facility until she reached adulthood, when she was released and her record expunged.

Silver wrote down the dates. She forged ahead with a Google search and several articles popped up about a pre-teen murder case involving Daphne.

For two more hours, Silver pieced together what she thought was the greatest scam of the twenty-first century. Daphne had a host of charges, including records tampering, checks and credit card fraud. The same attorney who had miraculously had all charges against Brandan dropped some months earlier, seemed to work magic in Daphne's life several times.

"That's probably why she was so confident during our case," Silver said aloud. She took a break when the words on the screen began to blur. She realized she couldn't continue to print items because she was leaving a paper trail. She tipped over to her office and retrieved a key ring hard drive. The gadget was no bigger than an extra-long thumb, but it could hold up to 128 megabytes of data and she could secure everything safely.

Silver helped herself to a bottle of water in Pat's fully stocked fridge and continued working. In a minuscule box in the right hand corner of one of the screens, Silver was able to access the most confidential information. She read it several times to make sure she was reading it right. Apparently Daphne had been married to a foreign diplomat for fourteen years, and he had all her delinquencies obliterated from her record. Daphne was riding on diplomatic immunity. Attached to her information was a situation Silver was sure Daphne thought would never come out. Silver saved everything on the key ring hard drive, shut down the computer, grabbed her things and fled.

Silver sat in the parking lot of Brandan's building until the wee hours of the night. She called her sister to assure Jill that she was all right and that she needed some space to clear her head. Silver couldn't bear to tell Jill about the truth she hadn't fully comprehended.

On several occasions the lights to Brandan's place flickered on and off, and Silver wished she could reveal everything, but no matter how much her ego desired it, her gut forced her to realize now wasn't the time or the place.

Silver rubbed her temples until they were sore. Her gut was speaking again, and it was telling her the one person to help her through the mess she'd uncovered lived not too far away. The notion was crazy but when Silver found herself in front of Paula Mitchell's condo at 3:00 A.M., she knew nothing was as it had seemed.

When Paula invited Silver in for a cup of tea an hour after Silver resolved herself to ask for help, Silver knew for sure that she was involved in a situation beyond retrieval.

"You have proof of what you speak?" Paula asked as she poured the steaming hot liquid. She fixed herself a cup as well and sat down. "Here, deah." She pushed the cup in Silver's direction. "This will help you to remain calm. No sugar. Enjoy the natural flavors."

Silver pulled the metal hard drive from her key ring. "You have a computer with a USB port?"

Paula nodded.

"Then it's all right here, every bit of deception that woman has perpetrated since being on this earth."

"Let's get to work." Paula sipped heartily, placed the cup down and led Silver into her home office.

Chapter 15

A Fish Bowl in a Glass House

Silver had been on a secret mission with Paula Mitchell for a week before Paula declared it was time to disclose all of the information they had gathered.

Silver felt like she was in the middle of a live soap opera and she desperately wished she could turn the channel. However, what was going on was not a soap opera, a reality television show or a fairy tale. It was real, and her best friend was being hurt by an evil, deceptive person who would bring Brandan down with her if she could.

Silver and Paula decided Silver would drop off the information at Daphne and Brandan's, figuring Daphne's behavior would determine if Silver would ever have to tell Brandan. They hoped Daphne would confess. Silver had decided, however, if Daphne hedged one millimeter, she would disclose everything, a task she wasn't particular about enduring.

Silver switched cars with Paula and they put their plan in motion. Scrunched down nearly under the dash, she waited in Brandan's parking lot until she saw him leave for work. Thank God his pattern hadn't changed, she thought when he skipped out the door and shielded his eyes from the bright sun with his forearm. He looked around suspiciously before entering his car. Silver noticed he had on what looked like an Armani suit she hadn't seen before. For a moment Silver became sad about his suit, which hung from his shoulders as if on a wire hanger. Brandan didn't know he was living a lie, so why wouldn't things go on normally?

When Silver felt it was safe to sit upright, she rummaged through her purse, found her cell and dialed. In seconds Paula picked up.

"It's done already?" Paula questioned, skipping the formality of hello.

"I haven't done anything yet. Paula, what if Brandan knows? I mean how can he not?" Silver rambled.

"We've talked about this, remember? Don't get off the task at hand. If Brandan knows and is living this lie voluntarily, you and I will deal with how you will accept this as his friend."

Silver listened intently to Paula's pep talk, ended her conversation then called Brandan's office. When he answered, she hung up since she knew he was safely thirty minutes away, so he couldn't pop home and surprise her.

Cautiously, she approached the front door of Brandan's building and inserted her key. Fortunately for her, Brandan hadn't changed the locks. Daphne sat in the front room puffing on a joint like she was the queen of the universe.

"Oh my God, I thought you were Brandan. What the fuck are you doing here using a key that you aren't authorized to use?" Daphne asked, trying to extinguish the marijuana. "Get out. I'm calling the police." Daphne wobbled to the phone. Silver beat her to it and snatched the cord from the wall.

"We're going to have a little talk first," Silver said. "I'm going to keep my comments brief." Silver's voice was steely. "I know your dirty ass secret and everyone in this community, the job, Brandan's job will know if you don't come clean."

"I don't know what you're talking about, bitch." Daphne picked up marijuana stick, flicked her lighter and inhaled heavily. The distinctive stench almost knocked Silver back out the door. "I'm not going to say it again. I know and everything I know is all documented right here. You have three days." Silver turned to walk away but every fiber in her body told her to turn back around.

With limp force, Daphne stood had picked up the heavy crystal ashtray, still filled with residue and flung it toward Silver's head.

Silver ducked and lunged back at Daphne with all of the rage her mind and body could hold and smacked Daphne so hard, Daphne's frail body fell backward into the seat. Silver clenched her fist to pound Daphne's face and caught herself on the edge of evil. "You have three days. You don't tell Brandan I will. And when everyone finds out what you've done, I guarantee you, I won't have to do anything because you won't have a moment of peace." Silver said out of breath. She turned back around and took a slow walk back to the door. She picked up the envelope with all of the proof she needed in the world and flung it toward Daphne. Daphne moved quickly, the envelope missed her head.

"You move fast for a dead woman." Silver sneered.

"I'm not the one's who's dead, bitch. But when Brandan finds out what you've doctored up, you will be dead in his eyes. He loves me!" Daphne yelled.

"Not after he and the world finds out who you really are. Can you imagine the torture you'll experience once the neighborhood, your former co-workers and manufactured friends find out you're a fraud? Think about it. Three days to tell him or I will. If I'm wrong, stick around and take your chances, if I'm right, I suggest you be gone." Silver stomped out of the house and left the door wide open. "Three days Daphne or you'll be the next one in the local paper." Her voice trailed the wind.

"That wasn't part of the plan, Silver. You weren't supposed to confront her," Paula said over the phone.

"I know but I couldn't help it. You had to see her face, Paula, and the way her voice changed was scary." Silver had stopped near her old apartment to catch her breath.

"Silver, this is serious business, and to get through this you're going to have to get over your anger quickly. You don't have that luxury. Now it's all about Brandan. I need you to stay focused. If there is an air of corruption in your actions, it will be a lot more difficult for you and Brandan to recover. Do you understand?" Paula asked.

"I hear you. I do."

"Great. Don't deviate from the plan again. I'm here to help you," Paula said and they hung up.

Three days had passed and Silver hadn't heard anything. She knew Brandan couldn't have been told about Daphne's secret, otherwise she would have heard from him.

Silver drove to Brandan's dealership a visit. No need in putting off the inevitable.

"What are you doing here, Silver? I don't have time for any crazy shit."

Brandan glared at her then gave her a look she knew meant he was fed up before shaking his head and continuing to work.

"Brandan, I do need to talk to you," Silver said cautiously.

"I haven't seen or heard from you in months, and all of a sudden you need to talk. Why not talk to that thug I saw you with at Applegate Farms?" Brandan placed some things in a file drawer and slammed it shut.

"His name is Diego, and he's just a friend, Brandan."

"Dude," he paused, "your life. You want to hang out with that character, go ahead. Just leave me and my wife out of it. Tired of you bitches and your shit, man," he mumbled.

"What did you call me?"

"Did I stutter?"

Silver took a deep breath. Brandan was angry but she couldn't let his mood steer her away from her plan. "Brandan, I need to talk to you. I know it's odd, me showing up out of the blue and all, but you have to know how serious this situation must be." Briefly she pondered that Brandan may have seen the information she left with Daphne, or maybe Daphne confessed. As quickly as she pondered Brandan's knowledge, she released the thought. Brandan was angry about something for sure but he wasn't enraged, not for what he was about to find out.

"Silver, speak or you need to go. I have a lot of work to do." Brandan got up and placed a file in the adjacent cabinet near the door, shoving Silver out of the way with sheer momentum.

"Not here. I can't talk to you about this here. Please meet me at this address as soon as you get off. Trust me, it's important."

"Silver, I'm not playing any games. I'm not meeting you anywhere. Say your peace and leave," he said as he sat back down.

"Like I said, I can't say it here. It's about Lemar."

Brandan looked up. He looked skeptical. "I'm sick of you and your crap. This better be about Lemar 'cause I swear, Silver, I won't have another thing to do with you or anyone else. I'm done."

Silver placed Paula's card with her address on it in front of Brandan. He picked it up and fingered the edges.

"Please meet me at ten-thirty. I know it's late but it's after Paula's last client."

"Since when did you and Paula Mitchell mend fences?"

"A lot has changed since you've been away," Silver said. "See you at ten-thirty." Silver left, gingerly she closed the door behind her.

Toni Staton Harris

Silver peeked through the window and watched Brandan climb the stone-walled steps. She sat back down on the couch and waited for Paula to escort Brandan in. His demeanor hadn't changed from the hostility she'd seen earlier.

Paula ushered Brandan to the couch next to Silver. He scooted to the edge, his legs wide opened, his hands clasped between them. "I don't have a lot of time. What's this about?"

"Would you care for something to drink, deah—tea, water or anything?" Paula asked, pouring herself a glass of water.

"No. I want to get this over with, now," Brandan asserted.

Paula handed Silver a glass of water but Silver couldn't drink. She held the glass between her fingers so tightly she feared it would crack.

"Brandan, we're here to discuss you and Silver. She's come up with some information that's critical to your life, and she thought she should share it with you here. Perhaps I can help make the news easier to bear." Paula sat down in a swivel office chair, somewhat of a distance from Brandan and Silver, creating a circle.

"I told you, Silver, if this isn't about Lemar, we're done. I told you." Brandan stood.

"Brandan, please don't be angry with Silver. I don't condone lying but she was really concerned that you wouldn't come, and it's imperative that you have this information," Paula said.

"I'm listening." Brandan stroked his goatee.

"Do you have any idea why you're here?" Paula asked.

"Do you?" Brandan said.

"I'm asking because I'm wondering if you had a conversation with your wife recently about some information we've uncovered," Paula said. Silver moved to the far corner of the room.

"My wife is in Texas. She skipped only leaving a note, so Paula cut the psychobabble bullshit and tell me what's going on or I'm leaving," Brandan yelled.

Silver rose and planted herself at the window.

"Silver, come sit back down and tell Brandan what you've found," Paula implored.

Silver sat near Brandan who emitted a cold breath of air. She rubbed her face and spoke. "It was brought to my attention that Daphne had some trouble with the law and stuff, so I started digging around and found out that the rumors were true. Daphne was fired from Sci-gex and—"

"Silver, I know all of that. Get to the point," Brandan interjected.

A deluge of tears fell to her feet. Silver couldn't imagine having to do anything harder than she had to at that moment.

Brandan's shoulders softened along with his voice. "Okay, stop crying. What's going on, Silver? Just tell me. What did you do?"

Silver kept shaking her head as the tears continued to flow. "I can't do it, Paula. I can't say it."

"Yes, you can. Just say it," Brandan begged.

"Brandan—" Paula pulled her chair toward him and grabbed his hand—"you have to understand, Silver uncovered some concrete and verified information vital to your marriage and your life as you know it. Daphne has some secrets that I suspect will dramatically change your existence. For all intent and purposes you were...are married to a woman, but Brandan, Daphne is a transgender."

Brandan snatched his hand away and wore a mystified expression. "What are you saying? What are you talking about?"

"Brandan, Daphne's birth name is Darnel Dixon. He had a sister named Daphne Dixon whom she murdered as a child. Daphne is actually Darnel. She was born a man." Paula's calm tone did nothing to ease Silver's loud wails.

Brandan stood and paced. He walked back and stood over Paula. "You're saying my wife is gay? You can't be saying she was a man. I would know. You know how many times we've had sex?"

Silver managed to pull herself out of her crying hysterics. "Think about it, Brandan," she said. "Remember the name Darnel kept popping up at the house? You even said mail was coming to her house in Darnel's name. That's because Daphne was once Darnel."

"This is bullshit. Bullshit, Paula. My wife is my wife, and she's not gay and she's not that crazy shit you're talking about," Brandan yelled. "What, Silver? You caught Daphne with another woman or something? Why would you say this?" He shook her.

"No, Brandan, Silver didn't catch your wife with anyone. We're not saying she's gay. We're saying she's a transgender—one who cross dresses as the opposite sex, but they are free to be the gender they were born at any time. A transsexual is one who chooses to live as the opposite sex but doesn't go through with the operation. A transgender is one who actually undergoes severe hormonal therapy for up to twenty years and has several gender-based operations to completely change his or her organs. Your wife is a transgender. In fact, she is featured on several Internet sites devoted to the subject." Paula offered copies of articles to Brandan.

He swiped them out of her hand.

"Brandan, I know this is very hard for you. It's almost as hard for us to tell you this, but you have to understand; we had no choice. It would have been worse for Silver to withhold this information," Paula said.

"Silver, why? What are you trying to do by making this shit up?" Brandan turned to her and pleaded.

"It's tr-ue," Silver said, hiccupping. She wouldn't look Brandan in the eye. Instead, she sipped on the water Paula had given her, which made the hiccups worse. "When I found out that Daphne was Darnel, I went online, and I was able to pull up the death record for Daphne Dixon. That was the sister. A copy of the death certificate is in the folder. Daphne was using her dead sister's identity. She had to keep going back to Texas because her grandmother found out and was pressing charges against her in Texas."

Brandan grabbed his head and shook it.

"That's not it..." Silver said.

"But it's enough." Brandan stopped Silver from speaking. "I'm not listening to another word. I'm going home and waiting for my wife, who hasn't been there in three days. Have you said this shit to her?" Brandan got in Silver's face.

"She's not there, Brandan. I told Daphne if I was lying to stick around, but if I'm not to be gone." Silver trembled.

"Who the fuck are you to make that decision about my life?" Brandan kicked a chair clear across the room. "Where did she go, Silver?" He grabbed and shook Silver by the shoulders.

"I don't know."

"What do you mean you don't know?". Brandan yelled.

"Ahhhhhhhhhhhhhhh!!!" He picked up the chair he had been sitting in and threw it through the window. Glass shattered everywhere and two short stories below on the pavement. Both Silver and Paula hit the floor. Moments after she realized she hadn't been harmed, Silver stumbled to her knees, her attention toward an enraged Brandan. "Brandan, you've got to understand!"

"Silver stay the fuck away from me. Stay the fuck away!" Brandan stormed out before she could finish her statement.

Silver fell to the floor and wailed. Paula wrapped her arms around her, all the while explaining how she'd done the right thing.

"Now the healing can begin." Paula said as she rocked back and forth with Silver in her arms.

As if her week wasn't heavy enough, Silver sat waiting impatiently for an appearance before an arbitrator to settle her pension claim on Lemar's behalf. The hearing couldn't have come at a worse time.

"I don't want you to say anything. Our position is clear. Ms. Boyd doesn't have a leg to stand on. It's already been deemed conclusive that your son is entitled to a fourth of his father's pension as one of his heirs. Cheryl Boyd can't block what's rightfully Lemar's. Do you have any questions?" Silver's attorney Mac asked.

Silver shook her head. Tears hadn't left her eyes in days.

"I advised you to be silent in there not out here with me. What's wrong?"

Silver didn't answer. She rubbed her eyes. It felt like tiny grains of sand were lodged between each lash.

"Ah, Miss James. Sir Elias MacDuffie, attorney fabulous, I take it this action will be swift." Kendrick Armstrong appeared with Cheryl Boyd by his side. "We're not enemies, Mac. Technically, we're on the same side."

"And if I stand knee deep in this shit long enough, you'll tell me it's mocha." Mac said.

Kendrick laughed. "Let me speak with you for a moment." He pulled Silver's attorney to the side.

Silver and Cheryl stood side by side. Silver didn't have the energy to send hate.

"You won't get a cent of my husband's damn money," Cheryl whispered.

"He wasn't your husband, but he was my baby's daddy. My DNA test came back conclusive. How about yours?" Silver shot back, referring to the questioned paternity of one of Cheryl's kids. Each one had a different daddy, only her youngest had been proven biologically Todd's.

"You bitch I'll see you in hell first," Cheryl said in an eerie hushed tone between grit teeth. "Come on, Kendrick." She yelled.

Kendrick abruptly ended his conversation and followed Cheryl.

Silver shook her head and followed Mac through the arbitrary doors. All she could do was pray.

"We really need to deal with this as a family, not just with the two of you hatching hair-brain schemes on how to tell a man—a black man— that his wife was a man. You know how crazy that sounds?" Jill said to her mother, Silver and Mom Savoy who were eating Saturday brunch.

"Have you heard from him?" Silver asked Mom Savoy, stirring Southern

Butter Pecan cream in her coffee.

Mom Savoy shook her head, wearing a look of despair. "I called the police, and they said we can't file a missing person's report yet because it's only been a couple of days."

"Silver, did you go by Daphne's place?" Jill asked.

Silver nodded. "Nothing. The doorman at Daphne's place said he hadn't seen Daphne in months, so that was before the accident. But that doorman to her building is always asleep. He was asleep when I went by there one day to inquire about Brandan or Daphne so I wouldn't hang my hat on his information." Silver sipped her coffee. "I wish I hadn't told Brandan."

"You had to, Silver. This was bound to come out," Jill said.

"Lord, I pray God's mercy on her soul—or his soul," Mom Savoy said, talking about Daphne. "How somebody with so much wickedness...the world is going to hell in a hand basket."

"I have to say this. We must keep our anger toward Daphne in check or when Brandan comes back around, we won't be able to help him." Paula looked around at each of them. It's healthy that we continue to refer to Daphne as a female because that's what we know her as. We don't need to keep throwing this mess in Brandan's face."

"That makes sense," Jill said. "Where do you think Brandan can be?"

"Lemar has been grouchy and hard to manage, and it's almost like he senses Brandan's absence and that something is terribly wrong," Silver said.

"Out of the mouth of babes," Jill said.

Silver reached down and pulled her vibrating cell phone from her hip. She pulled off an oversized earring so she could hear. "Yeah, hey...what's up? You sure?...For real?...Okay, I'll be right there...No, it's okay. Thanks, thanks so much...I'll see you in five." Silver placed the phone on her hip and put her earring in her jean pocket. "Diego said that Brandan's at the Nickel Bar. He's being volatile, and Diego's trying to keep him at bay."

"Why don't you take Sebastian with you?" Jill yelled.

"No. Just watch Lemar until I get back. I'll call." Silver was out the door.

When Silver entered the, dark room, aromatic of old beer and harsh whiskey, Diego was over in a corner near a pool table trying to reason with Brandan.

"You don't know me, nigga. I don't care who you date!" Brandan was shooting balls everywhere. "Back off, man. I'm not drunk."

Silver slowly walked over. "Brandan, let's go home."

"Silver, my best friend, my pal, my buddy. Where is home, Silver?" Brandan asked.

"How much did you give him to drink? Has he been here all night?" Silver asked the bartender.

"He just got here. He hasn't had anything to drink," the bartender answered.

Silver grabbed Brandan's head. "You okay? Huh? Come on, talk to me. Where you been?"

"Everywhere and nowhere," Brandan said. He pulled away and continued with his violent one-man pool game.

Silver didn't smell any alcohol emitting from his body. What was fueling Brandan was pure hatred and rage.

"Diego, that's your name, right?" Brandan asked after the last ball hit the wall.

Diego nodded.

"Did Silver do it?" Brandan asked.

"Do what, man?"

"Tell you about my wife?" Brandan answered.

"Brandan, don't. I haven't discussed anything with anyone outside of the family." Silver closed her eyes and silently prayed for Brandan to refrain from disclosing any information.

"Oh, my best friend didn't tell you?" Brandan sauntered around the table and planted himself in front of Silver who silently beseeched Brandan to quiet. "My wife was a dude."

"A what?" Diego asked. His head snapped back and forth between Silver and Brandan.

"You heard me, a fucking dude, man. But get this, she has a pussy. Ain't that some shit? And my best friend, my best friend over there is the one who saved the day, found all of the information and brought it to me." Brandan laughed and continued taking his anger out on the balls.

"Brandan, please. Just come home with me. Please," Silver pleaded.

"I'm not going home," Brandan said flatly.

"But you have to get out of here. It's too much. You have to go, man," the bartender said.

"Smitty, you kicking me out of your establishment?" Brandan asked.

"Yeah, man, I am."

"Brandan, let's go home, please," Silver begged.

Brandan threw the cue stick on the table, breaking the stick in half. He threw up his hands and stomped outside.

Silver reached in her purse and pulled out any spare cash she could find. "Smitty, I'm sorry for this. Give me a few days and I'll come back and pay for the damage, just let me get him home."

Smitty took the money, acknowledging Silver's deal with a nod.

Diego followed her. "Are you going to be okay?" he asked.

"I'll be fine," Silver assured him. She walked out and met Brandan who was in no condition to be by himself.

"Nice place," Brandan said as he emerged barefoot from Silver's new bedroom the next day.

Silver sat at the table, which was covered with the same papers she'd tried to show Brandan at Paula's office.

Brandan looked in the cabinets and the refrigerator.

"Grits are on the stove, Taylor ham and waffles are warming in the oven. You want some eggs?" Silver rose and grabbed a carton from the fridge. "How do you want them?"

Brandan didn't utter a word. He sat at the table and put his face in his hands.

"We have to deal with this, Brandan."

"Nothing to do," he said as he looked up. "My wife was a dude and I ain't know it. Nothing else to face."

Silver placed some scrambled eggs on a plate and set it before him. She pulled the meat, waffles and grits from the stove and sat down. "Did you know that there's a secret society of trans-genders and trans-sexuals. Everybody has been doing stories on it, all of the talk shows. I'm telling you, Brandan, some of these people you can't tell—"

"What makes you think I want to talk about this shit?" Brandan asked.

"Because you can't run from it forever," Silver said.

"And you make that choice? Again, another choice made for me but not by me," Brandan said.

Silver sat back at the table and pulled out a photo. "This is a picture of a Brazilian woman. This is a transgender. I don't think anyone would know otherwise. This thing is happening all over the world."

"But not with us. Black people just don't..." Brandan said.

"That's it, Brandan. That's not true. We have to stop saying what we as black people do and don't do. There is a worldwide society of this thing—blacks, whites, Asians, Indians, any ethnicity you can think of is a part. Nobody has a lock on this.

"When I first started looking into it, I wondered who would have the money for this. For a person to go from a woman to a man, the operation is a lot more costly but from a man to a woman, you can find doctors who would do it as low as ten thousand dollars. I've heard of breast reductions or augmentations costing more than that. In countries like Brazil and Thailand, you can find doctors who will do these things pro bono to gain experience or test out new techniques."

Brandan's silence lulled her into thinking he was at a place where they could discuss it.

"You talking about this shit like it's interesting, like you gettin' a kick out of learning about this shit. This ain't no game, Silver." He shoved the plate and glass on the floor, stormed to the bedroom and slammed the door. Silver was cleaning up the mess when he emerged from the bedroom fully dressed. "You can get that shit up from the side of the bed too. I puked. Couldn't help it," Brandan said and walked out of the door.

Silver didn't know where he was going, and she didn't try to stop him. Paula said extreme patience and time would be needed for this task, and Silver knew she had a long road ahead of her. Silver wanted to cry, but her tear ducts were dried up. She went to the bedroom to survey the damage. There was a large piss stain in the middle of her coral bedspread. Silver gasped and looked on the side of the bed, and Brandan had regurgitated like he had said. Clearly, the road would be longer than she thought.

Silver stabbed at her meal. Diego had convinced her to take a moment away from all of the ruckus going on in her life.

"How's your steak?" he asked.

"It's good," she answered.

"How would you know?" Diego laughed.

"I guess I don't really know considering I haven't taken a bite, huh." Diego continued to devour his. "I have to ask, is what your boy was spouting out at the bar true?"

Silver instinctively wanted to protect Brandan, but since he was stone-cold sober when he revealed the information, Silver thought it odd to lie.

"He's having some troubles in his marriage right now. Let's just leave it at that." Silver took a bite. The steak was tender and juicy.

"I hope it's not true. I couldn't imagine. If I weren't a cop and a fag approached me, I would blast his ass." Diego popped a piece of steak in his mouth.

"Sounds like you're a little homophobic. According to all of my research, you're the man to watch."

"You can watch me anytime." Diego grabbed her hand. "I would like it." Silver didn't respond; her mind was too numb.

"After dinner you want to go shoot some pool?" Diego asked, polishing off his meal.

"As long as it's not the Nickel Bar."

————————————————————————— *Toni Staton Harris*

Chapter 16

Pick Up the Pieces

Silver suddenly reflected on the past two years of her life. Enough had gone on and Silver longed for some peace. She nor anyone else had heard from Brandan in a month, since the day he walked out of her home, after vomiting on the side of her bed. He was definitely alive—his weekly check-ins with Mom Savoy had confirmed that—but not much else like where he was staying or with whom he stayed or where and if he worked.

Day by day Silver fielded the family's quizzical stares and rhetorical questions about whether Brandan had come to his senses and if she'd heard from him. The answer was still no.

Silver had her nose in a performance review document of an employee all morning, and her eyes were beginning to tire, so she stood to stretch her legs. She looked out the window of her corner office and appreciated the view. The downtown area was undergoing a major revitalization, and instead of a concrete jungle, Silver gazed at scores of full trees and a glistening waterfront that was once a swampy dump. She was still daydreaming when her assistant buzzed her to take an important call.

"Silver James speaking," she answered still standing.

"Silver, baby, this is Mom Savoy—"

"Everything okay?" Silver asked acknowledging the frantic tremble in

Mom Savoy's tone.

"No, baby, it's not. I need you to go over to Brandan's place. I just got a call from the property manager and the place has been trashed. They can't find Brandan anywhere..."

"What happened? Did they call the police? Who called you?" Silver asked, beginning to get hysterical herself.

"They don't know what happened. They think he was robbed or something. The manager's name is Merle, and she said to ask for her. Baby, I just don't have the heart to go over there," Mom Savoy said.

"No, no, no. Don't worry about it. I'll go right now and call you when I find something out."

"Thanks, baby. I'll be at home," Mom Savoy said and hung up.

Silver slammed down her phone, grabbed her suit jacket and purse and told her assistant to catch her on her cell.

Silver arrived at Brandan's apartment and walked through the door, which was already ajar. 'Excuse me, I'm looking for—" Silver pulled the piece of paper from her purse where she had written down the property manager's name—"Merle?"

"Are you Mrs. Savoy?" the woman responded.

"No, I'm Silver James. Mrs. Savoy can't make it, but I'm the next of kin." Silver extended her hand.

"Oh, I thought you looked rather young to have a grown son. I'm Meryl. Thanks for coming." She corrected Silver.

Silver tugged on her suit jacket. "What happened?" she asked as she walked around Brandan's apartment kicking debris. His sofa was slashed, chairs were turned upside down and his kitchen cabinets were destroyed. "Meryl, were the police called?" Silver asked, perusing each room. She climbed the stairs to the bedroom. It was a mess. The sheets smelled like they hadn't been washed in years and pizza boxes and plates with dried food were on the floor, and all of Brandan's clothes were yanked from the hangers and scattered everywhere. Silver held her nose as she surveyed the damage.

"The police were called and should be here any minute. I tried calling Mr. Savoy at work but his employer said he didn't work there anymore. We need to find out if this was a robbery or vandalism by someone else or Mr. Savoy himself." Meryl yelled upstairs.

Silver walked down the stairs, still holding her nose. "How did you get his mother's number?"

"Now that sounds like a question I should be asking." Detective Dowdy appeared in the doorway.

Silver sucked her teeth. "Always a pleasure to see you, detective," she said sarcastically.

He sneered. "More of your work, Miss James?"

Silver turned her back and spoke to Meryl. "Here's my card and my work and cell numbers. If you hear anything or need to contact me for any more information, please call me. In the meantime, I'll work on trying to find Mr. Savoy for both of us." Silver turned on her heels and stomped past Detective Dowdy.

"Wait a minute…" Meryl ran after Silver. "I need somebody to identify what may have happened here. I don't know if stuff is missing or what…"

Silver clicked her door locks open and turned, "I can't help you right now, but I'll be in touch." She hopped in her car and sped off.

On her way back to work, she decided to take matters into her own hands. She was going to find Brandan, whether he wanted to be found or not. She maneuvered her ear piece in her ear and commanded her auto dial to phone Diego. "Diego, this is Silver…I need a huge favor…I need to find Brandan ASAP…His place was ransacked…can I find a missing person's report?"

"Only if you really believe he's missing and there has been absolutely no contact with anyone in the family that could account for his whereabouts. And you need to be immediate family, meaning his wife or a parent of an under-aged child." Diego answered as if this question was common.

"I'm lost. His place is a mess and I don't know if he did it or not. His mom is the one who called me to find out what was going on…"

"I could put a trace on his license or credit cards for you. I'm not supposed to but anything to help you feel better." Diego said.

"Anything you can do to help, I really would appreciate it."

"It's done. I'll call you when I get something."

"Thanks." Silver said.

"Oh, oh Silver. How about we get together tonight. Love to see ya."

Silver paused only briefly and thought it not a bad idea. Diego was truly growing on her, the thought of his bulging muscles, milk chocolate skin and shoulder-blade length dreads certainly had appeal. "I'd like that." She finally answered with ease.

"Cool. I'll call you with plans."

"If I'm not at my desk, hit my cell." Silver disconnected her call and headed back to the office.

It was well after hours and Silver was still at work. The office was extremely quiet, and Silver took the time to catch up on some other tasks she had neglected, as her mind was still on Brandan and the apartment. She arranged for Jill to pick Lemar up from day care and thought to cancel her date with Diego, only to have her ringing phone interrupt her thoughts. "Whoa, déjà vu. I was just thinking of you," Silver said after Diego identified himself.

"I'd rather see you but if I can be in your thoughts, I'll take it for now," Diego said. "I found your boy—at least his car."

"Where? Is he all right?" Silver sat forward with her elbows pressed into the desk.

"I don't know about all that, but his car was actually abandoned on Route 95 just outside of Richmond, Virginia. A tow was called, and the car is still sitting in the state compound waiting to be claimed. If somebody doesn't get to it soon, it's going to cost him a fortune to get it out. He's already racked over five hundred dollars in towing, tickets and fines for abandonment, and the rate to be at the state pound is twenty-five a day—"

"Diego, I don't care about his car. I just hope he's okay. Richmond, huh?" Silver asked.

Yup. So now that I've done my job, how about we hook up after you finish yours?" Diego asked.

"Diego, I need a rain check. I have to make a run. I'll call you tomorrow. Cool?"

"Has to be," Diego said with obvious disappointment.

Silver hung up and decided to close shop. She had someone to see, someone she now knew could point her in the direction of Brandan's whereabouts.

Silver made her way to the Bloomfield/Montclair border where she caught an impressively chic Savannah Thayer, Brandan's ex-girlfriend, coming out of her condo. She was obviously stunned by Silver's appearance.

"Oh, hey Silver. What brings you to these parts?" Savannah asked, not breaking her stride.

"Hey, Savannah. Look, I don't mean to take up your time—you seem obviously in a rush—but I was wondering if you could help me out."

"Well, I really am busy. I have a minute but not much more."

"I'm not sure if you know anything, but Brandan has left town. Apparently, his car showed up in Virginia, and his family didn't think he had any contacts there, but I was hoping you could help us out," Silver said. She stood on the bottom step, eye to eye with Savannah who was

———————————————— *Toni Staton Harris*

on the top.

"Ahh, I would uh, love to help you out, Silver—" she ran her fingers through her hair and tossed it—"but I can't. I don't know anything about Brandan being in Richmond."

"Richmond? Who said anything about Richmond? I said Virginia, but I wasn't specific." Silver paused. "Look, Savannah, I'm sure you don't really know what's going on, but hiding Brandan isn't helping him. He has to face some demons and…"

Savannah placed both of her hands out in front of her. "How sweet it is."

"Listen, his place has been burglarized, and I need to get in touch with him—"

"Silver, please spare me. If there's an emergency, call Brandan's mother and she'll pass the information on. He's been in contact with her, or didn't you know that?"

Mom Savoy hadn't mentioned Brandan contacting her regularly and that fact unnerved Silver. However, now was not the time to reveal any anxiety.

Savannah placed her hand firmly on her hip. They eyeballed each other until Savannah looked away. "You know, it must not feel good."

"What are you talking about, Savannah?" Silver knew, but she wasn't about to give Savannah any satisfaction, especially since the last time they spoke she had tried to help her.

"It's funny. Now you need information from me. You need my help. Okay. Yes, I do know where Brandan is, but he doesn't want to talk to you. He doesn't want anything to do with you at all. You would do well to respect that. Now I have to go. Should something really come up, here's my card. Give me a call, and I'll be happy to oblige." Savannah handed over her card and skipped down the stairs, donning her shades.

"You *are* dumber than I thought." That comment abruptly halted Savannah's stride. Savannah turned around and looked at Silver with her glasses at the tip of her nose. "That's right. At first I thought you were real dumb—you know, hanging around a man who never wanted you. He even married someone else, and for almost two years, that same man didn't remember you existed. And now, he comes crawling back to you, and you take him back and take his shit. You're sad, girl. Doing his dirty work. Now the deal is this: Brandan's place has been robbed. If he doesn't do something, the management is going to sell off what he has left, put up an eviction notice and put Brandan out, then he'll have nothing. He needs to know about it and obviously you're the only one who has the connection. Do what you must, but I would hate to be the one responsible for Brandan losing everything," Silver said smugly.

"Fortunately, I'm not the one responsible for him losing everything. You are. *Ciao.*" Savannah pushed her glasses back to the bridge of her nose and strutted off.

Silver's vapid interest in Diego's karate match was evident. Lemar looked on, jumping around with excitement even though he was too young to know what was going on. Every so often Silver casually glanced in Diego's direction and gave him a wink. When their eyes met, Diego seemed to kick a little harder, faster or with more precision.

Silver and Diego had been casually dating for several months. Their relationship had progressed but; Silver wasn't close to being in love or anything, however she was grateful for his company. Besides, he was really handy around the house, fixing anything left by the general contractor.

Sebastian and Jill didn't think it was such a good idea for him to be around Lemar, but Silver had to find a way to get over her heartache concerning Brandan. And for the moment Diego was the person to help her. Silver, too, had her reservations, Diego was a cop but he casually knew of Todd, he'd explained. He assured her that he wasn't going to let anyone or anything prevent him from pursuing someone he wanted.

Diego emerged from the competition victorious. Silver was glad the early-morning match was over. She anticipated receiving a special package from her attorney that day and wanted to get home.

Silver wrapped a towel around Diego's neck and kissed his sweaty cheek. She scrunched her nose to hide her displeasure of contact with his sweat but the kiss seemed to make Diego melt like butter.

"Let's go get something to eat. The Office is a good choice," Diego said, referring to the Montclair eatery. "We could have some waffles and mimosas." He packed his bag and tickled Lemar who didn't respond.

"How about I meet you? I'm expecting a package between noon and one at my house. As soon as it arrives, I'll hop in my car and drive over," Silver said.

"What is so important for delivery on Saturday?" Diego asked.

"A very important package. No big deal."

"If it's no big deal then why are you rushing to get home?"

"What? I'm not rushing to…" Silver stopped herself and took a breath.

"Look, just drop it okay. I don't need an argument. Not today," she said.

"I'm not trying to argue with you, Silver, but you're always so damn secretive—"

"Watch your language around my son." Silver covered Lemar's ears.

Diego's tone was quieter, but he did nothing about its firmness. "—about everything. I help you out every way I can, but I can't ever know why. Your boy goes and acts crazy at the bar, and I help you get him home. Then he runs off, and I put out a search on him as a favor and now you're waiting for some mysterious package, and you blow off a date with me, and again I can't know why."

"First of all, since when did we get down like that? Diego, you're cool and all, but this—" she pointed back and forth at them—"this ain't all that. Now you call it secretive if you want, but there are things you don't need to know, and Brandan is one of them. I don't understand why you're asking about him anyway. And if I did ask for your help, you always have the option to say no, and trust me, I wouldn't sweat it."

"Okay, hey, hey, I'm sorry. Look, I want us to be all that. I'm digging you, Silver, and I just like to know what I'm walking into, that's all. Why don't we do this? I'll follow you home, take a shower and relax at your place, and once you get your package, we'll go. Cool?"

Silver nodded hesitantly. She was still steaming.

"Is that cool with you, little man?" Diego tickled Lemar under his chin. Lemar didn't move.

Diego hit the button on the CD player in his Hummer. The thumping bass came through the speakers, but the loud rap music failed to wake an exhausted Lemar from his afternoon catnap. Silver leaned over to turn the radio down.

"What are you doing? Didn't you see *Rush Hour*? You don't ever touch a black man's radio." Diego laughed to lighten the mood.

"You don't touch a man's radio if your son isn't in the car listening to Dip Set. I love Cam'ron, but I don't let Lemar listen to it," Silver said, looking out of the window.

"That boy ain't budging," Diego said, eyeing the toddler from his rearview mirror.

"It doesn't matter. Turn it off or you can let me and my son out and I'll take a cab."

"You're always so hard. Why do you need to be so hard?" he asked.

"Just how I am. I have to be strong for me and my son. We've been through a lot," Silver said with some of the fight leaving her voice.

"You don't have to be so hard with me. That's why I'm here. I want to be there for you if you let me," Diego said.

He seemed sincere. Secretly, Silver wished she could let her guard down. As they rounded, Nisuane Park, she watched children running with kites, and others playing basketball. Little girls were pushed on swings, while others frolicked through the jungle gym maze, and Silver thought of times she and Lemar did the same.

"So did you call your attorney and find out why the messenger never came?" Diego asked as they took the path back to her house.

"I left a message. That's all I can do. I know he's going to get a piece of my mind having me wait for an hour and a half." Silver continued looking out the window.

"Maybe the messenger left the package by now," Diego said.

"It had to be signed for so he'll have to bring it back," Silver answered.

"I would ask what's so important about this package, but I better not."

Silver didn't respond. "Ooh, "she said, pointing," there's a van in the driveway. Maybe that's the messenger. Hurry before he leaves."
Silver jumped out and ran to the guy. "Are you looking for Silver James?" she asked.

"I am," the deliveryman looked on his clipboard—"

"You're late," Silver said, signing the board and fingering the package. Diego was busy getting Lemar out of the car.

"I'm not late. This is my second trip, and no one was home the first time," the deliveryman answered.

Silver shook her head. "Never mind. Thanks," she said, relieving him and heading toward her door. She wasn't in the mood to argue. It was more important that the package was there. Diego followed her in the door, Lemar contoured to his shoulder.

Diego placed Lemar in his bed then poured two beers while Silver tore into the package. Diego sat on the couch and watched her while she quickly scanned the pages of a rather thick document.

"Damn, that's it? I'm not settling for this, no way." Silver flipped the pages. Finally she put the package down and went to the kitchen, where she got on the phone. She left a message and rejoined Diego on the couch, sulking.

"Okay, what's wrong? And don't tell me nothing. Talk to me. What's up?" Diego asked, handing over the glass of beer he had poured for her. Silver looked at the glass with disdain. She picked up what was left in the bottle and tipped it to her mouth. "I'm involved in a lawsuit, and my attorney wants me to settle for five hundred dollars a month but not lay claim to something else that I'm entitled to." Silver sipped. Realizing she was being secretive again and absorbing Diego's pleading eyes, she relented. "Okay, okay. I'm suing Todd's widow or baby's mama for a portion of Todd's pension and social security. I know for a fact that each of her kids is getting about a thousand bucks a month from his pension alone and another thousand from social security and all of her kids are not his. My attorney is saying his widow is willing to settle out of court for five hundred a month and no social security claim, but I'm not going for it." Silver sipped her beer. It felt good to get her anxiety off her chest for a second.

"Well, you don't need the money, do you? You look like you're doing fine," Diego said, looking around her place.

Silver didn't like what he implied. She placed her beer on the table, crossed her arms and cocked her head to the side. "That's not the point. My son's future is important to me. I could use the money to go directly to his college fund. It's not like I'm going to use it for myself," Silver said.

"Yeah, but Todd had his family to think of. No offense, but Lemar wasn't the brother's concern. He treated all of those kids like they were his and they did lose their father," Diego said. He placed his glass down, and Silver immediately gave him the eye to use a coaster. He complied.

"Yeah, and Lemar will never, ever know his father. I never knew my father because he and his family denied my existence. If it weren't for my sister, I wouldn't have any family. And when my mother died, there was nothing left for me. I was almost put in a foster home, but my sister was found, stepped in and stepped up. So how Lemar came about, or even why, is irrelevant. My child deserves the same as Todd's other children, and if I have anything to say about it, he's gonna get it or I'll die trying." Silver gulped the last bit of beer and retrieved another from the fridge. The full glass Diego had poured sat untouched. Silver huffed. She regretted pouring her life story and motivation out to him in one quick swoop. "Besides, how do you know what provisions Todd Boyd made for his children? You said that you didn't know Todd that well, just casual acquaintances on the force together?"

"Whoa. You're right. I was just speculating." Deon paused. "Okay, baby, I'm on your side. I was just trying to give you another point of view. Don't shoot a brother. Come here." He kissed her neck and passionately massaged her breasts. He got up momentarily, dimmed all the lights, closed the door to Lemar's room and turned up the baby monitor in the living area.

He planted himself between her legs and slowly unzipped her jeans. His tongue found its way from her belly button ring down her naturally lined belly to the tip of her pubic hair-line. With his teeth he tore into her panties and pulled her pants to her ankles then off. Diego then ate Silver into ecstasy. Finally, he carried her to the bedroom where he finished her off, placing his manhood perfectly between her thighs, sopping up her juices.

He quietly maneuvered her onto the pillow, gathering the T-shirt-soft comforter around her body. Afterward she rustled under the cover like a newborn. Disturbed by movement, Silver turned on her side, facing the door and opened her eyes. Her vision was blurry but she watched as Diego tiptoed to his duffle, and fumbled around. Silver sat up on one elbow and watched Diego's strange behavior as best she could in the dark.

"What are you doing?" Silver startled him.

"Just getting myself together. You know it's almost time to make that move." Diego answered coolly.

"In the dark?" Silver asked.

"I was trying not to wake you." Diego stood, brushed his knees and zipped his bag.

"Whatever. Silver rose and stumbled to the kitchen. She went to the fridge and retrieved a cold glass of water.

"Guess it's time for me to head out," he said. He knew the routine: Don't let the sun catch him going out the door. On several occasions, Silver made her position painfully clear. She and Diego were not a hot item, just something to pass away the time, even though Diego begged for more.

"So I'll see you tomorrow?" He grabbed her hips and swayed them to his rhythm.

"Give me a call and we'll see. We'll see." Silver stopped his motion like her feet were stuck in drying cement.

"You gonna get enough of putting me off, girl. I'll check you." She allowed him to softly kiss her lips. Silver didn't even bother to walk him out of the door. She peeped out the window and could have sworn she saw a lightning quick shadow pass by. She shook her head, assuming it was just Diego leaving after checking on things around the house. She reinforced the triple locks on her door and turned back in for the night.

Silver concentrated on her phone call to Jill. "I'm not going to hang with Diego anymore. It feels like Todd all over again, only there's no real attraction there. I'm just wasting my time," Silver said.

"I'll be the first to admit there's something creepy about him. And you can't replace Brandan through Diego," Jill said. "I know you miss Brandan more than anything. I miss him too. My mother thinks it's healthy that Brandan relinquishes his contact with you right now. She said it's obvious he still associates you with his misery and you both are better off away from each other until he's able to process his grief. I just hope he's getting professional help with it somewhere," Jill said.

"I doubt that. Paula offered, but Brandan wants no part of her either. He's running, Jill, and I just want to help him catch up, you know?"

"I do. But you can't help someone who doesn't want your help." Jill paused. "I must say that I'm glad for you and my mother's newfound relationship. It's quite refreshing."

Silver had to agree. It was nice to have some elderly wisdom in her corner. "Something positive did at least come out of this tragedy." Silver responded as she thought, *Why do I always have to forfeit one piece of happiness for another?* Nothing was worth her losing Brandan, nothing, and now she was in no position to help him, and it pained her soul. Friendship should never cost this much.

Silver ended her conversation with Jill and thought it might do her well to leave work early. Besides, she had to check on Brandan's apartment; go to her new favorite store of late, Home Depot; pick up Lemar; get some groceries and cook, all before seven. Lemar was on a nice sleeping schedule and Silver did her best to keep it.

Getting everything done would be nothing short of miraculous. However, some way she'd have to figure it all out. She had no choice. She bade Pat good night, having great confidence that her bid proposal to promote a new account was in order. Eclectic Designs was an organization that made elaborate gift baskets designed to fit anyone's personality, and the distribution was about to go international. If Silver cultivated it correctly, this small account would be in her large accounts division in no time.

Her first stop was Brandan's place. When she walked to the door, she didn't even know why she bothered. The eviction and notice to sell off the remainder of Brandan's things was posted to the door. Silver didn't even take the notices down; she just slumped off, devoid of all hope. She didn't call Mom Savoy to tell her what was going on. After she found out that Mom Savoy had been in contact with Brandan just like Savannah said, Silver didn't have much to say to the sweet old lady. Mom Savoy gave up no clues as to where he might be.

Silver crossed that chore off her list and planned to get Lemar, make a quick stop to the grocery store then head home for an early dinner. Much to her surprise, when she reached the daycare, Lemar had been picked up by Jill already.

Silver emerged from the grocery store in darkness. She tipped the stock boy who placed five bags of groceries in the back of her truck then headed home. The house was unusually dark. She decided she'd call Jill once she got in and got settled so Jill could bring Lemar home.

Silver gathered all of her bags so she didn't have to make more than one trip. At her front door as she fumbled with her keys, she received the hardest thump she had ever experienced to the back of her neck. It winded her and knocked her down immediately. She didn't even have time to scream or see who hit her. She dropped her bags.

The hits never stopped coming. "Over your dead body, the voice said in an altered human state. Thump...thump...thump repeatedly lodged against her head, neck and back in a smooth almost rhythmic pattern. Silver couldn't move. She lay there, unconscious, with a stream of blood coming from her mouth.

A cantaloupe from her discarded bag fell out and rolled toward the woods. The shadow that appeared suddenly disappeared beyond the trees following the rolling fruit.

Toni Staton Harris

Chapter 17

It's A Different World Than Where You Come From

The place was vague, but the scent of Black Love incense was unmistakable. Silver pushed through the curtain of red, black and green beads. There was a familiar portrait on the wall. It was a giant-sized man with a curly black afro, a generation of his people struggling etched on the canvas as if looking in his brain. A noose was around his neck and one tear formed a track down his cheek.

Silver walked in farther. The Al Green eight-track reverberated on the console. The smell—fresh collards, Brother's Barbecue, deep-fried fish, fried turkey, sweet-sauce ribs and barbecue chicken—came from the kitchen.

Silver walked through the doorless walkway. A strange woman was at the stove stirring the collards. She was silent but she smiled. She tilted her head in the direction of the back door.

Silver looked down. She was barefoot in a flowing yellow dress. She found herself walking gingerly on old rickety steps that led to the concrete backyard. She passed a table full of a variety of salads. Silver stuck her finger in the potato salad and savored the flavor. "Ummm," she said aloud. The mixture of pickles, the right amount of mustard and mayonnaise worked to delight her tongue.

"Don't forget the dessert table," somebody said. Silver looked around but people seemed to ignore that she was there. She didn't recognize too many folks. Like magic she made her way to a table filled with her favorite homemade desserts—seven-layer chocolate cake, pineapple coconut, 7-Up cake and pineapple upside down cake. But the biggest of all, the Red Velvet stood proud, and just as she reached to run her finger through the butter-cream frosting a stinging whack came across her behind. "I told you about sticking your tiny fingers in my cake," a familiar voice said. Silver turned around and hugged her mother with more energy than she thought her body could hold. "Welcome home, baby. Y'all, my baby's home." Silver couldn't have felt more alive.

"We have stabilized her, but there is massive swelling on the brain. We won't know if she has brain damage until she wakes up. She's suffered severe trauma to the head, and brain damage is very possible, almost inevitable." The surgeon squeezed Jill's arm. She wanted to fall apart, but Sebastian was there to hold her up.

"Has anyone gotten in contact with this Savannah person?" Paula Mitchell held an air of calm. No one answered. Brandan hadn't contacted Mom Savoy in the last two weeks so Savannah was their only link to him. "Mom Savoy, did you try the last number you had?" Paula asked.

"I did, baby, but it's disconnected. I don't know where my son could be now."

Paula tried to comfort her daughter. Silver had been beaten horribly. When Jill found her, she thought she was dead. Silver was lying in an inordinate amount of blood, her lifeless body cold. As a doctor, Paula knew Silver's survival was based on when Jill found her. The only thing that could sustain her from this injury was sheer will.

"Y'all, my spirit is telling me it's time to pray for this child," Mom Savoy said. Without a word everyone present complied.

Silver was exhausted. She walked around meeting relatives she hadn't known. She felt protected and loved and didn't bother to question why she was there or even how. That was until she saw the one person who stopped her heart.

"Hold her tongue. Nurse, get them out of here, please," the doctor barked. Hesitantly Jill, Sebastian, Paula and Mom Savoy stepped out to the hallway. "What's going on?" Jill asked frantically.

"She's having a seizure. You must stay calm." Paula gripped Jill's hands and stroked her daughter's hair. "She's fighting. That girl is fighting some demons right now. We have to be strong for her." Paula turned her attention to Silver who was on the other side of the glass. "Yes, fight, deah. Fight and be strong. You can do it," Paula whispered to the glass.

Silver stroked his face. It was old and worn but affable. His strong, wiry beard was colored with salt and pepper. He didn't speak. Instead, he put his head down. Her body reacted on its own. She hugged him and placed her head on his chest. At first he didn't respond, but finally she forced his arms around her. She responded with the relief of a lifetime of pain and misery. "Daddy," she called out.

"Baby, you have to go get some rest. She's stabilized. Besides, you have to go check on Lemar and Abigail," Paula said, having spent another night at the hospital.

"They're fine. I talked to Sebastian's parents already. I'm not going anywhere until I know my sister is all right. Besides, she could..." Jill couldn't say it much less think about her life without Silver.

Sebastian approached with a cup of chicken broth, courtesy of the vending machine. Jill sipped it and almost puked. It had the aroma of chicken, but it tasted like coffee grinds had infiltrated it.

"I have connections in the psych ward. Why don't you take a nap over there? It's not far, and if anything should change, I'll come and get you," Paula pleaded.

"You're not getting rid of me that easily. I know what you're doing, you're trying to commit me. No way. I'll get in there, they'll confuse me with someone else and try to strap a white jacket around me. No way,"

Jill said as she paced the room.

Paula and Sebastian laughed hard, and Jill joined them.

"What is he doing here? Mommy, I don't understand." Silver asked, pointing to Todd Boyd who sat in a corner playing chess with someone Silver couldn't name.

Silver's mother gave a wide grin and nudged Silver toward Todd. The ground sank beneath her feet as she remained barefoot, her yellow dress flowed in a cool and pleasant breeze.

Silver stood before him, but anger wasn't in her heart. Compassion seemed to replace any vile feeling she ever held. And even though neither one of them spoke, it was understood.

Paula was relieved she had finally convinced Jill to take a nap. When Paula dropped her off, Jill was surprised that the psych ward hospital rooms weren't draped in the nightmarish white padded walls she had imagined. Instead, there were serene browns and greens and comfortable furniture.

Now it was Paula's turn to release the anger, hurt and frustration she had pinned up and taken out on Silver for many years.

Paula tipped past the monitoring machines and planted herself directly in front of Silver's head. She looked at the young woman who could clear her of the guilt preventing Paula to be whole again. Paula knelt.

"I know you thought I hated you. I actually hated myself. I've always loved you, deah, and I wanted to love you. Everything about you was the goodness of your father that made me fall in love with that man from the first day I met him. You even hold some of the things I disliked about him." Paula stood and paced the room. "But his faults were not your fault, and I'm sorry. I'm truly sorry. Deah, I promise if—no when—you come back to us, I will make that up to you. Every time I made you feel unwanted or perverse for being alive and being present, I'll make it up to you. But, I need you to fight. I know all that you've gone through, and it pains me that your best friend isn't here to see you through, but you have to fight. You deserve to be here, and I need the chance to make up for all the pain I've caused you and to help you fight. Fight." Paula kissed Silver on the forehead and used Silver's bed sheet to dab her eyes. She stroked Silver's cheek and stood at the sound of someone coughing.

Paula turned and recognized the stark man whose eyes held sadness.

"Detective, how may I help you?" Paula asked, tugging at her clothes.

"I came to check on Silver's condition. We're working hard to find out who did this to her," Detective Dowdy said. "It's unfortunate we can't question her, but we do have some clues. I was hoping she'd be awake by the time I made it here."

"Well thank you. She's stable, but she's not ready to wake yet. She will though. She will," Paula said.

"Here's my card, ma'am. We're posting a uniformed officer outside her door for protection. Please call me and only me if something should change," Detective Dowdy said.

"Is there something else I should know or something you're trying to tell me without telling me?" Paula asked intuitively.

"No. Just be careful, and I'll be in touch," Detective Dowdy advised. Paula watched his strong gait as he walked out the door.

The pleasant breeze had turned into a typhoon and night was near. People scrambled to get the remaining food into the house. The crowd was quickly thinning. They were already home; it was Silver who had to leave. One by one the guests seemed to disappear.

"Where is everybody going?" Silver asked her mom as she picked up the bowl that was filled with potato salad.

"It's time to go home, baby. It's time for you to go too. The party is over, sweetness." Sweetness. Her mom often called her that even when she was bad. Her mom always said it was to remind Silver that she was sweet even when Silver had been mischievous.

"I'm not going anywhere. I'm staying right here with you." Silver dropped the bowl and clung to her mother.

"No, baby. I thought you'd gotten it, sweetness. It's all about forgiveness. That's how you let love out and in. It's all about forgiveness. That's how you replace all that venom with peace and tranquility." Silver's mother smiled and continued taking the bowls in the house.

Silver followed her, leaving her bowl.

"Besides, you can't stay here. It's not your time yet, baby. You have a lot of work to do. There's somebody who needs you more than he needs himself. And although he blames you, you have to fight for him and with him."

"Who? Brandan, Mama?" Silver asked.

She smiled, knowing full well that Silver knew the answer.

"I don't know how to help him, Mama. I don't know what to do or what to say." Silver shook her head.

"No, no, no, baby. Don't do that," her mom said as if she read Silver's change in aura. "You just have to give him what was taught to you here—the power of forgiveness. That's the key, baby. Forgiveness is one of the most critical properties of love and joy. Forgiveness is not an easy road but it's a conquerable one. Now go on."

Silver reached for her mother but she was gone. Everything around her was gone, and all Silver saw was blankness.

The night pardoned the day's stubborn intrusion. Jill pulled opened the blinds, and the sun streamed through. It had been a week, and while Silver's condition hadn't worsened, she hadn't awakened either. Paula kept saying since the attack, Silver's body needed rest and at all costs, her body was going to take it.

Every day, Jill was by her sister's side, wiping her brow, brushing her hair and praying Silver would come back to her.

"Sweetness, you've been here too long. It's time to go. You can't hide anymore." Silver heard her mother's voice but couldn't see her. "You have everything you need, now go. I'm always here for you. I'm always with you…"

"…we need you, baby. It's time. You've been away too long." Silver heard another voice. She also heard background noise she couldn't quite make out. She tried to open her eyes, but they seemed glued shut. She heard someone say, "Get me a warm towel. I need to wipe her face." The touch was soft and inviting. Finally, Silver was able to open her eyes.

"She opened her eyes, she opened her eyes," Silver heard the voice say. A noise sounded as if someone ran out the room. Silver heard someone say in the distance, "She opened her eyes, y'all. She's back."

Silver heard more noise as if bulls filled her room and surrounded her.

"Oh my God, Silver, baby girl, I'm here," Jill said.

Silver tried to open her mouth, only that seemed glued shut too. She finally formed enough saliva to speak. "Daddy gone. Daddy gone," she whispered.

"Silver, honey, I'm here. What are you saying?" Jill asked.

"Daddy gone. He's not here. I saw Daddy. He's not here, but he's okay," Silver said.

Jill asked a barrage of questions. In a broken tone, Silver answered all of them. She continued to repeat that she knew her father was dead but had made peace with him. Silver's doctor entered after hearing the commotion on the floor. "She's a little delirious. Is that normal, doctor?" Jill asked as he examined Silver.

"It is normal," he answered, "we need to take her for some examinations, check for brain damage and such. We'll have her back in no time. I'm confident she's going to be okay now." The doctor and nurses wheeled Silver out and the family rejoiced.

"Oh, praise the Lord. Lord, let your name be praised," Mom Savoy said. "My sentiments exactly, Mom Savoy. My sentiments exactly." Paula clasped her hands in joy.

"Baby, you need to get on your knees and thank the Lord for your sister coming back to us. You should pray, baby." Mom Savoy said to Jill.

"I don't really know what to say," Jill said.

"Baby, just say what's in your heart. God wants us to talk to him from the heart. Come on, let's all gather 'round." Everyone complied with Mom Savoy's wishes, and they formed a circle.

"God, um hello. It's me, Jill—"

"Yes, Lord." Mom Savoy's interruption startled Jill a bit, so she paused.

"Go on, baby. Go on," Mom Savoy urged.

"Um, I, we just want to thank you for bringing my sister back to us. We ask that she will be okay and in good health. And we—"

"Yes, Lord, we thank you," Mom Savoy said jubilantly.

"Yes, we thank you, Lord." Jill actually appreciated the help. "Yes, we thank you. And, Lord, we ask that you take care of Brandan too. He's hurting, and we want to help him but we need you to get him to want to be helped…" Jill was now on a roll. Mom Savoy kept praying as Paula and Sebastian looked around. "Thank you, Lord. Amen."

"We ask these things in your precious Son, Jesus's name. Amen," Mom Savoy ended.

"Wow, that was great," Jill said, feeling relieved.

"Yes, baby, God is good all the time, and all he wants us to do is just talk to him. It ain't no big secret on how to talk to God. I would love for y'all to come to church with me sometime. It would sure make my day."

"I would like that. Yes, all of us," Jill said. They then sat around in silent meditation.

Two hours passed before Silver was returned to her room. Some color had returned to her face. She still spoke with heavy pauses and hushed tones, but the doctor said she'd suffered no brain damage and her spine seemed well and intact.

Paula walked in the hospital room looking sad. Silver and Jill ceased their game of chess, waiting to hear what she had to say.

"Silver wasn't delirious when she first came out of the coma. She's right. Monroe Mitchell is dead. Here's the obituary." She threw the paper and it landed on Silver's rollaway table, toppling the pieces.

"My father is dead? When?" Jill asked, scanning the paper. His passing wasn't particularly shocking. He had been dead to Jill for many years. But what was disconcerting was the fact that no one from his family had informed them.

He had died five years ago from liver failure. "I wouldn't be surprised if he hadn't drunk himself into oblivion, wishing to be with your mother, Silver. He loved that woman with all his heart. He wanted to be with her, but I promised I wouldn't let him go. When your mother died and he couldn't be with her, I lost him for good. He was in our house in body but never in spirit. I knew all about you, Silver. And when you surfaced, I prayed every night you'd go away. When Jill chose to care for you herself, I shunned my own child, and you've paid ever since. Please forgive me. You didn't deserve my hatred and neither did your father, but I couldn't shake it. Hatred. It's a horrible thing that eats away at your very insides until you can rid yourself of it. I vowed if I had a second chance with you, I would fight tooth and nail to erase it and make it up to us both. I deserve happiness and joy too. I'm starting here and now. Will you meet me?" Paula bent over and held out her arms.

Silver looked up and remained silent. She heard a familiar voice again: "Haven't you gotten it? It's called forgiveness…" Silver yanked Paula toward her and buried Paula in her chest. It was that moment that she knew what she would do once she got out of there. If she and Paula could resolve their differences, nothing would stop her from helping Brandan, whether he wanted it or not.

Silver limped and needed a cane to help her into her house. Cards, balloons and streamers were all over the place. Pat and several of her workers with the help of Jill and Paula organized a welcome home. Silver embraced them all. She and Lemar laughed and ate. Guests arrived, bearing enough food to last Silver a month, others came with gifts or smiles, and Silver graciously accepted it all—until Diego showed up.

Jill without reservation asked him to leave. Silver limped to the door and accepted three-dozen roses. "Thanks, Diego." She thought his visit odd considering he hadn't called or visited for the five weeks she had been in the hospital.

"I know what you're thinking. But Leu—" Silver cocked her head, indicating she didn't know of what or whom he was speaking— "Detective Dowdy said your visitation was restricted. I hadn't talked to you since your accident and you weren't really interested in seeing me anymore so I thought it was best to stay away."

Silver squinted and looked to the left. "We had a conversation about me not being interested in seeing you?" Silver couldn't recall it. She couldn't deny it because, according to her family there was a number of things she couldn't remember. But that was from people she trusted. She didn't feel as though she could trust Diego.

"Um, yeah, we did. You know you broke my heart but I understand. I could tell you weren't really feeling me. But hey, if you change your mind, you know my number, right?" Diego asked.

Silver didn't answer right away. She was still trying to recall their conversation, but nothing came to mind. "I'm sure I do have your number somewhere around here. Hey, thanks for coming by," Silver said, limping toward the door.

"If you need anything, please don't hesitate to call," he said at the threshold.

Silver smiled, acknowledging his kindness and allowed him to leave. She made her way back to the middle of the room and continued to enjoy her party.

Some hours later, as the crowd finally dwindled to just Jill, Paula and Silver, the doorbell rang again. "Somebody want to get that?" Silver asked. She made no bones about the fact that she was uneasy about doors.

"It's okay, baby girl. Why don't you get that?" Jill prompted. "Trust me, you're safe. There's an armed officer who sits right outside your door. Nothing like what happened will ever occur again."

Reluctantly, Silver wobbled to the door. She hoped it wasn't Diego. She didn't have the heart to make him leave, but she didn't have the mind to desire him to stay. She opened the door slightly. When she mustered the courage to look through the crack, there Brandan stood, looking even more regal than she had remembered. His beard had more salt than before. He stood there in worn jeans, a black t-shirt, tube socks, open-toed flip-flops, and a diamond still sparking in his ear. It wasn't a dream. It was truly Brandan standing before her.

"Oh my God," she said as she flung the door open. She dropped her cane and with all of her strength wrapped herself around him and cried.

"So how long have you been in town?" Silver questioned. It was in the wee hours of the morning and once Brandan made his surprise appearance, everyone left to give them space. Jill and Sebastian swiped a sleeping Lemar from his bed to take care of him for a few days.

"Three days," Brandan answered, picking up dirty glasses.

"Three days, and you're just getting to me tonight?" Silver asked. Brandan didn't say anything. "So how long you plan on staying?"

"Where does this go?" Brandan asked, referring to a crystal punch bowl.

Silver opened a cabinet and pulled out a movable shelf. "You plan on answering my question?" she asked.

"I'm not sure. Depends on how I'm needed around here."

"What if I told you I need you for an eternity?"

Brandan looked at Silver awkwardly. "What are you saying, like permanent, as in relationship?" The words sounded foreign the moment they slipped from his lips.

"No, Brandan, I don't mean like that. Actually, I don't know what I mean. I can't say that I definitely don't mean it in that way. What I'm

saying is, my life—Lemar's life, Mom Savoy, Jill and Sebastian, even Paula—
is miserable without you. You've been the missing link. I'm glad you
came back, for whatever reason, but I need you to really get how much I
love you, man."

"Well good." Brandan paused. Silver hoped he might say he refused to
live without them too. "When I heard what happened, I wanted to be in
that bed right next to you. I love you, too, Sil, and I forgive you. I'll be
here as long as I can, but I can't promise you an eternity."

Silver sulked. Brandan didn't speak as she dreamed and hoped for.

"You know, when I got back to town, all of the mess I left—"

"You mean ran from," Silver interrupted.

"Left, ran from, whatever. I'm not going to fight with you to be right.
I didn't want to be here, and it took everything in me not to tell that
cabdriver to turn around so I could get on the next plane heading back
west."

"West?"

"Yeah, west. Silver, I went as far away from this shit as I could. I left
Virginia, only stayed in Atlanta for a few days then I made connections
with some folks from school who live in Sacramento. I stayed there for a
few months, but I'm in Oakland now. The only thing keeping me here for
the moment I'm here is you and your well-being. When my time is up,
I'm out. And I can only give you a piece of what I have. So if what I'm
offering is not enough, I'll go hang at my mother's for a minute and then
I'll head out. But if you understand what I'm saying, I'll hang here for a
minute. And we'll see where we go from there."

Silver thought about everything Brandan said. She had to remind
herself that none of it was personal and to be thankful Brandan had
returned home.

"Brandan, you don't get it. I don't want to take anything from you. I'm
just glad you're home. I just want to help you, that's all. I want to return
the many favors you've given to me." Brandan walked to her, and they
embraced so tightly it felt like eternity.

Silver was still working from home six weeks after she was released from
the hospital. As she had predicted, Eclectic Designs was boasting high six
figures in sales a month after going international. It was the fastest
growing account in seven years. She and Pat were discussing some minor

discrepancies when Brandan used his key and entered.

"Hey, Brandan. Welcome home. It's so good to see you," Pat said.

Brandan retreated to Lemar's bedroom, closing the door.

"Did I say something wrong?" Pat was obviously offended.

Silver shook her head. "He's just not willing to see or talk to anyone other than immediate family. Sorry about that. He just needs to deal with everything in his own time and his own way."

"Well damn, I said hi, not 'how is it knowing you were married to a crazed freak who ruined everybody's life.' I mean geez..."

"Pat, let it go."

"No, Silver, y'all need to deal with this or him being here is doing no good. He's still running and you're enabling him if that's how he's dealing with people. I mean come on, everybody gets knocked on their ass in life."

"Not like Brandan has." Silver defended him. "And don't go there because you have no idea what it means to be a black man."

"Neither do you," Pat said seriously.

"I know what it means to be black. Look, one of the reasons he left is because he was tired of people staring at him, knowing what happened. I couldn't lie to him. I told him you knew about Daphne."

"And?" Pat asked.

"He flipped. He wanted to know why."

"What happened to Brandan was tragic, but a year later, it's time to move on, Sally. Move on. The only thing he's guilty of is not truly knowing that wench. And if it weren't for me, putting my job on the line so you could get the information, none of you would have known. For you to help him isolate himself is not helping him. Has he even talked to you about what happened?"

Silver shook her head. She hated to admit it, but she knew Pat was right and she was avoiding the inevitable. Just then the phone rang. Silver interrupted their conversation to retrieve it. She looked perplexed at the 510 area code. Silver talked for a brief moment and then called Brandan to the phone. He had to take it in the living room since Silver didn't have a phone in the bedroom.

Brandan spoke in hushed tones and chuckled. Silver's attention was thwarted to the living room rather than her conversation with Pat. After finishing, Brandan walked in the kitchen, got a glass of water and drank it in one gulp. He poured another, gave an evil eye to Pat, closed the refrigerator and walked out of the house.

"Wow, you need to do something quick," Pat said, gathering her things to leave.

"I don't really know what to say," Silver finally admitted in a sheepish voice.

"Oh shoot." Pat snapped her fingers. "I saw something months ago on *Oprah*. It's a little similar. Oprah interviewed men who were married and became transsexuals. Some of them even stayed with their wives, and their families accepted it and dealt with it. I'm sure we can get the transcript or a videotape of the show. Maybe that'll help break the ice. It was actually pretty interesting. And you know Oprah, she didn't sensationalize anything," Pat said.

"I don't know. It sounds like those families knew though. The problem here is Brandan didn't know, and I don't know that he even believes what happened to him," Silver said.

"But you have to try something. What does Paula say?"

"She said for me to try and show Brandan the research again and go through it with him. She also said a year might not have been enough time for him to heal."

"But it's enough time for him to start. Hey, it's your life. If you're okay with tiptoeing around him like this, do you." Pat put her hands up in surrender, kissed Silver on the cheek and squeezed her hands before walking out the door.

As soon as Pat left, Brandan returned. "I'm not a fucking experiment. I don't appreciate you talking about me with Pat like that. It ain't cool, and what I'm going through is none of her business."

"I'm sorry, Brandan. I think she was just offended that you barely spoke to her, that's all, and frankly I'm at my wits' end. I want to get past all of this, but it's like a pink elephant between us," Silver said.

"I don't need to talk about it, and that's that. I'm going out. You want something?"

Silver shook her head.

———————————————————— *Toni Staton Harris*

Chapter 18

"All Aboard...Leavin' on the Midnight Train to Cali"

"What the fuck..." Brandan cussed as he sped across the intersection of Broad and Market in downtown Newark.

"Brandan, calm down. What's wrong? You act like you've never driven in the northeast before. Watch the woman," Silver screamed.

"She shouldn't be crossing in the middle of the street against the light. If we were in Oakland she'd get a ticket. That's the damn problem with traffic in this area: nothing but complete chaos that would be solved if people would follow simple damn rules like cross on the green and not in between."

"Okay, you need to take it down a notch."

"Normalized dysfunction. Why are people allowed to double park like being on the side of a parked car is a space?"

"I guess it has been a long time since you've been around." Silver gazed out at the worn-looking pedestrians lugging heavy bags against the whipping wind. "What's Oakland like?" she asked out of curiosity.

"Easier," Brandan said. "You might want to consider coming out there, permanently." Three months had done nothing for Brandan's choppy tones and succinct conversation. Just because he was running from his past didn't mean that Silver was getting aboard that train. She liked

Jersey, and her family was here. Not that she knew anything else or any place else but to just up and move and to transplant Lemar was not in her best interest.

Brandan pulled into Silver's circular drive and retrieved several bags out of the car. Silver informed Brandan that she would grab Lemar from Jill's and meet him at the house in a few minutes.

"Cool, I'll start dinner," Brandan said. He entered the house just as the Spiderman tune began playing on his phone.

"Jules, hey...I can't really talk now. I'm tied up. I'll call you later, okay...I promise, I'll call you later...No, I don't know when I'm coming back. She's okay, but...look we'll talk later," Brandan said, hanging up the phone abruptly.

Silver entered the house alone a few minutes after Brandan.

"That was quick," Brandan said, entering the kitchen where Silver was putting away the groceries.

"Well Sebastian and Jill were going out tonight and Abigail and Lemar were staying at Sebastian's parents. They asked that I pick him up later. I want to get out of these jeans. Be right back."

Some thirty minutes later, Silver emerged in a scarlet silk lounger. She went around the house lighting candles. Since she had been home candles brightened the house but she never burned them, thinking of Lemar's safety.

With the room engulfed in a romantic glow, Silver rejoined Brandan in the kitchen where he was making his famous linguine and white clam sauce.

"Um, smells good," Silver said, easing herself into a chair. Brandan had a cold glass of Pinot Gris in her spot. She took a small sip. "What's the difference between Pinot Grigio and this?" Silver asked, pointing to the bottle.

"Same type of wine but one is French and the other is Italian," Brandan answered, juggling two pots, one cooked the clam sauce, the other water boiled for the pasta.

"I'm impressed."

"I've learned a lot by living on the West Coast. We're not too far from Napa, and Jules and I take Sunday rides to some of the wineries sometimes. The drives are peaceful," Brandan said. He placed the pots down and began crushing whole dried oregano in his hands and wiping it in the pot of sauce.

"Jules has called you a couple of times. Who's she?" Silver asked, taking a sip of wine that wasn't bad even though she would have preferred a Heineken.

"My roommate," Brandan answered candidly.

"Nobody special? Just your roommate?" Silver asked.

"Nothing special...just friends."

"How did y'all meet?" Silver asked. She sipped the wine slowly.

"She needed a used car, I helped her get one. She needed a roommate, and I needed a place to stay. She's working on her Ph.D. at Berkeley," Brandan said, stirring the pot.

"And y'all aren't intimate, never was any desire to be?" Brandan shook his head. "Why?" Silver asked.

"Because we both have things to do. We have our own separate lives going on. She has her room, and I have mine. We barely even see each other when I'm home. She just checks on me from time to time." Brandan began cutting garlic.

"Interested?" Silver asked.

"Nope."

"Why not?"

"Just not."

"Because of Daphne?"

"For the most part."

"Wow, that was easier than I thought," Silver said. She placed the wine down. She was starting to get a headache.

"It's true." Brandan wiped his forehead with the back of his hand. "At least you're facing it." Silver paused. When she saw it was safe to continue, she said, "Brandan, what happened is not your fault. Daphne was a sick, sick person—or I should say she is a sick person. You know Detective Dowdy thinks she's the one responsible for what happened to me. They have an APB out on her." Silver resumed drinking.

"If they catch her, they better not bring her anywhere near me. I would kill that bitch."

"Killing her won't change anything." Silver waited for a response. When she didn't get one she continued. "You have to commit yourself to healing from this. I never met my father, then I met him in my dreams. Brandan, I thought if I ever had the chance I would give him peanut butter in the desert. When I found out Paula was the main reason for me never seeing him, honestly, I thought I would want to kill her, but when I met that man in my dreams all I could do was hug him, and this joy was released in me. I didn't know how or why, but then I heard my mother say I had to forgive him in order to be set free from my anger. Paula said the same thing. If I go around hating my father or Paula for where my life is now, there would be no way I could survive and fight."

"So you think I should forgive Daphne?" Brandan sneered, sweeping the chopped onions into the pot. "Like hell," he said with venom. His back was to her as he spoke.

"Eventually you'll have to in order to release yourself from your misery. One day, you might even be flattered. That woman was so crazy in love with you that she actually did all that deceiving to have you. It wouldn't be the first time a woman has concocted some crazy scheme to be with you. Remember Allencia, your college girlfriend and how she was pregnant but not with your child? You almost dropped out and married that girl. See, you're always doing the right thing, and there's nothing wrong with that. You came back to a place that represents hell to you, just to make sure I was all right. Your time is almost up here. You'll be going back soon. I can feel it. But just like you're so ready to do the right thing for everyone else, do the ultimate for yourself. Start healing, Brandan. That begins with forgiveness. I know you know this because it wasn't long ago that you were talking this same stuff to me." Silver smiled and stroked his cheek.

Brandan nudged her away and continued cutting onions. She didn't have the heart to tell him that he had put more than enough in the pan and with all the garlic and onions they would be keeping the vampires away for weeks.

"I went to this counselor out on the coast. You know that mofo had the nerve to tell me I need to explore my inner child and my longing to be with men. He literally said it was my fault, that I drew Daphne to me. He had the nerve to say that I'm suppressing my gay tendencies. I stepped to him to whip his ass, so I got out of his office."

"Well, I don't think you drew Daphne to you out of being a suppressed gay man but I think you draw needy people to you because you want to be needed, and you are. But you have to understand that you're needed because you're loved not because you can fix something or help somebody. Sometimes the helper has to be helped."

"That's what Jules said." Brandan reverted to simple responses.

"Jules sounds like a smart girl," Silver said.

"She is. She's real cool people. Miss Juliet Bowls."

"Oh, her name is Juliet?" Silver asked. Brandan nodded. "But you call her Jules?"

He nodded again. "Everybody does."

"So what happened with Savannah? Is she out there with you too? I tried to contact her a few times before everything happened but she had moved."

Brandan sighed. His expression was heavy again. He shook his head. "What?"

"Last I heard, Savannah's back in Virginia. I hurt her bad. I know that. She came down to Atlanta with me. She hoped we were going to be together and stuff, but I couldn't do it. I fucked her and fucked her and fucked her. Every time I saw Daphne, and one day I almost hurt her. Damn." He slammed the knife down. "That's when I went to Cali. I needed a fresh start without all of the noise."

"Did you rape her?" Silver asked, astonished.

"No, nothing like that. She's a little woman, and she was dry and she asked me to stop because she couldn't get wet, but for a second I couldn't. She tried to scratch out my eyes. I almost blacked out."

"Was she okay?" Silver asked with genuine concern.

"Physically, yeah, but I messed that girl up. I didn't want to use her anymore than I had. I said I was sorry, but I didn't feel like it was enough," he said sadly.

"Give her a chance to forgive you, Brandan. You should call her and apologize again."

"That girl doesn't want to hear from me."

"You don't know that, Brandan. Remember, you can only control your actions, feelings and you. You can't control other reactions." Silver poured herself some more wine. Brandan was still cutting and his eyes were flooded. He tried to wipe his face feverishly. "Damn onions," he said.

Silver smiled. He was back to cutting garlic.

Two A.M. had come fast and hard. Brandan and Silver were still talking in the living room, listening to some music when the phone rang. Silver scrambled to get it, so as not to wake Lemar.

"Hello?" Silver said in a raspy voice. She didn't hear anything. "Hello?" she said again in an agitated tone. "Hello." Dial tone. She slammed the phone down and re-joined Brandan in front of the fireplace.

"Who is calling this late?" Brandan asked.

"They didn't answer. Some prank caller. Well, I guess that's my cue. I'll probably get three hours of sleep now. I should make your butt get up with Lemar tomorrow."

"I might. I might not even go to sleep," Brandan said. He reached for the headphones to the electronic system then tinkered with the dials and buttons and began searching through CDs. Silver looked at him lovingly and kissed him on the forehead.

At 6:00 A.M. sunrays came bursting through. Silver heard Brandan rustling with Lemar who was bent on blasting Elmo's "Hokey Pokey." "You're going to wake your mother, boy. No Elmo." Brandan tried to sound stern. Silver knew that was an act since Lemar had Brandan suckered. When the phone rang again and Brandan summoned her from her cracked doorway, she had no choice but to take the call. When she finished, she headed to the kitchen.

"Who in the world was that? I hope not that Diego character," Brandan said, feeding Lemar his beloved Cheerios.

"What do you know about Diego?" Silver asked as she dragged to the coffee maker. Brandan had already made a pot and the aroma alone should have been enough to wake her up.

"I know that that clown means you no good. I saw him leaving your house when I came home. I waited because I didn't want to confront him just yet. I don't like him for you, Silver."

"I don't either, Brandan. We've been through a long time ago. That wasn't Diego. That was Detective Dowdy. He wants to put another car outside. Now don't trip, but they have locked in Daphne's whereabouts. They haven't caught her yet, but until they do, Detective Dowdy wants me to be safe."

Silver watched Brandan tense up. She poured herself a cup of coffee, took a sip and coughed violently. She beat her chest.

"You all right?" Brandan asked, ready to spring into action.

"Strong. What is this?" Silver made an awful face.

"It's Hawaiian Blue. They had it at the store, so I picked some up. You don't like it?" Brandan asked, surprised.

"If you had warned me maybe. It's so strong," Silver said, sniffing the cup. She was scared to take another sip.

"You'll get used to it. It's smooth. So they're looking to pick Daphne up, huh?" Brandan asked between gritted teeth.

"Yeah. How do you feel about it?" Silver asked, then braved another sip. Brandan was right, now that she was braced for the second swallow, it tasted like chocolate.

"Are you going to answer my question?"

Brandan continued playing with Lemar and spooning his Cheerios. "Captain Brandan to co-pilot Lemar. We're coming in for a landing, *vroommmm…*"

Lemar laughed as if he was filled with pure joy. Brandan and Lemar finished their breakfast. Brandan picked Lemar up and proceeded to the bathroom where he bathed and dressed the little tyke.

Brandan re-entered the room with Lemar in tow fully dressed and ready for the outdoors. "You ready to go, little man?" Brandan asked. He had dressed as well.

"Where are my two favorite men going?" Silver got up from the table. She rubbed Lemar's head affectionately.

"Tell Mommy we're going to the park," Brandan answered excitedly. Silver gave Brandan a quizzical look. "I called Jill. She's at the big house. Lemar can sit with her for a minute while we talk," she said to Brandan.

"Talk about what?" Brandan asked. He grabbed Lemar's Nerf football and placed it in Lemar's hands. Lemar gripped it with ferver.

"You know about what. You haven't answered my question and it's important that we discuss the whole—"

"Kill that noise, Silver. Nothing is more important than my time with Lemar right now," Brandan said in a commanding tone. "And if you were smart, you wouldn't be passing this boy off to your sister every time you had something to do or needed to talk."

"What?" Silver asked defensively.

"You heard me. This boy is starved for your attention, and it's obvious you've been too preoccupied to give it to him."

"What?" Silver was incensed. "You've been here for a skinny minute, at best, and now you're going to lecture me about how to raise my child?"

"Silver, not in front of the kid."

"My kid, Brandan. My kid or have you forgotten?"

"Silver, I'm not going to have this discussion with you. Now I'm going to the park with *our* son, or have you forgotten? We'll talk about this later." Brandan gathered his and Lemar's jackets.

"No, we won't talk about this later because if you read the birth certificate, it reads that Lemar Todd Savoy James's father is deceased. You never signed it remember so this discussion is over," Silver yelled as she watched Brandan and Lemar head out the door to the car. She slammed the door so hard, she thought the pane would break.

Silver was seated at the table working on her computer when Brandan returned with a sleeping Lemar in his arms. She looked up, saw that Lemar was in one piece, rolled her eyes at Brandan and resumed typing.

Brandan emerged from Lemar's room, having put him down for his afternoon nap. He pulled a glass from the cabinet and poured himself some water, all in silence. Silver continued typing, refusing to acknowledge his presence.

"I want you and Lemar to come to Cali permanently. You'll have to learn to drink organic coffee. It's stronger but it's smooth and better for you." Brandan sipped his water.

Silver looked up. "Ain't nobody say anything about moving to California. Brandan, please."

"Nothin' here for y'all," Brandan said.

"Oh, now you're making decisions for me?" Silver typed. "I'm not going anywhere. My life is here, my family is here, my roots are here. I have this house, my job. I don't even know why I'm talking about this. I'm not talking to you." She turned and continued typing.

"Lemar is not being fed here. Even you're too stifled, still relying on Jill for everything." Brandan paused. When Silver didn't respond he continued, "Well, you have about two weeks to decide, then I'm out. My time is up here." Brandan finished his water and walked out of the room.

The days of Brandan's east coast tour had wound down. He made his rounds, trying to make his peace with New Jersey. He wanted to return to California with no strings attached. He finally got the nerve to call Savannah, to once again apologize, but punked out when a man answered. Luckily, he had remembered to block Silver's number.

Silver walked in and caught him packing. She didn't smile. He knew his departure was paining her, but he had to move on. Besides, he was following her advice. She was fine. She was even planning to return to work soon. He had convinced himself he was no longer needed, no matter what Silver said.

Brandan followed Silver to her bedroom, but she had closed and locked the door. "Sil, can we talk?"

"In a minute. I'm doing something right now," she yelled beyond the door.

"Where's Lemar?" he asked.

"Oh, at Jill's. Abby was helping him color. That moody boy acted like I wasn't even around. I'll pick him up later." Silver seemed almost jovial. "Hey, we can talk but do me a favor, why don't you put on some music and pour some wine. I got some red in the kitchen. I went shopping."

Brandan put on Tony Toni Tone's *House of Music*. He had always loved the group but since relocating to the Bay Area, he had Tony Toni Tone fever, considering that was their hometown.

"This CD is hot." Silver came out swaying in a platinum negligee. She was down from a size twelve to a ten, and no one could deny how scrumptious she looked, especially Brandan. They laughed and did some old school dances, each one trying to top the other with the whop and the running man.

"You know Raphael Saadiq was at the PAC with Ledisi?" Silver said as she danced.

"Oh, I know that was hot," Brandan responded. He kept dancing with her, perfectly in rhythm and amazing step.

"Man, I wanted to scream when that man took his shirt off. Brother got bod," Silver said, sounding old even to her ears.

"Dirty old woman." They laughed.

Brandan moved in closer. Silver took in his masculine scent and the hair on her arm stood straight. The track, "Let's get down" was playing and Silver enjoyed reminiscing. She could tell they were both getting over heated. She pushed away toward the console and turned the music down. "What are we doing?" She asked solemnly.

"Just letting things happen like they should have a long time ago." Brandan said seductively. He moved in again. He pecked her lips and then her neck.

For a brief moment, Silver was lost. She thought of what was happening before her eyes and remembered when she may have longed to hear those very words from Brandan's mouth. At that moment, she understood, Brandan's undeniable charm and trance like abilities. But in a brief moment of clarity Silver pulled away.

"Stop…" She said but Brandan continued. "Stop!" She shouted again. This time she turned her attention to the stereo and completely shut it off. "This is isn't right. Let's sit down." She motioned to the couch.

Brandan followed, obviously his manhood was leading the way.

Silver looked down. "I'm flattered. I really am, but Brandan we know this isn't right. Not like this and not under these circumstances."

"No it's right Silver, I can feel it." Brandan said breathlessly.

"No it's not right, Brandan. You and I have far too much to go out cheap like this."

"You just being stupid." Brandan pouted.

"No I'm not. And when you're in your right senses, you'll see what I'm talking about. Brandan I love you more than a brother and I'm not willing to risk our love and friendship on a cheap night of us going out like suckers because we are both horny and lonely. We're better than that. Trust me on this."

"We're not going out like suckers just because we take our relationship to a different level." Brandan asserted.

"No Silver, I'm still a man dammit and I need this, I need you like this!" He cut her off.

"No Brandan you don't. You don't need me like this and you don't want me like this, trust me."

"Speak for yourself." Brandan said and stood. "I don't have to put up with this…" He stormed toward the door, mumbling all of the way.

"Brandan don't run, where are you going?" Silver followed behind him.

"Far away from you." He shouted and slammed the door in her face.

Several days went by and short answers to shallow questions had returned as the primary communication between Silver and Brandan. Everyone noticed the tension and just chalked it up to Brandan's departure.

Silver didn't even want to participate in the going away party the family threw for him. When Brandan and Silver did speak, he tried to convince Silver that moving out West was best for her as well, but she really wasn't budging.

The party was going on full blast. Brandan left cards with his address and all of his numbers, including Juliet's cell phone. Silver left the festivities, sick to her stomach that she was losing Brandan once again. She took a walk outside to answer her cell phone, which had been ringing since the festivities began. "Hello."

"Silver, this is Detective Dowdy. I've been trying to call you all day."

"Sorry detective, I was busy."

"Well, I wanted to give you some good news. Daphne Dix has been caught. She's being detained for questioning. With that said and done we're relieving the patrol car of his duties."

"Wow, really?" Silver said somewhat deflated. *There really is no reason for Brandan to stick around now,* she thought. "That's great, detective. Um, detective…have you contacted Brandan Savoy about this information?"

"No, I haven't. Why would I need to talk to Brandan Savoy about an attack on you?" Detective Dowdy asked.

"Well Brandan was once married to Daphne and him hearing that you've caught her might stir some ugly feelings. I don't want Brandan going after her, so can we keep this information between us?"

"Miss James, I think it's wise we end this conversation. I don't want to hear of any vengeful or threatening action against a suspect, who by the way is denying all action against you."

"Thank you, detective." Silver hung up her cell and retreated to her place. She noticed that the patrol car that had been at her door was gone. When Silver opened her front door, her instincts kicked in, and she became nervous. Her heart palpitated as loud as the music and laughter from the big house. She looked out the front window. She tried calling up to the big house, but the phone was dead. Then the lights went out. Silver immediately dropped to the floor. Someone pounded on the front door.

Silver patted the floor until she found the poker from the fireplace. Stumbling to get up, she knocked over a chair and end table. The door was kicked open. A flashlight was pointed directly at her, and someone moved toin fast.

Silver couldn't get up fast enough before the figure stomped on her arm and kicked the poker across the rug. The figure reached down and grabbed Silver by her hair, and she went kicking and screaming across the room.

Silver's arm hurt, but she managed to grab the assailant's leg, causing the person to stumble to the floor. The figure sprang like a cat and used a kitchen chair to crash Silver across the back.

"Uhg," Silver cried out. "Don't do this."

The assailant kicked her in her ribs with what felt like steel-toed boots. "Over your dead body it will be 'cause, bitch, I'm happy to fulfill that request."

Silver was barely conscious when she heard rumbling feet and shots behind her. She thought they were the voices of angels. Several shots rang out and the person who kicked her slumped over her legs.

——————————————————————— *Toni Staton Harris*

Chapter 19

Boomerang

"If you ask me, I think you did this on purpose to keep me here," Brandan said. He smiled and stroked her head.

Silver coughed. "Please, man." She looked around as best she could. She knew she was back in the hospital. She tried to sit up, grabbed her chest and plunged back down.

"You're doing okay. Your ribs are badly bruised. The doctor said he just wants to keep you for observation. You took a pretty hard blow there, baby girl," Brandan said.

"What happened?" Silver asked through the shooting pain at her brow.

"You were attacked again," Brandan said.

"I know that, dummy. Do y'all know by who? I mean I heard voices when I was hit. I assume somebody else was there," Silver uttered then coughed. She motioned for someone to give her some water.

"Yeah. You were attacked by Cheryl Boyd, honey. She's dead. She was killed by the officer who was leaving his post. He saw her making her way through the door," Jill said as she poured ice water into a plastic cup with a straw.

Silver sipped as she finally focused. The gang was all there—Brandan, Jill, Sebastian, Paula, Mom Savoy and Detective Dowdy. The scene of her attack played in her mind again, but this time Silver would not be a victim and succumb to feelings of doubt and self-pity. She forced herself up, and

Brandan helped her to prop herself against a metal rod headboard.

"So is somebody going to tell me the whole story?" Silver asked.

"Honey, why don't we talk about this in the morning, when we know you're feeling a little better?" Jill said.

"Again, is someone going to tell me the whole story?" Silver was adamant about the truth. She had no plans of going through hell on earth again, ever.

Detective Dowdy stepped forward. "Silver, you are the victim of a five-year investigation involving, Todd Boyd, Diego Bradford, Todd's common law wife and Diego's half-sister, Cheryl Boyd.

Silver struggled to prop herself against the headboard. She wanted to listen intently.

"Diego was the best cop we had on the force. Right about the time when Todd Boyd got involved in a major drug ring, Diego was pulled in as an undercover to track and help us gather enough evidence on Todd. But something snapped with Diego and he not only became involved in the same ring, a power struggle ensued between the two of them.

"Right about the time when you and Todd became involved, a million and a half dollars, came up missing. Part of that money was fronted by the department for the sting and we believed that somehow you were involved or at least knew where the money was.

"After you showed up in the flower shop, Cheryl figured you were the point person because of some flowers that Todd used to give you. She didn't know that Todd was actually having a relationship with you, until Diego had you tagged and started tracking your whereabouts."

Silver grabbed her head as she listened. She studied the faces of everyone in the room so silent, a spider crawling on the wall could be heard.

"When did you realize I had nothing to do with the drug ring?

Detective Dowdy cleared his throat. "We weren't sure until the second attack and Diego confessed and turned states evidence."

"But I don't understand, why would they try to frame me for Todd's murder? Why murder him in my place, was that Cheryl's doing too?"

"That too was coincidence. Diego went to confront Todd about the missing money. He was at your place, apparently a meeting place on occasion, a struggled ensued and Todd's neck was snapped. His decapitation was ordered by the higher ups of the cartel as a warning to whomever had the money. Everyone assumed it was you. I'm sorry we had to let everything play out because we believed you were a part."

"So what about the second attack?" Silver asked.

"That was courtesy of Cheryl Boyd. She was bent on destroying you and became impatient when Diego wouldn't complete the job. Diego was smart enough to realize we were onto him and tried to lay low." Dowdy answered.

Silver had to cough, but her chest hurt so badly she didn't want to move.

"I'm sorry about all of this, but we've broken this case and you won't have to deal with any of this again. You don't even have to testify," Detective Dowdy said.

"Is it because of Diego's admission?" Paula asked.

"Yes. He's confessed to everything," Detective Dowdy answered. "We've also released Daphne Savoy." Everyone looked at Brandan who squinted.

"I'm not impressed." Paula folded her arms and stepped toward Dowdy. "Silver could have been hurt all because of your irrational assumptions."

Jill's eyes bugged.

"Lady, we protected Silver. My guys are the ones who saved her." Detective Dowdy said.

"You wouldn't have to if you had disclosed the information that she was in danger," Paula shot back.

"Lady, we are the police, and I didn't have to tell you anything. There was an important investigation going on, and we couldn't compromise it so that you would be satisfied how we were doing things. For a long time, we really believed Silver was involved and there was no evidence to refute that." Detective Dowdy said defensively.

"Well, we'll see about this. You can be sure that we'll be speaking with our attorney about legal recourse for this situation," Paula said.

"Stop. Stop it. I want everyone to leave," Silver said.

"But sweetheart..." Jill said.

"Jill, I want everyone to leave," Silver shouted.

One by one they kissed her and filed out. Silver wanted to do something she hadn't done in a long time. She wanted to cry in silence. Alone.

It was three in the afternoon. *Dr. Phil* blasted on the kitchen television set as Silver stumbled in to find a cup of coffee. For the seventh day since she had been home from the hospital Silver hadn't bothered to dress or shower. She would, however, brush her teeth.

Brandan was going from the living room to the bedroom, perfectly aligning his shoes along the sides of the suitcase. Silver stood in the doorway sipping on some good old-fashioned Dunkin Donuts Hazelnut coffee.

"I guess this is the day, huh?" she finally said.

"Yes, it is," Brandan answered, placing folded sweaters in the black restraints and zipping everything in tight. "You might want to get some air today. It's going to be nice, a high of fifty degrees, and since you haven't been out in a week, air might do you some good." He pulled his suitcase to its upright position and rolled it next to his matching suit bag already at the door. Silver noticed he had done a nice job of replacing his clothes since his wardrobe had been destroyed when his apartment was vandalized. She didn't dare ask where he got the money.

"My offer still stands, you know," Brandan said. He poured himself a large glass of ice-cold water and gulped it fast enough to warrant brain freeze. Silver didn't bother to answer. She already had. Brandan seemed to be close to finding his place in California, and that was great for him. She understood that too much had gone on in the Northeast for him to handle. And if he was to heal completely, Silver sensed it couldn't be with her. Now Brandan had to discover it.

Silver still had a lot of healing to do on her own. Pat had informed her that the company was going to offer Silver an exit package. With all of the time she had missed, the company could no longer afford to keep her on. Silver just added that layer of misery on the pile with the rest of it, believing her time at Sci-gex was up long ago.

There was one thing of which Silver was sure, and that was she couldn't follow Brandan's dream to set up a life anew a million miles away from her family, her support system and everything she knew and loved. Despite everything that happened to her, Jersey was her home and she wasn't running. Besides, what would she do in a state where her only ally was her only friend—Brandan, a man whose emotions were as stable as a pair of stilts on a tightrope?

If her sessions with Paula had proved anything, they helped Silver understand that she took herself where she went. So all that running wouldn't do her a bit of good if she wasn't complete with herself.

Brandan also tried the argument that her safety was a major concern. But with one of the largest drug busts in the state of New Jersey solved, Diego safely behind bars and Daphne well in hiding, she didn't anticipate any more enemies surfacing.

Besides, she had never even been to the West Coast, and from everything she'd heard, Californians were fake and syrupy. Silver truly wasn't interested in that. She had to remain tough and stern. If there was one thing about the East Coast she loved, it was that New Yorkers told you how they felt, where to go and how to get there with no hesitation. There was no pretense with them, and Silver was actually shocked that Brandan seemed to fit so comfortably in California, a place that seemed like Mars. Nevertheless, that was Brandan, not her. What would he say if she asked him to stay in the area they'd known and loved and helped each to work things out? He believed his time was up in these parts. There was nothing there for him and he had to do what was best for him. And that was exactly what he said.

Silver finished her coffee and rinsed the cup before placing it in the dishwasher. She dabbed her hands on a towel and asked, "So what do you have on deck for today? I thought maybe you, me and Lemar could go to The Office or the park or something." Silver picked up the phone to call the big house and have Jill ready Lemar for them to go out. Lemar had been staying with Jill and Sebastian since Silver's return from the hospital.

Brandan gently had her place the receiver back into the cradle. "My plane leaves at eleven tonight. You and Lemar could take me to the airport. I have to be there an hour and a half before take-off." He kissed her forehead and cupped her chin in his hands.

"I'm going to say my good-byes to Mom and my crazy sisters. I'll be back in time to grab my things and go." Brandan donned a lightweight black jacket as his phone rang. After answering, he continued his somewhat clandestine conversation in the living room. Silver moved in close and listened. "Yeah, I should get in about 6:00 A.M. your time…Cool, I'm coming into Oakland not SFO…yeah…yeah…I'm glad I'm coming home…Oh, okay cool. I'll catch a little sleep, and when you get in from class we'll head out." Brandan laughed and ended his conversation.

He was walking back into the kitchen to leave when he saw Silver dart across the room. He gave her a knowing non-condemning smile. "That was Jules confirming my flight," he said as he tossed his phone in the air and placed it in his pocket. "Well, I'll see you in a bit." Brandan turned back around. "I know we talked about this but my offer still stands for you to come to California. If not tonight maybe someday."

Silver didn't answer; her heart was too heavy. She didn't want to see him go. Even though he said she and Lemar could come out anytime, Silver felt a sense of permanency with Brandan leaving, like this was his last time being here, in Jersey, in her space.

"Oh—" he snapped his fingers—"I called Savannah. I just wanted to get some closure on some things, you know."

"I do. What happened?" Silver asked.

"She listened to what I had to say for a hot minute then she had to go. She hung up before I could say good-bye. She didn't say whether she accepted my apology or not, but I gave it."

"Well, you tried, right?" Silver smiled, masking a brave front.

"Yup. Well, I'll see you in a bit," he said. He checked for his phone and wallet and left.

The silence in the house was way too loud for Silver to bear. She turned on the stereo. When sound didn't emit, she yanked Brandan's headphones out of the console socket. She heard the familiar bass line as Raphael Saadiq crooned how he was still standing. It was that song again, Brandan's new anthem, his declaration that he was still a man. Silver couldn't take it. She turned the stereo off without stopping the CD first, not caring if her actions damaged it.

Still desiring to deafen the silence in her surroundings, Silver took a hot lavender-scented shower. For forty-five minutes she remained under the almost scalding water, which also washed away her tears; however, it didn't do much for the pain in her heart.

After her shower, Silver picked up the phone and dialed Paula. She could use her advice at the moment and the peaceful sensibility of Paula's voice. She was relieved when Paula answered her cell on the first ring. "Hey, it's me, and I really need to talk to you...Yeah, he's leaving tonight. I'm torn, I admit. Well, can I come to you? What time are you done?...Sure, I can drive to midtown. That's not a problem. Okay, I'll call you when I'm in the area....Yeah, we can meet somewhere for tea....Thanks, Paula."

Silver tore through her drawer looking for something casual yet chic. Her hair wasn't dry since she hadn't worn a shower cap, so she couldn't style it. She reached in another drawer and found the perfect hat to match a pair of pink knit stretch pants and taupe ruffled top. Just as she tried to close the drawer, she scraped her hand across a somewhat damaged metal lock box. Silver's heart lurched. It was the box that held the map for her mother's gravesite along with some other memorabilia Jill had given her when Silver moved to Montclair. Jill explained that she hadn't given the box to Silver while she lived in her old place for fear it might be stolen, damaged or lost. Jill was right. If Silver had kept the box at her house, it would have been destroyed in one of the fires that consumed everything. There was nothing for Silver to say except thank you. She kept the box in a drawer into which she rarely ventured, having given up a young-adult fetish for the latest style hat many moons ago.

Silver grabbed the box, sat on her bed and placed it on her lap. Slowly, she opened it and unfolded the corners of the grainy blue map that pointed the exact direction to where her mother had been buried. She traced the red line that led from the George Washington Bridge to Harlem River Drive South, across 138th Street and down Broadway. She wasn't familiar with the area, but she knew the various landmarks.

Harlem wasn't her only deterrent. Silver hadn't visited her mother's gravesite since she was a kid. She never thought it would do her any good since in spirit, her mother wasn't there. She learned to call on her mother from her heart, recalling the sweet smells of Black Love incense and the sizzle of fried turkey in her comatose state, in the different world she once visited.

As if she was led by an unknown force, Silver sped right past the turnpike exit to the Lincoln Tunnel. Her car gravitated toward the George Washington Bridge, down Harlem River Drive South, across 138th Street and down Broadway.

From the gate Silver could see weeds that defied the wind had crowded most of the gray stones. In the dusk alone and starlight miles away Silver found herself at the foot of her mother's tombstone. Her attention was captivated by the dates. She repeated February 3 several times before realizing it was her mother's birthday. "Happy birthday, Mama," Silver said as she dropped to her knees.

After being still for a while, Silver looked around. She stood and checked her mother's neighbors whose grave markers were so old, weather and time had worn their markings dull. A slight chill gripped the air and turned Silver around.

There it stood. Across the street, erect as if it dared someone to knock it down, was the lone, pale blue house that haunted her as a little girl. The gargantuan white-painted door resembled the wicked smile of the boogey man with one tooth. The image of that house was terrifying for her and she remembered that if she got too close, the house would swallow her up and no one would ever find her.

Today, however, was a different day. Silver chose to stand and look that wicked toothed haunted mansion in the center of its being and scoff.

Today, she chose to smell Black Love incense, frying turkey and sweet potato pie. Today, she made peace with the house, which ultimately didn't look so strong but weathered and tired, ready to be put to permanent rest.

"Mama, I need your help. Brandan is leaving and I don't know if I should go with him. I mean, it's crazy. Why should I pack up Lemar and go halfway across the country, and for what? I love Brandan. I want to help him, and he's wonderful for Lemar—a blessing in his life—but man, I don't know what I want, if I want anything at all with Brandan. I guess I want things to be the way they were, you know, when there was no pressure or pain to have to deal with. I want the days when Brandan and I could go have a beer, a pool game and a good football game. I know I can't go back, but how do I go forward and where do I go forward? The hardest part is that I really don't know what I want from Brandan. I'm embarrassed. He tried to sex me and I almost let him just to keep him here. I know better than that. It didn't feel right, it…it didn't gel. It didn't work." Silver wrapped her arms around her head and interlocked her fingers as if to hold her thoughts in her mind.

Amid the dead grass, the moss and the dirt, Silver sat yoga style, with her legs crossed in front of her. She placed her head in her hands, propped her elbows jabbing her thighs and sat like that for hours until another chilled breeze caused her to check the time.

"Oh shoot." She shot up, regretting the lost time. "Mom, I'm sorry. I love you. I have to go. Brandan needs to get to the airport, and I think I know what I have to do, what I want to do…what I want. See you later. I love you." Silver kissed her hand and touched the tombstone.

On her way to her car she called Paula, advising that she'd explain her no-show later and sped as fast as Saturday night New York City traffic would allow. Traffic and the turnpike closure caused Silver to get home much later than she had planned.

She was met by a note on the kitchen table.

Silver,

Disappointment wouldn't begin to describe how I feel that not only did you renege on your word to take me to the airport but you lacked the courage to even face me knowing I was leaving tonight.

Everything we've been through, I would have sworn we've gotten past temper tantrums and avoidance techniques to get what we want. You know good and well I can't stay here any longer. I extended my heart to have you and Lemar to start your life anew in California. I respect your decision that leaving is not the right thing for you but to just not show up when you knew I was leaving…was that supposed to be your protest or something?

Well I got it, and you don't have to worry about me coming back. There is nothing here for me, and I'm going to continue to do what is best for me. I thought I had your unconditional support and understanding but I see that was a lie. It's the same as it's always been—it's about you, Silver, or nothing or nobody at all. Well, take care of yourself and Lemar. If you're ever in the Bay Area, holla. My number is 510-555-8739. But know this, I won't make the first move next time.
Peace,
B

Silver balled up the note and threw it in the trash. *He didn't make the first move the first time,* she thought as she planted herself at her table and put her head in her hand. It was just as well that she let him go. There was nothing left in Newark for Brandan and she feared there was nothing there for her to look forward to.

————————————————————————————— *Toni Staton Harris*

Chapter 20

I'd Rather Live in His World

Fifteen inches of snow ushered in a frightfully frigid reminder that the 2005 winter would be fierce. Normally the cold weather sent Silver into hibernation, but she was actually enjoying watching Lemar test out his new sleigh. He had plenty of hills and valleys on the property to ride, and he laughed heartily, tackling each and every one of them.

"Aunt Silver, I'm going in the house. It's too cold out here." Abigail said. "We'll be in in a bit. Why don't you pull the marshmallows out of the cabinet and get them ready? We'll toast them and have some hot chocolate," Silver said.

"Cool" was all Abby muttered with all of the teen attitude she could muster. Silver laughed, remembering her teen days, amazed Abigail had reached them so quickly.

After an hour and a half of playing, Silver convinced Lemar it was time to go inside. He was stomping the snow off his feet just outside the door when Silver heard the phone ring. Abigail was disturbed at having to interrupt her web surfing session to answer it.

Silver and Lemar entered the kitchen and dropped their wet coats at the door. Abigail was talking like roadrunner to whomever had called. Silver assumed it was Jill or Sebastian or even Paula. Silver was pulling off Lemar's boots when Abigail finally handed her the phone.

"Hello," Silver said, helping Lemar out of his sopping wet overalls.

Lemar went sliding across the floor in his socks and underwear. "Slow down, boy. Abby, catch him and stop him from running," Silver said, paying little attention to the person on the other end. "Hello," she said again.

"How's all that snow treating you?"

Silver hadn't heard Brandan's voice in a year, for a split second she almost had to ask who it was. "It's cool. What about you?" she casually answered.

"I don't have to worry about snow out here, but it's been pretty cold," he said.

"Um-hmm...So, I thought I wasn't going to hear from you again. I'm surprised. What prompted this call?" The twenty degrees outside was warmer than the tone in her voice.

"I miss you. I knew you wouldn't call me so I'm making that move."

"According to you, you weren't making the first move. So again, what prompted this little call?" Silver paused. "And am I supposed to get excited or be upset or what? How am I supposed to feel about you calling, Brandan?" Silver wasn't in the mood for a long diatribe about how hurt he had been without even giving her a chance to explain herself. He asked her to make a major life change on a whim, then basically called her selfish and unyielding when he snapped his fingers and she didn't jump.

"Silver, I'm sorry. I'm really sorry. I'm still going through a lot, and I didn't have a right to take my confusion out on you. I heard what happened with you and the airport."

"I accept your apology. Now I have to run. I have a child to take care of." Silver turned to hang up.

"Wait," Brandan yelled, prompting her to halt. "I was calling to say how sorry I was and that I was hoping maybe you and Lemar could come out for a visit."

"That's nice, Brandan, but I'm busy right now, and even if I wanted to, I can't take a lot of time from work. I just got with a new firm."

"I heard...Doing the same thing, right?" he asked.

"Yup."

"Cool. Well, y'all could just come for a weekend. The airlines have a lot of deals going on. I thought it would be nice for you to get out of the cold. I know how you hate snow," Brandan said.

"Thanks but no thanks, Brandan. I'm off the roller coaster with you. Take care. I know how to reach you if I need to," Silver said and hung up. She was determined not to regret her action. "Okay, guys, I have white hot chocolate and mocha. Why don't we make both and then put the marshmallows on the fire?"

Lemar yelled in agreement and ran to the living room. Silver looked at the phone and then turned off the ringer with the same determination she used to hang up.

"You need to call him," Paula said as she poured hot water over a tea ball of Mariage Freres, a fragrant herbal tea from France.

"Why?" Silver asked, setting her cup down to cool. Paula liked her tea lukewarm and Silver began to take on that same trait.

"Because you're miserable without him. You need closure on what you two decide your relationship is going to be. You both are playing games right now, but in a minute the games will have to stop, otherwise you'll both be lost."

Silver sipped in deep thought. She knew all along that she would have to make the trip to the Bay Area, but she was determined to make it alone for closure.

Things don't seem totally different, Silver thought stepping off the plane and taking the long walk to baggage claim. People bustled about but the groove seemed slower, a lot more relaxed.

Silver found her bags and followed the signs to ground transportation. The airport workers were extremely friendly, almost frightening. Silver had to remember she was in another state. People actually spoke, looked her in the eye and acknowledged her presence. Men scrambled to get her bags, and when she was escorted to her seat in the cab, she thought she might be able to get used to the treatment.

Getting used to anything was not her mission. Silver was in San Francisco to put her ill feelings to rest, to get serious closure on her relationship with Brandan and to determine once and for all if he should be shut out of her life for good.

The cab cruised pleasantly down the highway, which was surrounded by water. Silver smiled to herself, fully understanding why it was called the Bay Area for it was surrounded by an exquisite bay. She marveled at the yachts in water parks along the roadway. The traffic of which people often spoke completely eluded Silver as she wondered at the various homes that literally sat on hills.

The cabdriver exited on Sixth Street, and Silver realized the city looked no different than New York. Now in San Francisco proper, Silver eyed various missions and soup kitchens with lines around the block. The area looked blighted but that didn't squash her excitement.

"How far is Oakland from here?" Silver asked the cabbie.

"Not far. In traffic twenty minutes; without less than ten," he answered.

"Well, this is your stop," he said a few minutes later. "Please step out on the left. The cars speed around that corner quite readily."

Silver checked the meter, paid the tab and offered a generous tip. A doorman promptly grabbed her bag and escorted her into the most exquisite hotel she'd ever seen. It was beautifully ornate, and the first thing that struck her was the various chess, backgammon and checker boards all over the lobby, beckoning her to play.

Brandan recommended that she stay there even though his residence was in Oakland. Seeing that she'd never been to the West Coast, he wanted her to have the full Bay experience. She had a few hours to settle in before meeting him in the restaurant attached to the hotel.

Silver was greeted and checked in by a petite Asian woman with a balmy voice. She was directed to a suite on the seventh floor. When Silver first entered, she thought the room rather small but quaint. It was very modern and decorated with Asian flavor. The room held character, with porcelain vases, man-sized mirrors decorated with Chinese characters and a three-foot deep tub inviting her to take a luxurious bath.

And so she did. Silver figured out the elaborate radio beside the king-size bed, which was already turned down and laced with a chocolate. She ran a scalding hot bath and luxuriated until she fell asleep in the tub.

With plenty of time left before she met Brandan, she emerged refreshed. Silver adorned herself in a hotel robe and slippers. She relaxed on the bed and couldn't wait to dive into it that night. It already felt like heaven underneath her skin. She was having such a great time that she forced herself not to call home. She just wanted to relax. Silver picked up the keyboard console that controlled everything from the room lights to the stereo and decided to check out the weather. After twenty minutes of figuring out the console, she found the weather channel and was dismayed that it would be only a high of sixty degrees.

In her mind California was supposed to be hot. And though Newark was sitting under thirty-one inches of snow and record low temperatures, Silver didn't bring a thing that would be appropriate in this weather except a sweat suit, which wouldn't do because that was meant for her to relax in the room only.

Brandan had left strict instructions: if she were to leave, walk to the left of the hotel, not the right. Walk down toward the trolley and not up the hill. And whatever she did she wasn't to cross against the red light or an intersection that didn't have an official crosswalk. Also she wasn't to cross in the middle of the street like she did in Jersey if she wanted to avoid a jaywalking ticket.

Instructions or not, Silver wasn't about to greet Brandan in a sweat suit. She checked the clock. She still had one hour and fifteen minutes before meeting Brandan. Quickly, she dressed and made her way to the concierge who directed her to Union Square.

Silver walked out on Taylor, turned right as directed and landed in the high-end district after taking a quick trolley ride up a hill so steep, the sidewalk had stairs. She found and put together a few chic outfits from the largest Nordstrom's department store she had seen, that would accommodate the weather.

Upon arrival back at the hotel, Silver changed and applied fresh makeup before heading to Ponzu's, the restaurant where she and Brandan were to meet, only five minutes after schedule. Silver walked toward the bar, which was surrounded by freshwater fish tanks. The bartender explained the array of Damsel, Red Squirrel and blowfish that resided in the tank before taking her order. She ordered the house specialty, a Pink Croc, a drink with Cointreau, Remy Grape, fresh lime juice and some other special ingredient.

Silver was delighted when Brandan walked through the door. Only he wasn't alone. He was accompanied by a slender, beige woman, pleasantly pretty in her own right but rather plain. She had shoulder-length brown hair. Silver would have suggested a layered cut to offset the thinness. Silver also would have offered another fashion tip: a three-quarter-length shearling with a ruffled fur collar and stiletto knee-high boots to accentuate her long legs. A slight brow tweezing just to clean up around the edges wouldn't have hurt either.

"Hey, baby girl." Brandan hugged her with all of his might. The woman stood at a respectable distance. His hug felt good, and Brandan looked absolutely scrumptious.

"Hey. Nice hotel. I like it," Silver said, brushing off the seat next to her as the woman approached.

"Sil, this is Jules...well Juliet, but as you know, I call her Jules. Jules, this is Silver," Brandan said proudly.

Juliet gave Silver a hug similar to Brandan's. Juliet didn't waste anytime sitting between Brandan and Silver and ordering a Pink Croc as well as a bowl of edamame and duck spring rolls.

"What's that? How do you say it?" Silver asked, referring to the dish Jules had ordered.

"It's pronounced *ed-ee-mom-ee,* and it's a steamed soybean in the pod, dressed with salt. It's similar to a lima bean but with a different flavor. Great gnosh food," Juliet said excitedly.

"Oh." Silver was skeptical.

"Don't worry. You'll actually like it. The duck rolls are excellent too," Brandan chimed in.

"I don't know. First sushi and now eda...whatever you call it," Silver said.

"Just try it. If you don't like it, I understand, but a least you will have tried it," Juliet said. "Oh, if you want sushi, the best place is Yoshi's in Jack London Square. The food is so fresh and just gorgeous, just gorgeous."

Silver looked at her oddly. "Gorgeous food, huh? Never quite heard that expression before. I'm not really a sushi girl. I like my food cooked." Silver almost got annoyed but decided she'd wait until she had at least one more drink in her, then she could blame it on that.

"So how was your flight?" Brandan asked.

"It was relaxing." Silver slurped the last of her drink and pushed the glass to the edge of the bar.

"We have a great weekend planned for you. We're going to one of my favorite jazz places tonight, after we eat of course. Tomorrow we're going to the Wharf. We need to take you by Ghiardelli's and get some dungenous crab and Heinekens. Oh, and we planned a dinner cruise and wine tour, then on Sunday after church we're going to Alcatraz but not before we go to Royal Café. It's legendary in Oakland."

"We? Brandan I thought we—" Silver pointed to herself and him— "were going to talk." Silver didn't have time for games or beating around the bush.

"Silver, if you don't mind," Juliet cut in, her tone soft, almost apologetic, "I'm sorry, I tend to get carried away. Brandan did tell me you were coming out here to talk to him. He wants you out here permanently so badly, and I thought if we showed you a wonderful time, you wouldn't want to leave. I meant no harm. I just want to help," Juliet said.

Silver couldn't figure Juliet's angle, but she appreciated her acknowledgement nonetheless. "I appreciate that, Juliet. I'm sorry. I didn't mean to be harsh or anything. I just don't want to leave having not fulfilled my purpose for being here. I would love to do some of those things after Brandan and I have a chance to talk things out. I don't mean to exclude you, but there are some things—"

"I completely understand. No need to explain. So why don't we hang out tonight? You and Brandan can do your talk thing tomorrow. If you're up to it, I'll join you guys later. If you're not, trust me, my feelings won't be hurt. Girl, it's so rare that I get to hang out. I've been looking forward to this night, so…" Juliet said.

A blank look shadowed Silver's face, then a minute smile crept across her lips. There was something about Juliet she really liked. Silver lifted her glass as an offering. Juliet accepted and clinked her glass with Silver's.

Silver and Brandan walked along the perimeter of Berkeley's vast green campus. Silver could see how going to school there would not only enhance one's mind but spirit too. An element of peace surrounded everything. They settled on a bench.

"So what made you finally come?" Brandan asked, sipping on a bottle of water he had pulled from his knapsack.

Silver laughed. She looked down at his feet and thought what a difference a day, a year or a state made. He was wearing flip-flops and white tube socks again. Brandan was a different man. His presence was strong and stately like she'd known, but that day, he seemed settled and confident. "To answer your question, I came because I wanted to clear the air with you."

Brandan's eyes bugged at her candor. His shoulders tensed. He placed his water at his side and braced his back against the bench. "Well, start clearing," he said courageously.

"I need you to listen without interjecting. I have a lot on my mind, and I want to clear it all, once and for all. And I promise I won't bring up anything I say today ever again, but I want to talk about it until I'm satisfied. Can you give me that?" Brandan nodded and held out his hands. "No interruptions, please," Silver reiterated.

"I have been extremely angry with you for three years, Brandan LeMarr Savoy. I've been a good friend to you, in spite of my faults, and I felt like you abandoned me when I needed you most and you needed me most. You blamed me for incidents in our lives that weren't my fault. For example, Savannah—"

"Hold up. I didn't —"

"You said you'd let me finish." Brandan nodded silently and sipped his water. "Remember the first time when you and Savannah broke up?" Brandan nodded, and Silver continued. "I was just the messenger that she wasn't the woman for you and you weren't the man for her. Nothing more or less. It is my job, duty and my honor to look out for you. You even said yourself that you all were just 'doing the thing.'" Silver made quotation marks with her fingers. "And when you went back the second time, it hurt me deeply because you did it to spite me. And then you tried to make Savannah take my place, not talking to me, transferring messages to me from her. Not cool. If you ever even look like you're cutting me out of your life like that and pull some shit to make me jealous, I swear, Brandan, I'll cut you out of my life for good. It'll hurt, but I'll spend every waking day and all of my energy to get over it. I can take mistakes, but I won't take you spiting me on purpose."

Brandan nodded again. He didn't dare deny what Silver was saying.

"Now, the big one—Daphne. I know you didn't date and marry that girl out of spite, but I begged you not to get involved with her. I begged you. You didn't want to listen because you were in love. I accept that, but I will not take the blame for what that wench did. And furthermore, I won't be responsible for giving you the information and revealing the truth. For whatever reason, the truth came to me. I won't apologize for that. It would have been easy for me to avoid it all and just let things be, but I love you. I would stop at nothing for your happiness and your happiness in truth because that's what you wanted. You wouldn't have settled for less. But for you to turn on me the way you did, hurt me and damaged me more than you could even fathom. And to be honest with you, I don't know that we can truly recover from all of that betrayal or better yet that I can recover from it. For this friendship to work, a lot of trust has to be rebuilt, and I don't know where to start. And some days I don't know that I want to start.

"I love you dearly, Brandan, and I also love me. I love my child and my family, and I won't jeopardize loving me for anyone. I've gone through too much. So if you're willing to love me, respect me and begin to rebuild the trust and honesty we once had, we can go from here. If not, I'll pack my bags and get back on that plane without looking back once."

Brandan took another sip of water. "I was angry at you too. I had nobody else to be angry at, so you were the closest one. And Sil, baby girl, I'm sorry. I am sorry. Yes, I was in love with Daphne, and I'm able to admit that now. I was devastated—still am—with all that has gone on, but I couldn't handle it, didn't want to handle it. So like you said, I ran. And for a while I was still running. I'm not anymore. I just want to be who I choose to be. And I can do that here. I've started all over again, and I feel good about it. This is where I'm supposed to be, and I won't apologize for that. I want you in my life. I want Lemar in my life. Yes, I was being selfish for wanting you out here with me, but I have to be who I've evolved to be. I can't be Mr. Fix-it anymore. I don't want to be selfish, but I do want what I want. If I can't have you out here permanently, at least I can have you and Lemar once a quarter, maybe eventually once a month. I'm going to be here. I will do my best to bridge our gap, but from here. It's a long, hard road we're about to take, but we can do it, if you give us the chance."

He looked directly into Silver's eyes and saw the softness he knew as a child. They would be okay. With hard work and diligence, they would be stronger than ever.

"You're in love with her, aren't you?" Silver asked, referring to Juliet.

Brandan sighed and fidgeted.

"Just answer the question, Brandan." Silver already knew the answer.

"I believe love is possible with her. But right now, I want to take it slowly. There's definitely potential. Juliet is getting her Ph.D. in psychology with a concentration in counseling. She's not my counselor, but she helps me out." Brandan sipped more water.

"So you two have never been intimate?" she asked. She grabbed Brandan's water and sipped.

He looked at her, acknowledging her bizarre behavior. There was time when Silver barely drank after herself much less anyone else. *Things have definitely changed,* he thought before speaking. "Silver, hear me when I say I've been celibate for the last two years. When the time is right, I'll break that, but for now, I really have to discipline myself, be strong and push through. I'm standing up for my manhood. I'm really sorry for what almost happened that night. You were right and I'm proud of you for standing up for yourself and us. Like you've always done."

"Yeah, that night…. You know, I'm sorry for that too. I was confused. I was so scared for you to leave, I thought, *hey, I could go along with this.* Brandan, afterward I was ashamed. Until I visited my mother's grave, I didn't understand why, but then I got it. I got that I—we—weren't meant to be like that. Us on a sexual level is trite. It's easy. And you and me, we are past easy. You know what I'm saying?" Brandan nodded. "Anyway, I thank you because if we had gone ahead and did what was easy and surface, we could never have pushed to the point we have now. Sitting with my mother, I realized that I was coming into my own as a woman, as the person I want to be. And that person—Silver A. James—no longer needs you to be my father and certainly not my lover. I want you as my best friend. I want to defy all odds with you, and honestly we already have. So with that, I thank you. You are still a man and you're the man because it takes a real man to reach out like you have and do the work you're doing on yourself."

Brandan was silent. He tilted his head backward as he took a breath. "Damn, I really don't know what to say, but I appreciate it. All of it." He thought for another moment then spoke. "I never wanted you to be embarrassed by that. I'm not the saint you portray either. But after thinking things through I knew you were right. One night of indecision wasn't worth it. I had to really fight through that one. But I'm still a man."

Brandan paused and tipped the water bottle to his mouth. Before taking the last sip, he offered it to Silver. She refused and he gulped. When the time is right, Juliet could be the one. We'll see," he said.

Brandan didn't have to say that he loved Juliet. Silver saw it in his eyes, felt it in his heartbeat and heard it in his voice. And she wasn't going to fight it. Silver felt a sincerity with Juliet, a peace and a truth. And if that was what Brandan needed to be whole, who was she to stand in the way? Brandan and Silver continued on their walk.

"I'm not going to Alcatraz. We can do that Red Room tonight, but I don't want to do the prison," Silver said. "That's crazy."

Brandan laughed. "That's cool," he said.

"But if the two of you want to do sushi, I'm down. I'll even try it," Silver said as they walked on, laughing and talking like they were two school kids on the corner of North Seventeenth Street in East Orange, New Jersey.

Love Was Spoken Here
Silver's Epilogue

It was almost five years ago to the day when the smell of firewood on the 101 South burning amid a setting sun intoxicated me so completely that I dreaded getting back on the plane.

Brandan was right all along; the Bay Area was where we needed to be to fully cleanse our lives and find ways to start anew. It's different, but after being here that first time on a March day, I couldn't deny that I was bound to be out here permanently. It took me three months from the day I stepped off the plane in Newark. I was met by the same foot of snow I'd left behind, the wind whistling behind my ears and the crabbiness for which the Northeast is sometimes famous. I've been out here ever since and never once looked back. I settled in San Jose with Lemar who travels between me and Brandan in El Cerrito.

Now, as I take the brick-faced walk to the church where everything is about to happen, I smile. I smile because Brandan and I have come so far and for so long. It wasn't easy, but here we stand today, both of us participating in a life-changing event that we prayed for, desired and fought for.

Brandan was responsible for decorating the church, and he spared no expense, lavishing it with orchids, roses, birds of paradise and almost any other exotic flower California had to offer.

As I look around, I marvel at how far we've all come. "Jules, what in the world are you doing here? You're supposed to be making sure everybody is in place and ready," I needled her.

She chuckled. Jules and I have become the best of friends. She is an absolutely wonderful person. She helped my entire family get settled out here. Well, they haven't moved, but Abigail is studying music at Berkeley. Whenever Sebastian and Jill come out, which isn't too often since they have a change-of-life addition to the family that keeps them occupied, Jules makes sure they are pampered like a king and queen.

Mom Savoy can't stop crying. She's just happy all over. Whenever she prays hard enough to get her body on the plane, Jules makes her feel like the world has stopped for her. Even Paula and her husband are here. Paula and Detective Dowdy hit it off when Paula vowed to take down the entire police department for me because of the way she felt I was treated. I don't think either Paula or Detective Dowdy expected romance but it happened, and we are all grateful for it.

"So where are Brandan and Lemar?" Jules asked me.

Lemar is serving as best man and taking his role very seriously, getting Brandan to the church hours before time. "They're in the pastor's study hanging out," I answered.

"Well, I guess I better go get everything ready," Jules said. She grabbed my hands and looked into my eyes. It was serious; it was on, and we were all ready.

I was so nervous walking down the aisle. You'd think that I had never walked in heels the way I wobbled. But I made it safe and sound and without falling. Lemar was already down there, standing next to his "dad" looking debonair and proud. I wanted to pinch his cheeks and kiss him, but he was at the age where he wiped my kisses off in public.

The ceremony went off without a hitch, and it was right. It felt good and all was well.

"I don't know if I can top the speech that was given by my eight-year-old whom I'm so proud of," I said, "but this is not the time to talk about my son. This is the time to talk about two people who are truly meant to be together, who I pray in God's eyes are blessed and constantly remain in love and in like.

"It's important that I explain something. When Brandan first approached me to serve as the best woman, it wasn't until Jules pulled me aside and said that her wedding to the man she loves would not be complete without me. And for this jewel, precious ruby of a woman to not only include me in the most important and perfect day of her life, but to have me participate on a level that most other people would shun is selfless and giving. For you see, Jules, who has become one of my dearest friends, vibrates on a different level than most. I love you, Jules, and I trust and pray that you and Brandan are filled with joy, peace and happiness forever. You truly deserve it. And if he ever gets out of line, just call me and I'll help you straighten things out." People laughed. "I would like to leave you with this Bible verse, which is often read at weddings because it is so full of truth and love. I recited from memory:

"Love is patient, love is kind. It does not envy, it does not boast, it is not proud. It is not rude, it is not self-seeking, it is not easily angered, it keeps no record of wrongs. Love does not delight in evil but rejoices with the truth. It always protects, always trusts, always hopes, always perseveres, Love never fails. But when there are prophecies, they will cease; where there are tongues, they will be stilled; where there is knowledge, it will pass away. For we know in part and we prophesy in part, but when perfection comes, the imperfect disappears. When I was a child, I talked like a child, I thought like a child, I reasoned like a child. When I became a man, I put childish ways behind me. Now we see but a poor reflection as in a mirror; then we shall see face to face. Now I know in part; then shall I know fully, even as I am fully known. And now these three remain: faith, hope and love. But the greatest of these is love. Amen."

"God bless you all and remember, if you don't get on the other side of something, how do you know you were ever truly friends at all."
With that, there wasn't a dry eye in the house.

Toni's Charming Notes

I am so grateful to God in the precious name of Jesus Christ for all that you are doing and all that you've done. I send you the highest praise for my gifts, and I recognize that it is all because You chose me first.

To the love of my life, Injeel Harris, my rock, I thank you for tirelessly having my back.

To my family, friends and loved ones, you all support me effortlessly.

Chandra Sparks Taylor, as always, you are more than my editor, you are my friend.

To my author friends: Nancey Flowers, Jacquelin Thomas (my mentor), Fred Williamson, Jamise L. Dames, Crystal Ellis, Jeff Haskins, Terry B., Angie Daniels, and Mary B. Morrison. All of you have given selflessly. I appreciate you.

I learn from many. A special thanks goes out to two fantastic teachers and women of literarture: Susan Taylor Chekak, UCLA Extension and Kathleen Longo, Kean University. Your voices are still in my head.

My first readers: Mike Jones, Ametra Burton and Kenyatta Ingram, you are phenomenal individuals.

Ametra Burton my everything girl. Thanks for the Photo.

To all readers, your feedback is invaluable.

I thank every book club in existence because you are the reason writers are sustained. If I have not met you yet, I look forward to it. Many thanks to: Sistergirl Book Club, Virginia; Kaper Book Club, Oakland; Illuminations, New Jersey; The Book Club, New Jersey; the Woman of Bethlehem, Pennsylvania; Mocha Book Club, New Jersey; Nia Iman Book Club, California; African Violet Book Club, California; Just Us Girls Book Club, New Jersey; Ebony Eyes Book Club, New Jersey.

To all the booksellers, you, too, sustain authors. God bless and thank you for your support: Maleta Wilson, Heritage Bookstore and More, Rancho Cucamonga, California.

Several businesses profiled in this story are real and awesome. I couldn't help but give them their props: Eclectic Designs, New Jersey; Juzang Thang Caterers, Pennsylvania; HRL Equities, New Jersey, Baltimore, D.C. and Los Angeles; Up Up and Away, New Jersey. See my website, www.tonistatonharris.com, for links.

Thanks to my technical support team: Lydell Jackson, D'Juana Clark, Deb Edwards, Michelle Rush, Princess Parker, Joan Burke Stanford, David Anderson and Tom Cusmano.

Special dedication

As I sit in my parents' kitchen—they are at my sister's babysitting my nephew, Malcolm, and my niece, Simone—I am warmed at how Hilliard D. and Maudie Ruth Staton truly loved me from birth. I'm astonished how in my adulthood they are always here for me and stop at nothing to consider my well-being. Often I've said to and about my mother that I pray to be half the woman she is. With that strength I'll rule the world. My daddy, I have always said and continue to say is my hero. I love you both dearly. All that I am would not be possible if not for you.

I cannot begin to name everyone, so please know that even if not on these pages, you are in my heart and my prayers.

From the Bottom Up,

Toni

Insight

Writing this novel was a wonderful journey for me, personally and professionally. The idea came from two sources: 1) as I traveled domestically and abroad and found that the question can men and women be platonic friends? was a hot topic and 2) having to maturely deal with my own relationships with two male friends as well as with the fact that my husband has female friends.

I admit that in the beginning, balancing mature feelings and jealousy was tough. The turnaround came when my husband dropped me off at the airport one day. He made a quick comment that I wrote this book to spite him. I denied that fact and proceeded on my four-day trip. As always, with my laptop at my hip, I fired it up in my hotel room and re-read some of the story. I found that my husband was right. I wrote some things that weren't necessarily founded or grounded in research or anyone's truth. I scrapped the project as it was, got back to the drawing board, devised some questions, polled some people and sought to find truth in a situation far beyond the surface of what would be expected.

Researching the topic from a social standpoint was invigorating for me, and it caused me to grow. My friends stopped talking to me (*wink, wink*) because they'd say "oh, boy, here comes Toni. Remember, don't say anything you don't want to see in a book later because you will." Or if you say something, say "on the record" or "off the record." A secret to all of my friends and family: nothing is off the record, but know that I'll always change the names to protect the guilty.

As I polled more than 350 people of all ages, ethnicities, races, creeds and colors, here's some of what I learned:

Can men and women be platonic friends?

Women: 80% yes, regardless of age, ethnicity

Men (ages 20–30) 95% yes

Men (ages 31–49) 85% no but if one of the parties is homosexual, possibly

Men (ages 50 and up) 98% no

Some explanations:

"Men always have one thing on their minds, so no."

"It takes a certain level of maturity to get past the initial state of attraction, so maybe."

"Women can't only be sustained by women, so yes."

"Friend is a term defined too lightly, a friend is a friend no matter what the sex, so yes."

"I find it easier to be friends with men because women are too catty."

"I have male friends and prefer them over women."

"Heterosexual men who pursue friendships with women are after one thing."

Reading Group Guide

The following questions are designed to enhance the reader's understanding of the novel and spark discussion.

1. Was Silver truly at peace with a platonic relationship with Brandan? Why or why not?

2. Why did Silver reject intimacy with Brandan?

3. What was Daphne's motivation behind her deception?

4. Discuss the dynamics of Pat's and Silver's friendship.

5. Brandan desperately wanted Silver and Daphne to get along. How do you think Brandan helped or hindered the situation?

6. Barring Daphne's deception, was Daphne correct in her quest to minimize Brandan's relation with Silver and Lemar? How would you react if your mate wanted to maintain a relationship with a child that is not biologically his/hers?

7. Would Silver and Brandan have made a good couple? Why or why not?

8. If friends cross the line into intimacy, can they ever regain their true friendship? Explain. How does crossing the line impact that friendship?

9. What was the major lesson Silver had to learn in order to grow in all of her relationships?

10. Why didn't Brandan and Silver ever get together?

11. Why did Silver keep her baby?

About The Author

Toni Staton Harris is the recipient of several accolades including Author of the Year, 2003 SisterGirl Book Club, Virginia Beach, Virginia and Outstanding Alumnae, Benedictine Academy, Elizabeth, New Jersey. She authored the award-winning novel, *By Chance or Choice* slated for re-release at the end of 2005, and has completed the sequel, *Here We Grow Again,* due out 2006. Currently she is working on her fourth novel and several short stories. She resides in the Los Angeles area with her husband, Injeel.

Visit her on the web at <u>www.tonistatonharris.com</u> or <u>www.epiphanypublishing.net</u>. She would love to hear from you.

Coming Soon...
Here We Grow Again

Gem

"Wake-up Sunshine," Gemmia-Jewel Barner heard her assistant, Dale, say as Gem rolled over from her eerie dream. "We land in a little over an hour and you said you wanted to shower." Dale pulled the down comforter from Gem's lanky frame and dropped a plush towel at her feet.

Gem lumbered to her gold-trimmed shower off of the bedroom aboard her private state-of-the-art airplane. She rinsed, then plopped in one of the sixteen passenger chairs so her make-up artist could work some magic. Gem had become a stickler about her appearance and vowed never to look tired or worn. "So how much time did you say we have before we land?" Gem asked as she swirled around and turned her attention back to Dale. The make-up artist gently pulled Gem back.

"Now, a little under an hour. Hopefully we'll have no drama, kiss a few babies, answer a few questions from the press about the new album, make sure you plug the label and then the limo will whisk you off to the rehearsal studio, I'll be checking us in the hotel and..."

Gem held her hand up to halt Dale's diatribe. Gem was confident that Dale had the next six months of their lives in the palm of her hand via her Treo 650.

With the make-up artist done, Gem gazed out the window to the cloud-filled sky with nervous anticipation. It had been four years since her last album. Her new one, entitled *Brilliance,* was predicted to enter the marketplace on Billboard's top ten. With *Brilliance,* rested the hopes and dreams of Gem and her beloved husband, Vaughan. According to some critics, this album was the one to watch. This should be Gem's time and this album was supposed to showcase the pinnacle of her career, the one that would surpass all sales and Grammies she'd ever won. Everything hinged on its success since she and Vaughan were launching her album under their new label, Winter-Gem Records. They had also signed several new artists coming out with their own projects: a girl band, a duo and three solo performers.

Gem retreated to the bedroom to dress. By the time she emerged the pilot was informing Gem's entourage that they were approaching New Jersey's exclusive Teteboro airport. Gem sat back down and watched the wings of the airplane slice through the clouds where she was able to make out legions of fans toting banners, Welcome Home posters, T-shirts, CD's and other paraphernalia for her to sign. Gem also noticed the dreaded paparazzi on the opposite side of her fans.

Even though she had nothing pending in her life to fear, seeing the reporters caused doubt to rise in her soul. How would her fans take the new album, its new direction, the vocal chances she'd taken at the urging of her private vocal coach? She hoped they would recognize her new sound as growth and an increased commitment to her craft. Although, to date Gem had proven to be one of the world's consummate singers, she also knew you were only as good as your last project.

Industry insiders praised this album as her best work yet, but Gem knew the true measure of success was her fans. Soon enough she'd find out just how they felt.

The pilot indicated their final approach. Dale, as she often did, defied the flight attendant's instructions to be seated, when she answered the cordless phone from the center aisle console.

"Ma'am, no disrespect, but it really isn't safe for you to be on the phone as we're approaching our destination. Your call could interfere with the equipment and..."

Dale ignored the flight attendant and handed the phone to Gem. "Obviously we don't have a lot of time, but it's Vaughan from Japan, he sounds urgent." Dale rolled her eyes at the attendant who withdrew her orders.

"Hey beloved, I can't talk long. I'll call you as soon as we land...What is it? Can't it wait?... But I can't talk right now...I promise, I'll call you before I leave the plane ...Okay...I love you too." Gem turned off the phone and braced herself as the wheels hit. "That was lovely. We need to get this pilot more often," she said referring to his pillow top landing. Even as the plane rolled pass the crowd, nothing drowned out their roars. Gem was thrilled.

The plane stopped and Gem's make-up artist applied a last minute touch-up. The attendant opened the door, the air stairs unfolded and the shouts of the fans grew louder. Dale exited first, then the make-up artist, stylist, personal chef, masseuse and two bodyguards, Mojo and Cujo. Finally in grand diva form Gem appeared and the crowd went wild. The commotion was so intoxicating that Gem forgot to call Vaughan.

Gem clasped her hands together in prayer form, bowed her head, then blew kisses in every direction. She descended the stairs with the grace of a queen and opened her arms to receive her fans. She signed old CD's and T-shirts. She held and posed for photographs with several toddlers and children. The others handed out pre-signed photographs and Gem was led by Dale to the podium where she'd address the press.

Her adrenaline was high and all of the nervous anxiety previously built up had turned to pure joy. Gem began her speech: "This album Brilliance co-produced by me and my beloved, Vaughan is the beginning of new beginnings..." Her confidence illuminated and despite the lack of Vaughan's presence, (he usually traveled with her on mega tours) she felt at ease.

Light bulbs flashed in all directions and Gem was now ready for questions. She pointed into the face of one reporter who had an innocent almost angelic smile. "Where is your mega-star producer/husband, Vaughan, these days?"

"Oh," Gem said delighted to answer an easy question. "He's in Japan, promoting the latest artist on our label. They're called *Satin Dolls* and mark my words, keep your ears to your I-pods because they are going to be fierce. Where Destiny's Child has left off, *Satin Dolls* will pick up and take over the world." Gem radiated.

"What about the allegations that the lead singer of the group was ousted and is on her way back to the States because she's in, shall we say, a family way?" The same reporter asked. Her smile now turned wry.

"What? What are you talking about?" Gem asked, her voice sailing into high soprano.

"Yes, would you care to comment on reports that the lead singer, I believe her name is _ "

"Desiree." Gem answered the name of the lead singer she had handpicked and groomed.

"Well your lead singer Desiree is supposedly on her way back to the States as we speak. It is alleged that your husband fired her because she's pregnant and that your devoted husband Vaughan Winters is the father. How do you answer these allegations?"

Gem froze, visibly stunned, all grace drained from her face.